Ab:

MW00936906

The Beckett Series

By

Mary Martinez

Abandoned
Book six of the Beckett Series
Copyright @ 2018 Mary Martinez
www.marymartinez.com

Published by Canyonland Press

Released in the United States of America
Cover artists: Sheri McGathy
Editor: Cyndy Gleave

DEDICATION

As always, a huge thanks to my family and friends for all of their love and support.

To Ron, my wonderful husband, and Toni Batt, my traveling friend, for humoring me and exploring New York and documenting, with pictures, my characters' neighborhoods.

Thank you, Kim, Cyndy, and Sabrina for the help all of you have given me! I couldn't have done it without you.

Enjoy

Clanog Patrick & Finn

Mary Martinez

Chapter One

Glenna Beckett peeked around the sheer curtain at the window of Jessica, her sister's, old bedroom. The little generals, Gabby and Sophie, were busy with all the last minute details of her wedding. The up and coming wedding planners had turned the *Elders'* back yard into an elegant fairyland. Her nieces had a promising career in front of them. Though Reagan and Christine, their mothers, had laid down the law about a college education first.

Glenna smiled as she watched her nieces. Maybe they could fund their education with parties and weddings on the weekends. She exhaled and looked for the familiar figure of her fiancé. He was conspicuously absent. She glanced at the old bear figured clock of Jessica's childhood and confirmed the time. The clergyman had arrived a few minutes earlier, and the wedding was set to commence in twenty minutes.

It was looking more and more as if she were going to be jilted at the altar. Why? She'd been the one dragging her feet, she'd never been able to lose the tiny niggle of unease. But Lance Gordon was a force to be reckoned with when he'd set his mind to something.

And he'd wanted a fall wedding.

A rap on the door startled Glenna, her thoughts flew as the knob turned and her father walked in.

"Glenna, don't you look beautiful. It's enough to take my breath away." He stepped toward her and she launched herself into his arms at the same time almost knocking him over.

"Dad!" She wailed. Yes, she'd been known to wail.

"Oh, Glenna." He rubbed her back as he'd done when she was young in the midst of some teenage drama. "It's going to be okay, little one."

She couldn't hold in her worries anymore and stepped out of his arms so she could gather her emotions around her. A very unlike Glenna-of-the-past move.

"I don't think Lance is coming." She sniffed loud enough her mother would hear and probably join them to complete the *Elders*. "Everything happened so fast and then he was gone for months and I started to have doubts. And again he swooped in and…"

She paced to the window. Glenna felt her dad step up beside her, he placed a calming hand on her shoulder.

"Glenna, tell me at your own pace. I'm not going anywhere."

For a moment she'd been afraid he'd call in her mother. She loved her mother, but her confidences had always gone to her dad. Unless it was *female* stuff. She sighed, moved from the window to sit on the edge of the bed, or tried, her full skirts and slips didn't allow her to sit. She didn't really want to stand. *Oh, to hell with it.*

She reached behind her with both hands and drew up the yards of material and sat, the acres of lace and silk piled high enough to tower over her like the Alps.

"One day Lance walked in my shop and my first thought was…" She closed her eyes, had she really been a fool? "Dad, I thought he was gay. Tyler and Matt are right, my gaydar went ding, ding, ding."

She opened her eyes and her dad stared at her in bewilderment. The *Elders'* may be trendy for their age, but at times they could be dense.

"You mean you thought he was homosexual? But why would he ask you to marry him? More importantly, why would you say yes?"

"Well, that's my point dad. I didn't think anything more about him because that's what I thought. But he kept coming in my shop and looking around. Then he introduced himself and said he was an Arts dealer and had come in my place looking for treasures. We had a mutual love of art and rare antiques and before I knew it, he was taking me to showings. Then we'd go to fine restaurants and discuss our shared passion.

"Then he asked me to marry him, all very romantic, you know a candlelit dinner, expensive wine. He even had a violinist come to the table to serenade while he made a production of asking me."

The bed dipped, her father's arm snaked around her shoulders. She let her head drop to rest on his. She had to sniff back the tears that threatened.

"Dad, I had to say yes. It was a fairytale moment and I was caught up in the magic. Even more, he never tried to be, *you know*, intimate with me. He wanted to let the tension build until we were married. The romance of it all was overwhelming. The next day he had to jet off to some European country for a rare antiquities showing. International dealers would be there. He's always looking for that one treasure that will bring his name to the forefront of the inner circles. Get his face on the cover of London's premier art magazine, Blackmans. "

"You've seen him since then?" He hugged her a little closer.

"Well yes, he drops in and strolls around my shop as if he's still looking for something." She sat up to face her dad, as best she could with the hindrance of the highland of fabric weighing her down. "Alex, my assistant, told me that on my days off he would come in and look, no, search through things. I thought it was cute because he forgot I wasn't working that day. But Dad, he had told me after we'd started dating that he only used the excuse of trying to find something to come in and see *me.*"

"And you don't believe that?"

She didn't have a chance to answer, the door opened without warning and a waif of a woman slipped in. Effie her best friend. She couldn't help but smile when she saw her. Effie, as always, looked like a loveable mess. Her blonde hair piled on her head, strands slipping out of their restraints in every direction. One thin strap slid down her shoulder and her dress billowed around her knees. She looked like a disreputable pink elf.

"Oh, I'm sorry Glenna I didn't know you were talking to one of the *Elders'*." She started to back out of the room, the main problem was, the door had closed behind her, she met it with a thud. "Ouch."

"Effie, are you okay?"

The pixie rubbed her posterior but grinned. "Yeah. Just a bruised ass."

Her giggles brightened the mood that had fallen over the room.

"Has my groom decided to make an appearance?"

Her question caused her good natured friend to actually frown. It was a very rare occasion when Effie did anything but grin or smile. The slow burn that had started in Glenna's stomach an hour earlier flamed into a full blown inferno. Her hand found her tummy and rubbed.

Her dad frowned. "Glenna, are you okay?"

"Could you hand me my purse, it's over there on the dresser." She held her hand out as her dad retrieved her bag. She'd take her anti-acid the doctor had prescribed. Then things would cool down and she could cope.

"Effie, what is wrong?"

"No one has seen Lance. When you didn't come out at noon, we thought maybe he'd snuck in here with you. Reagan sent me in to see what the holdup was."

Her dad handed her a glass of water, she quickly tossed back the gel tab. Then Glenna dug through her purse to unearth her smart phone. She punched in the number to *Glenna's Surprisingly Vintage*. A few rings and her assistant picked up.

"Alex how are things going?"

Worry tightened her chest as Alex exclaimed in surprise about her call.

"Yes, I am supposed to be at the altar..."

There was another bout of excited chatter and Glenna let her assistant run out of words. Though she knew the answer, Glenna asked anyway.

"Have you seen Lance?"

After another smattering of exclamations Glenna finished the call and sat the phone at her side. Her insides were a twist of emotions. The bastard had left her at the altar. On the trail of that thought, fear gripped her with sharp talons. Where was Lance? Was he hurt? The air suddenly too thick to breathe she inhaled but nothing seemed to fill her lungs.

With a sensation of falling over, the room filtered from gray to black.

*****

"Come on Glenna, let's get you up. We need to get this blasted dress off you." Fred tugged at her arm. He shot a look over his shoulder. "Effie can you find Martha for me?"

The pink confection whirled as she pulled the door wide and dashed out the door, and then he heard an 'Ooof.'

Again he twisted to glance toward the door. Effie hadn't needed to go far to find Martha. His wife rushed in, bellowing orders about cold cloths, glass of water, and help in one giant breath.

Effie didn't bother to reset her other strap that was now falling down, the constraints on her hair had lost the battle, without a care she raced off to do Martha's bidding.

"Fred, what happened?"

"She was sitting on the edge of the bed, though how I'm not sure with this bundle of material she has on." He shook his head. "It was the weirdest thing. When Effie told her Lance wasn't here, she called her shop. She seemed so calm. After she sat her phone down and she literally in *slow* motion began to topple to the ground."

"Why didn't you catch her?"

"Well, Martha dear, that's the weird part." She tilted her head and raised a brow. "It happened to fast."

"But you just said it was in slow motion."

"Yes, but by the time it registered what was happening it was too late."

A soft groan pulled their attention to Glenna. Effie raced in with the armful of instructions and plopped down beside them, spilling the glass of water in the process.

Glenna sputtered. "What was that for? You didn't need to throw cold water in my face for God's sake."

"I'm sorry," Effie said. "At least you're awake now."

"If you say so," Glenna grunted.

Fred wished he could do more than to help Glenna to a sitting position. When his children hurt, his heart ached right along with them. It didn't matter how old they were.

"Come on little one, let your friend and mother help you out of your dress and meet us in the kitchen."

"For a family meeting?"

Fred couldn't tell if she sounded hopeful or sarcastic. Nonetheless he patted her shoulder and left. The family discussions always took place in the kitchen, he'd gather the others.

No one walked away from his daughter on her wedding day. If Fred got a hold of that Lance Gordon, heaven help him.

*****

Glenna let her mother help her pull the heavy fabric over her head. With Effie trying to help and mostly getting in the way. Finally, when she was free of her dress, she sank onto the bed and put her head in her hands and waited for the tears.

None came.

It appeared she'd just been jilted, and no tears. What was wrong with her?

"Are you all right, dear?" Her mother wanted to know.

She sighed, was she? Yes, but could she admit that? What kind of bride would be okay after being abandoned at the altar in front of *all of* her family and friends? The kind that got caught up in the romance of the proposal and not the man. Because really, did she love Lance?

She cared for him.

"Dear?"

"Sorry Ma, I'm not sure how I feel."

That at least satisfied her mother's question. But when she glanced at her friend, Effie hadn't been fooled. There'd be some answering to do later. She'd worry about it then.

Effie held her jeans out to her. "Time to slip these on."

Once she had the jeans on, she slipped her tee over her head. She caught sight of herself in the mirror and gave an inward groan. She could imagine what her brother's would say about the deranged mop listing to the side of her head.

"Hand me that brush over there, please."

She didn't care who gave it to her as long as she could do something. She needed to be confident when she faced the clan. Being the youngest was tough and her family could be intimidating to say the least.

"I'm going to make some tea, dear. Gabby made the announcement that due to technical difficulties, there wouldn't be a wedding today and Sophie is currently ushering people out of the yard." She chuckled. "Sorry dear, but those girls..."

"It's okay Ma, really." She gave her mom a hug. "I'll be there in a moment."

"Effie dear, thank you for taking care of our girl."

Glenna held in a chuckle. If anything she was taking care of Effie. She was always getting herself into one scrap or another. The woman was the most kind hearted, lovable, crazy, gullible, naïve, scatterbrained, and optimistic person she'd ever met. Effie had saved her life, maybe not literally but she had, when Glenna had first moved to Calistoga. She didn't know what she'd do without her friend.

"Do you believe me now?"

"What?" Glenna blinked. It took her a minute to understand the question. "About Lance? There are so many things you've told me about Lance, which one do you think I believe now?"

Effie giggled. "Come on, I've always wanted to be in on one of the Beckett family round tables in the kitchen."

She reached for Glenna's hand to pull her toward the door. With a surprisingly strong grip.

She let herself be pulled downstairs. Effie needed no directions, the sound of voices directed just fine.

"Glenna," her oldest sibling, Tyler said. "Come sit at the head of the table"

"The seat of doom," she muttered under her breath.

Unfortunately, her mother heard. "Honey, we're here for you. There is not going to be any doom."

The *Elders* busied themselves setting food that should have been for the reception, in the center of the table. Then drinks all round. Tea for some, beer for others. Glenna thought it would be prudent to keep to the tea side for now. After a few minutes had passed, everyone seemed settled with either a drink or food or both. As if on cue there was a collective sigh and their attention settled on her. A heavy weight of expectation.

She drew in a fortifying breath as she gazed around at her family. The younger Beckett's were in the family room with the generals in charge. She noticed her brother Tyler and her two brother-in-law's Gabe and David all had a small notebook, pen raised in anticipation. What did they think this was an interrogation?

Tyler tapped the end of his pen against is lips, she recognized the action. He'd been doing the same since school. His *thinking* persona. As if he felt her attention he lowered the pen to the notebook and pinned her with an intent look.

"When was the last time you saw *Lance*."

"Tyler you already know that," Glenna answered.

"No, I just know he didn't come with you from the airport and that he was to meet you here today."

All true, she'd needed to do some last minute wedding shopping and she wanted to spend some time with her family. She shut her eyes a moment and tried to picture the last time she was with him, what had he said?

"A week ago, he had a buying trip he wanted to go on before we left for our honeymoon trip."

"Where did he go?" David raised a brow, he used a pencil, and had it poised above the paper. "Could his plane have been delayed?"

"When was he supposed to be in New York?" Gabe shot his question off as if afraid he wouldn't get a word in if he didn't hurry. "What airport, airline?"

She should have thought to bring her own damn notebook to take down the questions. God. "He went to Brussels, he had a contact that informed him of a priceless piece."

No one said anything, clearly they were all waiting for her to tick off the rest of the answers. Matt, her brother sat to her left, nudged her leg and when she turned toward him he winked. Matt of all people knew what it felt like to be under the scrutiny of the *Cloak and Dagger* part of the family. She smiled and turned her attention to the conversation. Might as well give all the information they need, the faster to get this over and go lick her wounded pride in private.

Because she finally realized that she was actually relieved and it was just humiliating to be the one left at the altar.

"He was supposed to come in last night, but when I called he didn't answer." She gave a shrug. "Then I went with Jessica to do some last minute grocery shopping."

"And you never tried again?" Keira, her law enforcement sister-in-law asked.

It must be a telling sign to her family when she wasn't anxious, most couples were inseparable before their wedding. Yet the night before their wedding she hadn't even wondered why he didn't call when he received her message. Nor had he thought to let her know if he'd arrived safe.

"It wasn't uncommon for him not to return my calls. When he left, he said not to be surprised if he didn't call." She grinned. "He said it would make things more exciting when we saw each other for the first time at our wedding."

Her grin faded, was he hurt somewhere?

"What airport and airline?" Gabe repeated his question.

"JFK and Delta."

"I'll go make some calls." Christine her oldest sister stood and paused. "Do you know where he was going to stay last night?"

It would have made more sense had he stayed in Brooklyn, but Lance was a snob and had to stay in Manhattan. It didn't matter that Brooklyn was an up and coming city with all the millennials fleeing the crowded city.

"The Grand Hyatt on 42nd."

Christine raised a brow but didn't say anything, just turned. Glenna assumed she would call the airport and the hotel. If she were going to lose a bridegroom, at least her family had the knowledge and the contacts to find that person and bring him home.

The question was, did she want them to?

Conversation around the table turned to of all the possibilities of what could have happened. Much like the research sessions she'd loved when she'd been attending Stanford University.

Tyler had already filled two pages with likelihoods to follow up on.

Christine came through the arch from the family room and walked straight to Glenna, placed a hand on her shoulder. Dread galloped along Glenna's skin to settle in the pit of her stomach.

"His name was not on any of the flight manifests for flights in from Brussels yesterday." She squeezed Glenna's shoulder. "The Grand Hyatt didn't have a reservation for a Lance Gordon. I had the airline and the hotel check for the last four days including today. Just in case he came in early, or came in this morning."

Glenna looked round the table, their expressions reflected what she was thinking.

Had he planned to marry her?

Chapter Two

Muscle guy glanced around the room at _Glenna's Surprisingly Vintage_. "Are you sure the Bellini is here?"

The dark fabric stretched across his body builder frame defining each muscle as he stalked around the room. He stopped to finger a delicate ballerina that looked out of place in his large gloved hand. He'd grown to appreciate the delicateness of the figurines and art that he'd come to love in the last ten years.

When he'd joined the Yacht Club de Monaco, he'd been so excited. He'd never imagined that years later he'd take it all for granted.

The day it had all started, seemed like just yesterday.

Bored. The four of them had been so bored. All of them had more money than they knew what to do with, which their wives and girlfriends took great delight in spending. There they were sitting around tossing back shots of fifty-year old Yamazaki whiskey—the cost of one bottle more than most people's homes—as if it were two buck chuck. Or was that three buck chuck now?

The women had gone out shopping. The exclusive boutique shops, on the French Riviera, had monthly themes. That month had been cat burglars, for some unknown reason. The women had all been giggling about buying slinky and chic black dresses, and strappy shoes when they'd left.

He glanced down his solid body at his attire, dressed for that same theme. That had been what had started the idea rolling, until here they were, ten years later. _The Black Cats_. Looking for a priceless painting that had been stolen during the Nazi occupation.

The three men stood in the store room that doubled as the shop office. The fourth man waited in the car with the engine running and ready to flee.

They'd delayed until closing and well after dark, before entering. It came in handy that Stocky Guy was a lock expert, as having been a locksmith during University. Who needed to break in when they could walk in, get what they wanted, and then lock up and no one the wiser?

"Yeah, I bought Gordon a couple of drinks, flirted with him," the stocky one said in disgust. "So not my type. *If I were gay*, that is. The guy loved to brag so it didn't take long to find out that he was after the Madonna and Child. He even had a buyer."

"How did he know it was here?" The tall lankly beach boy type, out of place in his black clad garb, asked as he continued to search through items in the box they'd found stored in a corner.

Brought back to the present by the questions floating around him by his closest friends muscle guy answered. "Didn't you say he'd found the piece at some estate sale?"

"Yeah, except when he got to the sale someone had already purchased it. He found the manifest and followed the new owner here. She's the proprietor, Glenna Beckett," stocky said.

"Convenient she's out of town." This from the lanky guy.

"Gordon's idea. He somehow convinced her to marry him." Stocky chuckled.

Lanky guy turned to him. "I thought he was gay? You did said you flirted with him."

"Yes to both. Apparently she didn't know that, because he played her and now she's back east, and we're one step ahead of him." Again stocky let out a chortle.

"Let's get the art and get out of here. I checked Gordon's flight and he should be here soon." Muscled guy moved with deceptive calm.

A rattling of keys sounded in the door, and the light flaring nearly blinded the three men standing in the center of the office.

The woman's scream broke the silence. She turned to flee but stocky guy slammed the door shut. Like a wild person she kept screeching and ran through to the show room. The three men followed.

"We just don't have time for this," the lanky guy declared.

Before muscle guy could stop his friend, the other man pulled his gun out and shot her execution style.

"What the fuck?" muscle guy said. "Are you crazy, *The Black Cats* may have a reputation for going to extremes to get what they want, but we've never killed anyone."

Stocky guy seemed to be frozen in place staring at the woman who only seconds before had been alive, vital, and very beautiful. He looked up at his other friend, the moisture in his eyes sparkled through the black mask.

"There was no need, Jason. Fuck."

Muscle guy tensed and turned. "No names, I don't care if we're the only one's here. There's surveillance, which has caught this whole scene for the viewing joy of others, and it could have audio."

Placing a hand over his ear piece he spoke to the fourth man still in the car. "And we're supposed to have a warning. You fall asleep at the wheel?"

The other two looked at him and nodded. What started out as an evening of enjoyment for their favorite hobby, finding the treasure and selling it to the highest bidder, just turned deadly serious. After a moment a voice in their ear pieces sounded.

"I swear to God no one has been on the sidewalk since you went in the side door. No one went through the front door. No car drove in. I had no clue about a surprise guest until you did."

All three stood staring at the woman as if she'd magically get up and walk away. Then muscle guy sighed.

"Let's get the piece, get the hell out of here." Muscle guy continued to look around the store room. "It's not in here. I swear we've looked everywhere.

Where did that real estate dude say there was a hidden storage?"

There was a pause as all of them thought back over their planning conversations. Lanky guy scratched around his neck as if the ski cap rubbed him the wrong way. "I'm not sure he actually said where, just that in his experience of the area several shop owners have maintained the cellars for storage that were built into their establishments during the prohibition. He knew this was one of them. He did however say, the entrance to the storage was hidden."

Stocky guy snorted. "He knew?"

"I'll take another look in the back, see if I can find any hidden nook." Lanky guy, who'd been called out as Jason, walked swiftly through the door into the office area.

Muscle guy and stocky guy stayed away from the body and the windows and then moved toward the back office going out the back way they'd entered.

"Nothing here." Lanky guy said as he returned. "I don't know where there could be a hidden storage area. There's no trap doors, nothing. I even looked in the closet."

"Let's get out of here."

The three stood at the back door, while lanky beach boy, Jason, opened then leaned out to scope the area. "Come on, I can see the car over there under the trees."

No one spoke as they made it to the sidewalk and across the road. At the late hour no one seemed to be around. The bar scene was farther south on Fairway. They were on the north end, where it seemed everyone had hunkered in for the evening.

When they climbed in the car, muscle guy ordered his friend at the wheel to get them the hell out of there. Once out of the area, as if orchestrated, they pulled off their ski masks.

"Did you get the Bellini?" The driver asked.

"No, there was no fucking storage area either." Muscle guy punched the back of the seat.

The driver glanced in the rearview mirror to lock eyes with muscle guy. "Yes there is, that agent said he had been down in the basement, before it was a store. There's no guarantee the owner uses it, but it would be a waste of space not to."

"Waste of space? What are you a designer or something?" Stockier asked.

There was no answer from the driver as he concentrated on the road until he pulled in front of the only five-star hotel they could find in Calistoga, The *Solage*.

During the drive, the men had replaced their black turtlenecks with dress shirts, their black jeans finished off the look of casual elegance.

The driver had already been in his dress shirt and black jeans. They took turns being the one left in the car to drive for a quick getaway if needed. "God, from the sound of it, I'm glad it was my turn to drive. I'm not positive, but I'm pretty sure I'd be squeamish witnessing a shooting.

"What the fuck were you thinking, Jason?"

*****

Home. Glenna paid the driver, grabbing her bag out of the back seat before the man had a chance to help. As she walked up the drive she savored the sight of her small cottage on 3rd Street only a few streets north of the main drag, Lincoln Avenue. She dropped her suitcase on the postage stamp size porch and took a moment to survey her neighborhood and appreciate the cool fall evening.

She let herself in and smiled. She loved her home. It may be small, but it was hers. She would unpack and make a quick dinner and have an early night. She probably should check on *Glenna's Surprisingly Vintage*, but she trusted Alexis Hansen her assistant to keep things in order. One of the most organized and business minded people she knew, Alex would have called if she'd had any problems. Morning was soon enough to get her head back on the job.

She needed one more night. Time when there was no family, no one to try to comfort her. A loud hammering on her door made her sigh. So much for being alone. Effie probably thought she needed company. She finished hanging up the blouse she'd just placed on the hanger. When she opened the door it wasn't her friend, but her crotchety old neighbor.

"Mr. Barlow."

Glenna felt guilty when she saw Agnes, her tabby, in his arms. She'd forgotten to retrieve her precious cat from him. Poor thing. She reached for the furry bundle in the nick of time, as he practically threw the feline at her.

"Here's your damn cat." Without another word he turned to stomp to his house next door.

"Thank you, I really appreciate it," she called after him.

He didn't so much as miss one stomp before she heard the bang of his screen door. She swore she heard him cuss before the slam of the inner door shut him in for the night.

She gave Agnes a squeeze and scratched her head, the cat purred in delight. "I'm sorry I left you so long with Mr. Grumpy Pants. Come on, let's give you some dinner."

After she finished her unpacking and ate dinner, she settled in her favorite spot, to read one of her many romance novels. Unfortunately, her mind wasn't on the pages. Instead it wandered over the last week.

Thank God her family had offered to return all the gifts that had arrived at the *Elders* home prior to the wedding, or the non-wedding as her mind had labeled it. She wasn't sure if she'd been able to stand taking care of that chore. By the time she'd left Brooklyn her stomach had been a firestorm.

Her parents had insisted she stay a few days with them until they could locate her missing fiancé. Her family prided themselves on having the crème de la crème of law enforcement, and yet they had not found a trace of Lance.

One thing kept nagging at her. He had wanted to marry *her*. He was the driving force to get the deed done. Glenna had been the one to drag her feet. On reflection, she realized in her heart something was off.

She stood to pace her small living room, her mind still reaching for clues. She stopped in the middle of the room, Agnes let out a soft meow as if she understood her muddled thoughts.

"What did Lance want?"

The cat wound her way into a figure eight pattern between Glenna's ankles. She waited until the cat cleared the danger zone before resuming her pacing. There was something at *Glenna's* that Lance had been searching for, if she could figure out what that was then maybe she'd find him.

Again she stopped.

"Do I want to find him?"

She needed some sleep. There hadn't been much of that since her aborted wedding day, and though Alex had most likely kept everything running smooth at the shop there were invoices, receipts and a whole host of other items waiting for her.

Hours later, she still stared at the ceiling longing for sleep. She was more than tired, she was exhausted yet her mind kept going over the events of the last month. In hindsight, there were so many signs that should have shown her not to marry Lance. How had she missed them *all*?

She'd met him the year before last at the annual Calistoga Lighted Tractor Parade. An event that she'd loved since her first Christmas in the valley. She had loved the look of him, so urban and yet metrosexual at the same time. With his sleek expensive gray suit with a man bun, he just looked so sophisticated. Her family, especially her brothers, hadn't been as charmed by his looks, they'd dubbed him *bun boy*.

Lance had been holding, or more like gripping, his coffee and muttering about *how could he have known this was the backwoods? This was Napa Valley for God's sake.*

He was not impressed with the vehicles and their individuality in the creative lighting covering the rigs. She pretended not to have heard him mutter and asked him where he was from. They'd had a short conversation, only after he'd decided she wasn't a backwoods hick. But after only a few more trucks he'd tossed his to-go mug in the trash and strode angrily away. She never *had* found out what had made him attend the parade if he had felt so strongly against it.

What wasn't to like? Lots of festivities, bright lights, Christmas cheer, and where else could you find Gingerbread and wine pairing? She laughed just thinking about it.

She rolled to her side and punched her pillow and willed herself to sleep. It didn't work. A moment later, she was remembering how the next day he'd entered her shop. At the time, she'd was surprised to see him. She welcomed him like she did everyone. And he complimented her shop and she offered to show him around some of her treasures. He started flirting with her, in such an old world way. She'd been surprised because she had been positive he was gay.

She went along with the banter. She'd even taken him into her store room, something she never did.

She sat up. There was something about his expression when he'd scanned the room, it had been searching for sure, but... What had he seen or not seen? It was just out of her grasp.

She glanced at the clock. Five in the morning. Her brain was racing to pinpoint that fleeting feeling she'd had that first morning Lance had visited her shop. There would be no sleep. She threw the covers back and made herself get up for the day.

After she showered and had her first cup of coffee she sort of felt human. It was going to be a long day. She checked the cat food in the automatic feeder and made sure water filled the bowl. As if the feline could smell food on the horizon she edged her way around the door frame and then rubbed around Glenna's ankles.

"Agnes you be good while I'm gone." She scratched behind the gray tabbies ears.

Usually she walked to *Glenna's Surprisingly Vintage*, however the dawn was creeping in and the moon was just dipping behind the mountain. Even the breeze had a bite. She'd drive.

As she pulled into the store's parking lot, she noticed the lights were ablaze in the shop. Odd, electricity was not cheap. In fact there was a reminder on an antique cork board by the switch for the last person out to shut off the lights.

With a feeling of unease, she unlocked the back door into the shop. A wave of *something* rotting hit her like a solid wall. She immediately covered her nose with her hand. She tossed the keys onto the office desk and went in search of the stench. By the time she reached the showroom it was all she could do not to toss her cookies or more precisely, her coffee.

Everything looked fine. The glass counters that ran around the room gleamed as if Alex had just used glass cleaner. Nothing to note on the shelves. No windows were broken. As she stepped around the counter the full force of rotting flesh hit her.

In the center of the room lay her assistant. The body had clearly been there for longer than a day. Glenna couldn't hold on any longer, she lost the coffee and biscotti, adding to the already overwhelming smell.

She backed her way into the office to call *nine one one*. She stayed in her office until the officers knocked on the front door.

"Come to the back please," she called from that door.

The two officers came around the side of the building, one had a steaming cup of some kind of brew in his hand.

"You may want to put your mug on my desk before you go in there."

The two officers looked at each other and promptly covered their noses, the mug hit the desk with a thunk. They both stopped at the edge of the counter.

The tall cop, clearly more experienced of the two, turned to her. "Do you know the victim?"

"Yes, she's my assistant Alexis Hansen. She lives in Yountville."

He ushered his partner and Glenna toward the office. He gestured for her to have a seat at her desk. He settled into the chair on the opposite side.

"Karl I'll call it in and get the medical examiner out here." The other officer didn't wait for an answer. He opened the door letting the early morning breeze in for a moment before it shut behind him.

"I'm Officer Karl Beckworth, and he..." He nodded his head toward the door where his partner had left. "...is my partner, Dane Jones."

He pulled a small electronic device out of his pocket, it looked like a cross between a phone and an eReader. From a side band he pulled a stylus out and poised it over the screen, then gave his attention to her. "You called this in?" He glanced toward the business license hanging next to the desk. "You're the proprietor?"

Was this a trait of the law enforcement profession? Asking questions in a row instead of waiting for an answer before moving to the next question? When she didn't answer he ducked his head and looked at her through his lashes as if he were dissecting her.

She cleared her throat. "Yes, to both questions."

"I'm not a medical examiner, but even I can see she's been there for a while."

She wasn't sure if that was an accusation or a statement. He wrote something in his little tablet, then leaned back in his chair so he could see through to the show room. "I'll be right back."

He didn't give her a chance to respond. She thought he was going back to look at the body, but instead he went out the door and disappeared. She was about ready to go find him when he returned. He settled onto the chair, scribbled something and then without looking up asked a question.

"What I want to know is this, why didn't anyone call it in before this? The lights are blazing you can *clearly* see the body from the windows, especially the front door."

On the last word he finally looked up and pinned her with a stare as if she knew the answer. If he wanted to disconcert her with his interrogation style it was working.

"I would like to know the same thing."

"And why are you just calling it in?" He finally asked the question she'd been waiting for since the officers arrived.

"The examiner is on the way and so is the CSI team," Officer Jones announced as he returned to the room. "Why didn't anyone call this in before now? You can see the body from the front."

"That seems to be the question of the day," Glenna couldn't help the dry comment. Both officers glared for a moment. Then Officer Beckworth returned to business.

"Well? Why didn't you called it in earlier?" he repeated.

"I have been at my family's home in Brooklyn. I got home last evening. As soon as I discovered Alex..." She refused to call her friend *the body*. "I called *nine one one*."

"And you can back up your alibi?" This from Jones.

"May I?" She nodded toward her purse.

When neither protested, she dug through and found the receipts she'd left in her purse. Anything financial she kept in the shop office. She handed the papers to Beckworth. He took his time reading the dates, with Jones reading just as thoroughly from his vantage point, over his partner's shoulder.

"You've been gone for over a week. When was the last time you talked to your assistant?"

Glenna swallowed down her guilt as she realized she hadn't even checked on the shop since she'd called to ask about Lance on her wedding day.

"September 29th," she said. "It was around two in the afternoon. About noon here."

"That was shortly after you left and you didn't check on your business?" She didn't blame him for his skepticism.

Jones squinted at her, after a moment he asked. "How did you know the exact date and time? That was a week ago."

Damn, she hadn't really wanted to discuss why she'd been at her parents'. There didn't seem to be any way around the subject. Might as well get it over with, it wasn't going to get any easier.

"That was supposed to have been my wedding day."

Officer Beckworth lowered his brow at her, but remained silent. A good tactic to encourage people to talk—Tyler had once told her that little tidbit of information.

"I called Alex to find out if she'd seen my fiancé."

"Wasn't he with you?" Officer Jones asked.

"If he had been I wouldn't have called Alex." Dumb ass, did he have to make things harder?

"So what happened? The guy leave you high and dry on your wedding day?" Jones chuckled.

No, she did not like the younger officer at all.

"Dane, try to be a little more sensitive." The older officer admonished.

"Sorry," Jones muttered without a trace of remorse and he still had a smirk riding his lips.

"Something like that." She might as well answer the question, as he'd guess anyway. "Can we try to figure out what happened to poor Alex in there?"

"May I make copies of these papers?" Officer Beckworth asked.

Since they verified she was not in the vicinity at the time of the murder she didn't see a reason to refuse. Through the open door, Glenna saw a patrol car and a black sedan pull into the parking lot.

During the next several moments, her little office was crowded with people. Officer Jones led the two Crime Scene Investigators into the show room.

"God someone hurled in here, and it's fresh." His voice grated down her spine.

She closed her eyes in mortification, heat burned in her stomach and she could feel her cheeks warm.

"Dane we do not need a commentary." Officer Beckworth didn't say anything to her but sent a look of apology for his partner.

Two hours later, she knew her prediction of a *long day* had been a gross understatement. It wasn't even noon yet and she felt as if it had been days since she'd walked in and found Alex. She wasn't sure what she felt. The only thing she knew was that she was numb.

Alex had been shot, but the official cause of death wouldn't come until after the autopsy. While the officers seemed to be otherwise occupied, she stepped out to the landing for fresh air.

"Don't go far." Beckworth's voice echoed after her.

No sooner than she reached her car than she saw Effie sprint from her Bistro coffee shop. The parking lot serviced both their businesses. Glenna leaned her hip on the fender making sure she was in view of the window of the door. Not only did she want to see what was going on, but she wanted Officer Beckworth to see her.

"What the fuck is going on?" Somehow the F bomb didn't sound strange coming out of the little woman that was more elfin than... normal human.

"Someone murdered Alex."

"*What?*" Effie strode to the door, but the officer shooed her away.

"Who would hurt Alex, she was the nicest person I've ever met."

"I don't know, Effie. I feel terrible. I didn't call her all week to check on her. What kind of person am I? Maybe if I'd not been so self-absorbed and called her over the week, I could have alerted someone when she didn't answer. If she hadn't been such a loner or lived alone, maybe someone would have raised an alert about her missing."

Her chest tightened at the thought of Alex and confronting who had done this to her. She must have been so frightened. Before that moment, she'd had an entire life waiting for her, and now she'd never experience the joys of love, children, growing old. She would never see her family again.

Nor would her family ever see her again. The world had lost a beautiful soul. Glenna knew that Alex was in a beautiful place now, but she'd deserved to live her life.

"Glenna, there is no way you could have prevented this."

"I know, however if I'd called she would have been found earlier. The body has been here for a few days. Alex wouldn't have wanted anyone to see her like that."

"That can't be, I have been back in town for a few days and I've walked by the shop and didn't notice anything."

"Did you look in?"

Effie thought a moment. "I don't think so. You know when you're walking a familiar path you tend to take things for granted. Lost in your own thoughts. You just assume everything is the same."

"One of the officer's checked the front door, it's locked. If there were any customers who tried the door, they either didn't look in to see the body or worse they didn't bother to call and report it."

Effie made a face, which seemed so out of character that Glenna could only stare. She'd never seen Effie without a smile or at least a serene expression.

"I don't think anyone would *not* call it in. I don't think they noticed. The pedestrian traffic has been low this week. That has to be it Glen, otherwise I would lose faith in humankind."

"I think you're right. I would hope so anyway."

"Why don't you come over for a latte?" Effie started to walk, thinking Glenna would follow.

"I don't think the officer wants me out of his sight."

Effie turned and gazed past Glenna at the bustling shop. "How many guys are in there?"

Glenna frowned, why would she want to know? Then she realized. Effie was being Effie, taking care of everyone. "I think there's, let see, two CSI guys, then there's the medical examiner and then Beckworth and Jones."

Effie started to turn, then looked over her shoulder. "White chocolate mocha?"

"Skinny as you can make it. Oh, I forgot the photographer. "

"You got it, six coffees and a WCM, on the skinny." And her friend was on her way.

What would she do without Effie? She would've never survived without her, not after what happened when she'd first moved to Calistoga when she'd graduated from Stanford.

The jingle on her cell for her brother Tyler interrupted her thoughts. She pulled the phone out of her back pocket to answer.

"How did you know I needed to talk to my big brother, that just so happens to be a fed?"

"What's going on?" Tyler's voice sounded like he was standing next to her.

"Do you remember my assistant?"

"Have I met her?" Guys were so literal sometimes.

"No, I meant just me mentioning her when I called the shop?"

"Yes, I remember you called to see if Bun Boy was there." When she didn't take offense to his reference he continued. "Why?"

"Someone murdered her in the shop while I was gone. I discovered her body this morning when I opened the shop..." She swallowed. She could feel the water works threatening. She drew air in through her mouth, out threw her nose.

"Glenna, are you okay?"

"No."

"Dumb question, of course you're not."

"Why did you call, Tyler?"

"I was worried about you and my gut told me to call you."

Their family had always been close, but she had a special connection with Tyler. He wasn't just her big brother, he was her protector. He had a sixth sense when it came to Glenna. He had called during that dark time when she'd first moved. She'd only told him the partial truth about that terrible night. He'd still been on the next flight out.

"I don't know what to think, Tyler. Do you think Lance's disappearance has anything to do with Alex? She was the sweetest girl, no one would want to hurt her."

"Was anything missing?"

She paused, she hadn't even looked. "I don't know. I haven't really had time to look."

"Didn't the responding officers ask?"

"Not yet. But they've been pretty busy."

"Idiots," he muttered. "Look I have a few connections on the west coast. A friend of mine from my time at Quantico works out of the field office in San Francisco. I'll give him a call."

"Would you? Maybe he can figure out what is going on. I'm scared, Tyler. Do you think Lance could be involved? The more I think about it the more I think he sought my shop out for something. Even Alex said whenever he'd stop in he seemed to be searching for something. Yet, there is no way Lance murdered Alex, he genuinely liked her."

"Don't worry, I know someone who will figure this out. His name is Patrick McGinnis, expect a call from him."

"Thank you Ty. I really appreciate it."

They talked a few more minutes until Glenna spotted Effie carrying a tray of beverages from the Bistro.

"I need to go help Effie, thank you." She hung up before he could protest.

She plucked her white chocolate mocha off the tray, no sense taking a chance that one of the officers wouldn't snag it.

"Thank you, Effie, you're the best."

"Who was on the phone?" Her friend asked.

"Tyler."

"I should have known. Are you sure he's not your twin? I swear you two *got* the *twin connection.*"

"Reagan and I have the connection, it's just different than mine and Tyler's." She sipped and let the warm liquid slide down her throat. "He's going to call a friend to come and make sure we find who did this to Alex."

Effie nodded toward the office door as they walked toward it. "Do they know that your brother is sending help?"

"No, and I'm not going to tell them."

As they stepped through into the office, the smell of coffee drew the officers like cops to a donut shop. Though it had to have been more of a sixth sense. No way could they have *actually* smelled the brew. Once the coffees were divvied out, Glenna turned to Officer Beckworth.

"Do you want me to check to see if anything is missing? There has to be a reason my assistant was murdered."

Beckworth turned his attention to her in surprise. Obviously he hadn't thought she had a brain in her head.

"That would be helpful. As soon as the CSI and photographer are done, if you could go over your inventory and make a list of anything missing."

She nodded and returned to her vigil by her car. Effie kept step with her as best as her short legs would let her.

"Did Tyler say when this guy would call?"

"No, but he said to expect him soon."

"Good." She sipped her own beverage, which Glenna knew to be Chai. "Glen, you need to get your life back, it hasn't been yours since Lance walked through the door."

"You never liked Lance. Why?" Glenna had never really asked. She'd acknowledged, many times, her friend hadn't liked her fiancé but she'd never confirmed it by asking.

"Since you're ready to listen, first of all your brothers are right. He's gay. In fact, I've seen the way he watches men. Usually we both follow their cute little asses with our eyes."

She waited for Glenna to respond but Glenna just rolled her eyes at her friend. She had a feeling that everyone had been right on that subject. Not that it mattered, except that made it even more confusing that he'd asked her to marry him.

"Is that all?"

Effie laughed. "Oh, where to start? The list of reasons is so long."

Glenna couldn't resist another eye roll. "Just list them from top to bottom."

"First, he never looked at you with love. A guy with love and romance on his mind, one who wants to sweep a woman away, gazes at her with adoration. Sure, he went through the motions—elaborate motions I know. I never heard one drop of adoration, unless it was for himself."

Glenna thought about it for a moment. Countless times when they'd been at a restaurant, he'd sit across from her and whisper words of love, and now she realized how empty the words were. Looking back, she

Mary Martinez

admitted to herself that his words and actions had all been scripted. The man had been playing a role and if she hadn't been so caught up in it, she would have realized that it was fake.

He had romanced her with gestures and props but there had been *no touching*. In retrospect she couldn't believe she hadn't noticed.

As if reading her thoughts Effie asked. "Did the man ever hold your hand? Did he ever throw his arm around your shoulders?"

"No to both. There are more and more things I'm remembering now. I think maybe I was too close and caught up in his grand scheme." She leaned her head and rested it on the top of Effie's.

Effie snaked her arm around Glenna's waist. "Now we just need to figure out what that grand scheme was."

Chapter Three

Patrick McGinnis thumbed his phone off and dropped the thing on the table with a thud. What had he just agreed to? He held in a groan, *barely*.

"What's up dad? You look like you just ate a sour grape."

Finnegan, his sixteen-year old son, and the joy of his life, walked to the cupboard and pulled out a bowl. He filled it with cereal and added milk and then joined Patrick at the table. He dipped his spoon for a large scoop, and as he brought it to his mouth, Finn gave him the *I'm waiting* look.

"I just received a call from an old friend," he said in way of explanation, he really didn't like talking work with his son.

"It must not have been a good conversation."

"It was good to catch up. He was with me at Quantico." Best to focus on the old acquaintance part.

"Dad, I'm in high school. You can stop sheltering me now. He must have called for a reason. One you're not too thrilled about. What's up?" He repeated his earlier question.

Damn, Finn was growing up to fast. And the kid was right. He had a tendency to shield him from his work. Something he'd always tried to do, but more since Finn was three and the worst thing that could ever happened to a child had happened.

"Tyler is an agent in New York, however, he has a sister in Calistoga."

His son let out a hoot of laughter. "Match-making from the east coast."

"Ha, ha. No, his sister seems to have lost her fiancé and her assistant."

"What they elope and left her behind? Why'd he call you?"

"The fiancé never arrived at the wedding. And then when his sister went to open her shop she found the assistant had been shot."

"Oh." Finn ate for a few minutes in silence. "Does the lost fiancé and the dead assistant have something to do with each other?"

"That's one of the things Ty wants me to find out."

Finn suspended his spoon half way to his mouth. "What is the other?"

"He wants me to find the missing fiancé for his sister." He pulled his fingers through his hair. "It's a wild goose chase if you ask me. If the guy had wanted to get married he'd have been at the wedding."

"You'd think, unless he couldn't."

Patrick contemplated his son. He would make a good detective. He'd already helped solve a few of his cases, by just listening and making comments that brought other solutions to mind. Patrick wasn't sure he wanted that for his son. He loved being a federal agent. For a while, after the incident with his son, he'd tried something else. However, his true passion was law enforcement and he'd been placed back on duty within the year.

You couldn't help where your heart led you. No matter the consequences.

"That is what I need to find out." He stood and poured more coffee into his cup to warm up the cooling liquid. He leaned a hip on the counter while he sipped. "What's going on at school today?"

Finn finished his cereal and stood to wash his bowl out. He appeared to be thinking as he put his dishes in the dishwasher.

"I have an algebra test. Just a fair warning, Dad, it's kicking my ass."

"Language son." But he smiled, he'd heard a lot worse. "I have a few minutes do you need my help?"

His son gave him a skeptical look, which was well warranted. Algebra had thoroughly kicked his ass in high school, too, to the point he'd needed Saturday morning classes to pass the damn class.

After a moment he answered. "No, Mrs. Stewart said she'd meet me before school."

"Old Mrs. Stewart is still there? I had her for Algebra." He smiled and resisted the urge to ruffle his son's hair. Since the boy was almost as tall as he was, it'd be a little awkward anyway. "You're in good hands then. Do you want me to drop you on my way to Calistoga?"

"Sure, let me grab my bag."

"We leave in five."

Patrick watched his son, then turned, rinsed his cup, and set it in the dishwasher. He might as well get this duty over with, he'd call his boss on the Bluetooth on the way and give him the details. He needed to see if they wanted to be involved or if he was doing this on the side.

They settled into his ancient 4Runner. Living half way between San Francisco and the Napa Valley area, a sturdy reliable vehicle was a must.

He'd grown up in American Canyon and when he'd started his career by going to John Jay College of Criminal Justice in New York all those years ago, he hadn't seen any reason to move when he'd finished. Since he'd brought Finnegan home with him, all the more reason to stay. He couldn't raise a boy on his own without the help of his parents.

"Dad, you're going to miss the road."

Patrick was startled to find he hadn't been paying attention, so lost in his thoughts. He slowed and barely made the turn without screeching the tires.

"Sorry bud, thinking." He parked in front of the school and waited while his son grabbed his things and gave a wave then turned and headed inside.

"Have a good day," he called after his son's retreating back.

Gone were the days when his son wanted a kiss and a hug. Apparently he was too manly for those things now. Patrick smiled. Sometime he should embarrass him by doing just that.

By the time he'd arrived in Calistoga he'd received the go ahead on delving into the disappearance of Lance Gordon. The man had been missing for over a week, during which time the murder had occurred, with the key connection, Glenna Beckett. His assignment was to find if the two were related in any way, or a coincidence. He didn't believe in the latter.

He slowed as he drove Lincoln Avenue keeping a look out for *Glenna's Surprisingly Vintage*. What kind of name was that for a store? Tyler had said that his sister owned a shop of antiques and other knickknacks. He pulled into the parking lot between *Glenna's* and another place with a sign gently swaying in the breeze, *Effie's,* in elaborate looping letters. The words *Coffee Bistro and More* were in the same cursive style printed in gold on the front window. Both shops fit the Calistoga touristy area. The main street was a favorite for summer vacationers. Not only could they stroll and visit unique shops, they could toss in a few stops for wine tasting. After all, this was Napa Valley. Even after the devastating fires, the place had rebuilt. The area was full of determined people.

He had a feeling he'd be here for most of the day. He hoped the *and More* meant he could pick up a sandwich, preferably something that didn't contain anything organic.

Placing the SUV in park, he checked his messages. He was expecting some Intel on Gordon. Unfortunately, his inbox did not have the requested information yet. Sighing, he couldn't put off dealing with Tyler's sister any longer. He climbed out and made his way to the side door. He knocked and after a moment a woman pulled the door wide.

"I'm sorry we're not open for business today."

The first thing he noticed was the resemblance Glenna Beckett had to her brother. If he'd seen her on the street he'd still know she belonged to the Beckett family. It wasn't intentional, but he found himself surveying her from head to toe, and what he saw made him want to turn tail and run.

His ex-wife all over again. Elegant, arrogant, selfish—came with the territory of elegant. She was exquisite, almost too perfect. Where her brother had almost black hair, she had streaks of gold through hers bringing out highlights that lightened the dark color. If her hair curled like her brother's did, she'd done something to tame it. Instead, the locks flowed down her back in gentle waves.

"Done staring?" Her voice interrupted.

He cleared his throat, dammit. "I'm Patrick McGinnis, Tyler sent me."

God that made him sound like an errand boy.

"Oh, come in. I've been expecting you." She stepped away to let him enter.

The smell slapped him in the face, no mistaking the aroma of decaying death. He found himself in a small office, away from the crime scene. However, the doorway into the shop afforded him a view of yellow caution tape and he could barely make out the edge of the chalk line where the body had been.

"Have a seat. What do you need from me? I want to help in any way I can. Alex was a good person. She didn't deserve this." He saw her throat work as she swallowed, her gaze darted away and she blinked several times to check the tears.

"Tyler said that your fiancé is also missing?" She didn't seem upset about that part of the scenario.

"Yes. Lance left to go to Brussels a week before the wedding. He was supposed to arrive in New York the day before we were to marry. I didn't think anything of him being later than expected. I thought he'd changed his itinerary to arrive with just enough time to get to the wedding."

"I understand he wasn't on any of the flight manifests for the day of the wedding or for a few days prior. What do you think happened?"

She seemed surprised by the question, though it was a logical one. "I don't know. I stayed in Brooklyn for a week while my family searched for him."

She turned her head toward the doorway leading to the showroom. She bowed her head. After a moment, she raised it to regard him again.

"I hadn't called Alex since the day of the wedding. I asked if she'd heard from Lance and she hadn't. And then I forgot about her. I didn't check on her, or my shop. If I had, maybe she would have been found sooner and the clues of the murder would be fresh." She looked down and seemed to struggle to gain control. "What kind of person am I?"

The question surprised him as he'd labeled her in the category of Joyce, the ex-wife. She had been so self-absorbed she'd never thought about anyone but herself, and certainly wouldn't have asked that question.

He wasn't ready to change his opinion of Glenna Beckett just yet. Joyce had been nice and thoughtful when he'd first met her, too.

"You couldn't have known." Avoiding the actual question. "You trusted your assistant, correct? Had she watched the shop for you before?"

"Yes. I trusted her or I wouldn't have entrusted the shop to her. She took over when I was on buying trips."

"Could she be involved in anything that doesn't concern your store, but may have resulted in her death?"

He was reaching. He suspected the woman's death had everything to do with the shop. He just needed to eliminate all the other possibilities so he could concentrate on the real issue.

Had Lance Gordon and Alexis Hansen been connected?

"I never associated with Alex outside of work. She was much younger than I am, plus she seemed to be more of a homebody."

"Do you know her friends?"

"A few have visited her here. I can't remember their names."

"Do you know how to contact her family?"

"Yes," she said. She dug around in her desk and finally found an address book and transferred the information to a card. "Here. I hope you can find something."

"I do too."

He pulled out his smart phone and found the recorder app, it was better than notes. First, he didn't miss anything while writing. Second, he couldn't read his own handwriting most of the time.

"What are you doing? Have you contacted Officer Beckworth?"

"The Agency has, I'm sure he's *thrilled.*"

She raised a brow, clearly catching his sarcasm. She nodded to the device. "And?"

"I'm going to go over everything with you since you met your fiancé. Do you mind if I record it? I will listen to it later for clues to follow up on, or anything I missed. Sometimes listening even brings more questions to mind."

"I don't mind. Where do you want me to start?"

"How did you meet?"

For the next hour she told him about her two yearlong whirlwind courtship. Two years didn't sound like a whirlwind. However, apparently it was, because in reality the time the couple actually spent together consisted of only a few months. By the time she finished he only had a few questions, but one thing nagged at him.

"It seems he pursued you, correct?"

"Yes. And that's what doesn't make sense to me. I had wanted a wedding next spring. I love that season. But more importantly, which I've only figured out this last week, I wanted to know more about him as a person."

"What do you mean? Why would you agree to marry someone unless you were in love with him?"

She sucked in her breath, closed her eyes a moment when she looked at him again, he detected something in her eyes. Almost embarrassment.

"I'm sorry, you probably think I'm a shallow person. There are so many things that I'm learning about Lance and myself that my friend Effie tried to point out the time."

He had no idea what she was talking about. This was the first reference to a friend. His ex had been shallow, so he'd already categorized Glenna that way the moment he saw her. Which actually made him the shallow one. He held his silence and let her continue, hopefully to explain.

"Lance was *always* romantic. Dinners, carriage rides when we visited New York. Aware of putting me first wherever we went. I'm ashamed to say I couldn't see past the romance of it all. When he proposed I was swept up in the moment and said yes. That's when the doubts started. Marriage is a big step and when I take it, I want the growing old package like the *Elders.*"

He frowned, again he had no idea what she was talking about, he did however, understand being swept up in the moment. Hadn't he proposed to Joyce because he was swept up in the moment? Of course, she was pregnant and there was a certain feeling of responsibility as well. But he'd been thrilled. He couldn't afford to get married, he was still at the University at the time. But he wanted to marry her. She was so perfect. Now he realized she'd been eye-candy and nothing more. She'd wanted to be a princess and he hadn't been a prince.

"The Elders?"

Her face lit with a smile that quite simply knocked his socks off, if he'd been wearing any. He was still blinded by it when she answered, he almost missed what she said.

"Sorry, the *Elders* are my parents. Not sure who started the term, but that's what we've called them since before Rea and I were born. Anyway, after Lance proposed, he jetted off to somewhere for his beloved antiques. I love antiques too, hence the shop, but I believe he loved them more than he loved me."

"Wait. If he didn't love you, why did he want to get married and more importantly why push for a fall wedding when you wanted to wait?"

She gave him a *look* as she threw her hands up in a questioning gesture. "That is *what* I've been trying to figure out. As the wedding drew closer, he was gone more often and I had time to think away from his constant wining and dining. Yet, I was still caught up in the romance of it enough to agree to a wedding at the end of September. And then he left me waiting at the altar."

"And this is why you asked Tyler to have me brought in? So I could find him for you?"

"Yes."

Patrick regarded her for a moment. "Have you decided you did love him after all and want him back?"

Where the hell had that question come from? It was none of his business and had *nothing* to do with the case. Actually, it did. What bothered him, was the fact *he* wanted to know as a man.

"No. I don't think he ever planned to marry me."

"What?" That had caught him off guard. "Then why push? This is the most bizarre situation I've ever heard of, and I still need to find a connection to the vic."

"Tell me about it." She sighed she raked a hand through her perfect hair. "Look, do you mind if we finish this conversation over at *Effie's*. I haven't eaten anything since yesterday morning, which I lost the moment I saw Alex on the floor. I'm not sure I can eat yet. But a latte would be nice."

Since his stomach was on a low rumble and he knew from experience it was about to turn to a growl any moment, he shut off the recorder and stood.

"I could use a sandwich. They have normal ones, right?"

She pushed away from the desk, grabbed her purse and stood. "What do you mean by normal?"

"You know like ham and cheese or turkey and Swiss? Nothing with Kale or Spinach on it."

She laughed and again he was glad he hadn't worn socks to be knocked off.

"Come on, I'm sure you'll find something to your taste."

She reached as if she might take his hand. He was sure it was habit for her. She immediately dropped her hand and kept her gaze straight. Her cheeks turned a delightful shade of champagne pink.

Deep in his bones, he knew he was in trouble. He had no clue how to extricate himself. Because he sure as hell didn't want to go down that path again.

Ever.

Chapter Four

Glenna kept her focus on *Effie's* porch. What had she been thinking? She'd almost grabbed Patrick's hand. There was something comforting about him. She hadn't thought about what to expect when the man contacted her, she hadn't had the time.

As soon as he introduced himself a feeling of calm had swept over her. Unfortunately, she didn't think he felt the same way. During their conversation she felt the weight of his attention and before he could mask the look in his eye, she'd seen something close to contempt or dislike. Why? She didn't know.

Maybe moving the meeting to a more casual spot at *Effie's* would help him loosen up. He had seemed less tense for a moment when asking about the sandwiches. The *normal* sandwiches made her chuckle, which rewarded her with another glower from him. Maybe he didn't like women. Hadn't she missed the signs with Lance?

At least the coffee shop wasn't crowded. *Effie's* was a popular place in Calistoga, and sometimes you didn't have a choice but a to-go order. After they gave their order, for which Patrick seemed happy to be able to order something *normal,* they found a corner table and he brought out his phone to set to record.

She hadn't realized how embarrassing it was going to be to tell a stranger how gullible she'd been. Lance had duped her, plain and simple. The more she talked to Effie, and now Patrick, the more foolish she felt. Blinded by the fantasy of what Lance had offered.

"Glen! I was about to come and get you, force feed you if I needed to." Effie turned as if she'd barely noticed Glenna's companion. "Well hell, no one gave me the hottie alert."

Glenna burst out laughing, not because of her friends' announcement but because the look on

Patrick's face was priceless. She wasn't sure if it was Effie's appearance or her declaration that he was a hottie. His gaze traveled from the top of her friend's cone head of blonde curls, over her green checkered blouse, registering her overalls, with one strap dangling at her front, to her socks, one bright pink, the other electric blue clashing with her red chucks.

He turned his dazed expression in Glenna's direction.

"Agent Patrick McGinnis, this is my person. Meaning she has saved my life and now and forever more is my best friend. Effie, Euphemia Kennedy."

He held out his hand reluctantly, maybe he thought her *uniqueness* would rub off. Effie on the other hand ignored the hand and since he was sitting, wrapped her arms around his neck in one of her famous hugs.

"I'm so glad to meet you." She straightened and turned her attention to Glenna. "Tell Tyler he did good."

Someone in the kitchen called out to Effie, with a wave she was gone. Patrick stared after her for several moments then clearly bemused regarded Glenna, again.

"What the hell was that? And what does she mean *Tell Tyler he did good?*"

"That was Effie, I think she was *Tinkerbell* in another life. She means that she's worried about me and I told her Tyler was sending someone."

As he reached for the phone, their order came. He moved it back to his pocket, thanked the girl, then grinned at Glenna.

"I'm starved. We'll finish after."

She regarded her food. She hadn't had an appetite since she'd found the body, but knew she should eat. She blew a breath out through her teeth and picked up the Turkey and Kale and tested it with a small bite. When it stayed put and didn't try to make a return appearance, she tried a larger one.

"You okay?" He asked.

"Yes, I think I can finally eat. Want to try my turkey and kale?" She grinned at him.

He eyed it dubiously as if he may actually try it. "No, I'm fine with my turkey and bacon."

They ate in silence for a few minutes. She wished she'd only ordered a half-sandwich. She'd take the rest to go. Apparently she'd have the same meal for dinner tonight.

"What did you mean by Effie's *your person*?"

"I told you, she saved my life."

"How? Did she give you CPR or something?"

If only that had been the case. "No. I moved to Calistoga right after graduation from Stanford. I didn't know anyone, something happened and she helped me pick up the pieces."

He took another bite and waited for her to continue. Glenna wasn't sure she wanted to. She didn't know him and the ordeal she'd gone through was such a private thing. But it still haunted her, and she had been keeping the worst part inside, telling her friends and family only part of it. Effie was the only one who knew the entire story. She'd encouraged Glenna to at least tell her family, but Glenna had refused and her friend had respected her wishes.

"There's more to the story, but I respect that it's private." He took a deep breath dusting off crumbs at the same time. "That was good. Now before we get back to business tell me exactly what the *person* means."

She decided to give him the abbreviated version, because without going into details of what had happened she couldn't really answer his question.

"Apparently, I have poor judgment when it comes to men."

He raised a brow at this bald statement but kept his thoughts to himself.

"As I said, I didn't know anyone when I moved here. The ink wasn't dry on my degree but I was ready to set up shop. I had no money, what was I thinking? I hadn't been thinking and I'm glad, or I probably wouldn't have the life I have now." She grinned. "At the moment it's a mess, but on a whole it's been a wild adventure."

"And your friend, what is her name?"

"Effie?"

"Yes, and Effie saved you from a wild adventure."

A chuckle slipped through her lips. "No, as I said I had no money. However, I was determined to have my shop on the main drag of Calistoga. Way above my price range. I was lucky to find an agent who would even talk to me. We met at an art showing in the area, one of the things we had in common. Love of art." She frowned. "That had been what drew me to Lance."

He raised a brow, but refrained from voicing his thoughts. She swore she actually heard: *Is there a pattern here?*

"His name was Danny Collins. He was so helpful. I thought at the time it was because we *did* have something in common. He found my property and negotiated a deal. I'd hadn't dared dream I would be lucky enough to find a place. After the papers were signed he asked me to dinner. I, in my naivety, thought we were going as *just friends*. After a few dinners he made an advance. Clearly he wanted more and I wasn't attracted in that way what-so-ever.

"I let him down as gently as I could. And we parted friends." She remembered the night she'd heard the key turn in the lock. "Or so I thought."

"Bastard."

She studied him through her lashes. "Exactly. Anyway, unbeknownst to me, he'd kept a copy of the key to the shop."

The scrape of Patrick's chair echoed over the conversation in the room, quiet settled in its wake. He glanced around, instead of standing as it looked like he had been about to do, he leaned forward and placed his palms flat on the table.

"What happened?"

She called upon the calm she needed to recite the details, she hadn't been ready to divulge. As she had with the police, the hospital, and her family she distanced herself—telling the story as if she were repeating something that had happened to someone else. If she didn't, all the emotions would come rushing in and overwhelm her. She couldn't do that right now, not with Alex's murder and Lance's disappearance.

"I was in my office working on the startup business plan the bank needed for my loan. Then I heard the key in the door to the office, not the front door. I may have had time to think of something if he'd come in that way. He was on me before I could stand."

Even though she planned to distance herself, it never completely worked. She swallowed the panic she'd felt, and the initial shock at seeing someone she trusted step through the door with the purpose to attack her.

"Effie was leaving work and saw Danny leave my office. We hadn't met yet, but she had a gut feeling something wasn't right. She found me laying in a pool of my own blood from the broken nose he gave me. She's the one who called the police, the ambulance, and Tyler."

"Bastard," he repeated.

"Then she set about helping me put the pieces of my life together again. I had trusted Danny. I truly thought of him as a friend and I was so grateful to have someone to introduce me to the community."

"How long ago was this?"

"About ten years ago, I believe." Though she knew the exact date. Why she didn't tell him, she didn't know.

"Anything else happen? He just broke you nose?" he asked as if he knew there was.

"No."

"So he's probably out of prison by now. Do you want me to check?"

"Danny never went to prison. He was never charged."

This time he shot to his feet and towered over her like an avenging angel. "Why the fuck not?"

She glanced around and nodded toward his chair. "Patrick, please sit down."

He followed her gaze around the room and finally returned to his seat. "I'm having a hard time understanding why he's not. Did he run? I'll find him. I can't believe Tyler didn't."

This was the part that was the hardest about her story, she hadn't told anyone because she knew she'd relive it during the telling. Most sane people would have reported who had attacked her. Now that she'd confided Danny's name as the real estate agent, she realized her mistake.

"Tyler doesn't know his name," She confessed. "I refused to identify him by name to Tyler and when the police came, against Effie's advice. I told them and the hospital that it was an unknown assailant. That I'd been working late and neglected to lock the door. He had intended to rob me, but Effie yelling had run him off. That was the story I stuck to."

Damn, damn, damn.

The expression on his face told her he suspected something else had happened. Well, she wasn't going to appease his curiosity. She couldn't believe she'd actually confided in him as much as she had. He must be very good at his job. He had an air about him that invited confidences. He would probably be very good with children. She had no idea where that thought had come from.

"To answer your initial question..."

"What?"

Obviously he'd been distracted by her story. "Effie is my person, remember?"

"Oh, yeah. You're not going to tell me more, are you?"

"No. I will explain the best I can what a *person* is and why Effie is mine. Because she saved my life even if it was more emotional than physical, she now feels responsible for me. She has my back and I have hers, and we've been as close as sisters since this happened. I miss my sisters back east, so it's nice to have Effie.

And someday, I hope to save her in some way, hopefully not the same way. Basically she's my person and I'm her person." She stood and gathered her plate, she always bused her own table. "Let's get back to business. I'm sure you're busy."

He followed her example but she knew there was more he wanted to say. She hoped he wouldn't.

"I'm going to say goodbye to Effie," she said.

He followed. She thought he'd wait.

"Thanks for the lovely meal, as always it was excellent." Glenna gave her friend a hug.

"Thank you, Ms. Kennedy, the meal was delicious."

Glenna laughed. "Especially since it didn't have spinach or Kale on it."

Effie tilted her head to regard Patrick who stood a head and shoulders over both of them and then to Glenna in confusion. Glenna just gave her friend another hug and turned and left with the agent close on her heals. Once they were settled in her office, the smell hit her anew. Maybe they should have stayed at the bistro.

"Whew, the smell isn't getting any better. Is there somewhere else we can finish in private?"

She wasn't sure she wanted him at her place, she barely knew him, but she couldn't think of any place else, except... "We can return to the bistro."

"Let's go to your place, I want to check it out."

"Why?"

"If the vic's death, and your missing fiancé are connected then you may be in danger also."

She hadn't even thought of that. And why not? She'd been around Tyler and her brother-in-law's enough she should've at least suspected it. That she hadn't, proved how upset she was over Alex. She tried to appear calm, but her insides were a gooey mush. She couldn't think straight and she just wanted to sit down and cry.

"Are you okay?"

"What? Oh yes sorry. I don't know why that thought had never occurred to me."

"I'm sorry, I didn't mean to frighten you."

"No, I should have figured it out on my own. Knowledge is better than going into something being surprised. I know that better than most. You are more than welcome to come and check things out. Hopefully the only thing you'll find is Mr. Grumpy Pants nosing around."

"Who?"

"My neighbor, Mr. Barlow. He watches my cat. He hates me and my cat. But he offers to watch Agnes while I'm gone." She gave a shrug. "It's beyond me why."

As they left, she locked her office. Since she'd walked to work that morning, she rode with him to her small house a few streets over.

When he pulled in the drive he let the engine idle a moment while he looked over the property. "This is your home?" He sounded surprised.

"Yes, not much but it's mine." She smiled. "If you count making monthly mortgage payments *owning*. I seriously love it. It's the perfect size for me."

He didn't say anything, she got the idea he was thinking about someone else in that moment. Finally, he turned off the engine, climbed out, and walked around the car and opened the door for her. When was the last time that had happened? Even Lance in all his gallantry, had never opened her car door.

He surveyed the neighborhood, nodded his head to the left.

She turned and saw Mr. Barlow standing on his walkway, in all his scowling glory. "Good evening Mr. Barlow. How are you this evening?"

His frown deepened to the point his eyes almost disappeared. Then he sniffed, huffed, turned and stomped to the screen pulled it open and let it slam in his wake.

Patrick looked down at her. "Nice fella."

"That's why we call him Mr. Grumpy Pants."

"We? Do you have a roommate?"

"No. I meant my cat, Agnes, and I call him that."

"You have a cat who calls people names?"

She just grinned at him and led the way to her small porch.

"Hang tight." He took her elbow and led her back the way they had come. "I don't know what I was thinking? I'm going to check the perimeter. Wait here, it will only take a moment."

As promised it had only taken a few minutes before he was at her side again.

"Things look clear."

Together they returned to her door, he waited while she slipped the key in and as the door opened a low forlorn meeeeoooow echoed.

"Agnes?"

She called out for the cat several times and heard another mournful meow. Her home was just a cottage really, not that big where could Agnes have gone?

She tossed her keys and purse on the table and hung her coat on the rack and went to search in earnest. When she entered her bedroom she stopped cold.

Patrick, close on her heels bumped into her. "Whoa."

There in the center of her bed was Agnes. Thank god she seemed to be all right. But who had put her in a cage and placed it on her bed? She *never* kenneled the feline.

"Ms. Beckett, what's wrong?"

Ms. Beckett? Where had that come from? Come to think of it, she hadn't heard him use her name yet. She glanced around the room but didn't answer or move. Agnes was looking at her in disapproval.

"Do you keep her in a kennel all day?" By the tone of his voice, he had an idea this wasn't her doing.

"What do you think?"

"Have you touched anything?"

"What do you think?" She repeated and raised a brow.

"Sorry, routine question, just slipped out."

He stood as still as she had and did a sweep of the room with his gaze. He bent at the waist to look at floor level. "Do you see anything out of place?"

She couldn't see anything out of the ordinary. "I don't think so, but I can't really tell from here, I have a lot of antique jewelry on my dressing table."

"The table looks like an antique itself."

"It is." She let her gaze wander around her room and land on the table again. "It's a Golden Walnut Victorian Antique Dressing Table circa1860. I need to sell it soon, but I can't seem to part with it. Maybe in a few years I'll be able to keep a few pieces for myself. I didn't want to have it in the inventory while I was gone. It's too valuable. Now that I'm back I'll have to take it to the shop. I'm sure it will go fast."

She would be sad to see it go. Someday she would furnish her little cottage the way she'd envisioned when she purchased it.

"Let's back out and I'll call the local PD to do a dusting and when they're done, they'll do a sweep. Adding this break-in to the other things that have happened, I can't help but assume they're all connected."

As she started to follow him, Agnes let out another mournful entreaty. "I can't leave her in that thing."

Patrick looked from her to the cat, then he pulled a couple of latex gloves from his back pocket, and whipped them on. Luckily her bedroom wasn't that large and they'd been standing at the end of her bed so all he had to do is lean over to open the kennel door. He was careful not to move the cage as he picked the cat up and then backed out of the room.

He stroked the cat's fur. "So you're Agnes, aren't you a beautiful Tabby?"

To Glenna's point of view, he just kept getting better. A man who liked cats. "Do you have a cat?"

"No, my parents have a couple. We had some while my sister, Margaret Kathleen, and I were growing up." He held Agnes toward her, and once the cat was safely in her arms he removed the gloves. "I wouldn't mind having a cat now, but Horace rules the household and I'm not sure a cat is in our future."

He called his sister by her full name, how endearing. "Horace?"

"Our dog, he's a hulking English Mastiff. He'd eat little Agnes for dinner. He's Finn's dog."

"Finn?"

He paused as if that last part had slipped out. She thought maybe he wouldn't answer.

"Finnegan Kendal McGinnis my sixteen year old son. He's my person you would say. He saved my life and then I saved his."

He had a son, she hadn't seen that one coming. Instinctively her gaze sought his ring finger and found it bare. He'd notice and grinned.

"Joyce isn't in the picture."

"Oh I'm sorry, did she pass away? Is that why you said he'd saved your life?"

They had moved to the kitchen and were sitting at her table waiting for the department to dust for prints. She'd assumed he'd get back to questions about Lance, but he'd kept up the chatter. He still hadn't answered about his wife, anyway she assumed she had been his wife or Finn's mother.

Before he had time to answer, a black sedan pulled in, she recognized it as the same car Officer Beckworth drove. He stepped out the car at the same time Officer Jones got out. Both turned their heads to the right Mr. Barlow must be outside. She could only imagine what he thought. The worst, she was sure.

She went to the door to greet them. They both nodded at her and stepped through into her living room. She could tell they weren't happy with Patrick's presence.

"Agent, what would you like us to do?" Beckworth's rude tone was almost on the verge of insubordination. Good thing Patrick wasn't their supervisor.

Chapter Five

Patrick eyed the two officers, their stances suggested they'd rather be waiting for the guillotine then help a federal agent. Some officers were grateful for the extra help, others resented it. Typically, the smaller the town the more resentment. Instead of taking the help, thankful for the extra manpower, they choose to take it as an insult as if they couldn't solve the crime on their own.

Most the time that was not the case. Patrick opted to hold his judgement until he determined if this was the case here or not.

Ignoring their disgruntlement he brought them up to speed. As Glenna led the two to her bedroom, the thought of an intruder in her private domain, made his blood boil.

"Watch that, officer. Ms. Beckett has some antiques in here."

"Oh we'll be careful with the princess's toys." Jones grinned at his partner.

"Jones, be respectful." Beckworth admonished the other man as if he were a child.

Patrick took Glenna to wait in her small kitchen while her bedroom was thoroughly dusted. He was beginning to think, this is one of those case where the town department needed someone else to solve the crime, because the idiot Jones couldn't solve anything.

By the time they were finished with the room, Patrick was reluctant to let Jones into the other areas of the house because they'd made such a mess. He'd seen worse of course, but there was no excuse for tossing Glenna's room. It was one of his pet peeves when officers left such a mess.

"Are you going to clean up your mess before you leave?" Patrick asked, even though he knew the answer.

"Sorry Agent, we have other assignments more important." Jones answered before Beckworth had a chance. The older man gave Jones a frown.

Beckworth turned to Patrick. "Where else do you need dusted?"

"The only place we know for certain was her room, though there is no evidence the intruder spent any time in any of the other rooms. It's anyone's guess. What is your recommendation?"

Beckworth's brow shot up in surprise. Patrick had learned if you ignore their rudeness and answer it professionally with a request for their opinion it usually defused the situation.

"I don't think there is any way to know unless we dust the rest of the rooms." He tossed a glance at his partner, Jones looked far from happy. "Let's finish up, and be as careful as you can."

Now that he knew Beckworth would watch Jones, he would take Glenna outside where she wouldn't have to see the cops make more of a mess. He could tell she found the situation disturbing on top of everything else.

"Come on," he said to her as he walked to the door and held it. She seemed reluctant to leave her home at the mercy of the two officers, but she finally followed.

"I'd like to ask some more questions about Gordon, but it's getting late. I would like to do a little research. Can you write everything you *do* know about your fiancé? Also, if you have any idea why he seemed to be looking for something at your shop."

She bit her lip and gazed toward her little cottage. She swallowed and then turned her attention to him. "I've been trying to figure that out ever since Alex told me he seemed to be searching through the antiques, and that was before the non-wedding."

"Non-wedding?"

"I can hardly call it my wedding day. Do you know how humiliating it is to watch friends and family, all gather only to be told, whoops sorry groom was a no-show?"

"I can only imagine, but you seem to be recovering just fine."

"Well, only because I came to the realization that I wasn't really in love with him. And it was my non-wedding day I discovered that little fact."

"And how did you discover that *little fact?*" Patrick figured being in love with the man you were going to marry should have been a *big fact.*

"I realized I was more worried about the trouble the *Elders* and the little generals had gone to. And that's not even counting all the food. It was almost as an afterthought I wondered if Lance could be hurt. When I found he hadn't even made a reservation at the hotel nor was he on any of the flights, I was just mad and humiliated. The hurt from being jilted wasn't even more than a small pinch." She raised a perfectly shaped eyebrow at him. "I think that's a bit telling about my feelings for the man."

He'd heard everything she had said, and he was appalled at the fact he was so relieved to hear she wasn't still in love with the bastard. He buried the feeling to pull out later and examine. He tapped on the note app he used on his smart phone and handed it to her. She bent her head over his phone and entered in what she knew about Lance.

He wasn't sure how he felt about Glenna Beckett. He'd been ready to dismiss her as a carbon copy of Joyce. But during the day, she'd been knocking down his preconceived notions. One by One. Dammit. It was a lot easier to disregard his fascination with the woman when he thought the worst of her.

The screen opened and the two officer's stepped out, they did not address her. Jones looked sullen and avoided eye contact with Patrick. He must have been reprimanded.

Officer Beckworth came toward him, flipping off his latex gloves at the same time. "Agent McGinnis, we have all we need. We'll be on our way now. We've cleaned the best we could. Probably need a cleaner to do a better job."

And with that they climbed into the car and left. Glenna's gaze followed their progress to the corner where they turned and were out of sight. She turned to look at her little house, with a frown creasing her brow.

"It feels like such an invasion," she said.

He nodded at the list she was making. "Are you finished?"

She handed his phone back and then turned to go into the house.

"Wait, let me help clean up. Then I better go home and fix dinner."

He followed her inside. They'd done a credible job, it wasn't anywhere as bad as usual. He helped her tidy up until her home was back in order. "You really love this place?"

She regarded him for a moment and then let her gaze wander around the room, pausing on certain items. Her expression said it all. She more than loved this place, this was something she was building for herself piece by piece. And she felt violated because someone had broken in when she wasn't home and *touched* her things. He suspected it would be awhile before she felt safe again.

"I really do, it still has a long way before it meets my vision. I'm not going anywhere."

"Before I go, I need to do a sweep. Are you going to be all right alone here?"

"Yes. Maybe I should invest in an alarm system."

"That might be a good idea." He left to do the sweep before he did something dumb, like kiss her.

Unless there was new technology out on the Dark web he didn't find anything, and he hadn't heard about any new listening software. It appeared whoever it was wanted something. The disturbing part was that he or she had wanted Glenna to know, did they?

"Glenna, did Lance like Agnes?"

She barked out a short laugh. "He hated Agnes, and the feeling was mutual."

There was no message left other than putting Agnes in a cage. It could have been Lance. Or it could have been they had put the cat in the kennel to keep her out of the way.

"Your house appears to be clean of listening devices. Meaning, I didn't find anything. The problem is the fact whoever did this, put the cat in that cage to get your attention, or simply keep her out of the way."

He made one last walk through. As he did so he noticed all the attention she'd paid to the colors, the furnishings. Some weren't new, but they were all in good condition.

"You really do love this home."

"Yes I do." She placed her hands on her hips. "You sound so surprised."

"I'm sorry. I'm just thinking of my ex."

"Joyce?"

So she'd figured out Joyce was Finn's mother. She wouldn't be flattered if she found out he'd compared her to be the same type of woman.

"Yes. She would have hated this house. She had to have everything on a grand scale. I could never keep up with her tastes."

"Why did you marry her then?"

"Finn. She was pregnant, and though I wasn't finished with my degree, I was thrilled to be a father."

"Where is she?"

"Last I heard she was on a yacht with her current husband heading to Monaco."

"But why is Finn with you?" Her eyes widened and for a moment she looked horrified. "I didn't mean that in a bad way. If she's in another country, is he with you while she is gone on her trip?"

"Finn has never met his mother, well that is, since she gave birth."

"What?" She almost shouted. "How on earth could she just leave her child?"

"She had no problem what so ever. She had expected me to keep her in the way she felt she was entitled. What I don't understand was how she expected me to pay for her tastes. She knew I was going into criminal justice to be in law enforcement. She stuck around with us until Finn was about three months old. As soon as she had her figure back she snagged a rich husband and that was the last I saw her."

She reached over and laid a hand on his arm. "I'm so sorry. Have you had any help with your son? Is your sister able to help at all?"

He felt the warmth run up his arm. "My parents live close by, without my mom's help I would never have been able to do it. Margaret Kathleen has a couple of kids of her own. Our kids are close. I imagine from what I'd gathered from Tyler, my family is much smaller than yours, but just as close."

"I'm glad you have that support. Drive safe, I'll see you tomorrow."

Dismissed.

"Lock up after I leave."

"I plan on it."

As he left, he noticed the old neighbor next door. He took a detour on the way to the car. The man regarded him with distrust.

"What do you want?" The gruffness of the older man's voice was rusty from lack of use.

"I wanted to ask you a few questions." Patrick tried to sound as friendly as he could. "Someone broke into Ms. Beckett's house. I was hoping you had seen something?"

Barlow's gaze landed on Glenna's house. For a moment Patrick didn't think he'd get an answer.

"Only person snooping around was that young fop that's always coming and going."

Fop? Patrick wasn't sure what that meant. But he caught the reference. It could only be Lance. "Can you give me a description of the vehicle he drove?"

The old man deepened his scowl, which hadn't seemed possible. "The young scallywag came on foot, if he drove he didn't park anywhere I could see."

Frustrating, he'd hoped to have some type of car or partial license plate. He pulled out a card. "If you see him around here again, would you please call me immediately?"

"How you expect me to call? Ain't got no phone, nobody to call."

Well that was inconvenient. "Do you mind keeping a look out? And the next time you see me, let me know?"

"You planning to hang around now?"

"I'm a Federal Agent on a case."

"Case for what? I didn't think it was against federal law for young folks to go cavorting around."

Cavorting? How old was this guy? He peered closer at him in the waning light. He did look old. He may have even been in his 90's.

"A young woman was murdered at Ms. Beckett's antique shop while she was out of town."

"Yeah, I watched that damn cat for her. Thought she went and got herself hitched to that young fella, the one snooping around here earlier today."

Bingo!

"If you see him again, will you borrow someone's phone and call me?"

"None of my business."

As he started to turn away, Patrick decided to play a hunch. "Ms. Beckett is in danger."

The old man whipped around, as fast as any old person could whip around that is, and stared at him.

"That young poppycock means that girl harm?"

Poppycock? God, had he stepped back in time?

"We can only assume he's looking for something he believes she has. He may harm her in order to get his hands on it."

"Well what is it? Seems to me the problem would be solved if you got rid of whatever he's looking for."

"You're right, but we need to figure out what it is."

He huffed and again turned toward his house. "I'll keep an eye on the young gal, don't you worry."

He wasn't sure if he felt reassured or not. One thing he did know, Lance Gordon was alive and well, snooping around Calistoga. He glanced toward the little cottage. If he was the murderer, Glenna wasn't safe.

He looked at the time, after five in the evening. Not that late in New York. He went to his SUV and climbed in. He didn't start the engine, instead he punched in Tyler's number. As it was against the law to drive in California while talking on the phone, he automatically set the call to Bluetooth, even if he was just idling. If he remembered correctly, Glenna's twin lived in San Francisco. Maybe Glenna could stay with her. It would be inconvenient but better than being dead.

"Tyler, sorry it's so late."

"Is something wrong with Glenna?"

"Could be. Someone broke in to her home. Actually there was no sign of a break in, thought Glenna had locked her door."

"Was anything missing?"

"Nothing that Glenna could see, they were looking for something. But I'm pretty sure it was Gordon."

"There in Calistoga?"

"I spoke to the neighbor and he said that the young 'fop' that's been coming and going for a while was at her house today."

"Oh you've been talking to old Mr. Barlow."

"Yeah, how old is the guy?"

"Not sure, but I think he reads historical novels or something because I swear whatever comes out of his mouth sounds like it's from a couple of centuries ago." There was silence on the line. "Glenna can't stay there alone."

"Didn't you say her twin lives around San Fran?" Patrick asked.

"She did, but she now lives in D.C. with her husband and daughter."

"I'll see if she can stay with her friend Effie."

"Aw, so you've met the pink elf." Tyler ended in a chuckle.

"Yes, Glenna thinks she was *Tinkerbell* in another life."

"She could have been. That's a good idea."

"If that isn't going to work, does your family have anyone else out this way? She can't stay alone, I'd ask her to go home to Brooklyn if I thought she would." Patrick ran his free hand through his hair, glancing over to the small cottage.

"No, I'm sure that's out. Glenna is a strong woman, she'll want to see this through, not turn tail and run."

"I was afraid you'd say that. Finn and I may end up with a roommate for a few days. I have a spare bedroom for when my sister's kids stay over."

"Won't cramp your style with the ladies?"

"There are no ladies to worry about. I'll keep you updated on any developments."

After Patrick thumbed the phone off, with his attention still on Glenna's home he let his thoughts wander a moment. That morning when he'd met her, he wouldn't have entertained the thought of her staying with him. However, even though he hardly knew her, he'd learned enough that other than having physical attributes similar to his ex, that's as far as the similarities went. Glenna cared about more than herself. She wasn't a snob.

He might as well go back inside and give her the news and wait for her to pack her bags. Hopefully, Effie had a place for her *person* to stay.

At the door he knocked, it swung open immediately. She didn't seem surprised that he hadn't left. But then she could see the drive from her window.

"What did Mr. Barlow have to say?"

She'd been watching.

"He said Lance was here."

"He knew his name?"

"No, he called him a young fop."

"A what?"

"I don't know, I'm going to Google it tonight. But the thing is, if he's the murderer you can't stay here."

"He may be a lot of things, but he's not a murderer."

"Are you willing to stake your life on that?"

She was quiet for a few moments. Then she went to the couch and dropped down onto the brown cushion.

"Do you think you could stay with Effie for a few days?"

"Ordinarily yes, but..."

"But? Is she going somewhere?"

"She's staying at her parents' home. She had some plumbing issues and it's going to be another few days before she can move home."

For a moment, he was tempted to ask if she couldn't stay there. If he took her home he could see all kinds of complications in his future. Not to mention he always tried to keep his home life separate from his work life.

"A hotel stay would be prudent for a few days."

It took Glenna a moment before she answered, she seemed to be avoiding his gaze. "I will be extra careful. There's really no need. First thing in the morning I'll change the locks."

"Locks won't keep someone determined out. You're not staying here. Tell me what hotel. We'll get you settled before I head home."

Another pause. "I don't think my bank account can handle the added expense after my disaster of a non-wedding."

Damn. He hadn't considered that. So much for keeping his home life and work life separate.

The two were about to collide with a vengeance.

Chapter Six

Glenna watched the expressions race across Patrick's face. He clearly didn't want her to stay. She didn't want to stay. There were no other options.

"Pack a bag," Patrick said. "Where's the cat food and bowls? I'll get Agnes ready."

Glenna didn't move. "I can't go to Effie's."

"I'm not taking you to Effie's. I'm taking you with me. I have a spare room for Margaret Kathleen's kids. It's not great but it is safer than here."

"I can't go home with you."

She didn't have any real argument about why she couldn't, she didn't want to stay home and face Lance. He wasn't a big man, nothing like Patrick who if you put him in a kilt would look like he stepped out an episode of *Outlander*. But she did not wish to have a repeat performance of her earlier encounter when she'd first moved to town.

She stood to pace and think.

Patrick watched her with a scowl. "You can't or won't?"

"Patrick, you hardly know me. What will your family think?"

"That I'm doing my job and protecting a damsel in distress."

She laughed. "You've had one conversation with Mr. Grumpy Pants and he's already rubbing off on you."

"Let's not waste time arguing, because you're going to lose. Go pack and I'll get Agnes."

"Just like that? I have no say in the matter? I'm a grown woman, I can make up my own mind. I will stay here."

"Tyler said you were not the type to turn tail and run."

"You talked to Tyler?"

"I thought your sister still lived in San Fran, I only called to find out if you could go there."

"You could have asked me. I would have told you Reagan moved back east. I'm not your responsibility just because my brother called you. I'm sure you have other assignments more important. I'm really mad at you, now you have my family worried about me."

"First, your family is already worried about you, your brother called me. However, the Agency opened a case. This is my assignment and you are my responsibility whether you like it or not."

She stomped her foot, a left over reaction from childhood—one she had in common with Jessica. And then she folded her arms over her chest.

"How old are we? Stomping your foot and pouting. Glenna Beckett go pack a bag."

She decided to go along with the reference to age. "You're not the boss of me."

At which he burst out laughing. It went a long way to ease the tension. He was right though, she was being childish. It wasn't a trivial matter, her life very well could be in danger. She'd have to commute to work for a few days, but wasn't it worth her life? Besides she wanted to meet Finn and Horace.

"How long do you think I'll need to stay?"

"Until we catch Gordon and or the murderer or at least until Effie's place is fixed and you can stay with her."

That last part made it seem he didn't really want her at his place. She didn't want to be a burden.

"Are you sure I can't stay here until I can go to Effie's? I can call an alarm company tomorrow. I don't want to put you out."

"You're not going to *put me out*. Is this because I said until Effie's place was fixed? You can stay with me as long as needed. I just figured you'd rather be with her than two stinky males and a dog."

She thought about it. She really did want to stay with the two stinky males and their dog. A jolt raced over her as she realized, she trusted Patrick.

"Okay. The cat food is under the sink..." She paused in the doorway. "Horace isn't going to eat Agnes, is he?"

"I hope not, but how about this, if there are any problems tonight, when we go to your shop in the morning, we'll bring Agnes and ask Mr. Grumpy Pants to watch her."

Her tummy rolled, so many things to consider. She'd have the kennel to keep Agnes safe if needed. "Give me a few minutes, I'll hurry."

It was a little longer than a few. Every time she thought she had everything, she'd think of something else. She was used to being able to run home if she forgot something. Knowing she wasn't going to be living close to her shop, she grabbed just about everything.

"I guess if I've forgotten something I can come back during the day," Glenna said as she threw her bag in the back of the 4Runner.

"No, you cannot return until we know who was in your house. You could walk in on someone."

"Wouldn't I know if someone was in the house?"

"He's not going to pull into the drive. Which Mr. Grumpy Pants confirmed 'the young scallywag came on foot'." A chuckle escaped before he continued. "People who break into homes are a careful lot, parking on another street among other things."

"Okay, I get your drift."

She closed her eyes and pictured herself walking through her home, checking her routine. Had she picked up her laptop? Yes. Had she picked up the receipt book she'd brought home yesterday to work on? Yes.

"I'll be right back."

She opened her eyes and saw Patrick go talk to Mr. Barlow again. She was at least 99% positive she had everything. That would have to do. By the time he finished talking to the neighbor she was in the vehicle and waiting.

"He is going to watch your place. I'm going to check in with him every day to find out if anyone has been here."

"Why doesn't he just call you?"

"He doesn't have a phone. He doesn't have anyone to call."

Glenna glanced over to her neighbor. He was staring at them as they pulled out of the drive. She rolled her window down and waved at him, which he didn't return, that was normal.

"That's just sad. How would it be to have no one?"

She watched Patrick's hands on the wheel as he navigated out of the drive onto the road. Once they were on the road he seemed to be deep in thought, she figured he was going over the case, until he spoke.

"Do you know his story? Does he have any family?"

Glenna thought over the years she'd lived next to him. How long had she lived in her house? Now she felt like the worst person.

"I've lived there about seven years and I don't know anything about him." She looked out the window a moment.

"That's just sad." She repeated her earlier statement.

"Don't beat yourself up over it, he's not the easiest or the most forthcoming person."

"Well from now on I'm going to go out of my way to be nice to him." She sat up in her seat and twisted to look at him, as best she could with the seatbelt restraining her movement. "Maybe I shouldn't call him Mr. Grumpy Pants, that's rude."

"I think you're okay with that, he is Grumpy and he does wear Pants."

"Thank God for that."

As Patrick negotiated the Silverado Trail road, he'd decided not to go through Napa on 29. The evenings in the valley could be become stop and go with all the travelers and locals vying for parking at restaurants, shopping, and wine tasting. He'd said he'd rather go a few miles out of his way than fight the traffic, and she was fine with that. She'd done the same on many occasion.

The silence in the car was a comfortable one, Glenna appreciated that. They didn't know each other well, it could have just as easily have been awkward, but there was something about Patrick that calmed her and made her feel safe. She hadn't decided if he'd changed his opinion of her yet. She didn't know what it had been or why, but he seemed to be coming around.

Patrick's phone jingle shattered the silence, startling her out of her thoughts. She placed a hand over her heart to stop its racing.

Even though the SUV was older, Patrick must have had it upgraded to make sure he could be hands free for the phone. In his profession that was most likely a must.

"Hello Bud. Did you get dinner?"

"Naw. I've been at football practice, just got home."

"Ready for the big game?"

"Yeah, hopefully we go to regionals, otherwise this is the last one."

"You guys are doing great, I bet you go. Oh, while we're on the subject, will you write the time of the game on the calendar? I want to be sure to arrange my schedule."

"Dad, you've never missed any of my games. I'll write it down. When are you getting home? I'll wait to eat if it's going to be soon."

So this was his son, their voices sounded very similar. She could picture a miniature version of Patrick, though if he was on the football team, he could be a bit larger than she had first thought. She watched Patrick glance at the clock and then to the road again.

"Why don't you call in an order for pizza at that new place, what was it called?"

"Pizza Stop?"

"Yes. Anyway tell them I'll pick it up in fifteen minutes, oh and make sure there is enough for three, we have a house guest for a few days."

There was a pause. Finn must be surprised. She didn't know how many house guests they entertained, but by the length of the silence he'd caught his son by surprise.

"Um, okay. May I ask who and why?"

"She's sitting right here," Patrick said.

"Hi Finn, I'm Glenna and your dad is a life saver literally."

"Um, okay," Finn repeated.

"I'll explain over dinner. See you soon."

"Wait dad, what kind of pizza? Ms. Glenna what do you like?"

Glenna usually didn't eat pizza, in fact she couldn't remember the last time she'd had any. But Patrick and Finn were giving her a safe haven she wasn't about to be difficult.

"I'm easy, you pick your favorite and I'll be fine."

"Okay, see you guys soon."

And with that, the connection was broken. He seemed like an easy going kid. "He seemed to take a visitor in stride, though he seemed surprised."

"He's a good kid. He knows to expect the unexpected with my line of work. Though, he did take the first time having a house guest in stride, especially since you're a woman. This should be interesting."

Glenna considered the man she would be staying with, what did she know about him? He was a federal agent, which didn't necessarily make him one of the good guys, but the fact her brother called him did. He had manners, which went a long way with Glenna. It seemed like many of her generation didn't know what manners were. He seemed to be honest and speak the truth, she felt she could trust him.

He hadn't earned that trust yet, so she'd hold back if for nothing else but self-preservation. She'd learned the hard way not to give her trust to everyone. Since the attack ten years ago, she tended to keep people at arm's length. It was a precaution, and she wasn't about to change now.

"You're pretty quiet over there. What's going through that head over there?"

He hadn't taken his eyes off the road to look at her, but she still felt the weight of his words. She needed to be honest. This wasn't a game of flirting and dating. This was her life. And he was her protector not a potential boyfriend. A situation she'd never been in before.

"I was thinking over the situation. Just so you know, I don't give out my trust to everyone. I've trusted in the past and been hurt." She again twisted in her seat so she could see his expression in the dim light. "Though I'm trusting you to keep me safe, I'm still holding some of that trust back until you earn it."

He didn't answer for a moment. She could see he was considering his answer.

"That's fair enough. And since we're being honest, I have a confession to make."

"Oh?"

"You'll have to earn my trust also. I may not have been hurt physically like you from trusting the wrong person, but my heart has been permanently damaged by Finn's mother."

"Joyce?"

"None other. She was perfect in every way, or so I thought when I met her."

Glenna pulled her legs up on the seat and sat cross legged to face him. The belt cut into her neck, she pulled it out and situated it so the strap was under her arm. Probably not safe, but she wanted to watch his expressions. They'd barely known each other for a day, yet it had been such a full day that she felt she'd known him for years. The closeness of the darkened car made for confidences. There may not be another chance to hear about Finn's mother and Patrick's heart break. She didn't want to waste the opportunity.

"How old were you?"

"Young. I wanted to be in law enforcement for as long as I remember. I did my homework and found the best college for criminal justice. John Jay College of Criminal Justice."

"The City University of New York."

"You know it?"

She laughed. "You forget I grew up in Brooklyn. I probably would have gone there, but being the youngest I wanted to be out on my own, so Stanford it was. I fell in love with the area. Many of a girl trip to the Valley helped me pick my location for my shop. But this is your time. On with your confession."

"Joyce had an affluent family on the Upper East Side. I met her at an Irish bar. Little did I know she was slumming. It was my birthday, twenty-one. Anyway, she saw in me the bad boy her parents would hate, and I didn't disappoint."

"Oh dear, I can see where this is going. You fell hard for her. But she was using you to get away from overbearing parents, right?"

"They weren't really overbearing as much as they spoiled her rotten. She had everything handed to her. I think she had just had enough of prissy boys from her expensive university and circle of friends. I was the boy toy to trot out for them all to see."

"And it helped that you looked like something out of an *Outlander* movie set." She grinned. "I've not known you long, but I've already imagined you in a kilt."

He took a moment to glance at her, the wicked gleam made her heart do a pitter patter. "Oh you have, have you? Well I just so happened to have one in my family Tartan."

"Be still my beating heart." Though she made it sound like she was joking, her heart was beating like it didn't understand that.

He laughed. "Anyway, I loved her. No. That's not quite true. I had her on a pedestal so high she couldn't help but fall off. She got pregnant and I did what I'd been taught to do my entire life. Take responsibility for my actions. I wasn't ready to get married, but I didn't see any other option. I was thrilled to have a child. She wasn't. Her parents gave her a choice to have an abortion or marry me."

"I'm glad she chose to marry you."

"She wasn't. She wanted the abortion. She didn't want to marry me. I couldn't give her the things she wanted. But I told her I'd go to court to stop the abortion, and just in case she tried to sneak to do it, I let her parents know this. They knew I was studying law, though it was for criminal justice, I knew enough to stop the abortion, and they knew it. So they forced her to marry me."

"That must have been awful. Did she try to make it work?"

"Not really, she rebelled by almost bankrupting me. We didn't even live together. I lived in my dorm, she at her parents. As I said earlier, as soon as she had the baby and got her figure back, she filed for a divorce and ran off with a rich financial analyst from Wall Street. I think she's on her fourth husband. Luckily, I'd graduated by the time Finn arrived. I moved home with my son, and my parents helped."

"I like your parents already."

"They're the best. They've never chastised me for my mistake and they adore Finn. The hardest months of my life were when I had to train at Quantico and leave Finn with them. But I knew he was safe, and that's what matters, right?"

"Does she see him or do her parents see their grandson?"

"No, they never even came to the hospital. I think they knew she wouldn't be staying married to me. And Finn was the red headed grandchild they never wanted."

"I don't understand people. I'm so sorry. But I'm a little confused. Why is this your confession of trust? Because you trusted her? It really doesn't sound like you did. You had to threaten a court order on her to keep the baby."

He took a deep breath and pursed his lips to blow out the air before he gave her a quick glance before watching the road again.

"This is hard. And embarrassing. As I said I thought she was perfect. She had every hair in place. She wouldn't step out in public if she didn't pass the mirror inspection. That's what she called it. She had no patience for people who didn't understand that her needs and wants came first. High maintenance."

Glenna thought she knew where he was going with this. And though she wasn't very flattered, she hoped he'd changed his mind.

"And though when Tyler called me, I didn't have any preconceived notions about you. You could have been a pink faery like your friend. But I'll be honest, when you opened the door, all I could see was a perfect selfish bitch. But then you cared about Alex. You wondered what kind of person you were to have not checked on her sooner." He paused a moment. "You ran your hand through hair and left it ruffled and you didn't care. You had a *person,* and Effie is so different than any of the friends Joyce had, she would have *never* dreamed of being seen in public with someone that wore different color socks. Let's see, oh and though you call Mr. Barlow Mr. Grumpy Pants, you're nice to him. And you care. You are ashamed that you haven't learned more about him."

"So you've decided that I may not be so bad?"

"Yeah. Oh, one more thing. Well actually there's probably more, but you love your house. No, you've made it your home. I can tell how much you care by the way you've made it your own."

"I don't understand, why would my house make you see me differently?"

He gave her a surprised look. "You're kidding me right? After the picture I've painted of Finn's mother, can you *really* picture her living in something so small and quaint? She would look at that property in disdain."

"That's why you looked so surprised when you realized I lived there. I had wondered."

He turned down a residential street. The houses were modest but well kept. Nice family neighborhood. He pulled into a beige stucco rambler. He put it into park.

"Dammit, we forgot the pizza."

Just then a young man came out of the front door. A younger version of Patrick. There was no mistaking who his parent was. He went to the side of the SUV leaned in.

"Hand me the pizza."

"Hmm, I forgot to stop and pick it up."

The boy ducked in and looked at her. She smiled at him. He straightened.

"Yeah, I can see why."

That surprised her. He didn't sound upset, just sounded like a normal guy. She couldn't help but laugh.

"I'll stay here with Finn."

Finn bent down again to look at her.

"Is that okay?" she asked. "You can help me settle in, and I can help you set the table."

"Hmm, okay."

He helped her take in her bags, eyeing Agnes a little dubiously. Her room or what would be her home for the next few days was small but clean. Twin beds, so she piled the bags on one, and set Agnes' kennel on the chair.

"Do you think Horace will eat my poor cat? Her name is Agnes."

He was almost as tall as his dad. He looked down at her, then the cat and at that moment the dog bounded in. He was a lot bigger than she'd imagined. Maybe she'd keep the cat in the kennel, Agnes wouldn't be happy but she'd be alive.

The dog nosed up to the cage door, the cat sprung against the back and hissed.

"I think maybe Horace needs to be afraid of your cat."

Horace wasn't intimidated by the hiss, he nosed around to the side and looked the cat straight in the eye. Glenna sucked in her breath and watched. Dog and cat had a stare down. *The O.K. Corral for animals.*

Chapter Seven

Patrick placed the pizza and breadstick boxes on the counter and stopped to listen. It was unusually quiet. The spare room was only across the hall, shouldn't he hear voices? Worried, he decided he best investigate.

The door stood open giving him a view of the situation. Dog and cat stared each other down, boy and woman stared at the scene. It was as if no one dared to make a sound or move for fear of what would happen.

"Anyone want pizza?"

The interruption caused chaos. Glenna threw her hand over her heart with a little squeal. Horace launched into a stream of ferocious barking, Agnes arched her back in a stance to rival any black Halloween cat, hissing for all she was worth. And then Finn burst out laughing, which miraculously caused both animals to pause and stare at him.

"I suggest Horace come with us and Agnes can stay in here, with the door closed she won't have to stay in her kennel," Patrick suggested.

He left them to decide whether to follow or not. He chuckled to himself, as he set the table that he'd thought would be ready when he returned. It was going to be an interesting next few days.

Horace didn't want to leave Glenna's room. He could hear Finn try to coax the huge beast out. Maybe he thought the boy was keeping him from his dinner. Finally, Glenna and Finn joined him without the dog.

"You didn't leave Horace in there did you?"

Glenna winked at Finn, then answered Patrick. "It seems the two have formed a truce. I thought Horace had left with Finn and I let Agnes out, and Horace was at her side in a moment. Best friends. Who knew? And after all that drama."

All he could do was hope that they hadn't mistaken Horace's friendship for something else. For all they knew, Horace was making friends with the enemy to size her up and determine went to launch his attack.

He needed to go over some things with Glenna. He had come up with a few questions on his ride to and from the pizza retrieval. He always did his best thinking driving or exercising. But he wasn't sure he wanted to include Finn, so he'd wait until after dinner.

Glenna had other thoughts though. "No one has said anything about the surveillance equipment I had in my shop. Do you know if the local police have reviewed the tapes yet?"

Patrick looked to his son, but Finn seemed interested. "They said they want you to look at coverage and see if the men seem familiar in any way."

Glenna's checks went from fresh pink to milk, her throat worked a moment before she replied.

"I am not sure I can watch the murderer harm poor Alex."

He laid a hand over hers. "We'll watch the end, we do not need to review all of it, just enough for you to see if you recognize any body language on the guys."

"Guys? There's more than one. I knew it wasn't Lance." Glenna put her fork back to her plate. "Can't they run their faces on that facial recognition that your agency has?"

"You watch crime shows?" Finn asked with a grin.

Glenna gave him a weak smile, better than her washed out look she'd had since he mentioned she watch the tape. Then she turned her attention to Patrick waiting for his answer.

"Actually, we could if they weren't wearing masks. Gordon could be one of them, we're hoping you may recognize a mannerism or his walk. Just something for us to go on."

"As long as I don't have to watch anything to do with Alex, I will be okay."

"What were they going after?" Finn asked.

"Good question, bud." Patrick grabbed his paper plate and started to clear the table. "We haven't figured out if anything was stolen."

"I need to do an inventory, and there's all the stuff in the basement."

Patrick paused and turned to stare at Glenna. "What basement?"

"Oh, I don't think I've even told the local PD. It's a basement that I keep new items until I'm ready to add them to inventory. Only then do I move the item to my storage in the back of the shop. I should have taken my vintage dresser there months ago. " Glenna sighed. "It comes down to the fact I love that thing and I don't want to sell it. I can't afford to keep it at this time." She chuckled as she slid her chair away and helped finish cleaning the table.

Finn followed their actions and before a few minutes had passed, the kitchen had been put to rights, and Patrick led them to the living room to finish their discussion.

"Why would you need to tell anyone about it? When the police went through your shop, didn't they check it out?" Patrick glanced to his son. "Don't you have algebra to do?"

"Dad..." He looked to Glenna when there was no help in that corner, he pleaded with Patrick. "I can do my homework later. I can help you two brainstorm."

He thought about it for a minute. "I'll make you a deal. You said you were having problems with your Algebra. We're just getting started with this case. You do your homework tonight and tomorrow night after dinner we'll get together and you can help us brainstorm and figure out what to do with all of the information we come up with."

"Really?"

"Yes."

Patrick waited until he was out of the room. "I hope I don't regret my decision."

"You're a good dad. I'm sure he'll forget about helping us by tomorrow night."

"No I won't." Finn's voice drifted from the hall.

"First rule of kids, they can hear from great distances." He grinned at Glenna. "When they want to."

She laughed as he had intended. He needed to keep her mind off reviewing the tapes.

"Tell me why the police didn't check over your basement."

"As I said, I didn't think to tell them about it."

"Weren't they thorough? It's standard to open every door, even closet doors."

"It's in a closet. I'm sure they thought it was just that." When he was about to ask the obvious question she continued. "I don't know much about Calistoga history concerning the prohibition era, but I like to think maybe my basement was a Napa Valley version of a Speak Easy."

Well that didn't clear up anything.

Glenna let out a delightful giggle that totally belied the seriousness of the situation. "I've bewildered you."

"Understatement to say the least."

"It's a hidden door in the closet. Unless you know it's there you'd never find it. It's behind the rack. I use it as a coat closet. When I go to estate sales...." Her voice trailed off and her expression changed.

"What?"

"I think I know what Lance wanted."

"What?" he repeated.

"Well I don't know exactly. Right before Lance came to Calistoga I went to a large estate sale in upstate New York. I brought home a box of collectables."

Patrick watched her forehead pucker. He wanted to reach over and smooth it out with his lips. He swallowed and tried to concentrate on what she was saying.

"I don't remember anything of much value. My customers are mostly tourists and locals looking for good deals or something unique."

"Why do you think this particular box has something?"

"Two things, and I won't really know until I go through it. Anyway, first the estate belonged to an old Nazi war criminal. No one knew who he was until after he died though. They found some of the missing art that was stolen during World War II. And second reason is the timing."

"If it's something that valuable, why don't you know what it is?"

"After a buying trip I don't always display everything right away. Most the time I store the new things in the basement until I can go through them. I try to tie it in with a store promotion or weekly deal." She shrugged. "Sometimes, as with this box, I am not sure if there is anything of value, so I'm not that anxious about it. It's not like I saw something and couldn't wait to get it home. At the estate sale, I looked around and there were so many interesting items that day. Most of them above my budget. I didn't want to go home empty handed. On a whim I took a chance and bought the box of odd items. I looked over the manifest on the side of the box and figured it was worth it."

"You put it in the basement, but if you thought it had something interesting why have you waited so long. How long has it been?"

"I always have a lot of paperwork to get through when I get back from a sale. It's usually at least two weeks to a month before I get to the inventory in the basement. Not to mention it was around Christmas time, so I was looking for holiday items for the shop. I'd decided to wait until after the New Year to go through the box. I can't remember why."

"When did Gordon show up?"

"It was before Christmas. I saw him at the Calistoga Lighted Tracker Parade. He was *not* enjoying the moment. He said a few disgruntled things and I can't remember what I said but after a moment he left. Then a day or two later he turned up at my shop.

Flirted with me. Which surprised me since I'd originally figured he was gay."

"If he was gay he wouldn't have asked you to marry him."

"He didn't marry me." She gave him and exasperated stare. "I think for some reason, he thought he'd find whatever it was he was looking for before the big day. Maybe he did find it."

"No. If he had, Mr. Grumpy Pants wouldn't have seen him at your house today. If he or his gang, or whoever was in your shop and murdered your assistant had found it, they wouldn't be still looking."

Glenna was silent for a while. Patrick knew she was still processing everything. In a matter of two weeks, her entire life as she'd known it had been shattered. Lifelong plans had changed in a blink of an eye and her safe environment had not only been violated, but a person she knew and considered to be a friend had been murdered.

A lot for anyone to process.

"Lance doesn't have a gang." A delicate shudder seemed to ripple over her. "He doesn't seem to play well with others. For that reason, I can't stop the little voice in the back of my mind that tells me there might be someone else after what he is. Either they found he knew something about it, or they tracked me down the same way."

"That's a good point. I don't know much about antiquities sales or estate sales, how would they track you from something like that? I know there would be receipts but would it list *all* the items?"

"Most collectors go to the same sales, or they're aware of them. Estate sales keep a list of everyone who purchased something and what that item was. In my case my name would be attached to a copy of the manifest. Stores do not give out the information of their clientele. Estate sales on the other hand are a little less formal."

"Meaning? Do they just give out the information to everyone?"

"Sort of..." She held up her hand. "Let me explain. They have a book or a folder with a list of everything for sale. As people purchase something the person jots down a name by the item. The sale I went to was quite large and it was popular because of the notoriety of the owner being a war criminal known to have priceless stolen art."

Still, can anyone look at the list?"

"The list is actually for people to read over so they're not spending hours looking. So, yes. Everyone goes to *look*. But if you're searching for something in particular then it's easier to read over the list. Some estates just write 'sold' next to an item but I noticed this one was keeping track of names."

"Why would they do that?" Patrick asked.

"Because of the stolen art. Many of the countries are asking for the art back and offering a reward. There are a few of the collectors who have had art stolen that are doing the same, offering an incentive for the return of their treasures."

"Why didn't the authorities go through the sale items and confiscate the stolen art?"

"Because there may not have been any stolen art from World War II for sale that day. Just because some of the art was found to be stolen after the owner died, and given back to the original country or owners, doesn't necessarily mean there was any left. I certainly wouldn't recognize any stolen pieces without a lot of research, or unless I was actually looking for something I'd seen."

"That makes sense. Most law enforcement officials don't have time to investigate on a *maybe*."

"Maybe I have something Lance wanted that doesn't have anything to do with the missing art. I'm an antique shop owner, which is very different than art dealers who search the world wide for unique and priceless finds. They research and they actually track certain items."

"Why didn't he just ask you?"

"Because even though it may not have been part of the stolen art, doesn't mean it wasn't something priceless that could be sold on the black market for an ungodly amount. He never behaved in a way that led me to believe he dealt in the black market. But I am aware of an even more lucrative place. The cyber black market. The Dark web. People kill for priceless items. We're just going to have to go through the box. If we don't find anything, we'll be back to square one."

Patrick looked through the doorway to the kitchen clock and noticed it was well past ten. "Let's get a good night's rest and we'll tackle the videos first and then we'll explore your Speak Easy."

"I'll make breakfast."

"You don't have to do that."

"I know, but I never get to fix breakfast for more than myself. And I love to cook."

Patrick had been in the process of locking the front door, he turned. "You just keep surprising me."

She just grinned and winked at him.

Chapter Eight

Glenna opened the fridge for ideas of what to cook. For two big boys, she figured bacon, scrambled eggs, and some potatoes. Did they like spicy? Unless they were like her dad, who loved spicy but spicy didn't like him. She'd settle for just a little kick.

She was surprised to find Patrick's kitchen well stocked. He was a good dad. He must make sure that they ate well instead of fast food all the time. She liked that about him. She took a mental inventory as she pulled breakfast items out. She'd do a Sheppard's pie for dinner. Unless they were extremely lucky on catching the murderer, she figured she'd be here at least another day or maybe two.

She eyed the whole coffee beans and the grinder. Did she dare? She didn't want to wake the boys. And when did she start thinking of them as *her* boys? Dangerous territory. First, he had *ex*-baggage. Second, he was law enforcement. She swore she'd never be attracted to the hero type or anyone with baggage from a former relationship. Yet here she was, half in love with his son already. Not to mention she loved Horace, if for nothing else, for not eating her Agnes.

"Are you going to make coffee or will it to brew on its own?"

Patrick startled her out of thoughts. She whirled to face him, his damp hair curled around his ears as he entered still buttoning his shirt. The glimpse of bare chest dried her mouth.

"Must you sneak up on people? If you must know I was trying to decide if the grinder would wake you two up."

"Looks like you already have a good start on the breakfast and that is what woke me up. Why don't I tackle the coffee?"

"Sounds like a plan." She gave a stir to the potatoes making sure they cooked evenly. "What time does Finn have to be to school?"

"In about an hour." Finn answered for himself as he entered the kitchen. "Damn, that smells good."

"Son, language."

"Sorry, but it smells better than cereal and toast."

"Hey, I cook eggs." Patrick protested above the grinding beans.

"On weekends."

Glenna smiled, enjoying the banter as she cooked. If she were honest she'd admit it made her homesick for the *Elders* and Brooklyn. Mornings before school. Reagan arguing about eating, she was never hungry. Glenna on the other hand always was. Matt complaining about Tyler eating all the bacon. Jessica and Christine counting calories. Home.

"What are you thinking about?" Finn surprised her with his question.

"The *Elders*."

"The what?"

Patrick chuckled and answered for her. "Her parents."

"Do you have a big family?"

She could tell by his tone he longed for a brother or sister. "If you call five siblings, big, then yes. I'm a twin, and Reagan and I are the youngest."

"I was at Quantico with her oldest brother Tyler."

"Oh yeah, so this is the sister."

"What?" Glenna looked from son to father.

"Yeah your brother called and dad did not look happy."

He hadn't been happy with the call and that was *before* she reminded him of his ex. Her stomach rolled. She was putting him out. Dammit. She'd finish breakfast and pack, she could stay at a hotel or something until it was safe to go home.

"Hey, I didn't mean to make you look sad." Finn laid a hand on her arm.

"Glenna," Patrick placed a hand on the other arm to force her attention to him. "I thought your brother was sending me on a wild goose chase to find some putz with cold feet. It had *nothing* to do with *you*. So get those thoughts out of your head. You're welcome here until it's safe."

"Yeah Ms. Glenna please stay." Finn added.

She looked at one hand on one side and then the other. Even their hands were similar. And how could she stay mad or sad. He was right. He hadn't known her. She'd probably have felt the same way in his shoes.

She grinned first at Patrick, then Finn. "How am I supposed to finish breakfast if I can't move my arms?"

They let her go like a hot potato and she laughed. It only took a few more minutes before everything was ready to serve. Once they were ready to eat she waited for one of them to say grace, when it was evident they were about to dig in, she cleared her throat and raised a brow.

"What?" Finn asked.

Patrick looked a little abashed. She knew he was brought up catholic, if his sister's name was any clue.

"Grace first."

Patrick gave a quick prayer, Glenna thought was too short, but he'd barely said amen when both of them started eating as if they hadn't had a home cooked meal in years. The stocked pantry and fridge belied that assumption. Maybe Patrick wasn't a good cook?

"What are you guys doing today?" Finn managed between bites.

"Glenna is going to review the surveillance video and then we're going to do some inventory." Which came out with a pause between each word as Patrick talked while eating.

Men.

"I need to shower before we go."

"Just to get dirty?" Finn paused forkful halfway to his mouth.

"Inventory isn't really like an archeological dig. However, you do have a point. Okay, after I do the dishes I'll just throw on something and I'll shower before I make the Sheppard's pie this evening."

"Sheppard's pie?" they chorused.

"Oh, you don't like it?"

"Yes we do," Finn said.

"Glenna, you don't have to feed us and work off your stay here. You're our guest we should be cooking for you."

"You forget, I like to cook. It will take my mind off what's going on. I'm your responsibility not your guest and I don't want to be a burden."

"A burden," Finn snorted. "You're not a burden. Hey maybe you could come to my football game Friday night. If we win we go to the championship."

"I remember."

He looked at her in bewilderment. She stood and started to gather plates.

"I was in the car when you told your dad. I would love to come to your game, I haven't been to one since... I actually can't remember when."

Patrick looked like he might argue. She was perhaps overstepping, but on this, she didn't care. It would probably be nice for Finn to have someone cheering him on other than just his dad and grandparents.

*****

Glenna contemplated herself in the mirror. She didn't want to look the frump but Finn had been right, she would be rummaging through old dirty and dusty boxes. Oh well, Patrick was just going to have to see her that way. Once and for all he'd realize she was just Glenna and not his ex-wife. She liked to be girly and dress up. But sometimes you just had to wear old jeans, a grubby tee shirt and pull your hair into a ponytail. It was a tomboy kind of day and she wouldn't care what he thought. She pulled a ball cap on then pulled her hair through the opening in the back and she was ready to go.

It didn't matter what she wore anyway, the shop would be closed for a few more days until the authorities gave her permission to open for business.

Finn had been about to climb into the back of the 4Runner when she walked out, he stopped and grinned. Patrick just stared.

"What?"

"You look about Finn's age and ready for a softball game or something."

She thought about it a moment. "I'm okay with that. Let's go."

They dropped off Finn in front of his school. Patrick waited until he was out of sight and then turned onto the road. Glenna tried to stop all the thoughts running through her mind. She really didn't want to watch the videos of the night Alex was attacked. Even if it was after the fact. Most likely her body would still show on the screen.

Patrick placed a hand on her knee, his warmth calmed her, and she was going to need to be very careful of her heart. She had to remember he was off limits. No matter his calming and safe presence. He had two strikes against him. True, he had a lot going for him, too.

"Glenna, I promise if you can't watch I'll turn them off." His words confirmed he had known her thoughts.

"No, I'll watch. If one of them was Lance I want to know. I'm finding out a lot of things about him, but I really don't think *murderer* is one of them."

"I hope you're right."

A few minutes later they were pulling into the shop parking lot. The police officers Beckworth and Jones were propped up against the fender of their car waiting. They both straightened once they parked and got out.

"Are you ready to watch these?" Beckworth patted a black case sitting on the hood. "I have a question."

"Another one?" Patrick's toned leaned toward sarcastic. But the officer didn't seem to notice.

"Why go to all the money to put surveillance in and not add it to the store room?"

Glenna was surprised by the question. "Why would I go to the added expense? No one is allowed in the back."

"Duh, thieves usually don't follow the rules," Jones, said. "They would go in the back."

"Jones." The older partner barked.

"It's all right." She turned to Jones. "Your point is taken. If I'd had it in the storage room, we may have figured out what they were looking for, or if they had taken anything."

"Yeah, when *are* you going to take some inventory?" Jones asked.

This guy had no filter. "Today. And don't worry Officer Jones, you'll be the first to know what we find. Now, can we get started? I'm sure the two of you have *other* things you'd like to do."

"Can't wait to be alone with the fed huh?"

"Enough Jones." This time it was Patrick who berated him.

Her stomach flipped and flopped as she waited for them to set the video to the time right after the murder. She purposely looked away from the monitor not wanting to see anything, even in fast motion.

"Glenna?" Patrick asked.

She realized the others were waiting also. She swallowed and turned her attention to the screen. Luckily most of Alexis' body was out of view blocked by the counter. If she looked through the glass she could probably make more out, but she wouldn't be doing that. A tall figure stepped into view his face fully covered with a black ski mask. He motioned with his hands toward the back. The other figure was a bit shorter, not by much but enough to notice. He nodded and continued to look over the counters. Then another man came out of the back, he must have gone in before she started watching. He said something and shook his head. Then the other guy emerged again, he was by far the tallest. All three were muscular, not fat, but built. And two were about the same build and height, leaner.

Nothing at all struck her as Lance. "None of them are Lance."

"How do you know? They all have ski masks on."

She looked at the younger officer. How on earth had he passed through the academy? His partner rolled his eyes.

"Glenna?" Patrick prompted her to continue.

"None of them had any mannerisms that matched his. More importantly, Lance wasn't built, he has a lean runner's body. In fact, he ran every morning."

"You could tell all this?" Jones asked.

"That's why we had her watch them," Beckworth barked. Clearly exasperated. "At least we know whatever Gordon was looking for has the interest of someone else."

"Now we know we're looking for three other interested parties. What we don't know is what they were looking for, art or antiquities." Patrick picked up where Beckworth had left off.

"Come on Patrick, the sooner we go through the basement, the faster we'll have a clue." She paused. "Hopefully."

"What basement?" Beckworth glanced in the direction of the store room.

"There is a hidden door to a basement. Glenna keeps her new finds there until she can take inventory," Patrick explained.

"Once I know what I have and it's been cataloged in the computer I bring it into the main store room. My assistant knows..." Glenna closed her eyes a moment, swallowed then opened them. "...knew that meant she could find a place in the shop for them."

"Good. Maybe today we'll have a direction to go in our investigation." Beckworth motioned to his partner and the two left.

"Well? What are we waiting for?" Glenna asked moving toward the closet.

Chapter Nine

"Latte's."

The exclamation stopped Glenna before she reached the closet leading to the basement. Patrick watched her turn to grin at her friend who stood in the doorway holding up two coffee to-go cups.

"You're a life saver!"

"It's WCM on the skinny, just the way you like them." Effie grinned and turned to Patrick. "And for you a dark, bold, black as sin, the way you ordered it yesterday morning, hopefully it's *just the way you like it.*"

Patrick gratefully took the cup, then frowned. "WCM on the skinny? What kind of concoction is that?"

Effie pulled herself up to her full height of what he guessed to be five foot nothing and answered as if instructing a class. "White Chocolate Mocha, and on the skinny means it's made with non-fat milk, sugar free syrups and no whipped cream."

Then the woman giggled, the sound reminiscent of *Tinkerbell* from *Peter Pan.* "She takes all the fucking fun out of it."

Tinkerbell with a trucker's mouth. Patrick grinned at both and raised his cup in toast. "To finding some clues."

He took a sip and it was every bit as delicious as the French press. "Effie are you up for some sleuthing?"

She gave him a horrified look, then glanced down at her green and pink striped skirt, orange blouse, then back to him. "No thanks. I don't want to ruin my clothes." She turned to Glenna. "If you need me to, I'll run home and change."

"I think Patrick was just joking. We're okay. You have a business to run." Glenna stepped close to her friend and gave her a hug. "Thanks for the work fuel. Chat with you later."

Effie was gone in a wisp and swirl of some flowery scent as fast and dramatic as her entrance. He'd never met anyone like her.

"She's like a real life animated character from a book." He watched her skip, hop, and walk across the parking lot. Only then noticing that one sock was striped and the other polka dot. At least they were pink, green, and orange. "I mean that in a nice way."

He flipped the door shut, twisted the lock. "Ready to tackle those boxes?"

In answer, Glenna pulled the closet opened. "Can you see the door?"

He stepped forward and searched. He finally moved some brooms and mops and still could not see a door. "No. I think you're right. A carry over from prohibition."

She motioned him to step a foot back and then cleared away the shoes and other things on the floor and pulled up a trap door revealing a staircase into the basement.

"Wow. I'm just glad it's not a ladder."

Glenna chuckled. "There is no way I'd be able to move boxes down or up a ladder."

"Ladies first."

She led the way to the basement and then sat her WCM on the skinny on the workbench, placed her hands on her hips and surveyed the area. Her stance reminded him of a super hero one. Then he remembered Tyler telling him once that his sister Reagan would stand like that when surveying a crime scene. Patrick wondered if the like mannerism was one of those twin things.

After a few minutes, Glenna went to a box shoved into a corner and tugged it into the center of the room. For being a storage area, it was remarkably organized and decorated. She'd made it homey with bright yellow walls, though they weren't plaster, but cement. The shelves were done in orange and he had a moment's inspiration that her elfish friend had lent a hand in the decorating.

"I think this is the box from upstate New York." She read over the manifest, then grinned at him. "Yes it is. Let's see what is in here."

He set his cup next to hers and pulled up a chair. "I have no idea how valuable these are, I don't want to break anything. What do you want me to do?"

"As long as we're both careful and take turns taking things out we'll be fine."

She pulled out an object and carefully unwrapped it, checked the list that was sitting next to them on an empty chair. She pursed her lips and surveyed it for a moment.

"I don't believe this is anything of value, or that would cause a break in anyway. It's only worth a couple of hundred dollars."

Patrick raised a brow, in his opinion he'd been thinking a couple of dollars, forget the hundred. Following her example he brought out another piece. Once he unwrapped it, he frowned. What the hell was it?

"So what about this?"

She looked up and frowned. "What the hell is that?"

Well at least he didn't feel so uneducated now. He shrugged at her question. She reached for it and turned it this way and that, she finally referred to the list and checked it off.

"Well?"

"It's a *Schematic figurine of the Kusura type marble Anatolian Early Bronze II period 2700-2300 BC.*"

"Oh, okay. Is that valuable?"

"Yes it is. But Lance had no interest in the early Bronze Age, he leaned more to art."

Confused he asked. "Aren't artifacts to all concerned, *art*?"

"Sorry, I meant art as in pictures, like Van Gogh or Monet, or like the Italian Maestà by Duccio, 1308–1311, or Medieval or Renaissance art."

Not that he fully understood what she meant, but at least he was familiar with Van Gogh and Monet, it gave him a general idea of what to look for, and not those little weird statues. Even if they were worth thousands, to someone anyway.

Patrick glanced up as Glenna swiped a hair away, which had escaped her ponytail, from her face. He wanted to reach over and wipe the dirt smudge from her face. How on earth had he ever thought she was like Joyce?

"What are you thinking over there?" Glenna hadn't looked at him, but she must have felt his thoughts.

"Just thinking that we've been at this all morning and I'm hungry."

She straightened to give him a shocked look. "After that huge breakfast you and Finn put away? I swear I won't be hungry for a week."

He stood and looked down at her. "I'm a mite bigger than you. Takes a lot of fuel to keep this body going, you know."

She tilted her head to regard him, he was delighted to see twin pink cheeks. "You've been doing nothing but sitting here. How does that burn fuel?"

"You should know that you burn calories even sitting. Someone my size, about 66 calories per hour. And it's been a couple, plus I drove here and we talked to the detectives..."

She held up her hand. "Stop! I get your point. I could use a break. I'm going cross eyed and I still have no clue what Lance could have wanted. This is the only sale I know we both attended."

"As you said, the only one you *know*."

Patrick held out a hand, she grasped it, and he pulled her to her feet. He took a deep breath and tried to ignore the electricity running up his arm. She let go of his hand as quickly as possible. Did she feel little shocks also?

He would have to explore the possibilities after the case. His number one rule, never get involved with someone he worked with, no matter what capacity.

Effie made a big fuss over their lunch causing the other patrons to glance at them more than once. Most likely wondering if they were in town for the art festival. And if they were anyone worth noting. They'd be disappointed to know they were just residents and Effie was just being herself. And by the time most of them left, they'd all received the *Effie* treatment. Must be why the Bistro was such a popular place.

Patrick sighed when they returned to the basement. What he needed was a nap after that lunch. Instead he looked around at the boxes. They only had one more box to go through from the New York estate sale. Squaring his shoulders he bent to the task. The sooner they went through it, the sooner they'd be finished.

*****

Glenna watched Patrick from under her lashes. She had always wondered what that meant when she read one of her many romance novels, and now she knew. You had your head bent as if looking down, but your eyes were actually focused on something across from you. And the point was for people not to notice. She'd never had any particular reason to try this until now.

He was such a delight to watch. A big highlander, his huge hand gently unfolding the protective paper away from delicate objects of art. Then the little crease between his brows would appear and she'd know that he didn't have a clue what he was looking at. She found it delightful.

And in that moment she knew she was in deep trouble no matter that he had not one, but two strikes against him.

"Are you done staring at me?"

She raised her head and glared at him for catching her. Drat the man.

"I was just wondering when you're going to ask me what you're holding."

"I wanted to figure it out on my own." He picked up the paper and started reading the list. "Ha, found it. It's this ancient fertility God thing."

"You better put that down unless you want to have a dozen kids."

His eyes widened in dread and he at least had the forethought to wrap it and put it to the side and not drop it, like she'd feared. She should have thought that through before she scared him.

"I was only joking. I honestly have read no modern day evidence that they actually work."

"Good to know. I love Finn, but twelve of him is a little daunting."

Glenna smiled and then returned her attention to the next item. She pulled it out, peeled the paper away. And froze. This had to be it. It was a small delicate frame, within it, the Madonna and child.

"What?"

"I think this may be it, but I need to grab my laptop. Oh, never mind, I won't get service down here. Take a good look." She turned it so he could see. "Come."

Glenna placed the frame on the work bench, then led the way toward the stairs. Once in her office she logged onto her laptop.

"If I'm not mistaken it's a Giovanni Bellini. And if it's the one I'm thinking of, it's one of the missing pieces stolen during the Nazi occupation."

Her heart raced as she navigated through her bookmarks for the article she'd saved. If it was what she thought it was, the piece was priceless.

"Found it."

"Found what?"

"The article, it's about all the art and objects that are still missing from when the Nazi's confiscated and destroyed homes in the cities and countries they occupied. Give me a minute and let me find the list."

As she scanned through the pictures and the descriptions, her excitement built. And then there it was.

"Here it is, *Giovanni Bellini, Madonna with Child, c.1430.*"

Patrick leaned over her shoulder and read aloud. "This was evacuated in the early 1940s from a museum in Berlin to be housed in a flak tower in Berlin-Fried.... Something or other, located within Russian control at the time. Most of the objects in the tower were either looted or presumed destroyed, including Bellini's Madonna."

"How did this find its way to upstate New York?" She glanced up at him. "Museums and countries are offering awards for the return of their art."

"And we've found motive for your fiancé's interest." He stepped back to give her room to stand up. "Correct me if I'm wrong, but wouldn't the piece bring even more on the black market?"

"Oh, yes." She led the way back to the basement. She picked up the frame with much more care than she had when she'd just suspected its worth. "Not to mention the network on the Dark Web. I hear that they're the *new* black market. We need to find a safe place for this. Because I'm afraid there are hacks out there good enough to access the Calistoga Database, they're not as tech savvy as the feds. As soon as Beckworth puts in his report, I have a basement storage and what we found, they may know."

"As much as I want to pretend you're wrong, I know most likely you're right. The FBI has a full time task force monitoring who hacks in to our servers on a daily basis. From what I understand, almost as fast as our IT geeks can write a script to block a hack, there's a new breach."

"Do we have to tell them what we found?"

"Yes." He ran his hand through his ginger hair. Glenna immediately wanted to do the same. "However,

I don't think we need to tell them right now. We'll take this to my place and come up with a plan. I want to let Tyler know or better yet, your twin. From what I hear, she's had experience with cyber terrorism. She may be able to help. If the three guys who broke in found out about it through the Dark Web."

She thought about it and paced. Then stood in what she referred to as her strong woman stance. Fists on hips, feet a foot apart.

"What?"

"Is that a twin thing?"

She frowned, what the hell was he talking about? He was grinning and looking at her. Did she have dirt on her? But then why would he call it a twin thing?

"Twin thing?"

"Your super hero pose."

She looked down at herself and understood how he could get super hero from her stance. "This is what I do when I need to be strong and take care of things. I've been on my own for a while. It gives me confidence."

"Makes sense, but did you know your sister does the same thing when she's taking in a crime scene? Tyler told me she calls it her Super Hero pose."

Surprise ran over her. Reagan may be her twin and there were a few things they had in common, but mostly they were different as night and day. She had more of connection with Tyler.

"I can see you had no clue. Well I have yet to witness your sister's super hero, so until I do, I'll go with the *Strong Woman*. Because I think I like the idea that you know you can handle the situation." He gave her a look that she couldn't decipher, but it had butterflies vying for position in her belly. "What are you thinking? Do you have an idea of who might want the art?"

She'd think about those butterflies later, now they needed to figure out what was going on before someone else got hurt. What would she do if the art thieves came back and somehow Effie was hurt? She'd never forgive herself.

"I had no idea we'd find something this priceless. This puts a whole new prospective on things. This art ring or whatever it is, and for all I know Lance could be a part of them, is far more dangerous than I thought. I thought maybe they'd killed Alex by accident. She surprised them, or threatened to call the police or something. But now, I don't think they care who gets hurt."

"Let's get this to my place, I'll report what's going on. This has to be an International ring, the department may have some background and a direction of where we can look. Then we'll figure something out."

Glenna nodded. She had a roll of bubble wrap on the bench and measured out the length she'd need. She wrapped the picture up, then wrapped it with brown paper. She looked around and finally found a box double the size of the art.

"Good idea, if they're watching they won't have a clue what we're taking with us is what they're looking for."

A chill ran down her spine when he actually voiced her thoughts. Somehow it made it more real, more dangerous, and suddenly she didn't feel like the strong woman she wanted to be. Suddenly she wanted Patrick to make it all go away.

She couldn't do that, she owed it to Alex to help catch her murderers. She handed the box to Patrick so she could rummage through her purse for her lifesaving antacid. She really should make an appointment with her doctor, she probably had ulcers. Her stomach boiled whenever the situation turned stressful. The last few years she'd been pain free, until she was abandoned at the altar, and now the murder.

The first half of the trip to Patrick's was in silence, both lost in their own thoughts. The hands-free phone buzzed with a call breaking the peace. Patrick glanced at her briefly before he answered. Beckworth's voice filled the inside of the 4-Runner.

"Any news? Did you find something?"

Patrick paused and again threw her a look that said clearly follow my lead. Okay maybe she read too many romantic suspense novels. But she nodded just the same.

"Nope, we went through all the boxes. There were several valuable items, but according to Ms. Beckett nothing that would warrant a break in or murder. We have to be missing something. She even checked the internet to see if an item was worth anything."

This was the truth, he just didn't clarify what she'd been looking for and found. The conversation went on, and Glenna let the words flow over her, while she contemplated her growing feelings for the agent. She'd barely met him, and she knew feelings could escalate over intense situations. The best thing to do would be to guard her heart and when all this was over, see how things went. Now that was a good plan.

Then she thought about Tyler. He'd barely known Keira when he took her to a safe house and he fell in love with her and now she was working in the agency with him. Not to mention they had little Lucy.

Still... she was jumping way too far ahead of herself. Remember two strikes... Law enforcement and ex-baggage.

"...let us know if you find anything." And then Patrick broke the connection.

"Sorry, I was woolgathering. What are they going to find?"

He gave her a questioning look but didn't ask the question. Thank goodness. After a moment he explained.

"Since we didn't find anything, Beckworth had the idea to bring in an art expert to inventory your stock in the basement."

"And since we have what the thieves want, the expert won't find anything. And it will give us time to come up with a plan." Glenna grinned.

"Yes. I like your Strong Woman."

Warmth filled her at his words and she did her best to wrap her heart in steel to keep it safe.

"At least I'll have a free audit of what I have, right?"

He flipped her a grin as he pulled into his drive way.

*****

It was now more important than ever to keep his personal feelings out of the case. When Tyler Beckett had first called him, he thought it was a harmless favor the man asked of him. To be fair he figured Tyler had felt the same way. Neither could have determined that looking for his sister's missing fiancé would turn into a murder investigation involving priceless antiquities and an Art Thief ring. Now Glenna's life and possibly those around her were in danger. He was busy making a mental list of all he needed to do to start in the new direction when Glenna broke into his thoughts.

"Earth to Patrick..." She raised a brow at him.

"Sorry. Just thinking about the turn this investigation just took."

"I can understand that, but do we have to do it sitting in your driveway? It's getting a little hot in here." She grinned taking any sting that might have been in her words, away. She didn't wait for him to open her door, he was busy grabbing their treasure from the back.

Patrick placed the box on the table and then glared at the damn thing. He didn't want it in his home. If they found out, Finn could be in danger. They all would be. He could take care of himself, but he was only one man and he had three lives to protect.

"This can't be here."

He drew his attention from the box to Glenna, had she read his mind? She was glaring at the box too, with an expression that he had a feeling matched his.

"What should we do with it?"

She finally looked at him. "Put it in a storage unit."

"If they're watching, which I'm sure they are. They will still suspect it's here. What we need to do is have someone put cameras in both your store room and your basement, today. If they come back and can't find it. They'll know the big box is what they want." He plopped down in one of the kitchen chairs.

"That means we need to figure out who they are and come up with a plan before that happens."

She took a chair across from him and sat down much more graceful than he had.

"You're right..."

"...you just don't want any harm even coming close to Finn." She finished for him.

Yeah, he was in trouble as far as she was concerned. He'd do whatever it took to be impartial until this was over. Then, and only then, would he see if anything would come out of a relationship with Ms. Glenna Beckett.

"Right. I better get on with it. I'll call a company I know to place those cameras."

"While you do that, I'll use the shower. Then we'll call Reagan."

He raised a brow. "Not your brother?"

"I love my brother, but you said it. My sister has the experience we need. Besides I'd love to talk to my sister. I barely met her new husband and my niece I didn't even know I had."

He opened his mouth to ask for an explanation and then thought better of it, family talk was far to intimate. Maybe when he had his heart wrapped firmly in Titanium, he'd ask.

"Sounds good. I shouldn't take too long. They also may have some resources I can check out."

She stopped by the arch leading to the hall. "Promise me something."

"Sure, well if it's feasible I will."

"Keep me in the loop. I know I'm not a trained agent and there may be some things I cannot help with. But knowledge is power and I need to *know* every step whether I'm to be involved or not."

He thought about it for a moment. She wasn't asking to go on a stakeout or anything, just for information.

"I agree. The more you know about what is going on the better. I promise to keep you up to speed."

"Me too."

They both turned to see Finn coming through the back door, Horace at his side.

This case was going in directions he'd never dreamed possible. The last thing he wanted to do was involve his sixteen year old son.

Chapter Ten

"Finn, you surprised me." Glenna placed a hand to her racing heart.

She glanced to Patrick who was staring at his son, she knew he didn't want him to be involved in any capacity. She felt since she had brought the danger to their door, she needed to put in her two cents. Whether Patrick liked it or not.

"I agree with Finn. He needs to be kept up on things also."

His head whipped around to her, the fire in his eyes almost made her step back out of the heat. His love for his son was fierce and she understood it. Before he could say anything, Finn stepped further into the room. The boy placed a hand on his dad's shoulder. Patrick turned to face his son.

"Dad, I know you want to protect me. But if I know nothing, that puts me in more danger." He raised a brow and when Patrick was about to interrupt he gave his dad's shoulder a squeeze. "Think dad. If someone comes to school because they know I live here. How will I know who may be the bad guys if I don't know what to look for?"

Patrick's chest expanded and she heard his sigh from where she stood. "Dammit, you're both right."

"Sit." Patrick motioned Finn to a chair then glanced at Glenna. "I'll bring him up to speed while you take your shower. We'll all call Reagan when you're done."

"Awesome." Finn grinned. "Finally, you trust me enough to let me help."

The expression that crossed Patrick's face at his son's words was not a joyous one. As much as she wanted to be in on the conversation she decided it would be prudent to do as he asked.

Glenna made her shower quick, she threw her thoroughly disgusting clothes in the bag she'd brought for her dirty laundry. Going through treasure boxes from her shopping sprees could be very filthy work.

She threw her hair up in a lose bun, pulled some jeans on and pulled on a tee-shirt. Glancing in the mirror she figured she'd do, and raced out to see if she'd missed anything.

"Wow that was fast. All the girls at my school take forever to get ready for anything."

Glenna grinned. "I'm not just any girl, I'm super girl."

"Woman," Patrick corrected.

Glenna wanted to know what was racing through Finn's mind. His gaze was bouncing back and forth like a tennis match, as if trying to figure what that super girl and or woman meant. Apparently he decided to let it go because in the end he just turned to his dad with a question.

"Now what?"

"We call Glenna's sister."

Finn frowned and turned to her. "Your sister a super woman too?"

"No she's a super hero and works with a special agency that handles cyber terrorism. We're hoping she can help us track these art thieves on the Dark Web."

"Cool. I think I want to be a special agent."

Patrick looked at his son in horror for a moment, then resignation settled over his features. "It's not as exciting as it sounds."

Finn just chuckled. "So far it's been pretty good. I think I'd make a great agent, after all I have a live-in text book example to follow."

Glenna could feel the *proud* bouncing through Patrick from where she still stood under the arch to the kitchen. Someday she wanted to have a son or daughter who had a love for the profession she'd chosen. Anything of the arts. Hell, she knew she'd be proud no matter what her children did.

And why was she thinking of her children? She hadn't thought about a child since she was a little girl playing with Cammie from down the street when they'd pretended to be grownups with families of their own.

Patrick was playing havoc with her well-being. She could *not* fall for him. But every second with him pounded another chink away from the armor she'd been trying to pull over her heart.

"Are you going to stand there all day or can we get this show on the road."

Finn's voice startled her and she realized she'd been standing there in her own thoughts for several moments. She rubbed her hands down her jeans and then took the empty chair at the table.

"Okay, what's the plan? Should we make a list of what we need to ask Reagan?" Glenna had no idea how these agent things worked.

"For someone from a family full of law enforcement you're a little on the clueless side."

Patrick didn't expand but picked up his phone and waited with a raised brow.

"What?" She asked.

"I don't know your sister's number."

"Oh." She felt silly as she took the phone from him and punched in the number.

After a couple of rings her sister's voice came on the line, it was always a little unsettling to hear her own voice, or so it seemed.

"Reagan, we need to pick your brains on a case, I'm putting you on speaker."

There was a pause and then her sister's voice filled the room.

"Case?"

"Yes, did Ty fill you in on the agent he called to help find Lance?"

"Yes, he did. You're working the case with him? Isn't that a little out of your expertise?"

"Yes. Not the art part though. We found what the thieves' who murdered Alex was after."

"Whoa, what? Tyler didn't tell me anything about your assistant. Start at the beginning. I, apparently, know the bare bones."

Glenna nodded to Patrick to explain. For several minutes his voice was the only one heard. She was impressed with how thorough he was and yet to the point with no extra words. Even a civilian like herself would be able to follow the details. And then she realized he'd probably done that for her and Finn's benefit, even though they mostly knew the details.

"Well, that puts an entire new twist on the missing groom. I knew I didn't like him the moment I saw his little man bun."

Glenna frowned. "Why the f..." she glanced at Finn. "...heck does everyone hate man buns?"

"There are so many reasons it would take too long to list." Patrick answered before her sister could.

"Yeah." Finn agreed.

Glenna let it drop, she'd never understand. She thought they were cute. Though she couldn't imagine Patrick with one. His thick copper hair looked good just the way it was, a little longish and resting on his collar with just a hint of a wave.

"We through talking hair and fashion? Let's talk Dark Web. The first thing I'll do is run a few feelers out for the stolen artifacts. Whoever bites will give us a place to start. Then we'll need to decide how to get them to walk into a trap."

"How do we do that exactly?" Glenna wanted to know.

"By figuring out how to let them know we have what they want," Patrick said. "But mostly we want to be in control. And in no way can they suspect the authorities know about the art they are after."

"That's going to be hard. They know you're an agent." Finn frowned at his dad.

"No, I've never shown up in a squad car or under any capacity with the local police. They may suspect. But all they know I'm Glenna's love interest."

"Unless Lance is part of the group." Glenna bit her lip. "However, he did jilt me at the altar. You could be my rebound."

"Now *that* sounds interesting."

"Dad, I'm right here."

Glenna almost laughed as the blush crawled up his face and actually seemed to clash with his ginger hair.

"Glenna, I'm right here." Reagan's voice held a hint of amusement. *"But it could work. Let's see what we can do to get you two to drop the bait. If they know about this art that means they're professionals."*

"And most likely they're in an International group." His voice didn't give a hint of embarrassment, though Glenna was amused to see a bit of pink still lingered.

"And if the time is right, I have the perfect location to drop the bait." Glenna stood and held a finger up to stop any questions. "Hold on..."

She raced to her room and grabbed her laptop. Once back in her chair started the log in process.

"Backmans House of London deals in rare art and antiquities." She didn't bother to look up as she tried to find the site on her computer. "It was their monthly publication where I found the article on the missing Nazi art."

"You would put an ad in that? What would you say? It's stolen you can't really advertise it legally."

"I know. I have another idea. Most of the countries have a reward offered for any missing art or artifacts returned to them. I'll check to see if this one has one, but I'm sure it does." She concentrated for a moment ignoring the others' growing impatience. "Found it."

"Found what?"

Reagan's question was echoed by the two guys.

"Sorry. I knew that Backmans has a grand gala somewhere every year. This year it's in New York."

"And you're going to take it there and show it off?"

"Give me some credit. I may not be in the law enforcement branch of the family. But I *know* art and antiques. My thoughts are that I bring my new rebound date to the gala and we have a few conversations around the right people. You know whisper about the art we found and I want to auction it to the highest bidder on the Dark Web, but my morally honest new beau wants to take the reward from the country of origin."

"Or since it's a possibility that they may suspect that I am law enforcement, maybe I should be the one who wants to auction it?"

"Or maybe Dad just wants to be a bad guy since it's for a good cause." Finn grinned at them.

"I like this kid. Maybe when they come to New York for the gala you could come home for some coaching and meet the Elders."

Whoa there Reagan. Glenna looked first to Patrick, who wore an expression she couldn't read. When she glanced at his son, there was full on grin of delight.

"Yeah, that would be awesome. Like I was in on the whole operation *Find Lance*. I like it. Besides Dad, you're going to need a little help with the dancing." He tilted his head to regard his father. "Can you even dance?"

"I can dance."

Patrick didn't voice his thoughts. Glenna would have offered her savings to know what they were. But Reagan jumped back in with her thoughts.

"Operation Find Lance, it's a keeper. Okay kid lets you and I plan this out. I will prompt Glenna on the cloak and dagger, as Matt calls it, role and you coach your dad on the romance stuff. Glenna will be the expert on art. Sound like a plan?"

"I'm not sure..." Patrick began with a worried frown at his son.

Glenna knew he wanted to protect Finn, they'd already established that. "Think Patrick, Finn would be far more safe with us staying at *The Elders* than here without us."

There was silence in the kitchen. Reagan kept silent as if she sensed how difficult this decision would be for a father. Reagan now had a daughter to consider. Glenna imagined she would have a hard time involving Gabby in a case. Though Glenna knew that's how Reagan found her daughter. Gabby had been involved in a case and Reagan had rescued her without knowing that Gabby was her daughter. Glenna couldn't even imagine how hard that had been for her sister.

"You're probably right. The idea is growing on me. Finn you will not be going to the Gala though."

"I don't think minors are allowed anyway. He'll be safe with the family." She grinned at Finn. "More or less."

"What do you mean more or less?" Patrick demanded.

"I think she means he may come away with some ideas. The next generation of Beckett's are turning into quite the entrepreneurs".

"Entrepreneurs? I didn't see that one coming. You guys win. Finn will go with us and I'll have Mum and Da watch Horace and Agnes. They can keep an eye on the house too."

Glenna still wasn't convinced he was completely sold on the idea as much as he felt outnumbered. And maybe even a little manipulated. She'd talk to him later and if he was truly against the idea she'd support his decision. *And since when do I even have the right to have a voice?* Scary thoughts on her part. With effort, she returned her attention back to the case at hand.

"I will do some research and see if I can find anything about who may benefit from attaining the art. Backmans has information about known rings and what dealers need to watch out for, among other things." Glenna opened a document to make a list of things she could do to help. "I will take care of the *art* portion of this case as you suggested."

"Find out how you get an invite to the gala and make sure you're registered. I will run my feelers on the

Dark Web and then run down any leads with my contacts. Patrick, I will keep you up to speed on what I find and you can run it by your department to see if they have leads I might not have.

"And Finn you take care of coaching these two on the romance, it's got to be believable they're a couple."

"I'm not sure they need coaching in the *romance* department but I'll have Rebekah help me coach dad so he won't embarrass himself on the dance floor."

"Who says there'll be dancing?" Patrick asked.

"Oh there is always a band and dance floor." Glenna thought a moment. "You know that maybe a good place to be *whispering* things to each other about the piece. We'll find our..." She glanced at Patrick. "...targets, is that right? Anyway, once we know who might want the portrait we can stand next to them or dance by them and just loud enough for them to hear but low enough they think we're trying to be quiet, we can drop the bait."

Glenna was very proud of herself for picking up the lingo, she just hoped she was using it correctly.

"Well done, sis, there may be hope for you on the law enforcement branch of the family yet."

"Ah, never. I'm not cut out for cloak and dagger any more than Matt. However, now I know I'll be visiting the family next week I am looking forward to getting to know Bryn and Paco. With all the wedding drama I really wasn't in the frame of mind to visit."

"And you will be now?"

"Yes, why not. And besides, Tyler and the rest of you will be trying to tell me everything to do or not do at the Gala so I don't blow my *cover*. I think I may need to take my new sister-in-law for a girls shopping spree. Jessica would like to join us I bet."

"Wait a minute. We're not going to have time for *shopping spree's*. We're going in for the Gala only, dropping the bait. and getting you and Finn out of there."

"No, that won't work..."

"No, I agree with Glenna. These guys are most likely international professional art thieves they're going to do their due diligence. They will know you're an agent which will make it all the more important for you to pull off the romance thing. It's a good thing you're not in a department that specializes in art theft. Anyway, what better way to reinforce your cover than by meeting the fam? Do a little recreation with the brothers. Just so you know we have an excellent gun range and simulator."

Glenna could tell that piqued his interest. "And Reagan would be the first to challenge you."

"This is not a vacation, however, I do see the point. And Finn would have a good time seeing where I went to school."

"I would? I'd rather go to the gun range. Hey, Agent Beckett..."

"Reagan."

"Reagan do they let civilians in the simulator?"

"Yes, I was able to take Matt and Bryn for some training. It took a special permit, I will see what I can do. But only if your father approves and will be in attendance."

The look Finn gave Patrick would be hard to say no to by any parent. Glenna knew he felt on the spot. More reason to talk to him later.

"I hate to admit it, but the more I think about going a few days early the more sense it makes. They're watching us, I can feel it. Up until now we've been doing nothing to give the impression that *I'm not on the case.* It is time to make some moves that I'm more interested in Glenna than art."

He was quiet for so long, Glenna thought he was done. And it seemed he was when he stood, but he went to the calendar frowned and said over his shoulder to Finn. "Your game Friday, if you win you go on to playoffs, right?"

"Oh my goodness, Finn you may have to stay home if you guys win." Glenna couldn't let him miss something as important as a playoff game.

"When is the Gala?"

Finn reached over and grabbed the calendar out of his dad's hand. He sat it on the table and studied the dates circled.

"It's a week from this Sunday." Glenna consulted the site again. If we fly in on Wednesday or Thursday we could hang with the family. But if you have games that weekend..."

"That works great. If we win this Friday, the next day we play the winner of San Jose County. Then if we win that game, we go to state which will give us the next weekend off and we'd play the following. See?"

He pushed the calendar across the table and sure enough there was the weekend of the Gala that had *no* circled dates. Patrick leaned over Finn's shoulder and contemplated the same thing. Glenna couldn't tell if he was happy or disgruntled by the fact he didn't have an excuse to pull his son out of the trip.

"It's settled then. We'll leave Wednesday and come home on Tuesday. Give us a day to consult with Reagan and Tyler after the event."

"Sounds like a plan. I'm going to let you guys plan your trip and I'll start sending out some feelers. Patrick I'll be in touch. Glenna you do what he says, he knows the criminal element, you stick to the art element which none of us know."

The phone disconnected without a goodbye, which was true Reagan. Glenna didn't remember Reagan being so diplomatic, but she had been. She made sure not to make Glenna feel inadequate but needed. She looked forward to seeing her family without the emotional trauma of being dumped on her wedding day. Now she realized she'd never loved Lance, but *loved* the romance of it all, she felt a little ashamed.

Was she so hungry for love that she saw it where it wasn't? And what about her new and tentative feelings for Patrick? She would have to guard herself well through this trip. When everything was solved she'd know he was interested if he contacted her. Then they could build something.

Maybe.

She just knew she wasn't going to be so easily swayed again. Maybe she needed to stop reading romance novels.

No.

She just needed to be wise.

"So, are you going to just stare at that computer all day?" Finn's voice broke into her thoughts.

"Sorry about that, I was just thinking about the upcoming trip."

That wasn't a lie. It just wasn't in the way they thought.

"So what is next? Should I search some airline tickets? We won't need a place to stay, we'll stay with *The Elders*. Now all the kids are grown and flown the coop, there's plenty of room. I will see what I need to do to get us in on the list for the Gala."

"And we need to start looking like a couple." The look he gave her made her toes curl. And she wasn't sure if it was in a good way. She wished she knew his thoughts. "And what better way than my son's football game?"

He ruffled his son's hair, Finn grimaced but then smiled. "Great. You're going to love Nanna and Móraí"

Glenna knew Finn must be referring to his grandparents. "Mo ree?"

"Yeah, my grandfather is Irish so I like to call him by the traditional Irish name or one of them anyway. The Irish word for grandfather is *seanathair*, literally meaning "old father." But grandchildren usually use instead, *daideó* pronounced DADJ-yoh or *móraí* as I do. And since my grandmother is Scottish I call her Nanna, but a lot of kids around here call their grandma's Nana."

"My nieces and nephews' call *The Elders* nana and papa, not sure if it has any meaning other than Sophie was the first to start calling them that and it stuck"

"Finn, I think it's time for you to do some homework. Glenna and I need to discuss a safe place to store this piece of art."

"We can do that while I throw the Sheppard's pie together."

Finn let out a little whoop. "Yes. I was afraid you'd changed your mind."

"I promised."

Patrick didn't join in, but continued from where she'd interrupted. "When you're finished with school work, maybe we should go out for dinner tonight. It wouldn't hurt for those following us to see this *rebound* thing. Right?"

By the tone of Patrick's voice, Glenna now knew he was not a happy camper to be on the romance train. Just great.

Chapter Eleven

Patrick waited until Finn was out of the room before he turned to Glenna. He needed to calm down. She wasn't the one who railroaded him into this scenario, but then he hadn't stopped it. At the moment he was feeling... what? Trapped? Intrigued? Excited? More scared than he'd ever been in his life?

Bingo! All of the above. God. What was he going to do? From the moment he first realized that his animosity for Joyce wasn't going to be any protection against the beautiful, put together, immaculate Glenna, he'd been in trouble. His first thought that was she was his ex-wife all over again had been blown out of the water within minutes of meeting her.

Now he knew that was so far from the truth, he'd been swimming against the emotional current. He was so tied in knots he didn't know whether to grab her and shake her or kiss the living daylights out of her.

There she stood. Several emotions had crossed her face during the conversation and most of them had mirrored his.

"Patrick..."

He held his hand up, he needed to go for a walk to cool off before he took his whatever his jumble of feelings were, out on her. "I need some air and perspective. Give me a minute."

He nearly pulled the damn knob off the door in the process of leaving. At first he concentrated on putting one foot in front of the other and not thinking. Hell, he just knew he needed to get away from Glenna, the situation, the feeling of not being in control.

It sucked.

He blinked. He'd been so lost in thought he was surprised to find himself standing in front of the home he grew up in. After a moment he realized he was staring at his father, who was on the porch as he had been after dinner every night, whenever possible, for as long as Patrick could remember. It was where he found him whenever he needed to talk. It was where he'd first told him about Finn and how scared he was of being a father when he was little more than a kid himself.

And that was *before* he knew he'd be a single dad.

"Patrick."

One word that's all it took for his feet to start eating the distance to the chair waiting for him. Next to his Da. Where he could say or ask anything and know he'd get the best advice a man could want. Didn't mean he was going to like what he'd hear, but whatever it was it would be the best.

"Da..."

His mum pushed opened the screen door took in the scene and disappeared. A moment later, still neither of the men had spoken, his mum appeared with a bottle of Jameson and two shot glasses.

She shrugged when Patrick raised a brow. "I thought it looked like a whiskey talk. I'll leave you two."

Without waiting for a response she was gone. His da poured and handed him his glass. Then raised his own.

"May you always have a clean shirt, a clear conscience, and enough coins in your pocket to buy a pint!" And slammed it back a second before Patrick did the same.

Heat funneled to his gut and burned. He poured the next round.

"*Slainte chuig na fir, agus go mairfidh na mna go deo.*"

Patrick slammed it back and let the fire roll its way to his belly. He father sat the glass down with a small snap and chuckled.

"I haven't heard that for a bit. 'Health to the men and may the women live forever.' This is about a woman then?"

"No." He shot to his feet, had to stand for a bit and get his bearings. He took the two steps to the railing and held on for a moment. "Yes."

He swung back ran a hand through his hair, "Sort of. Oh hell, I don't know what it's about."

"A woman. You're mom had me tied up in so many knots I'm not sure how I took a shit."

"Kendal!" Aw the voice of his childhood. Only it wasn't directed at him. It also proved she still eavesdropped. She may *pretend* to give the men their space, but she had to know what was going on.

"Caroline shut the door." And so it went as it always did. And his mother never shut the door.

"Finn is involved..."

"What? Finn has a woman?"

Before he had time to answer the screen blew open and his mother stood over him like an avenging angel.

"Who is she? I will go have a little talk with her."

"Jeez guys, if you'd let me finish. It's not about Finn and a woman. It's about a case that Finn wants to be involved in..." He inhaled and let his breath trickle out before he finished. "And a woman."

This time his mother took up the third seat on the porch. "If it involves my boy Finn, I'm staying."

Patrick sighed. He really needed his dad's advice about Glenna. After all he'd found the perfect woman, and that's what Patrick wanted. His mother, as mother's can do, patted his hand and smiled then said the words that proved she'd read his mind or sigh.

"After, you can talk to your da about the woman part. Now what's going on with Finn?"

"It's not that easy to separate the two."

"So it is about Finn and a woman?" His mother demanded.

"No. Well yes. No." He shook his head. It was the whiskey on an empty stomach. "It's about a case that Finn wants to help with, and the *case* involves the woman."

His father poured another round and they did the required toasts and then he looked at Patrick. "Son are you ever going to tell us what's going on?"

"If you'd stop liquoring me up, I might be able to."

He sighed. "Sorry, that was uncalled for. I just don't want Finn to be involved."

"Why does he need to be?" His mother asked.

"I did something I promised myself I never would. I brought my work home with me. Now, though I don't like it, Finn feels he needs to be in the middle of things so he's prepared. And dammit I think he's right."

His da regarded him a moment. "You're taking us around the bush here, you better start at the beginning."

For the next several minutes his parents let him talk and listened intently. They were good at that. It was why he always came to them. He'd always been close to his parents, even during his rebellious teen years, which was a totally different story.

"Dear, I don't want to worry you, but that black van just a little down the road has been there since you came. They pulled over the minute you stopped at the gate. I didn't think much about it. And I haven't seen anyone get out of it, and with the tinted windows I can't see anyone in it."

"I noticed it too, but like your mum I didn't give it a second thought."

Patrick resisted the urge to turn. "If they're here that means, they're not at the house with Glenna and Finn."

"Your *case* is right about one thing. Finn needs to be informed. I also think you need to take the boy with you to this Soiree thing." His father didn't so-much as look in the direction of the van either. His mother was facing it.

"Maybe I better go."

His mother placed a hand on his thigh before he stood. "They may follow you home. Wouldn't it be prudent to let them think you've just gone in the house? Maybe go out the back door?"

He raised a brow at his mother, she'd been watching too much television.

"Or I'm sure your mother wouldn't mind going back in the house and calling Finn and your *case...*"

"Exactly what do you mean my *case?* You've said that twice now. My case isn't a person."

"Yes it is. It's this Beckett woman who owns that vintage shop in Calistoga."

"Oh, it's *that* Glenna? I didn't put two and two together because you never said the name of the shop." His mother said this as if he'd purposely misled her. "You need to take care of Glenna, she's a sweetheart."

He thought she was done, but then he saw a gleam appear in her eye and he really didn't think he was going to like what she said.

"Dear, she's a good girl, she'd be good for you." Then she gasped as if, he didn't want to think about what he was about to compare it to. "She is the *WOMAN* you're in knots about, oh I love a good romance."

"Mum."

"Caroline, man talk! Go make that call."

They waited until his mother disappeared into the house. They could vaguely hear her on the phone. Patrick was hard put not to turn and take a good look at the black van. But they'd know they had been spotted. He took a deep breath and resisted the urge to take another shot of his favorite whiskey. His dad didn't offer either, he must have come to the same conclusion.

Things just got a little dicey and he would need a clear head. He just hoped it wasn't too late for that.

"Your mother is right? Is it because of Finn? Son, the boy needs a mum. And not because you're a single da but because the boy needs a woman to learn the softer side of life. You know? So he knows that's it's not all farting and scratching."

Before Patrick could chuckle, his mother again proved she'd been listening by bellowing his father's name.

"Quit being so nosy woman."

"I don't know what I feel, Da. I know that if I'm to keep my boy safe and Glenna, who I care too much for already, I have to keep my head in the game. And that means unemotional."

"Aye, I understand where you're coming from then." He scratched his chin looking out over the field across the street and Patrick was proud of his will power not to turn and look to see if the vehicle was still in the same spot.

"How does she feel about you?"

Patrick grinned for the first time. "I think she has the same knots."

"Then what the *ifreann* is the problem?"

"I got off on the wrong foot. I was a little cool toward her at first. She reminded me of Joyce. I thought she was going to be a spoiled, self-centered *soith*, and would cry over a chipped nail."

"Nothing worse than a woman being a self-centered bitch. You were wrong?"

"Yes. They're different as night and day."

"And what is the problem? Did you apologize?"

"Yes. But I don't think she wants to get involved with law enforcement and I've got baggage. Hell, I'm not sure I'd want me."

"Finn is not baggage." Now his father sound indignant instead of amused as he had been.

"Not Finn. My baggage is the fact I have an ex-wife who I initially compared her to, and not in a good way. Wasn't the smartest thing I'd ever done."

"What wasn't the smartest thing, was to tell her." He lowered his head and gave him a look that clearly made Patrick feel like he was ten again. "Does Finn like her?"

"Horace already loves her and Agnes, and I'm pretty sure Finn adores her, especially her cooking."

"She cooks?" This with a shaggy raised brow. "Who's Agnes?"

"She's a great cook. Agnes is her very uppity cat who seems to tolerate Horace."

"A new case, a new gal, and a cat. Seems like I might as well stick a fork in you because you're done my boy."

"Da. I came for advice not a glib observation. I need to get going so I can get home before the van notices I'm gone."

"I'll be quick then. Let things work themselves out. And since I love you and Finn, I want you safe. Keep your head on the case until after, then if it's right you'll see things will fall into place."

The door swung open. "That's what happened to us dear, we were both stewing about our feelings and over thinking every little thing and it was causing all kinds of problems."

"Knots in the gut. As soon as I threw up my hands and walked away and gave us both some space. The kinks worked themselves out."

"Hun, I walked away."

"No, I did. I remember I thought, this is just too much. Then I walked away and two days later I couldn't eat or drink..." His da had a pained expression. "Son, no man should have trouble drinking. So I went back with flowers and that was all it took."

Patrick looked at his mother who winked and shook her head a little. Apparently, there were two sides to this story. But he'd think about it later. He really needed to get home.

"I love you both, thank you." He held the screen open a moment looking at his mum. "Call my cell if it leaves."

Over his mother's shoulder he'd been able to get a good look at the vehicle. It was too far to read the plates, but he knew he'd seen it a few times driving past the shop in Calistoga.

He went through the back door and raced to the end of the yard. As he leaped over the fence, memories raced through him of many a night sneaking out and even though the situation didn't warrant the smile, he felt better for it.

*****

The walls were closing in, Glenna walked from one kitchen wall to the other. If she didn't know better, she was positive the walls *were* moving in. Where the hell had Patrick gone? She'd been right, he'd felt trapped. She needed to talk to him. Make sure they devised a plan that didn't include Finn, if that was what he wanted.

She closed her eyes a moment then when she opened them again, she started to pace again. Her stomach rolled and she resisted the urge to slap a hand over her mouth, bend at the waist, and give a silent scream.

"You can stop pacing. Nanna just called to let me know dad is over there talking to Móraí."

Glenna turned toward the boy. "Does he always just take off like this?"

Finn grinned like it was all a joke. *Kids.*

"Nope. You've got my dad wound up like a top. He doesn't know if he's coming or going." He nodded as if he had found the secret to the Holy Grail. "This is going to be fun to watch."

A vise settled around her throat and gave a squeeze. The air left her lungs, her knees buckled and only through Finn's fast reflexes did her butt meet a chair instead of the hard wood of the kitchen floor. Her stomach rolled and pitched. She closed her eyes and willed it to stop.

Somehow she managed to drag some air into her lungs. "What exactly do you mean wound up?"

Finn pulled a chair over so they were knee to knee and bent over until they were almost nose to nose.

"You're not going to faint on me now are you Glenna?"

Glenna let her eyes focus on Finn and realized she loved him. Who knew you could fall in love with a child at first sight. He was a great kid. Horace picked that moment to leap with as much grace as a cannon ball into her lap causing Finn to slide his chair back in a rush.

"Horace!" Finn yelped and gently disengaged the dog from her lap.

Glenna watched all this in a numb haze. She loved the damn dog too. She wanted them for her family.

Patrick.

He was law enforcement. She swore that would never happen.

He had an ex, true she was out of the picture permanently. She'd sworn she would never do baggage.

What was she going to do?

"Damn. You're wound up like a top too." He chuckled.

Glenna focused in on the boy again.

"What do you mean wound up?" She repeated.

"Glenna do you love my dad?"

"No. Yes. I don't know. I can't love him. I've only known him for a heartbeat." She felt the first drip slide down her cheek. "I love you and Horace though. But... I just can't."

Finn regarded her for a moment. "You can't or won't? You said it was a *heartbeat*. The heart doesn't know time. It could take a second or years. He's a good man Glenna and he deserves a good woman and..." He slid his chair in again. "...you both deserve to be happy."

Glenna thought about it. She couldn't let anything happen until after they found the murderers. Alex deserved to have justice brought against her killers. Her parents needed closure.

"I know my dad well enough that I can tell you he won't let himself or you get emotional while we're on *Operation Find Lance*." He'd been tuned into her thoughts. He patted her knee. "You have time to mull this over, Glenna."

She felt herself melt a little more this amazing and wise boy. "How old are you, again?"

He drew away a bit. "Sixteen, why?"

"You're pretty wise for a sixteen year old. How did that happen?"

"I don't know, maybe it's because dad treats me like an equal, most of the time, instead of a kid. But I'm not wise, I just know my dad. He won't let anything get to him when he's on a case."

"Well, good to know."

Finn's cell rang, he pulled it out of his pocket, "Nanna, what's up?"

He listened for a moment and then said good bye. He drew in a breath, stood and walked to the window.

"We need to watch for dad, and make sure he wasn't followed."

Glenna stood from her chair so fast her head swam, her vision blurred. She stilled for a moment then went to stand next to her Finn.

"Why are we looking this way?" The view was over the back yard and not the street.

"He's coming the back way, he went through their back door so the black van doesn't realize he's gone."

"What black van? What's going on?"

"Nanna said that they noticed a van when Dad got there and it stayed so Dad went through the house and out the back."

"Finn, this isn't good. That means they found where I'm at, you're in danger. Maybe it would be better to have you stay with your grandparents."

"Not a chance."

Before she could argue, his phone rang again.

"What's wrong? Was that your dad on the phone?"

"It was nanna again. The van left."

"That's good?" Dread ran over her. "No, they're coming here."

"I think so."

"Did your nanna let him know?"

"I'm sure she did. As soon as I see the van though, I'll let him know."

Glenna ran to the front to watch for the van while Finn kept watch over the back yard. Five minutes went by, then ten and neither the van nor Patrick appeared.

"This is not good," Finn called from the other room.

She couldn't speak, she swallowed and finally managed a weak, "I know."

Chapter Twelve

Patrick bent, placed hands on knees and took a deep breath. Well, tried to anyway. He wasn't sure how he'd managed to get so out of shape. True, they'd pulled him off any interesting cases because he'd taken charge in the last investigation and hadn't followed protocol. The victim came out with hardly a scratch, he wasn't sure the woman would be alive if he followed protocol, so yeah he got his ass chewed and put on frou-frou duty for six months, he'd do it again. If it meant he saved a life.

He couldn't think about that now, he had to get home to Finn and Glenna. They were vulnerable. At least they knew what was going on. Dammit everyone was right, Finn had to be informed.

Never again would he bring a case home with him. Even if that case was a beautiful brunette with...

He stilled. There was someone coming. He was in the middle of a damn field, the grass was high, but not that high. He was bent, and but not out of sight, but if he straightened they see him like a Jack-in-box pop up.

This is what happens when you're distracted dumb ass.

Blowing the air out of his lungs he made the decision to stay as he was. Keeping his head as still as possible he tried to look around. With his line of vision there wasn't much he could see, but he could hear.

They were coming up behind him. He'd been wrong, he'd been the vulnerable one and he'd let the bastards get the upper hand. His muscles bunched without any instructions from his brain. He drew in a breath and straightened. And began to walk in the way he had been headed.

He would let them think he was clueless of their presence, when every instinct told him to run or confront. He continued one foot in front of the other.

Closer. They were gaining on him, he could tell there were at least two. The crunch of grass was too loud for just one.

"We're a coward then?" English accent.

Sucking air into his lungs he controlled his turn slow and measured. There were four.

Four.

Big was the first word that came to mind. Not that Patrick was small, since he was from good highland stock on his mum's side and Irish rugby stock on his da's, but his six foot three inches, and what he liked to think full of solid muscle, wouldn't be a match to four of the same.

He would not show fear.

"Coward?" he hoped he growled.

He stood his ground, let them take the lead. He refused to lose control and rush in halfcocked. Patrick took stock of each of them. One lanky, most likely a runner, fast. One solid muscle, body builder slow. One running a little chunky around the middle, probably the brains, again slow. The last one was a combination of lanky with muscle, he would be the toughest one.

Finn... He purposely cleared his mind. People were depending on him to stay calm, clear, and stay alive. Think.

He hadn't moved and neither had they. Staring contest then. It had probably only been a few seconds, but time seemed to be running in slow motion. His mind wasn't though, and they were at least giving him time to run through all the scenarios the four of them presented. He didn't have any form physical weapon, his brain would be the weapon at hand.

They were waiting for him to lead, which would be plain stupid under the current circumstances. He could see no visible guns, knives, or anything else on their person. That did *not* mean they didn't have something.

Chunky broke the standoff to take a step toward him. He felt his muscles tense in anticipation, but held his ground. Then Lanky moved to the left, lanky and muscle went to the right and muscle boy walked around him.

Surrounded.

He was dead.

*****

"Where's your dad?"

Finn didn't move from his vigil. "Where's the van." He slowly glanced over his shoulder. "This is bad."

"Let's go. Call your Nanna and tell her to call Beckworth and Jones."

Glenna grabbed the keys to the 4Runner raced through the door knowing that Finn was on her heels. She pulled the door open and hesitated, did she even remember how to drive a standard?

Finn stared at her from the open door on the other side. "Do you need me to drive?"

"Do you have a license?"

"Learners permit, I know how to drive a damn stick, do you?"

She tossed him the keys and raced around the back as he went around the front. As soon as she climbed in, the engine roared and she'd barely had time to pull her door closed before he took off.

"Slow down, I can't look for Patrick."

"I know where to look."

He didn't say more, just concentrated on taking the corners without killing either of them, but faster than the speed limit. She trusted him and didn't distract him with words.

Though she held on for dear life.

In the distance she could see a car or was that the van parked on the side of the road?

"Hurry, there's the van."

"Four. Where's Dad?" Finn muttered almost too low for her to hear, worry weaving through each word.

Finn was keeping his gaze on the road, but she saw him glance to the left of the van and she saw four guys running toward the vehicle. By the time they were almost even with them, the black van gunned and pealed past them like a bat out of hell.

"Where's Dad?" Finn repeated.

He pulled into the spot the other vehicle had just vacated and jumped out. In the distance Glenna could hear sirens. She wasn't about to wait, and neither was Finn. He'd hopped the fence and was already racing across the field calling his dad's name. She swallowed and climbed the fence as fast as she dared, then she was racing after the boy. No way could she catch him. He stopped and let out a yell, she couldn't understand what he said but he was waving at her frantically.

As she drew close she realized he wanted her to call for an ambulance. Her heart stopped.

"Glenna call 911." He bent down toward his dad.

She was too far to see how badly Patrick was hurt. She couldn't move. What had he asked her to do?

"Glenna. What the fuck is wrong."

The F-bomb coming from Finn jolted her out of her whatever it was and she punched in the number while racing the rest of the way.

Blood. Her first thought.

The sirens had stopped but she could hear shouts of the officers as they drew closer. And then the ambulance arrived. Everything was a blur she wasn't sure how long they'd been with him waiting. A minute? An hour? A day?

She dropped to her knees and reached for him intending to do, what she didn't know, Finn grabbed her arm.

"Don't move him."

Right. She let her hand drop and stared helplessly at Patrick's battered body. She couldn't tell if he was breathing. He was so still. It took her a moment to realize the pounding in her chest was her heart, like it was going to jump out. She drew in a deep breath and slowly let it out. And repeated.

She glanced over her shoulder, why was it taking so long for the medics to get there? As the thought crossed her mind a kind gentleman nudged her aside but didn't make her completely leave Patrick. There were three medics, they quickly assessed the damage and then next thing she knew they were moving him to a stretcher.

She walked with them through the fields, it was slow progress, the waving green may look pretty but it was a bitch to push something with wheels through it. She didn't hear one complaint from the medics, no it was all her mumbled frustration.

There was a man on either side of the stretcher, about to lift him in, Patrick grabbed her hand, or rather placed his hand on top of hers. Startled she looked at him, his lips moved as if he said something.

"What?"

Again he mumbled something. She stopped the men from putting him in, they allowed her to move closer to his head so she could lean over.

"What?" she repeated.

"You should see the other guys."

She wasn't positive she had heard right, the words were slurred and so soft she'd barely heard it.

The men lifted him into the back of the ambulance. She wanted to go with Patrick, but they told her she needed to meet them at the hospital. She ushered Finn back to the car and let him drive again. She knew it wasn't a good idea, but she actually wanted to arrive before the next century and she had a feeling she'd stall the car at every light.

Finn followed as best he could without breaking the speed limit. Neither of them wanted to take the time to be pulled over. Glenna was lost in her thoughts, worry nibbled and the usual roll and pitch rocked her stomach. She started when Finn broke the silence in the car.

"What did my dad say?"

"I think, but I'm not a hundred percent, he said 'you should see the other guys.'"

Finn barked out a laugh. "He's going to be okay."

****

Frustrating. Glenna couldn't get her heart under control. The pounding matched the drums in her head. Her stomach rolled, she could be in the middle of the ocean during the storm of the century the way it pitched. She did what she always did when worried. Paced the waiting room, around the perimeter like a track, then across and back again.

"Hey, sit down you're driving me freakin' nuts." Finn followed his words with a smile. "I know you're worried but he's going to be fine. He's a tough old bird."

Glenna stopped and stared. "Old?"

"Yeah. He didn't get to be his age in his profession by being a ninny. Sit. They'll let us go in soon."

"How is he?" A tall man strode in followed by a woman with the ginger hair she had passed on to her son, worrying the strap on her purse.

"Nanna, Móraí!" Finn jumped up and raced into their open arms for a group hug.

He'd been more worried than he'd let on. She swallowed the lump blocking her airway. She needed a hug. She needed to know he was going to be okay. Not long ago Patrick was safe and now because of her, he was in the hospital. Would they come after Finn next?

She needed to talk to Tyler. She stood intending to go somewhere private and do just that, but as she passed the group hug, Finn reach for her hand and pulled her in. Warmth encircled her and to her horror the water works started. Patrick's mother, whom she vaguely remembered seeing browsing her store a few time before but had never actually met before this moment and here she was blubbering all over the woman's blouse, steered Glenna to a chair and settled her in.

A moment later his father handed her a bottle of water with a gentle 'drink'. She sniffed, and now that the worst storm was over she gratefully took a sip and then took a deep breath.

"I'm so sorry." She sniffed again. "It's my fault Patrick's here."

Then horror of horrors, she started to boob again. She couldn't seem to stop. It was more than her guilt. She was petrified for the worst. Patrick wouldn't make it. No one had told them what his injuries were. She couldn't get the picture of his battered face and body, blood everywhere, out of her mind.

"Are you the McGinnis family?"

Glenna glanced up at the woman who'd entered the waiting room. She held a tablet and seemed to be studying it, and then she smiled at Patrick's parents.

"He's got several cracked ribs and several contusions. Luckily there were no broken bones well except his nose, which is a wonder. He's going to be fine." She paused, and Glenna thought she was finished. "We're keeping him overnight to watch him. We want to make sure there is no internal bleeding. He does have a slight concussion. He took a beating, but by the abrasions on his knuckles, he gave as good as he got."

"There were four." Glenna's voice sounded weak even to herself.

The doctor's brow rose almost to her hairline. "Four?"

Finn grinned. "Yeah, that's my dad. Nothing can stop him."

Apparently, Finn's worry was over because the doctor said Patrick would be fine. But Glenna knew that things could happen in a flash. She still needed to talk to Tyler. Patrick would want to stay on the case and she couldn't let that happen. Not when he'd been beaten within an inch of his life, and no way would she let anything happen to Finn.

The only way she could protect them would be to get out of their lives.

"Can we see our son?" Patrick's mother asked.

"For a few minutes and only two at a time."

So lost in her thoughts, Glenna started when Patrick's father reached a hand toward her. "I'm

Kendal McGinnis and this is my wife Caroline. You must be Glenna Beckett."

She took his hand, his firm and warm. Then she stood and held hers out to Patrick's mother. But the woman pulled her into a hug. Of course, that set off her emotions again. Damn, sometimes it was a pain in the ass to be such a girl. But she couldn't help it.

"I'm so sorry Mrs. McGinnis."

"Dear, it's going to fine. He's tough, always has been. And it's Caroline."

"He didn't sign up for this when my brother called him for a favor."

Patrick's father frowned at her. Glenna was sure he was going to agree with her, but he surprised her. "I believe when he *signed* up for the Federal Bureau of Investigations as a special agent, he knew exactly what he was doing. He was protecting you and Finn."

"Mr. McGinnis..."

"Kendal."

"Kendal, he wasn't assigned to the case until *after* Tyler called him and asked him to babysit me."

"I highly doubt your brother asked that of him. Patrick had been climbing the walls on his light duty, you offered him a challenge."

"But he's in the hospital."

"And your point?" Kendal raised a brow.

"He's hurt, he could have been killed." They were his parents, didn't they understand she'd put him right in the middle of an international crime ring?

"Glenna, give it up. Nanna and Móraí know how much my dad loves being an agent. He's been a bear to live with since his boss put him on pansy duty as he called it."

"What are you talking about? Pansy duty?"

Finn grinned. "Well he was on a case and if he'd followed protocol there was a good chance..."

His grandfather snorted. "More than a good chance, that woman wouldn't have survived if it hadn't been for your dad."

"...if dad hadn't gone rogue and rescued her and saved the day."

Glenna was beginning to understand. Tyler had gone rogue a few times. He called it Froufrou duty though. "And I've got him back on a case with meat, is what you're saying."

Three chorused 'yeses' was her answer. She smiled for the first time in hours.

"Okay, you guys win. I would like to go in and see him after all of you have."

"I'm sure he'd rather see you than my ugly mug."

"Speak for yourself Kendal," Caroline said. "The doctor said two could go in, why don't you and I go first. Once I know my boy's okay you can have some time before Finn and his Móraí visit."

Glenna took the proffered hand and together they went to the room Patrick had been moved to for the night.

Caroline walked in, as if she was in charge, up to the side of her son. He'd been lying there dozing and she smacked him on the shoulder. Glenna cringed at the pained expression as Patrick's eyes flew open.

"Fu..." his mouth snapped shut when he saw who it was. "Mum, what was that for?"

"For worrying us. You said you'd be fine on the back way."

"Well, hell. I thought I would be. And I didn't know there were four of them." He gave a lopsided grin that looked pretty painful from where Glenna stood. "I did pretty damn good against four. I'm alive to talk about it. Doesn't that count?"

Caroline McGinnis who'd been so stoic through the entire wait and speaking with the doctor bent over and kissed her son on the head and then burst into tears.

"What would I do if you hadn't have been able to handle *four*?"

Glenna slipped out the door to give mother and son some time. As she was shutting the door behind her, a tall redhead nearly bowled her over going to the room, and her words could be heard throughout Napa Valley, Glenna was sure.

"What the fuck were you thinking, Paddy?"

Glenna grinned at the nurse who had been about to enter if she hadn't been pushed out of the way by Patrick sister, Margaret Kathleen.

Family came first. She'd take the time to go check in with Tyler.

Chapter Thirteen

Glenna found a quiet spot in front of the hospital. She didn't want anyone sneaking up on her. She may feel better knowing Patrick's family didn't hold her responsible, but in her mind, that didn't let her off the hook.

She calculated the time, it was going on midnight in Brooklyn. She figured that was better than two or three in the morning. Could it wait until morning? Yes, but she needed to talk to her brother.

Family.

After several rings, a sleepy Keira answered the phone. She was instantly worried when Glenna asked for Tyler. She reassured her sister-in-law that all was well, *now*. A moment later Tyler came on the phone.

"Glenna what's wrong?"

"Nothing." She paused, she wasn't sure what to say now she had him on the phone.

"Glenna?"

"I don't know Tyler. I'm worried. Can you ask for someone else to take on the case?"

"What? I know Patrick, he's good. Where is this coming from?"

Glenna took a deep breath and filled her brother in on what had been going on, some of which he knew from Reagan.

"I can't have him hurt."

"Why Glenna? This is his case, he needs to finish it. Especially now."

"What do you mean *especially now*?"

"It will look bad to his fellow agents if he turns tail because four guys got the best of him..."

"*Four* is the key word. He could have been killed."

"Yes, he could have. Have you ever heard the expression that if you fall off a horse the best thing to do is to climb right back on?"

Glenna closed her eyes and counted to ten. Her brother was taking this too lightly. "Yes, dammit I know that cliché. But you're missing the point. Patrick is a single dad he has responsibilities. He needs to stay safe."

"He's an agent, it's his career. What kind of dad would he be if the example he gave his son was one of taking the safe road."

There was a pause and she could hear Keira in the background but couldn't make out the words.

"Glenna, I know you and Tyler are close, but he's missing the point." Her sister-in-law repeated her earlier words to her brother. "He's looking at this from Patrick's point of view, and I get it. I get it because I feel about my career as strongly as Tyler. I may not have planned to be an agent. But the rewards of helping people and the thrill of a catching the bad guys, getting them off the streets and making *those* streets safe for kids and my Lucy to walk on makes the danger worth it."

"I..."

"Let me finish, I've been where you are. When Tyler was shot I thought half my soul was taken from me. I couldn't breathe, I didn't know if I could move on. There was one thing I *knew*. I was going to get the bastards who hurt my baby. Partners, spouses, friends, family all react differently to the dangers of the career. Your mom cooks and *mothers*, your dad gets all gruff and protective. I get fierce."

There was a pause, and Glenna let the words sink in. Tyler had known she needed a woman's prospective. Maybe she should have called Reagan, but she'd have reacted like Tyler. And she highly doubted her new brother in law Paco would have been able to understand any better. But Keira did, and better, she belonged to the club of agents. She knew it from both sides.

"If you're going to love Patrick, Glenna, you're going to have to find a way to cope."

"Whoa, right there. What do you mean *love*? No one said anything about the L word. I care about him, he's a good man, a good dad, and he's been wonderful taking care of the break in, the death of my assistant who was also my friend. But *love*? No, I'm worried that he's going to get hurt again on my behalf. I need you guys to get someone else to take over. Patrick needs to recover. Finn needs his dad and the McGinnis' need their son. How could I have brought these terrible criminals to their door? What kind of a person would I be if I pretended everything was fine?

"Let him get out of the hospital and step in harm's way again."

Glenna waited for the response. She swiped a hand across her eyes to get whatever was blurring her vision away only to find she'd been crying. She swallowed and her stomach tightened. No, she was *not in love with Patrick*. She barely knew the man. She couldn't let herself. What would she do if she had to worry about his safety every day? Every single minute of that day? No.

"Glenna?"

She pulled in a breath. "Yes?"

"You care. Don't argue, you can call it what you like, but you care. You're scared. Again, this is me on the other side I get it. Don't you think I worry about Tyler? We're not always together on a case. Gabe is his partner and I have Monica as my partner. We worry every day about Lucy losing one of her parents. But have you ever thought what this world would be without the policemen? The firefighters? All the people who defend our country? All the people who put their life on the line *every day*.

"Glenna, do you worry about your family and friends every day?"

"No. Effie is a Barista and shop owner, she doesn't put herself in the line of fire every day. She's a normal person."

"Well, I wouldn't exactly call Effie normal," she said a bit on the dry toast side. "Have you thought about the desperate drug addict who sees her shop as a means to get his next fix? The one who is going to walk in and demand money and doesn't care who he hurts?"

Glenna closed her eyes, Keira had painted a picture she'd never thought of, nor did she want to, again her stomach rumbled and jumped.

"If you didn't have the Patrick's of the world that would happen more than it already does. We need him. Care for him, but let him do what he loves. He is an agent because he feels as I do. Glenna you'll need to come to terms with this."

She'd known that they wouldn't do anything to get Patrick off the case. However, as usual Tyler had known what she needed when she called. Even though it wasn't what she wanted to hear, it was what she needed to hear.

"Thank you, sis. I don't know how you do it." Glenna brushed at her face again. "I'm not sure I can."

"Glenna, take care of you and remember Patrick is trained and knows what he's doing. He'll find the ring of criminals and take them off the streets. And we'll be safer for it." There was a click. "We're on speaker."

Tyler's voice rang out next. "Sister of mine, I love you and you'll be fine. As will Patrick. Trust him. Good night."

Keira was next. "Take care of him. Good night, Glenna, and Glenna? I love you too and so does Lucy. Remember we're *all* always here for you."

And the connection broke.

Glenna sat on the bench cradling the phone in her lap. She watched the people coming and going, all with dramas of their own. It was time for her to visit Patrick and make sure he was okay. The call had accomplished one thing, she wouldn't ask Patrick to step away. She understood he needed to finish what he'd started. He needed that. She'd follow through with the plan, but she'd hold fast against her feelings for him.

She could *not* do this every day. As she stood, she felt her heart beat faster and knew what a battle it was going to be to shield it from Patrick.

He was fast becoming embedded in her heart.

When she walked into the hospital quiet surrounded her. She glanced at the clock in the waiting room and realized it was almost ten, she'd kept her brother and sister in law on the phone longer than she'd meant to.

Patrick's sister was gone when she reached his room, only Finn was in with him, she didn't think his parents were gone. They must have gone for coffee or something. She stood in the door and watched father and son for a moment.

As if he knew she was there, Patrick's eyes lifted to hers and locked. A bolt raced over her and she knew she was in trouble. She sucked in her breath and did her best to strengthen the shield to stop the crumbling of the wall around her heart.

Finn stopped talking as he looked over his shoulder, he grinned when he saw her. She saw this through her peripheral vision, as she hadn't taken her eyes off his father. Somewhere in her heart she was afraid if she did, he wouldn't be okay that it was all an illusion.

"Glenna! Dad's going to be okay." He turned his attention to Patrick again. "I told you he was a tough old bird."

The emotion in the boys' voice, broke her heart. If it weren't for her, they'd probably be getting ready for bed, or already turned in for the night. Instead they were in the hospital.

Patrick had finally broken the electrical current between them and turned to Finn. "What do you mean *old?* I am not old, I have a long way to go before *old.*"

"You're getting up there old man." Finn slid from the side of the bed, placed a hand on his dad's shoulder, and then leaned down and kissed him on the forehead. "You're going to be around until I'm an old man with you."

Glenna swallowed down the love that wanted to overflow of these two who'd come to mean so much to her in such a short time.

"I'm going to see if I can find the older folks, they may be lost wandering aimlessly."

He chuckled at his own joke. Two steps and he was by Glenna's side, he grabbed her and swung her around. When he sat her down, he held her a moment to steady her. He leaned down and looked in straight in the eye.

"Dad's going to be fine. He wouldn't be the man he is if he didn't protect those he loved, and those who need protecting." Then he straightened and looked at his dad and back to her. "He needs you."

Glenna watched him leave the room wondering how he'd known her feelings.

"He's a smart kid."

Patrick drew her attention. She shut the door then went to his bed side. He patted the place where his son had just vacated. She hesitated for a second too long. He gently reached for her hand and gave her a tug until she settled next to him.

"What are you thinking Glenna?"

She blew the air out of her lungs, closed her eyes for a moment. She couldn't think with him watching her. How to put into words her feelings? They were so new to her, she'd *never* felt anything like what was in her heart before. It seemed like years ago that she'd been abandoned at the altar. If nothing else told her she hadn't been in love with Lance, the turmoil in her heart warring with the rolling of her stomach did.

"Glenna? Talk to me."

He almost died for her trying to get home to her and Finn before the art thieves who were far more dangerous than she'd first thought. Until Patrick was hurt she'd thought Alex had been a onetime accident, a knee jerk reaction when she'd interrupted the burglars search. He deserved to know the truth of her thoughts.

"You could have died. I couldn't live with that, I brought these people to your home."

Patrick's chuckle cut itself short ending in a grown. "Oh, don't make me laugh it hurts."

"This is not funny Patrick. You could have died. Then what would I..." she placed a hand on his arm. "...what would Finn do without his father?"

"You were going to say what would *you* do, be honest Glenna. You are not responsible for me being in the hospital. I've been here before and I'll most likely be here again. Though I'll do everything to avoid it. It's just not fun. And you know what? They poke at you... A lot!"

"This is not a joking matter."

He tried to scoot up, when he failed, Glenna slid off the bed and fiddled with the controls. "Better?"

"Yes. I need to be as close to looking you straight in the eye when I say this."

She wasn't sure she was ready for whatever it was. She started to turn. But again he grabbed her hand and tugged until she perched on the side of the bed. Once she'd settled he touched her face, then he placed his other hand on her cheek so that her face was cradled. Warmth spread through her. He leaned in, slowly more from his injuries than prolonging the moment and kissed her at first tenderly, then deepened until he stole her breath.

He didn't let her go, with his words whispering against her lips he said, "I'm falling hard for you Glenna."

She pulled away and shot to her feet nearly knocking over his water in the process.

"You can't."

"Oh but I can, and I am. Hard."

Her entire body tightened, as if turning to stone. Yet her chest burned. She wasn't falling for him. She'd already leaped over the cliff and landed hard. As much as she told herself she was protecting her heart, she'd done a damn poor job of it.

"Glenna. Come back and sit. We'll talk about this rationally."

Without turning toward him. "The heart is never rational Patrick. I don't know that I can do this. Every time you walk out the door I'll wonder if you'll return."

"Glenna I'm not going to talk to your back. Please come here."

She could hear the rustle of bed sheets and turned in time to see him struggling with tubes and other medical equipment to come to her.

"Stop that."

She went to him and pushed him back and then sat in the chair. No way could she touch him at that moment and be *rational*.

"You're going to sit there?"

"I am."

"Okay. It's better than you walking out the door. We have to talk Glenna. We haven't known each other very long. Before you give me your thoughts, can I tell you mine?"

Could she hear him out without her resolve crumbling along with the barrier around her heart? She gazed at him a moment, his features battered and bruised and she wanted to cry. She blew the breath out of her lungs, again. It seemed like she was always taking deep breaths or releasing it in order to calm and focus. After a moment, she decided this matter of the heart wasn't going to go away if she didn't listen.

"Okay."

"And when I'm finished you'll tell me what you're thinking?"

Would she? Could she? She wasn't sure how to put into words the emotions swirling and bumping around her body until every nerve ending sparked.

"I'll try."

"I'll take that."

He struggled to get into a better position to look at her straight. He was having such a difficult time, she finally stood so she could slide on to the side of the bed again. Just being in the room with him made her aware of his rugged handsomeness, though a bit battered at the moment.

"Better?"

"Much, now I can do this." She'd expected him to take her hand, but he leaned for a brush of lips. "Now let me tell you what I'm feeling."

"I'm falling hard for you Glenna." He repeated as he took her hand. "Heaven knows I didn't want this, not while I'm trying to focus on doing a job."

She tried to pull her hand away. "This is my fault..."

"Shush, it isn't your fault. I was focused today. I don't know how they knew I left the back way. One of them must have been watching.

"The point is, I'm here now talking to you because of my training. I know every day what I may face. Most days are danger free, but there are times when I'll be facing obstacles and dangerous situations, it's what I do. I'm trained for it. Art is your career, you know it. This is a career for me. I know you're scared. I'm scared of leaving Finn an orphan. *Everyday*."

He leaned his head back a moment. She wasn't sure if he was thinking, or in pain, or just needed to rest. A few seconds later she determined it was a mixture of all three.

"I thought I'd never fall in love. And before you say anything, I believe I've told you this before, I did not love Finn's mother. She was my first serious relationship, as serious as a young college boy ever lets it get. I was full of raging hormones and though I thought we were careful, I have Finn to prove I wasn't. And I *thank* God for him every day.

"If she'd walked away and *took* him, I'd have moved heaven and earth to find him and have a life with him. Even though the last thing I wanted by that time was to spend time or have a life with her. I'm so glad she gave me the gift of my son. I will always be grateful."

"He's a wonderful young man, you should be proud."

"I am." He grinned, then winced. "But this is my turn, remember? Anyway, I know that my having an ex-wife is one of the things that you're not comfortable with, most people aren't comfortable with an ex. luckily mine is a distant bad memory..."

When she opened her mouth to agree, he held up a hand.

"Not yet. The next thing holding you back is my career, and we've covered that. It's not going away. I know it's asking a lot but I want you to think of a few things. Do you worry about your parents?"

He nodded to let her know she could actually speak and she almost laughed. But this was serious. She had an idea this was going to go the same route as the conversation with Keira she'd had earlier.

"Well they're getting a little older, I'm worried something might happen and I'm too far away."

"Do you worry about your friends?"

She'd been right. "If they're sick or if they have an accident, yes I do. However, my friends are all healthy so I don't worry that something will happen to them every day."

"Good choice of word. Accident. Something can happened to a person every day. An accident. A sudden heart attack. Or in Effie's case a break-in because someone wants her coffee recipes."

This elicited a short chuckle from Glenna. He was making light, but she knew he took every word serious as did she.

"True, my duties place me in danger more often than most. I do a good thing. I help take the bad guys off the street so my son can be safe at school, the store, or when he's out with his friends."

His words were almost an echo of her sister-in-law's. Did they teach them this at Quantico?

"I can't do anything about the fact I have an ex-wife and I *can't* do anything about being a federal agent it's who I am. But I can promise to take care of myself to the best of my ability. I plan to live a very long life. And if Finn thinks I'm a tough old bird now, I'm just going to get tougher and older."

What could she say? She realized as he spoke, the words that repeated her thoughts.

"I have an idea. We've already come up with the idea of being a couple to catch the bastards who broke into your shop."

She pursed her lips as she interrupted his *idea*. "And knocked you senseless. And they must know you're working the case."

"They thought they did. But I told them I was *hanging* around you because I was in love with you. When they didn't buy that I told them I'd met you through Tyler, your brother, who I'd met at Quantico for training. And that made them pause. They'll check it out. I'm sure even if they have a shadow of doubt, I've laid the ground work and we need to keep with the plan."

"Maybe we better let Tyler know, so he's not caught off guard."

"They're not going call him, they'll use their resources and check the dates, etc. Let's not get sidetracked. Glenna you care about me.

"Have you called your brother today?" He asked with far more insight than she wanted him to have.

"Yes, I did."

"Was that just to tell him about the four guys who thought they could best me?"

"Yes."

He waited. He gave her hand a little squeeze when she didn't say anything. Finally on a sigh she told him the reason she'd called.

"It's my fault you're in the hospital I asked Tyler to call your superiors to take you off the case."

He struggled to sit up straighter. "What?"

"Don't worry, Tyler explained that you wouldn't want him to do that, nor would he do that to *you*. He said you were the best agent and I had to have faith in you."

"Good, because there is no way I'm going to quit now. We're going to get these guys and they are going to pay for what they did to Alex and to you."

"Patrick, I know you will. That wasn't the reason."

He stilled. "What was the reason?"

She swallowed it seemed it was her turn. "I told him that I couldn't stand that you were battered and bruised because of me. He told me in no uncertain terms that you needed to finish the job and to get over myself, it wasn't my fault. If you weren't working on this case it would be another one."

"He's right. Is that the only reason? Because I'm hurt, or as you said battered and bruised. It's not your fault, so why do you want me off the case?"

Hadn't she just explained? He waited a questioning expression graced his face along with the colorful bruising. *Come on Glenna, for once in your life be truthful to a man, don't hide because you've been hurt by someone you trusted.*

Her pep talk should have calmed her, but it just made her more anxious. She'd trusted Danny Collins, he'd hurt her physically but the emotional scars ran far deeper. Then there was Lance, she'd basically hurt herself on that one, and mostly her pride had taken a beating. *Her fault*, she'd held herself away from him emotionally so he *couldn't* hurt her. Not something to base a marriage on.

Patrick was different than either of those men. He was a kind, protective, and a genuinely good man. He didn't want to be hurt either so why was this so hard?

"Have you gone into a coma or something?"

Though his words were joking, she could hear a thread of serious in them. She took a deep breath and decided to go with the entire truth, not just part to protect her now completely vulnerable heart. Some things were worth the risk.

"No-holds-barred?"

He titled his head, winced, and seemed to consider her words. Then when she was about to speak because he didn't seem inclined, he answered.

"Yes, even if it's going to give me more bruises. I'd rather hear now than fall harder and then find out."

"I have tried since the moment I met you to shield my heart. After all, you have my number one and two reasons *not* to get involved with a man. One, you're law enforcement. The Beckett's are full of those, why do we need another one?"

His chuckle filled the room, but even that sounded a little nervous and forced. But he kept quiet waiting for her to continue.

"Two, you have baggage of the female kind. Finn's mom, and *no* Finn is not part of that package. Joyce is out of the picture but she hurt you. She was your first love." She held up a hand when he started to speak. "Oh, I know you said you weren't in love with her. It still did a number on your head. Proof of that is the fact you have had no serious relationships since. Am I right?"

He looked over her shoulder as if he couldn't look her in the eye, which told her more than anything that she'd hit the nail on the head. She raised a brow and waited for his answer.

"No." He gave her hand, he was still holding, a squeeze to prevent her from commenting. "Only because I have Finn to consider. He didn't have a mom, and I didn't want him to get attached to someone and have it not work out."

"And yet here I am. Why did you bring me into your home then? I know you were unwillingly attracted to me from the beginning, correct?"

For that she got a grudging, mumbled, "Yeah".

She chuckled this time. "We're a pair aren't we?"

This time he grinned. "Oh don't make me laugh it hurts. Now quit stalling and tell me *why* you wanted me off the case."

"Fine."

Where to start? He knew about the two men who'd hurt her, but not really the reasons she was so relationship shy. She'd never told anyone what really happened with Danny, other than Effie. Even Effie didn't know all of it, she'd guessed most and had the insight not to ask questions, just given her support. Glenna had a feeling she could confide in Patrick, though he may take it upon himself to make the man pay. It was so long ago, she really didn't think anything would happen to Danny.

"I did my best, really I did, to keep you out of my heart. I've lectured myself more times than I can count since I met you, that you're not relationship material. That I've only known you for a nanosecond so how can I judge. The big problem is; that you *are*. I know it here." She patted her stomach with her free hand. "You're a wonderful father, a caring person, you love your parents. You have family guy written all over you. You remind me of Tyler, Gabe, and David. And once I get to know my other brother-in-law Paco, I'm sure you'll remind me of him also. *All* law enforcement and *all* good family people. And David had baggage of the number two kind and also has a daughter from a woman who left his heart damaged. So here I am in your hospital room trying my hardest not to care because I literally don't know if I can wonder every day if you'll come home."

"And yet every day I could go to a boring every day office job and not return."

"Yeah, I know I've heard the arguments from you ten minutes ago and ever since Tyler joined the feds. You could be hit by a car, be in a car accident, have a sudden heart attack. But you wouldn't be putting yourself in added danger on purpose every day either.

"I have dealt with that since Tyler became an agent, one of the reasons I moved to California. I miss my family, but I fell in love with the Napa valley. I have promised myself to visit more, and dammit they better come and visit me more also."

His hand left her hand and before she missed it's warmth he gently wrapped his fingers behind her neck and pulled her in and softly kissed her. Before it got out of control, he released her and lifted brow as if telling her to continue.

She had to settle her stomach's gymnastics. The man could pack a punch to the gut. That moment was when she realized even though, as she'd thought earlier, they hadn't known each other for longer than a split second, *he* was the one.

A lightning bolt struck her in the chest.

Her ma had told her that it had happened like that with her. Her mom had met her dad and zing, in love at first sight.

Glenna had never believed her until now. Was she still nervous? Yes. Hell yes. She needed to be cautious.

"To continue. Yes, those are two issues that I've had to overcome. And I believe I have. I love Finn and..." She grinned. "And Horace, mostly because he didn't kill my Agnes. I think you're working around my heart and together we can work through your ex issues. I alone have to deal with my worry, and I don't think it'll ever be easy, but I promise to work on it."

"So no-hold-barred? I am falling hard for you too. I have a suggestion or as I mentioned before, a plan."

"I'm listening." Though she still needed to be honest with him. Completely. About Danny and Lance before they could go on, but she'd hear him out first.

"As I said we're a couple or so we want everyone to believe."

"Whoa, I know you told the four about meeting me through Tyler, but I didn't think they really believed."

"Yeah, at first they didn't believe me. I insisted that, yes, I was an agent and knew you'd been robbed but the only reason I was around was the fact you are my fiancée."

"And that was all it took even after you'd told them about Tyler, they left you battered after that?"

"Well, not exactly. They still were a bit suspicious so that's when I described in detail about Quantico and how I'd known you since then and we're newly engaged. I'm sure they're still going to check it out."

"They were asking you between punches or something?"

Horrified didn't begin to describe what was going on in her rumbling stomach, her nerves were tinging at the thought of him going through what he had. She needed a Tums...

"No, one of them came up behind me and locked my arms so they could quiz me. And yes, there were a few punches here and there along the questioning."

She winced but didn't say anything. If she opened her mouth she was afraid she'd throw up all over his clean hospital sheets.

"I know they'll figure out a way to check the dates we were there and I believe when Tyler went to Quantico you were still in Brooklyn."

"Yes, but I left shortly after."

"I know, back to my idea, plan, and suggestion whatever... We're already going to be putting on a show but I think we should make it real."

"What?"

"Glenna, I want you in my life. I need to stay focused right now, but part of that is staying close to you. This will be a trial engagement. The bad guys have to believe it, so if we tell everyone, Effie, my parents, your parents that we're in love the easier it will be for them to believe. When this is over we'll talk again. If at that time you've still got doubts we'll face them together. But I'm not letting you walk away until I know that we've talked everything through and there is no chance for us. But I believe that we belong together and we'll find a way. Because I want a chance to have you at my side."

She ignored the last part, she wasn't ready to think of that yet. "My parents are going to know because of Tyler."

"We'll make them believe. We need to keep up the fiancée bit. It's not very romantic, but here goes, Glenna will you be my fiancée? We'll tell my parents, your parents, and Effie and make it official.

"Let's take it one day at a time until we catch the bad guys. When this is all over I'll go the romantic route if need be, but I hope by then we're ready to call this what it is. Two people falling in love and wanting to spend their life together, have a family."

"Finn would make an awesome big brother."

"Yes, he would. What do you say?"

Chapter Fourteen

"I think there are a few more things I need to tell you before you ask that question," Glenna said.

Patrick struggled to sit up straighter, not an easy task when every fucking muscle in his body screamed in outrage at the prospect of moving. What hadn't she told him? He had been feeling pretty positive when she'd admitted she'd got past the first two hurdles.

"I need to be honest about Danny Collins and Lance Gordon."

"Collins is the bastard who broke in, right? I knew there was more than you were telling me, what happened?"

Finn poked his head in the hospital room. "Hey dad, I need to go home because I have football practice before school."

They both jumped at the interruption. Patrick held in a groan only by sheer will.

"I'm sorry Finn, I didn't realize it was so late."

Glenna smiled at his son, and his world got a little better. She did love Finn. Patrick would do everything in his power not to let Finn get hurt regardless of what happened between them. He knew that Glenna would do the same. This time it was worth the risk.

Glenna stood, and immediately he missed her. It had seemed so comfortable having her perched on the side of his bed.

"Patrick, I'll come back after I take Finn home, I need to check on Agnes anyway. We left in such a hurry."

"Now we know our boy is going to be fine we're going to head home also. We'll take Finn with us so you can stay, Ms. Beckett," his father said.

They'd walked in with Finn. The room seemed smaller with his family gathered around him. In that moment, he knew things would work out with Glenna.

He was well on his way to being in love her and his family would love her too.

"It's Glenna, please."

His mother wrapped an arm around Glenna. "Glenna, it is then. Take care of our boy, we'll be back first thing in the morning."

They were gone before he could even say good-bye. When Glenna turned toward him again, he patted the bed. He wanted her back where she belonged.

"You're not going to let me off the hook and discuss this another time, are you?"

He scooted over as best he could without his body screaming at him and shook his head.

She sucked in a breath as if what she was about to tell him was not a pleasant subject. He'd already gathered that.

"You know the first part of the story. He'd wanted a relationship, felt he deserved it after he'd found such a sweet deal for me. I was so naïve. I truly thought we were friends."

He saw pain enter her eyes and almost told her she didn't have to tell him. He had a feeling she needed to tell him for her own healing. She closed her eyes for a moment, shielding whatever she was feeling from him. He reached for her hand and held on hoping to give her strength.

"That night, I was so immersed in my accounting that the door was opened and he was walking toward me before I even noticed. Then it was too late to react. I scooted my chair back intending to stand, but that only gave him the advantage of a clear avenue of attack."

Could she really go through this again? Would he make her go to the police? She wasn't sure she could tell it to them. She wanted to be honest, for the first time. Let the emotion and words come out so she could let go of the shame and the hurt. Though Effie had guessed she didn't know the true depth of her shame.

She'd told no one the full details of that night.

"Glenna. I imagine you are about to tell me that the bastard got away with far more than what you told the police. If you're worried that I will want you to press charges after all this time. Don't. It's been over ten years, I believe in Karma. If he hasn't gotten what he deserves and been punished for his deeds, I believe sooner or later they will come back and bite him in the ass. Just get it out and then it will be time to let go and heal."

He'd read her mind. The relief was almost overwhelming. He would listen and she could move on. But would he want to move on with her? Because no matter how hard she tried not to, she was ashamed and the guilt ate at her insides. Maybe it *had* been her fault and she'd deserved what he'd done to her for leading him on.

"Come here."

He pulled her hand. She could tell it caused him pain to move over a little more so she could lay beside him. It made it easier to snuggle in and reveal the terrible events of that night without looking him in the eye while revealing her dark secret. She took in a fortifying breath.

"He grabbed me by the shoulders and pulled me from the chair. I fought, oh how I fought, but he was so much bigger than I." The same fear gripped her in the gut. "He screamed at me 'you fucking tease, I'm going to take what you promised.' Those words echo through my mind at the most odd moments of the day. Anyway, then he raised a fist and belted me in the nose."

Pain shot through her head as if it had just happened. "Everything went dark for a moment. The pain, I can't even explain the pain. I wasn't left alone to gather my wits. With his other fist he socked me in the stomach and I couldn't breathe. Stars exploded behind my eyes and I couldn't see the next punch coming, but it knocked me on my ass."

She had to stop a moment, gathered her wits because she was back in that night. She swallowed to clear the block stopping her words, clogging them at the base of her throat. Trying to get out, but a ball of emotion wouldn't let them pass. Patrick waited, gathered her in to share his warmth. After a moment a small opening let the words flow.

"He stood over me, glaring at me, while I lay on the floor trying to think. What had I done? What did he mean by being a tease? I honestly didn't understand how this man could be my friend and yet do the things he'd just said and done. Yes he'd said a lot more. How I'd led him on, I'd let him think we were a couple. Then once I'd gotten what I'd wanted; *I* wanted to be *'fucking friends'*. Well he was going to have me no matter what, he said."

She closed her eyes to picture it. One last time, and then she'd let it leave her mind with the words she was about to say. And if Patrick didn't understand, then he was not the man she thought he was. And once again she'd picked the wrong person.

A little niggle of hope told her that wouldn't be the case that he would understand. It was the only reason she was able to continue.

"He reached for me then and ripped my blouse off along with my bra. Had they been of sturdy fabric it wouldn't have been so easy for him. When my breasts..." The air in her lungs trapped she struggled to release it, after a moment she let the breath rush out. She gulped in more air so she could continue. "...he grabbed them and pinched and pulled and bit at them.

"I never let the hospital see them. They would have reported it. I told them that he'd broke my nose and that was when Effie had arrived so there was no need to remove my clothes. They tried to insist but I was so upset they let it drop."

Again, Patrick waited. Before she could continue, a nurse arrived to take his vitals. Though she made Glenna move and gave her a disapproving look, she didn't say anything.

After the woman had left, she gently shut the door and Glenna returned to the warm haven of Patrick's bed. She wished she could just stay like that and not think, but she'd started the story and it needed to be finished.

"You know, maybe now, I can finally tell my parents what happened. I need to be honest with them and my family."

In answer he drew her a little closer, but he must have realized she needed to go at her own pace. The nurse had interrupted at a crucial turn of the story, at precisely the part she'd never let herself reveal to anyone. She wasn't sure she could pick it up again. She inhaled deeply and every muscle tensed as if her body didn't want her to relive those moments.

She had to let go in order to move forward. She may have thought she had, but she'd just been going through the motions of life.

"After ten years you'd think the events would start to fade and blur. But because I haven't let them out, they've been locked inside all this time. Patrick, I need to let it go so I can be whole again."

"I know you do. If it takes all night, that's fine. I'm not going anywhere."

Though his attempt at humor fell flat, it still made her smile. Again she gulped in air to fortify her.

"After he pulled off my top he leaned back so he could look at me and sneered, 'You think you're so special, well you're not. If I didn't need to teach you a lesson, I wouldn't bother. You're nothing.' And then he grabbed at my leggings I'd been wearing and ripped them, I think he used a knife or scissors, by then I think my mind had gone into protective mode or something. The rest is a blur of pain and embarrassment.

"The things he said, he never shut up. I remember those words as if they're seared into my soul forever. Over and over again how I was the worst kind of tease. I didn't have any self-confidence so I used men to make myself feel better. I was ugly and he was doing me a favor. How I owed him for helping me. All the while he was raping me. Maybe that is what he liked because he hurt me, he was aroused to the point his movements were frenzied. I do remember the more he talked and degraded me the more excited he became."

She would not repeat the actual words, it had been hard to repeat the few things she had, but most of which were peppered with names and words she'd never heard her brothers' say, or any man say, for that matter.

Patrick reached up with his free hand and brushed the hair off her face, then brushed a kiss across her forehead. It calmed her enough to return to her story.

"I think he must really hate women. I must have been screaming the entire time because Effie said she'd heard me in her Bistro, and my cries grew louder as she ran closer across the parking lot. She said he'd been leaving when she was half way to my back door.

"She knew what happened the minute she saw me. I didn't need to tell her. But she honored my wishes and let me tell things my way. I was so devastated at that point, I think I believed every vile thing he'd said to me. I felt dirty and ashamed, mortified, and many more things I can't even put into words. So many times since that night I've gone over my relationship with that vile creature from the day I met him until he left me broken on my office floor."

"And?" Patrick finally broke the silence as if he knew the beginning of the worst was over.

"And I can never find anything I could have done to make him think I wanted him in any way other than a friend. Everything was very professional, or so I thought, during the search for the property. The paperwork, the closing, everything. Then after he asked me to go to a celebratory dinner because the shop was now officially mine—with a mortgage."

"A normal man would have taken all of that as it was meant. You can't judge all of us by one twisted bastard."

She chuckled, it went a long way to untie the knots currently in her stomach. She wasn't finished yet though.

"I don't. You'd never treat a woman like that, and neither would my brothers. He masked the fact he was a bad person. He was always kind and considerate. After that dinner, I thought we'd become friends. He asked me to dinner a few more times, but I always had things to do. Then we went to lunch a few times and I enjoyed the lunches. Then he asked me to dinner again and I was available.

"That night he brought flowers and the warning bells in my mind went off. I was flattered but I had no feelings for him. When he gave them to me I said as much, well that I was flattered. I said I thought of him as a good friend and hoped we could remain as such. I told him that I was busy with my business and really didn't have the time to commit to a relationship and that he deserved someone who could. I swear I tried to let him down in the most compassionate way possible."

She gave him a squeeze this time and when he groaned she mumbled an apology, she'd forgotten that he was as battered as the story she was telling.

"No one likes to be rejected no matter how sugar coated you make it. I realize that. I thanked him for the flowers and the dinner when the night was over. He dropped me off at my home and he seemed a little hurt but understanding.

"It was two nights later that he walked in on me. I was completely taken by surprise. Obviously, the next day I changed the locks on my shop and my home. He'd helped me find my home also and I didn't want to have a repeat performance there. I think it was shortly after that he packed up and left town. I haven't heard from him since."

"Thank you for sharing." He gathered her closer. "You're shaking." He tugged the cover out from under her and put it over her. Not without a groan here and there.

"I really should let you rest."

"You're not going anywhere, I want to hold you. Glenna, you know all the things he said to you were *only* to hurt you and make him feel like a man, right?"

"In the logical part of my brain yes. Emotionally? It's been long enough that I'm starting to understand he was taking his insecurities out on me. I'm just glad he's gone and I never have to deal with him."

"Everything in me, especially the agent part, wants to go after the bastard and make him pay. But I promised you I wouldn't. Can you finally get past this? Can you move on? Glenna, my feelings haven't changed for you in the past hour. If they had, they wouldn't be real."

Glenna tensed afraid he was going to back away. Tell her that he couldn't get past what had happened.

"Relax, I want you to know I still want you. I am still in for the plan to let everyone know we're a couple. And when we get the bad guys we'll have had enough time to know if you can get over my law enforcement and baggage."

She grinned into the side of his chest where she was content to cuddle.

"I'm pretty sure I'm half way there already. I know I am over the ex-stuff. It's the worry every day that I'll have to work on. Can you get over what I've just told you? Because there's more."

"More?"

"Yeah I'm a hot mess."

He laughed and then groaned. "I told you not to make me laugh. Okay, tell me the rest of your messy story."

"Before you and I can move on, I have to let go of what happened that night. That means when we're in Brooklyn I need to talk to my parents alone. Maybe when you and Finn go with Reagan to the range. I have to forgive myself, understand I'm not at fault. After actually reliving the events of that night with you, I feel like a weight has been lifted and I can see a glimmer at the end of the tunnel.

"I've held my emotions in for over ten years, it's going to take time. I thought I'd let it go and moved on when I met Lance and actually allowed myself a relationship."

"You do know he's gay, right?"

"Exactly, had I not been going through the motions and caught up in the romance and the fact that I *actually* felt better about myself when he was around, kind of like I'd found a new girlfriend. I may have caught on a little sooner to that fact."

"You have no feelings for him?"

"None whatsoever. I realized that the minute you walked in to the shop. The bolts woke my body and emotions up from a ten year coma. And it scared the hell out of me."

She could feel him grin where his cheek rested on the top of her head.

"Good to know it wasn't one sided."

"Definitely not. And now you know all my dark secrets. Please be patient with me, I'm sure my insecurities about my self-worth will raise their ugly heads if or when you get a little too close."

"For you I have more patience than you'll ever need. By the way, if I didn't think you were a good woman you wouldn't have been invited to my home. I'd have put you up at a hotel before I'd expose you to my son."

Warmth and his love, yes they had met only days before but the intensity of their situation had brought them close at lightning speed. She felt like she'd known Patrick and Finn for years. She couldn't imagine her life without them.

Yet fear burned deep in her soul that one day the worst would happen.

"You're thinking again, you tensed up. Talk to me."

"Nothing you haven't heard before this evening. Let me just say this..." She swallowed and pulled in her courage because she was about to jump.

"I think your plan, idea, and or suggestion is a good one. We'll be solving the case and we will be testing our relationship one day at a time. So, yes to your proposal, such as it is....I'm ready to give this trial fiancée or couple thing a go."

Instead of words he pulled her into his side with one arm around her and tilted her chin up with his free hand. He looked into her eyes as he lowered his head. Tingles and pops exploded over her at the first brush of his lips. Soon the kiss was deep with a tangle of tongues and emotions. If it weren't for the hospital with all its tubes and beeps, things may have gotten more out of control than Glenna was ready for, and still might have.

The nurse had arrived to take Patrick's vitals again. "I guess your blood pressure is going to be a little elevated?"

He was there for observation throughout the night. They'd both forgotten where they were apparently. Glenna scrambled out of the bed as carefully as a scramble could be so she didn't hurt him. Her stomach jumped with nerves as they had when she was a teen and her ma caught her sneaking in after curfew.

Glenna gave the woman, who appeared to be somewhere between thirty and sixty, an embarrassed smile. Fit, tanned, with frosted hair, she looked like she would have been more at home on a tennis court than walking around a hospital in scrubs in the middle of the night.

"Ah, don't worry about a thing I am sure the young lad is all the better for your bedside manner."

Young lad? Glenna grinned at Patrick, he was anything but that. "Patrick, I need to get home and make sure Finn's okay and asleep. I'll come back as soon as I drop him at school."

Patrick gave her a look she couldn't decipher and then grinned. "I like the sound of that."

Funny thing, she knew exactly what he meant. He'd like that fact she'd called his place, home as if she were already there to stay.

"I do too."

She glanced at the nurse who stood at the computer entering notes. She walked to the bed side and leaned in.

"I can't make any promises, but I can promise that I want this to work."

"I'm good with that. Now go take care of our boy."

Chapter Fifteen

Glenna unlocked the door and crept in the kitchen as quietly as possible, she didn't want to wake Finn. He'd had a long emotional day. He needed his rest for the big game in two days, she glanced at the clock and realized it was well after midnight. Tomorrow she corrected.

"Hey, Glenna."

She'd been in the process of locking up, she swung around a hand going to heart. "Good grief, Finn, you're always sneaking up on me."

She blew the breath out. She was more on edge than she thought. She pulled a chair from the table and sat to give her heart time to stop racing.

"I'm sorry. I couldn't sleep. I was reading until you got home."

"Finn, I should have called. I was afraid of waking you. I should have known you'd be worried."

He settled into the chair across from her. A serious expression on his young face. He reached across the table and took her hand.

"Before we get into the adult emotional stuff I need to know how Dad is."

"Adult emotional stuff?"

He just raised a brow.

"Your dad is doing okay. He's very sore and I have a feeling tomorrow or Friday is going to be the worst. But he's on the mend. We were lucky there were no broken bones."

"Other than his nose, it was a little crooked from a school incident. Maybe now it will be straight." Finn grinned at her for a moment, then his expression was serious again. "Adult emotional stuff now."

"And what exactly would that be Finn?"

This must be about what she'd interrupted when she'd gone back to the hospital room earlier. He had been in deep conversation with his dad. Glenna glanced at the clock, he had football practice in the morning.

She held up a hand. "Finn, you have to get up early. Can this wait until breakfast? I promise you, I won't avoid whatever this *stuff* you want to talk about. But you need your rest."

He tossed a look at the clock himself. "Give me five minutes then I'll go to bed and sleep like Horace."

At the mention of his name Horace thumped his tail on the floor but otherwise didn't move a muscle.

"Five minutes."

"Did you agree to Dad's plan?"

So this was what the two had been talking about. They were close. She should have guessed Patrick would have told his son.

"What are your thoughts Finn?"

"I know you're scared. I saw how seeing my dad in the hospital tore you apart. I hope you can overcome the scared, Glenna."

She brushed the lone tear that had escaped away and sniffed. How old was he again? A wise sixteen year old, that was for sure.

"I'm terrified of loving both of you. I don't know what I'd do if something happened."

"I know. I can't say that it gets easier. But there are times when you don't think about it because Dad's on an easy case, and then there's the hundreds of times he doesn't let me or my grandparents *know* what he's up to, but he always comes home. I'm sure with your family you've heard this a lot that anyone can get hurt every day, not just special agents."

Refraining from rolling her eyes she answered, "Yeah, I seem to remember hearing that a time or two."

"Well did you agree?"

"I agreed to a trial engagement or couple whatever we want to call it, but yeah, I agreed to take it one day at a time."

"That's all we could have hoped for." He slid the chair back and knelt beside her. "Don't you think it will be easier for both of us if we have each other to make it through the scary times?"

And then the blubbering started in earnest. Finn gathered her in his arms and awkwardly patted her on the back. He murmured words of comfort and if she hadn't been crying so hard she would have laughed at his young inexperienced attempt to comfort her and stop her tears. He was growing into a good man.

She eased a way, picked up a paper towel that had been on the table and wiped away the damage. Probably making her resemble a raccoon if the dark smudges on the paper towel were any indication of the state of her mascara.

"You're a wise young man, Finnegan McGinnis."

"Finnegan Kendal McGinnis, that's my full name. I'm just a kid who wants his dad to be happy." He gave her another hug, stood and grinned. "Glenna you make me and Horace happy too."

He clicked his fingers at the dog and the two left the room. Glenna swiped at the tears again, then realized she needed to wash her face and get ready for bed. She couldn't seem to summon the energy to move though. It had been an emotional day.

*****

Glenna flipped a pancake and stifled a yawn. She had fallen asleep at the table waking around three in the morning and managed to wake up enough to finally go to bed. And then the alarm had gone off at five. It hadn't seemed like more than a minute.

"Good morning," Finn said as he came into the kitchen.

"Good morning yourself, are you ready for tomorrow night?"

"I will be after practice."

He reached across to snatch a piece of bacon managing to avoid her attempted swat. He dumped the books he'd had under one arm and swung a chair around to straddle it.

"Hey, that's no way to sit at the breakfast table."

A memory from her childhood danced through her, her mother had said those same words to Matt. He'd always had a swagger and tried to act macho. Glenna had always figured it was because as a math boy, as they called him, he had to keep up with Tyler in the manly department.

"Man, you sound just like Dad."

Nonetheless, he swung the chair around and sat properly. A feeling of love so strong nearly buckled her knees. How had she come to care so much for a motherless boy of sixteen in such a short time? She marveled at the fact a few weeks earlier she was dumped at the altar, and single again and relatively happy about it, just pissed and embarrassed.

And now she had a temporary and maybe a permanent family.

"These are almost done, then I will take you to practice on my way to the hospital."

"Have you heard from Dad this morning?"

Placing the steaming pancakes, with a generous side of fresh fruit—his coach had advised the team not to eat bacon. Apparently, the grease floats to the top of the stomach too quick with all that exercise.—onto the plate she placed it in front of him. He hadn't waited until the dish hit the table before diving in.

"Whoa, it's not going anywhere."

"Sorry, but you cook so much better than Dad." He gulped some milk to wash it down. "Don't tell him I said that."

She chuckled. "I promise. As to your question, no I haven't. I figure if something was wrong the hospital would call and if he's sleeping I don't want to wake him."

"Yeah, Mrs. Bigely, that's my health teacher, says the best healer is sleep. It's why some trauma patients slip into a coma."

"That's true, and sometimes the doctors induce the coma for that reason."

For a few minutes they ate in comfortable silence. Glenna enjoyed the time. This is what it would be like if she made the engagement real. It was all up to her. Or was it? People drew close during intense situations. It was best for all of them if they kept this to a trial until after the intense settled down.

"Do you go right to school after practice or do you have a break?"

"I have athletics, first period. It gives the team time to change and get ready for school."

"But don't you have to do something for gym, or I mean athletics, to get a grade?"

"I'm graded on my participation in football. That's my athletics."

"That makes sense."

"What's your plan?" Before she could answer he continued. "Speaking of plans what will happen to the case?"

"Medically speaking, I'm sure the doctors will tell your dad to take it easy the next couple of days. I'm sure he'll be given a list of instructions. Which I will do my best to make sure he follows."

Finn's laughter carried over the room and most likely to the neighbors. He finished up his breakfast before he commented.

"Good luck with that. I'm sure it's going to be business as usual." For the second time since she'd met the young man he reached across the table and took her hand—Patrick and Finn both tended to do that when they were going to say something important. "Glenna, I trust you to take care of my dad."

As with the previous evening she had to swallow down the emotion.

"I know you do, I will make him toe the line." To break the tension she added. "You do know he outweighs me by probably a hundred pounds, right? I will do everything in my puny power to make him rest."

He grinned. "That's all I can ask."

Together they stowed the dishes in the washer and straightened the kitchen. He took care of Horace while she fed Agnes, who ignored her since she'd been gone so much. Apparently she was in the cat house for neglecting her little furry friend.

"Let's go, Finn."

After she dropped him at school, she took the travel time to the hospital to consider what she'd agreed to, and waited for the dread, the nerves, or any of the other emotions she usually felt when someone got to close to her. But nothing happened. In fact, the opposite occurred. As she pulled into the parking lot, anticipation of seeing Patrick filled her with joy and a happiness she couldn't remember ever having.

Nearing his room she could hear voices, she stopped outside the door. Should she enter? It didn't sound like doctors, no it sounded like.... She peered around the door she'd been correct. Officers' Beckworth and Jones. She should give them time to take Patrick's statement. She could call Effie. She spoke with her briefly yesterday before she'd called Tyler.

No, she would talk to Effie in person later. Glenna wanted to hear what happened, because she had a feeling the story she'd heard had been sugar coated for his parents, Finn's, and her sake. When she stepped in all three men stopped talking and pinned their attention on her.

"This is official business Ms. Beckett, please step out." This from Jones, she did not like him. He was so full of himself.

"She can stay." Patrick patted the side of the bed.

"I don't..." Jones began.

"She's involved in this. After all these are the same perps who broke into her shop." Beckworth moved to the bed so she could reach Patrick's side.

"Now where were we?" Beckworth asked.

*****

Patrick had never been so glad to see someone in his life. It was as if the light entered with her. She was young, fresh, beautiful, and real. All the things he never thought a beautiful woman could be. Joyce had really done a number on him when it came to judgment. Glenna was showing him how, he realized now, most women were. Joyce was the exception, not the other way around.

Once she settled next to him, her bottom sidled up to his, making it hard to concentrate on the questions the officers were asking.

"Um, you said there four?"

Patrick started. "Yes, I know we only saw three on the tapes from the shop, but the fourth seemed to be a little less athletic than the others. Before all the action, I did my best to take mental note of their builds, as their faces were covered as they had been during the break-in."

"So you don't *know* if they're the same guys?" This from Jones.

"Because of their masks, as any *trained* agent I studied their body movement and any of other their characteristics while viewing the video. They're the same men." Patrick's raised brow challenged Jones to contradict.

Jones frowned, seemed to be about to say something, then reread his notes again. He continued after another heavy sigh. "Describe them as you remember."

Patrick closed his eyes to picture the day before when he found them coming up on him.

"One was lanky, most likely a runner. I remember thinking this one will be fast. Another one was solid muscle. A body builder, most likely slow. The third one ran a little chunky around the middle, probably the brains, again slow, and also the one we did not see on the tapes. The last one was a combination of lanky with muscle, stocky, he would be the toughest one. Then the action started."

"Did they say anything?" Beckworth asked.

"Oh, they said plenty." He straightened in the bed and refrained from groaning. He'd hoped to feel better by now, not worse. "Most of which I'd never say in front of a lady. It was the questions you'll want to hear."

Jones poised his stylus above his tablet in readiness. "And they were?"

"Mostly about what they were looking for, they never said exactly what that was. I don't believe they're convinced we know what they're after. And if we don't, there is more chance they'll be able to find it before we figure out what is so valuable.

"And of course, there was a lot of grilling about me assigned to the case. I gave them enough to check into my story that while I knew what happened at Ms. Beckett's shop, that wasn't why I was with her. They were justifiably skeptical, they thought it was too big of coincidence."

"I agree with them it is rather far-fetched. What are the odds that you just happened to be dating her, especially if they're connected in any way to the missing fiancé?"

Patrick fisted his hand hidden behind Glenna on the bed. He really wanted to wipe that sneer off Jones face. Beckworth seemed to be content to let his younger partner take the lead. Maybe for that reason, he figured Jones would get more information out of him by pressing his buttons.

It was working, dammit.

"As my superiors have contacted your department, you know I'm officially on the case. That is *not* all the history there is here though. Don't worry, I gave them something to follow up on. I'm sure they're using their sources to check out my story."

"Which is?"

"I met the beautiful Glenna through her brother, Tyler. We started out together at Quantico and we've been together for other training several times over the years. All of which, with the right hacks, they can verify."

Beckworth finally decided to step in, and Patrick let himself relax.

"Now the bastards think the two of you are an item, what are you planning? What does this have to do with whatever they're after?"

For a moment Patrick was confused by, *'whatever they're after'*, then he remembered they'd never actually gotten around to filling the cops in on the plan and what they found. He felt Glenna stir next him and chanced a glance at her, and sure enough she was giving him a questioning glance. Now was the time to fill the two in, and he had an idea they could be of help.

"We actually have what they're after." He threw up his free hand. "Now don't get your panties in a wad. It isn't that we didn't trust you, it's that we wanted to buy time in case the bad guys have a way to access to your reports."

"We're secure as the feds, just because we're a small department doesn't mean we're not professionals." Jones words were punctuated with indignation.

"He didn't say you weren't. But we wanted my sister to have a chance to track these guys through the Dark web, and figure out a plan all before we revealed anything. If these guys have professional technical resources, the minute you filed your report, we'd have been vulnerable. And yet..."

Patrick felt Glenna tense next to him, and heard the emotion gather in her voice as she answered Jones.

"...Patrick was still attacked even with our precautions."

"Have you heard anything from Ms. Beckett's family? Her sister or brother?" Beckworth asked.

"I heard from Agent Reagan Beckett this morning right before you two arrived." He looked down at Glenna. "I wanted to tell you first, but since they're here I might as well fill everyone in now."

She gave him a brief nod. For the next several moments he brought them up to speed on the events in New York, and their plan to flush the culprits out.

"We'll leave for Brooklyn to stay with Glenna's parents, so they can get to know the new fiancé. The gala is a week from this Sunday. Tomorrow night Finn has a big game..."

Glenna patted his thigh and finished for him. "...and we'll be there to support him, after all where would we be? I'm getting to know my new soon-to-be-son, and getting to know Patrick's family also."

"Now we know the plan, what are they after?" Jones asked.

"It's a Giovanni Bellini. The Madonna with Child circa 1430. Part of a collection that was stolen during the Nazi occupation. Very rare and valuable. Most of the art, when found, is either sold to the highest bidder on the black market or given back to the country of origin for a reward. Now, though with the Dark web, it's become even easier to find a home to the highest bidder."

Patrick wanted everyone to go but Glenna. Mostly he just wanted to go home and rest. But he knew they had things that needed to be done. So the sooner they finished with the officer's the sooner he could get on with his day and hopefully rest a moment or two before the game.

"Are you all right?" Glenna asked.

"Yes. Sorry, just gathering my thoughts. We have the picture at my house. It's not very large so we have it packed in a large box so they wouldn't know what we were transporting. However, they know where I live and will be watching for us to move anything. That's where we're going to need your help."

Jones perked up. Beckworth looked bored.

"While we're out of town, we need you to move the box to a safe place."

"Given they're not watching." Jones broke in to add.

"Oh, someone will be. From what Reagan said this morning, most likely they'll be at the Gala, which is exactly what we'd hoped for, if her sources are correct."

"You know who they are then?" Beckworth asked.

"We *believe* we know what organization. There's a large group of international thieves, but they call themselves collectors. They go after rare art and antiquities and do what all thieves do; sell it for the highest bid. They obviously don't let things like people get in the way. Reagan said they're one of the most ruthless groups. Most of the art rings try to stop before they commit murder. In other words, they'll lie and cheat and go to great lengths to get what they want but they won't harm anyone.

"This group goes for the crème of the crop and will stop at nothing to get what they want. This particular piece is something they *want.*"

Glenna straightened away from him, and he felt the loss. He stifled the sensation. He had to make it through until the end without letting her distract him. This was her wheelhouse, she knew more about it than he did. He had assumed she'd take over the reins and he'd been right.

"This particular piece is believed to have been evacuated in the early 1940s from a museum in Berlin to be housed in a flak tower in Berlin-Friedrichshain, located within Russian control at the time. Most of the objects in the tower were either looted or presumed destroyed, including Bellini's Madonna."

Jones gave a low whistle. "How the fu... sorry, how in the world did you get your hands on it? I mean, let's face it, your shop is just a tiny little tourist trap on the north end of the Napa Valley."

Beckworth sighed and shook his head. "Jones that was uncalled for, *Glenna's Surprisingly Vintage* is a very popular place, and some people come to the valley exclusively to visit her shop."

Patrick could see that while Glenna wasn't happy with what Jones had said, she was pleased by his boss coming to her defense.

"Thank you, Officer Beckworth. He's right in the fact that I'd never be able to sell the piece for what's it worth. It's simply over my patron's budgets. Hey, it's over my budget. It was packed away in a grab box I found at an estate sale in upstate New York. Since they keep an inventory of what's sold at those sales, I can only assume the thieves found the manifest of items and sales."

Patrick took over from her and turned back to the law enforcement officers. "That brings us back to how you need to move the art. We'd planned to find a safe storage unit, but now if they see us move anything, they'll go after it in case it's what they want."

"If Ms. Beckett..."

"Glenna," she told Beckworth.

"If Glenna is your fiancée wouldn't she be moving some of her things to your house and packing up some of her things for storage?"

Glenna turned to him, and he saw she wasn't ready to give up her little cottage. He didn't want to push. He also thought it was a good idea. But this would be one thing he stood firm on. *No pressure.* She had to come to terms with his profession and other things before she took that step.

"I'm not exactly in the best shape to be moving things. There isn't much time before we leave for New York on Tuesday. That's only five days."

"He's right, sir. But if they're watching how can we move it."

"And what would they be doing at your house Patrick?"

Another good point. *Think.*

"I don't want my parents involved at all."

"In what dear?"

His mother's voice startled him. His parents were standing at the door. He hadn't noticed their entry, obviously. How to answer her question without doing exactly what he'd just said he didn't want to do. His mother was the most stubborn person he knew. His dad would say Patrick was the stubborn one. He'd heard it a lot during his growing up years. *Ye'r a stubborn laddie.*

Beckworth came to his rescue. He *almost* wanted to hug him.

"It's a police matter. We really can't discuss it ma'am. We need to be on our way."

He turned to Patrick and gave him a brief glare as if he'd like nothing better than to walk out the door, take over the case, and push the unwanted fed out of the picture.

Not going to happen, boyo.

"When can Glenna open the shop for business?" Jones pursed his lips and gave Glenna a look that Patrick couldn't decipher. "We still need to have that expert come in and look at your inventory. Oh wait, we don't need to do that anymore do we? Were you ever going to tell us?"

"If my superiors hadn't wanted you to know, you wouldn't know now."

That didn't go over well, to say the least. The two officers slammed out of the room, as much as anyone could in a quiet atmosphere.

Unfortunately, they still hadn't solved the dilemma of moving the art. Gauging his mother's expression she wasn't going to let what she'd overheard drop as he'd hoped.

"What don't you want us involved in dear, and do *not* say nothing." Then as if she just noticed Glenna, she asked, "And why is Glenna *sitting* on your bed? Is that wise? What would the nurse say?"

At that moment said nurse walked through the door. "She would say, they've been hanging together on that bed since he got there. I don't think it would do any good to tell her to move. She'd just crawl back in when I left."

She grinned at Patrick, then Glenna. "Okay missy you will need to move while I get all these lines out of the man. I think he wants to go home."

As the nurse worked, she kept up a running litany of what he could and could not do. Mostly he'd do what he wanted, and the woman seemed to know that.

Patrick's mother insisted on following them home to make sure he was settled and safe. Glenna had a feeling this was her way of coping. And she wouldn't stand in the woman's way. Though mostly quiet during the drive, because Patrick didn't like to be out of control by not driving, they decided to announce their engagement to his parents.

Against his mother's arguments, and even Glenna had grumbled a bit, Patrick insisted on talking in the living room. He made his overstuffed Lazy Boy his bed. Once settled in and all the fussing was over, Patrick called Glenna to his side and patted the armrest.

He winked at her. How he wished he didn't have to take things slow and catch the bad guys. For the first time in his career he wished he wasn't in the middle of a case. Usually it was the case that made him feel alive. Glenna was starting to replace that feeling. Who knew, maybe he'd be willing to take that management position and sit at a desk while delegating when all this was over.

NOT.

"Mum, Da have a seat."

His mother threw a hand over her heart and slumped into a chair, his father placed on hand on her shoulder and stood like a sentinel as if protecting her.

He glanced at Glenna then back at his parents. "Exactly what do you think I'm going tell you?"

"They found something while you were in the hospital, didn't they?"

His da barely let his mum finish before he asked his question. "They take all those blood tests and they found out you had the big C. We were worried when we saw all those tubes and machines."

His parents were fairly savvy people, or so he thought. At the moment there were sounding more like his grandparents. Glenna wiggled and he knew she was trying not to laugh. Though having cancer would be horrible and wasn't a laughing matter.

"No. I'm a little rough around the edges but mostly I'm healthy as a horse. Da have a seat. I hope this is good news."

"You've decided to come to your senses and take that job your boss keeps asking you to take so he can retire." His mum sounded so hopeful he *almost* wished he could grant her wish.

"No. Can you two just let me tell you my news?"

His da gave him the *father look* then glanced at Glenna and grinned. "Please do."

He put his arm around Glenna's back and gave a tug until she was on his lap, which elicited an unwilling groan. For a moment he'd forgotten he hurt in every molecule of his body.

"Glenna and I are, not exactly engaged, but we're a couple."

Silence settled over the room. His mum's eyes fell to Glenna's hands, and she frowned when she didn't see the evidence of his statement, she apparently had missed the part about *not exactly*. His da just grinned.

"It's about damn time. I want a few more wee grandchildren."

"But you've just met. How can you be in love?" Then a horrified expression danced across her face. "Oh, Glenna, not that you wouldn't make a wonderful daughter."

"Wonderful daughter?" The voice came from the other side of the room.

Apparently they'd left the back door unlocked for his sister had entered unnoticed. She took in Glenna on his lap, then to her parents who had totally opposite looks on their faces.

"What exactly is going on?" Margaret Kathleen asked.

"Your brother just told us he has asked Glenna to marry him. But I don't see a ring. It must be for this assignment they're on. You know undercover and they want us to go along with it."

Patrick was a little disgruntled to have his mum come so close to the truth. He needed to come across convincingly if they were going to pull it off. Because his mum definitely couldn't lie with a straight face and if she were confronted by a neighbor about his engagement they'd see through her announcement.

Glenna wiggled in to get a little more comfortable. Desire warred with his screaming thighs. He'd never realized a man could use thigh muscles when using his fists in a down and out brawl, a little one sided, but that was what it had been. But then when the bastard had his arms pulled behind him, he had made good use of his legs.

"Patrick and my brother, Tyler, trained together at Quantico and have had several refreshers together since." She snuggled in, and again he managed, barely, not to groan. "You've met Keira also, haven't you?"

"Yes, that's Tyler's wife. She's an agent also. I believe a couple of years ago, she did some cyber training with us."

"Anyway, I met your brother..." She glanced at Margaret Kathleen then grinned at his parents. "...and son, through my brother."

He was impressed. She hadn't lied. Everything she said was the truth. Though it had been phone call to have him check on the missing Lance Gordon, which was sort of meeting through her brother, wasn't it?

"And you fell in love in what a week?" Margaret Kathleen was going to make this difficult.

"Did you miss the part about I've met Tyler years ago, I met Glenna because of him?"

His sister raised a brow, no she wasn't buying it. "And I didn't miss the part where you *never* said you didn't just meet her a week ago."

Glenna turned away from him to get a better look at his sister. She gently extricated herself from his lap. When she stood in front of Margaret Kathleen she held out her hand.

"I'm Glenna Beckett, it's nice to finally meet you. I've heard so much about you. I'm using the room your kids stay in as my office." she giggled a little, something Patrick had never heard. "I'm sharing it with Agnes. I needed someplace to work while I can't be at the shop."

Nicely distracted his sister took the bait. "Who's Agnes?"

The cat wandered in at that moment, Horace lazily following in the feline's wake.

"That is Agnes."

All three of his family stared at the round gray tabby and the huge dog. Then astonishment took over when the two curled up together for what looked like a long afternoon nap.

"Horace let her live? Horace hates cats. We have one and I can *never* bring Stripes when the kids visit."

"That's why I fell in love with Horace first, because he didn't kill Agnes."

Margaret Kathleen ignored the hand Glenna held out, and grabbed her by the shoulders and pulled her in for a hug. "Welcome to the family. I've always wanted a sister."

And apparently that was all it took for his family to believe. Cats and dogs. If animals were involved then it must be true. He grinned at Glenna when she returned to the armrest.

"You never told me you wanted a sister," Patrick's mother said.

"I was afraid you'd have another boy, look at him. Even when he was young he was never little. He intimidated all of my friends or all my girlfriends fell in love with him." She turned to Glenna. "It was awful. Either my friends wouldn't come over because of Patrick or they only wanted to come over because of Patrick."

"I know exactly what you mean, I have two brothers. Not as big as Patrick, but Tyler could be very intimidating and Matt was just cute."

"God, you guys are making me feel like some kind of oversized freak."

"Well you're my oversized freak. Except I picture you more as a highlander in your family plaid. Bagpipes and all."

"Oh, then you're in for a treat. The valley has a Highland Festival they do every year. The Scottish Games, my da, Patrick, and Finn all dress in the Dughlas plaid, that's Gaelic for Douglas, my mum is Scottish and my da has some Scottish relatives in Galloway."

"All my fantasy's coming true." Then she must have realized the connotation, she swallowed and turned to his mother. "I have a thing for kilts. And I just meant..."

"Oh, I'm not so old that I don't remember what it's like."

His mum pulled herself out of the chair she'd plopped in and came over to Glenna and gave her a hug maybe a little longer and tighter, by the slight bulge of Glenna's eyes, than his sisters had been.

"We welcome you to the family, also."

His da gently disentangled his mother from his fiancée and gave her a hug. "I can speak for myself. Welcome Glenna Beckett."

"When's the wedding?"

That was one question he hadn't been prepared for, leave it to his sister to bring it up. Luckily, it must be a girl thing because Glenna saved the day.

"I can't decide. But I am thinking next fall, or maybe a Christmas wedding. What do you think, Patrick?"

He raised a brow. Though he was only half joking when he said, "This Christmas?"

Glenna gave him a playful slap, Oscar performance in his opinion. "That's only a few months away, no way could I have the *huge* wedding I want in that short of time."

He chuckled for he knew that was payback, he hoped.

After his family left, all the energy drained out of him. He felt like a wimp. He was trying to decide how to let Glenna know he needed to rest without her turning all maternal on him when she solved the dilemma for him.

"I need to talk to Effie. I am not going to tell her about our engagement until you're with me." She paused leaned in and kissed him and when he was ready to haul her up in his arms and take her to bed, his injuries be damned, she pulled away.

"You know I think I like this plan of yours, more and more. Anyway, will you be okay here alone?" She straightened and frowned. "I can't leave you. What happens if they come back?"

The moment when she'd kissed him and knocked his socks off passed in a heartbeat and brought reality bashing in. He reached for her and settled her back in his lap.

"Glenna, now is the time to trust that things will be okay. You can't control anything in this world. You can't worry about everything. They probably assume after the attack, that the locals are keeping a closer watch on the situation." He didn't see any of the worry lesson, so he added, "I'm sure they, meaning the local PD, are. Go have a latte. What was it that you liked? I need to remember. A skinny something or other."

"A WMC on the skinny." He must have looked confused. "White mocha chocolate."

"As your new beau, yes my mum still uses that term, and I like it, I will have to learn all kinds of things about your *desires.*" He gave her a look.

She laughed and climbed out of his lap and chair. "It is hard for me to see that as a wicked look with two black eyes and a big white bandage over your broken nose."

"Oh, yea I forgot about that for a moment. I hope it's better looking by the Gala."

"If it's still green and purple, Jessica is pretty good with the make-up. We'll just have to do what we can. Do you want me to bring you an iced coffee or something?"

"It will be warm by the time you get home. Why don't you call when you're on the way?"

"I can pick up Finn after school, and we'll stop and grab something for dinner."

"Sounds good, now I'm going to catch some shut eye."

Glenna hesitated, he looked so vulnerable.

"Go woman."

He hadn't opened his eyes as he said, but he'd tried for a stern frown, but with his split lip it came out a little lopsided.

*****

Glenna felt the last of the armor around her heart she'd been struggling to hold on to slip away.

Her heart was officially his.

Chapter Sixteen

Glenna pulled to a stop in front of *Effie's Coffee Bistro and More*. She'd wanted to talk to her friend, true, but mostly she wanted to walk through her shop, *Glenna's Surprisingly Vintage*. She'd worked so hard to make it what it had become. As Beckworth had said, people came from all over to Calistoga to visit her shop. When a customer walked in with so much excitement claiming how far they'd traveled just to see her and her *amazing* treasures, she still had to pinch herself to remind herself it wasn't a dream.

She glanced over at her poor forlorn building the yellow tape rippling in the breeze. Could she ever feel safe again? Now that she was here there was no way she could bring herself to walk across the lot and let herself in on her own. She longed for Patrick, his strong presence would have allowed her to do the few things she needed to do. She knew he wouldn't like the fact she was there on her own. Especially since they'd planned to come together and start the clean up on Saturday.

Glenna had been so positive she wanted to walk through by herself the first time with no officers or chaos as it had been since she'd been home. Grieve for her friend. Be angry with those thugs, and though she'd never thought of art thieves as thugs before, these were. They were bullies and didn't care who they hurt as long as they got what they wanted.

If and when she'd ever thought of an art thief an image of *Cary Grant* in *To Catch a Thief* flittered across her mind. No more.

A knock on her window startled her and she turned from her contemplation of her shop's back door to find Effie standing at her window, which she rolled down.

"Are you going to just sit and stare? Come in and catch me up."

Relief ran through her. "You scared me."

Effie pulled the door open for her and then she followed her in, Glenna grinned as she watched the flowered skirt sway in the breeze. The green and white sock on her left foot and the pink and green sock on her right sort of matched some of the flowers in the pattern. Her bright orange shirt at least went well with the big poppies. Her hair as usual was a perfected mass of disarray.

What would she do without her friend? She hoped to never find out.

They settled in the corner table, *their* discussion table. A few moments later her usual WCM on the skinny sat steaming in front of her and her friend her usual a cold Chai.

"Well?"

Where to begin? There was so much. She took a sip and then went over the events since she'd seen her last. She couldn't decide if she wanted to let her know about the couple thing or wanted Patrick with her when she told her about the fiancée part. She'd wait. There was a possibility one of the men would come in and chat her friend up for information. It would be critical that her friend make it believable. And the only way for that to happen would be for her to *believe*.

Effie was a terrible liar.

"Wow." Effie sipped her chai and for a moment she was silent, unusual for her friend. "Wow is all I can say. What intrigue, it sounds like something I'd watch on *NCIS* or one of those cop shows. So you're leaving for New York next week? The *Elders* will be thrilled. They miss you Glenna, your Mom told me."

"I know they do, I miss them too. But this is my home. I love it here."

She let her gaze roam over the lot to her shop for the hundredth time. The safe feeling she'd worked so *hard* to find after what Danny had done had wavered. Thanks to Patrick it wasn't completely gone and for once she was positive she'd be able to feel that safe again. It was weird to rely on a person so completely. It seemed she'd known him for years.

"Hey, what are you thinking?"

"I was thinking how hard I'd worked to feel safe and now this."

Effie sat her drink down and gave her a hard look, which people wouldn't equate with her friend. "Now you listen to me. You're going to be just fine. I have a feeling there is more going on with that hunky agent than you're letting on. I know he wouldn't let anything happen to you."

Glenna just grinned. "Do you have some time you could walk over to the shop with me? I was going to do it myself, but I'm not sure I'm ready yet."

"Of course, let me go tell the guys I'll be gone for a while."

Not long after Glenna unlocked the door and the smell hit them as they walked in. She left the door open and went through to the front and opened the door to let the breeze help air the place out.

"God. We need to figure out how to get that smell out or you're never going to have any customers."

"I know. I was going to clean up myself, mostly because I have so many breakables, but maybe I should call in a professional cleaner."

"You could have them clean everything but the displays. They are mostly just dust left over from the police doing their fingerprint thing."

"Patrick is coming back with me on Saturday, I'll let him decide."

Effie raised a brow but didn't say anything.

Glenna's phone jingled, her generic ring, she looked and saw it was Patrick. She'd thought he'd still be asleep.

"Are you okay?"

"Yes." He chuckled. "You're not at Effie's, it's too silent. I figured you wouldn't just visit with her. So how is the shop?"

"It looks and *smells* the same."

"We'll take a look at it Saturday…" She could hear the faint sounds of him moving, probably trying to get comfortable. "…you know the more I think about it, I don't think I we'd be able to get the odor out of the place. Take some pictures of the place and tomorrow I'll check around and see if we can hire someone to clean up the worst."

How many times had he echoed her thoughts? More proof they were good together. She resisted the urge to break into a grin, somehow it felt wrong to be so happy standing in the room where her beautiful assistant and taken her last breath. Sadness filled her.

"Glenna, I understand how hard this must be for you."

"It is." She glanced around again, turned and returned to her office. "Patrick, I'll take the pics but I'm sure I can call around tomorrow. You need to rest. I think Saturday is too soon for you to be up and around."

"I'm already bored and want to get up and about. If my muscles didn't remind me every time I got up to take a p… Sorry. Anyway, I need something to keep my mind occupied. I can find someone tomorrow. Then you and I can go over what we're going to do in New York."

She smiled into the phone. "Your mind has been busy. I'll finish up here then I thought I'd stop at Calmart and grab some things at the deli for dinner before I pick up Finn."

"What? You're not getting pizza?"

"I figure something different would be healthier for Finn."

He chuckled. "I was kidding. Let me know when you're on your way. Take care."

He disconnected and she turned to find Effie smiling at her.

"What?"

She wagged her figure under Glenna's nose. "There's something going on there."

Glenna considered telling her but wanted to wait until Patrick was with her, it would be more convincing with him at her side. The want was so strong, she even opened her mouth to spill the beans. Then she reminded herself about Effie's lying abilities in case she didn't believe their engagement. Though more and more it felt like the real deal and not the take a one day at a time trial variety.

"I need to place an ad for an assistant." Successfully changing the subject. "Do you think I need to place it somewhere other than the Calistoga Tribune?"

Effie perched herself on the edge of the desk. "Don't think the discussion has ended. We'll revisit soon."

Glenna busied herself looking through drawers for the want ad sign she knew she'd stowed somewhere after she'd hired Alex. She heard Effie sigh and knew the discussion on her love life was only over for the moment.

"What are you looking for?"

"My help needed sign. I thought I'd place it up front again, after all that's how I found Alex."

She almost hadn't been able to say her assistants' name. How could she ask someone to work for her again?

"Glenna, you and Patrick will get the bastards who did this, you're going to be safe as will whoever you hire to help."

"How do you do that? How do you know what I'm feeling sometimes before I do?"

"Because we're sisters of the heart. We've been there for each other."

"I told Patrick."

Effie stared at her for a full minute before she responded. She didn't pretend not to know what Glenna referred to.

"You never told me."

"You knew. I didn't want to put myself through the scene again." She dropped her gaze to her lap where her hands had come to rest. She felt the moisture gather in her eyes. "I'm sorry, Effie, I should have. Maybe then I wouldn't have carried around these feelings of guilt, inadequacies, fear."

"You're right. I knew. You know you didn't need to tell me. I was there for you to support you. The moment I walked in that door I knew what had happened."

"I know. I wouldn't have survived if it hadn't been for you, my friend. Letting the words out, reliving that awful night freed what was trapped in me."

"And Patrick?"

"Listened, held me, and promised me he wouldn't go after Danny. He understood I didn't want to dredge up everything after all this time."

"He's a good man, Glenna."

"Yes. Now how did we get on this subject?" Before she burst into tears she started searching through her drawers again. "Now where in the hell is that sign."

"You let me borrow it. I'll go get it for you while you call the Trib. I think you should put it on the Chambers web site also."

"Good idea. Thanks Effie."

She powered up her ancient desktop. She had her laptop for serious computer work, but the old computer on her desk worked for what she needed at the shop. Unfortunately it took forever to boot up. Somewhere there was a list of local business that she hoped had the Tribune's number.

Found it. She punched in the number, placed the ad and by the time she disconnected Effie had returned with the sign and the desktop was ready to place the information on the town site. She just hoped that people would actually apply after what happened.

"I put the sign on the front door. Do you have any idea when you'll be open for business? You may want to print out some information to put up also."

"The officers, Beckworth and Jones, called this morning and told me they were through with everything they needed here. The investigation of course will go until we find who did this. Hopefully, we'll know after the Gala. And when we return from New York I'll reopen."

"I wish you luck my friend. I better get back, it was starting to fill up with the afternoon crowd when I went in search for your sign."

Effie gave her a hug and then left and silence remained.

Glenna pulled up a word doc and created a sign with the information about the reopen. She placed it next to the Help Wanted sign, made sure the front door was locked, and then skirted around the tape from the murder scene and left through the back door, making sure it was secure also.

She sat in the car a moment and contemplated checking on her little cottage and then determined two things, Patrick wouldn't be pleased if she went alone. She also didn't want to go alone, just in case she interrupted another search party.

She made a quick stop at the deli and then was on her way to pick up Finn. Her mind was so busy going over the events of the past month she almost flew by the school.

Good grief, she didn't even remember driving how many miles? At least she had apparently not injured anyone, including herself.

Finn came out of the school not long after she parked in front to wait. His tall lanky body flowed as he walked. She smiled, he was so handsome. And the girls all paused as he walked by totally unaware of the stares. Patrick must have looked like that when he was young.

"Hey Glenna, how's dad?" He asked as he climbed in the passenger seat.

"I left him sleeping while I went into Calistoga. He called though, so he didn't rest as long as I'd hoped."

"He's stubborn."

She grinned. "Yes he is. So are you ready for tomorrow night?"

"Yup, we're going to kick some as... er butt."

She didn't have much experience with teenagers, should she reprimand him for his almost slip? Naw.

"I bet you are. And you know what? I cannot wait to see a future NFL star."

"Now don't get to excited. I wouldn't go so far as to say I'm a contender. I enjoy football, but I really think I'm going to John Jay College of Criminal Justice. I'm pretty sure they don't have a football team."

Glenna paused. Two cops? Could she worry about two of her loved ones in law enforcement, then stopped that thought, she had a family full of them. She'd survived.

One day at a time. She could do this, and if she kept telling herself every day she could, she would.

"That's part of The City University of New York, correct?"

"Yes it is, it's where Dad went."

"I remember he said something about that. Well you'll do well there, even if there is no football team."

"I was thinking, Glenna, it will be nice to get to know my new family in New York."

She glanced at him and then back to the street. "They're going to love you. I will feel better knowing you have the *Elders* close by."

He chuckled. "I love that you call them that. Are we going to go over our plan tonight?"

"No. I want your dad to rest tonight and tomorrow. The weekend will be soon enough to go over everything."

As she pulled the car into the drive, the back door opened and Patrick leaned against the frame. She wasn't sure if he needed the support or not.

"Good luck with getting him to rest."

"We'll keep his mind off it." She climbed out and grabbed her packages from the back seat. "Do you have any board games?"

Finn pulled the groceries from her arms and carried them toward the house calling over his shoulder, "Oh, yeah we have board games and I'm the resident champion of all."

Patrick moved into the kitchen to let them enter. Glenna was relieved to see he seemed to be moving better if not free of stiffness.

"Board games?" He asked as he poked around in her selections for dinner.

"Yes, I'm making a rule. No shop talk tonight or tomorrow. You're going to rest."

He paused and contemplated her for a moment, she could almost see him thinking. And she knew his separation of work and home was going to be hard. Though before she'd entered his life it had been a normal thing. And if she was going to make this trial into permanent she would work to make that a normal thing again.

Home was off the clock.

"I hope we don't embarrass you tonight."

Glenna looked from father to son, both wore identical smirks. "Why would I be embarrassed?"

She busied herself putting out the deli meats, arranging the cheeses and breads she'd purchased. And tried not to think, that if this were a real engagement, shouldn't he have given her a kiss?

She felt him come up behind her, lean in and kiss the side of her neck, as if he'd been reading her mind.

"Hmmm, you smell good."

"Oh guys, don't do that in front of the child."

Which of course successfully ruined the romantic mood that had been about to wrap around her. But the warmth lingered.

"Sit, both of you."

They followed her direction and Finn barely restrained himself from doing what he'd done at breakfast and pounce on the food before the plates hit the table.

Over dinner they regaled her of stories of nights spent playing Monopoly and how she didn't stand a chance. And unfortunately, they had been right. She hadn't played board games for years. However, the evening had been a success, not one word had been said about the men who'd used Patrick for a punching bag.

As Glenna cleaned up the evening's dishes, the men cleared up the games and put the living room back to rights as they'd decided to move things out of the way to sit on the floor. As she'd done when she had played with her siblings growing. Memories flowed over her, and new ones had begun.

Patrick checked the doors to make sure they were locked and secured, along with the windows. Finn surprised her by giving her a big hug, then calling Horace and the two went off to bed.

She felt Patrick's arm go around her, and she turned into his arms.

"Thank you for a lovely evening, Glenna. I think we make a great family."

She smiled into his shoulder. "I do too."

"We best get to bed, Finn has practice and though you said no shop talk tomorrow, I do want to find a professional cleaner and there are a few things I need to do before we go to New York."

She stepped back and gave him a stern look, or she hoped it was anyway. "I promised Finn I'd make sure you were resting tomorrow."

"I will use my laptop and veg in that overstuffed chair I'm fast coming to hate. It may be comfortable, but I'm not used to sitting in it longer than watching the Golden State Warriors kick some opponent's butt."

"You're just going to have to tolerate it for one more day."

She bent to scoop up Agnes. When what she really wanted was to lead Patrick to her bed and make love. Holding her feline friend seemed like a safer choice. For one thing, she wasn't ready to take their relationship to that level yet. And another, Patrick looked like he was about to drop. Though she was sure he'd deny that.

He reached around the cat, who gave him a stink stare for the inconvenience and cupped her face for a swift kiss, or so it started out. A squawk from Agnes broke it up before it got out of hand. Patrick took a step back, and she was glad to see that his breathing indicated that he'd been as affected by that punch as she had.

"I want to take you to my bed, Glenna." He raised his hand to stop her from commenting. "I am going to wait though, because when I make love to you I want it to be perfect. I want to have all my strength back because I have a feeling I'm going to need it."

His last comment broke the sexual tension that had been thrumming around the two. She chuckled and took a step and with her free hand grasped the back of his neck pulling him down so she could kiss him. Keeping it light. She turned and threw a 'good night' over her shoulder as she walked into her room.

After the door was closed she leaned against it to wait for her breathing to even out. She ruffled the cats' fur. A loud meow in protest echoed over the room.

"That was hard, Agnes."

Chapter Seventeen

She woke with a start. Had she heard something?
The room was still dark with the exception of the glow
of the clock on the bedside table. Three in the
morning. She sat up and listened. Then she heard it.
Someone was in the kitchen.

Dread ran over her. Carefully so as not to let the
culprit know she was awake. She got to the door
without mishap, she eased the door opened and light
spilled into the room.

Finn was at the counter in the process of making
a sandwich. Relief flooded her. She didn't like that
every sound, creak of the floor, innocent rattling of the
windows brought dread. Would things ever be normal
and sane again?

She gently closed the door. The boy needed his
rest, if she went in they'd have a conversation and it
would be much later when he made it to bed. Let him
have his middle of the night snack and get back to
sleep. He was a growing boy and needed his energy.

It seemed she'd barely laid her head on the pillow
and the alarm went off. She would make a substantial
breakfast, run Finn to practice and shower later. She
pulled her hair into a sloppy ponytail, and threw on
some sweats. No need to dress up for kitchen duty.

First order of business, coffee. While it brewed she
pulled the eggs from the fridge and began the
preparation omelets. The boy needed a good breakfast.

"Something smells awesome in here."

As was fast becoming the routine, Finn reached
over her shoulder to grab the first piece of bacon as
she moved it to the plate.

"Hey." Again she was unsuccessful in rescuing the
bacon.

"I need my energy," he said echoing her earlier
thoughts.

"You checked on the old codger yet?"

"Old codger?"

They both turned to watch Patrick walk in, straight if a little on the stiff side, he looked almost fifty percent better than he had the night before. He was on the mend.

He grabbed the boy around the waist and began to wrestle him around. For which Glenna was going to have none of. She grabbed an arm, and until she pulled Finn away she hadn't known whose.

"You two are going to knock things over and my delicious breakfast will end up on the floor. Now both of you behave and sit down."

"But mum, he started it!" Patrick sat down with a mock frown.

Glenna burst into welcome laughter. She was still smiling as she dished up the omelets and placed all the serving dishes on the table. She glanced at the clock it was barely six in the morning.

"Come on, Finn we need to have you to practice at 6:30."

*****

The men in the van watched. The lights had come on not long after they'd pulled into their spot.

The leader frowned. "The kid must need to go to school soon."

"Football. That's where he went yesterday. A big game tonight."

"Good, maybe we can check things out while they're otherwise occupied." The words sounded bored as the man flipping through a magazine.

The leader twisted in his seat to get a look at his friend. "Good point."

"Distraction. The agent's mind will be elsewhere."

Thoughtful, the man in the front settled again to watch as a few minutes later the 4Runner slid by them, the Beckett woman behind the wheel, with the kid in the passenger seat.

Oblivious to their presence.
Good.

*****

Lost in thought at the kitchen table where she'd
sat up a temporary workstation, Glenna stared at the
laptop. Her mind was far from whatever the words
were on the screen. She kept replaying the trip to the
school that morning. Something was off, Finn had
been chatting a mile a minute about the game that
evening. Whatever she was trying to remember this
morning was on the edge of her subconscious. There
was a detail she'd thought of or noticed she'd filed
away to tell Patrick when she got home. What?

"Hey beautiful."

Glenna jumped, nearly spilling her water she'd
been about to sip. "Why do the men in this family
insist on sneaking up on me?"

"It's fun?"

Patrick pulled the fridge open, she noticed he bent
like he was the tough old bird Finn had called him.
After retrieving a bottled water he pulled a chair and
sat, more than a little gingerly, across from her.

"What are you working on?"

"You mean what am I pretending to work on?"

He grinned. "That too."

"Something about the drive to school is bugging
me," she said. She thought a minute, then snapped
her fingers. "That's it."

He raised a brow, gulped down some water
replaced the lid. "And that would be?"

"A van." She slid her chair back and went to stand
to the side of the front window. She motioned for
Patrick to stay back. "They're still there. I saw them
out of the corner of my eye and I didn't want to
interrupt Finn's enthusiasm. I meant to tell you when I
got home. But then you were sleeping and I started
reading my email...."

Careful not to be seen from the window she returned to her seat.

"They've been there since I got up."

"And you didn't tell me?" Her surprised tone said it all.

"I know you and Finn both wanted to be kept up on things." He gave a shrug and winced. "The same reason you didn't say anything. I planned to tell you when you returned as you pointed out, I was taking a bit of a beauty nap."

She chuckled. "As if you need it. Seriously though, why are they watching us here? Do you think they guessed we have the painting?"

He stretched his legs out to the side of the table. "Maybe they do. But I think it's a distraction. The want us to *know* they're watching."

"You're right, and I have an idea about that."

His brow hiked a little higher this time. "And?"

"You're cute when you do that."

"Didn't your brothers tell you, a man *never* wants to be cute?"

It felt good to laugh. "No. But talk about distracting."

She put up a finger to pause the conversation for a moment. She reached to the chair on her left and pulled the laptop bag off of it and held it up. Patrick frowned in confusion.

"Luckily our treasure is one of the smallest of Bellini's work."

"I'll bite. What does that have to do…"

Glenna cut him off by standing and going to her room returning with the Madonna and Child.

"It's about 14 inches by 18 inches, a little snug but look." She carefully slid the wrapped picture into her bag. "We can transport it with us, without the men outside knowing."

Patrick started to slide his chair away from the table, placed a hand on it to push himself back.

"Wait, I just checked. Remember."

"Yeah, but I wanted to make sure it's our guys? It was too dark this morning when I caught sight of it."

"Well I didn't get a good look with all of Finn's football talk. I bet it is though. It's a van, just a different color this time. They've been there all day."

"How do you know?"

"After you'd been asleep for an hour or so, I got curious and decided we needed a few things from the grocery store." She shrugged. "They were still there when I left and though they'd moved by the time I came home, I saw their van parked down around the block."

"I like that."

"That they're watching?"

"No." He chuckled. "The sound of you saying 'home.'"

Warmth filled her. She did feel at home. As much as she loved her cottage, this was fast becoming home to her.

"Back to the bad guys. We have until Tuesday to figure out where to stash this. If we take it in a box again, they're going to be alerted."

"Brilliant. I don't think I've seen you more than two or three times without that bag slung over your shoulder."

"Exactly, it's going to be a tight squeeze to fit my laptop in also, but it's doable."

In order to check it out, she put her laptop to sleep, folded it and slid, shoved, and shimmied until the computer and picture fit nicely. She slung the bag strap over her shoulder and walked around the kitchen.

"No one will be the wiser. You're doing great at this espionage stuff. Maybe you should become my partner, what do you say?"

She considered him while she pulled her laptop out. Placing the bag, with the painting inside, on the chair. Only when she decided he was messing with her did she answer.

"I think I'll be the perfect partner." He tossed her a surprised look. She smiled, dropped into the chair, and continued. "For this case only. Then it's back to boring shop keeper for me."

"Speaking of the shop, while you were in their sounding like a freight train, I made a few calls."

"I do not snore."

She didn't deem to comment on that one. "Anyway, I found someone to clean up. I will do the glass cases but they'll do everything else. We're meeting them there tomorrow morning at nine."

"Sounds good. What are we doing for dinner?"

The change of subject caught her off guard for a moment, then she heard a loud rumble. She chuckled.

"You must be recovering, because you're hungry. I think maybe I'm a little hungry too." Her stomach rumbled on queue. "Will Finn come home before the game? He said he'd call if he needed a ride."

"The coach usually has them carb up before the game. A few of the boys go to the little mom and pop Italian café by the school and order very large portions of spaghetti. I'm not sure how they eat like that and then go run around the stadium."

"Why don't we join them?"

"What and embarrass our boy by having us show up?"

"Oh, I didn't think of that."

"Glenna, I'm joking. Let me get ready and we'll stop on our way to the game."

He stood with effort and then look down at her. "We'll be taking your laptop, if they're watching it will be the perfect opportunity to come snooping."

"What about Horace and Agnes, you don't' think they'll hurt them."

"As much as the animals will hate it, we should probably kennel them for the night."

"They will, but I'd rather them be in a huff with me, than the buggers hurt the furry kids."

She pushed away from the table. She was sufficiently out of the mood to work, she snapped the laptop shut and did the shimmy to shove it into the bag again. He'd barely reached the kitchen archway when she glanced up and caught him watching her.

"What?"

"I think you're the most beautiful woman I've ever known."

"I thought that would be your ex."

"That porcelain woman couldn't hold a candle to you."

He walked back to her and pulled her into a hug, with only one small wince. "In case, you've got any crazy thoughts in your head that you have competition for my heart."

He dropped his lips to a breath away from hers, she felt the words more then heard them. "You *are* my heart."

Just a tender graze at first turned into a heated tangle of tongues. The air stilled, her heart pounded against her ribs in rhythm with his. For the first time in she didn't know how long she felt safe, loved, and home.

There *was* such a thing as love at first sight.

"Oh man, get a room!" They both started apart like guilty teenagers. "Horace is watching, you're going to traumatize the poor guy."

She barely had enough room between her body and Patrick's to put hand to heart. "Jeez, did your dad teach you how to sneak up on people. You scared the living daylights out of me."

Finn chuckled and shook his head. "Kids, do I need to have the *talk* with you?"

"We weren't expecting you home." Patrick ran a hand through his ginger hair, leaving it with a rakish look. Glenna saw his hand shook and knew she wasn't the only on rattled with the connection or whatever it was that had happened when his lips touched hers.

"That was obvious." Then he turned his attention to Glenna, she felt the burn roll up her neck over her cheeks. "Weren't you supposed to be making sure he was resting?"

"Aw…"

This time he threw his head back and laughed. "I'm just messing with you, Glenna. It's going to be awesome around here."

He took a few steps to where they both seemed rooted to the spot and threw an arm around both of them and pulled in. "Group hug."

Glenna stepped into the hug and put her arms around her two men. That was the moment that no matter what the next week brought, she knew she'd spend her life with Patrick and Finn.

"Dinner?" Finn asked.

"Your dad said you carbed up with the team. We were going to meet you at the café."

Glenna went to the fridge to check the ingredients, she could throw together a descent pasta dish. When she straightened she realized two things, Patrick hadn't moved and he looked as if he been poleaxed.

"You okay, Dad?" Finn beat her to asking.

Only then did he seem to take in what was going on around him.

"I've always wondered what it would be like to have a family."

"What? I'm your family." Finn ruffled the dog's hair. "Come on Horace, let's get you fed."

Patrick still didn't move, but watched his son leave the room. Then his eyes followed Glenna's movements as she tossed a salad. Patrick had talked about her and his heart and the big fiancée plan and making it real. She had an idea the full impact of the change in his life had just hit him.

Glenna divided her attention between the man who seemed to be running over the meaning of his life and throwing together a nutritious meal for an active growing boy. And then it struck her. She was a Mom. Her life was forever changed.

In a good way. She grinned. Life was good. She let Patrick have his space. Set the table even though she needed to walk around him, in the process. By the time Finn returned, dropped his bag next the kitchen door dinner was ready. She placed the salad in the middle of the table and Finn grabbed the bowl of pasta and placed it next to it.

"Dinner's ready dad. Dad? You alright? You haven't moved, you turn into a statue or something?"

Patrick blinked looked around as if being in a daze for a month. He finally moved, but it wasn't to take a seat as Glenna expected. He took two steps until he was between the two of them. As Finn had earlier he placed an arm around both of them and pulled in.

"You two are the most important people in my life. I promise that I will keep you both safe." He dropped a kiss on both of their foreheads. "Thank you. Now let's eat."

And he let them go and took his seat.

"Jeez Dad, I'm too old to be kissed by my dad." He wiped his forehead off, but Glenna could tell, the boy was touched by his dad's gesture.

"You eat up, Finn. You need your energy for the big game tonight." Glenna settled into her chair and dished up a portion of salad and passed the bowl to Patrick. "Patrick you'll have to give me a brush up on the game, I haven't been to one since high school."

"You went to the games?" Finn asked.

"Don't talk with your mouth full, Son."

"I was a cheerleader. Mostly I had my back to the game. But I remember a thing or two."

"Rebekah is a cheerleader also. She said we have the game in the bag."

Patrick chuckled. "She have a crystal ball or something?"

"No, her friend goes to the other school and she said their team sucks."

Glenna grinned and then realized both the guys had on a red tee with black lettering an A and C interlaced for American Canyon High School. She looked down at her green blouse.

"Either of you have a school shirt I can borrow?"

Patrick was about to say something, but Finn jumped up, two moments later he came in and handed her a black tee with the lettering in red.

"Dad shrunk it and I can't wear it anymore."

Patrick just grinned and shrugged as if *to say what can you do?*

And so the meal went until they'd cleaned up. Before long, the animals were kenneled and they were in the car on the way to the big game. All in team colors and flying high on team spirit. As they passed Fortworth lane, she glanced over and sure enough the same van was parked where it had been earlier.

"Oh, I forgot." Glenna said.

"What?" Patrick didn't take his eyes off the road.

"I was going to call Beckworth and let him know about the van, and ask him to check on the house."

"What van?" Finn wanted to know.

Silence followed his question for so long, Glenna didn't think Patrick was going to answer. But then he frowned and tossed a look in the rearview mirror to see Finn.

"Glenna noticed there was a van similar to the one those guys had the other day. They were just down the road this morning when she took you to school."

"They were still there when I went to the store and though they'd moved by the time I returned they were still watching."

"Glenna has the art in her bag."

"What? Is that safe?"

"Safer than leaving it at the house while we're gone."

"That's why you kenneled the animals."

Patrick nodded. "Don't worry about Beckworth and Jones, I called while you were changing earlier to let them know we'd had company all afternoon. They're going to send a few patrols throughout the night."

"They're not going to break in the front."

"Yeah, Dad. I would bet they go the back way." Finn lifted a shoulder. Placed a hand on the front seat to lean forward as best he could in a seat belt. "I told

Rebekah to try and be positioned in front of you guys. You both better cheer loud."

Subject officially changed, Glenna felt a wave of relief. Tonight she'd think about the game and be a part of the family. She knew that Patrick's parents would be there, she imagined they would all sit together in a show of support.

Several minutes later, her hunch was proved right. The McGinnis' had saved their seats. It seemed they'd been running later than she thought because Finn barely had time to run off and change to be on the field and the game was underway. Game Time!

Memories of another time in Brooklyn washed over her. She hadn't realized how much she missed home. Oh, she was going to enjoy this.

Chapter Eighteen

Patrick kept his attention divided between the game and scanning the area for something out of place, like four men in black. Though he knew they'd have no reason to confront him or Glenna in such a public and crowded area. Didn't mean there weren't there. He wouldn't know them if he saw them without their ski masks. Jostled out of his thoughts, he grinned.

Glenna jumped to her feet, cupped her hands like a cone around her mouth to help the sound carry and yelled at the top of her lungs. "Are you freakin' blind? 57 grabbed his facemask!"

His mother leaned back and smiled at him. "I like her."

At least his parents seemed to be taking their coupleness at face value.

"It's a good thing you do," he said.

Before his mother could reply, Glenna had plopped into her seat with a disgruntled, "Dumb officials."

"I say that every game, dear." Kendal leaned forward to answer.

Patrick smiled, Glenna was thoroughly engrossed in the game. That warmed his heart. He wished he didn't have to keep on the alert for anyone suspicious.

"Don't let them ruin the game. This is Finn's night." Glenna had placed a hand on his leg. "Don't..."

Glenna jumped to her feet again. "Go American Canyon!"

Patrick saw the rest of the play. A touchdown. AC seventeen, the opponent six. The rest of the game went by fast. Glenna made sure he kept his attention where it should be.

His mother grabbed Patrick's arm as she stood. "Come on."

The four of them started toward the field looking for Finn in the melee of American Canyon students who'd stormed the field after the game. They were also currently trying to pull the goal posts down in a victory celebration. There was his boy, pride rushed over him. So tall and handsome in his dirty uniform. He'd played hard.

"Dad, Glenna, Nanna, Móraí," Finn called out.

He rushed toward them. He launched himself at Patrick, knocking him a step back.

"We're going to the championships."

He hugged his grandparents, then turned to Glenna. "I'm so glad you were able to come tonight. Especially now."

"Why now?" Caroline asked but his mom had a smile as if she knew what was coming next.

"Because Glenna is going to be my mom!" As he said it he drew Glenna in for a one armed hug. "Isn't that awesome."

"I'm so psyched about winning, I just have something to say. Dad you know I love you, you've been both mother and father to me, and Nanna and Móraí have always been there for me. I have always had food on the table, a roof over my head. I'm getting a great education at American Canyon High, they have wonderful instructors. And if that isn't enough, now I'm blessed to have the best woman stepping in to be my mom. I've had a good life."

Patrick thought his chest was going to burst with pride. Glenna's and his mother's eyes, glistened, and his dad was about to pop with the same pride.

Finn had kept his arm around Glenna's shoulder and took the opportunity to turn her and begin to lead the way to the parking lot. Patrick took a step to follow and froze. To the side of the vehicles stood four men, though it was still a good distance away, even without the masks, he'd known their body types and builds. After all he'd spent some quality time having the shit beat out of him by them.

After a moment Glenna halted their progress and looked over her shoulder at him.

"Patrick, are you coming?"

He glanced at her, seeing that she was watching him in puzzlement. Then he looked past her and realized his parents were almost to the vehicles and thank God the four men had disappeared. They'd made sure he'd seen them though.

He managed a small smile for Glenna. He took two steps to her threw an arm around her so she was sandwiched between him and his son. "Let's go home and celebrate young Finn's win."

"Your parents said they're tired so they're going on home. Though they did make me promise to drop by before we leave."

"Okay," Patrick answered absently.

"What?"

As much as he wanted to keep her in the dark, he'd promised not to, and Finn needed to know. In fact, maybe he could miss one extra day of school and not go back until they were back from New York, the plan was to have everything resolved and he'd be safe.

"What are you thinking about so keenly?"

He sighed. "We'll talk at home and I'll explain."

She was plainly puzzled. After all, in her mind nothing had happened on the case since they'd left the van watching the house.

The drive home was a jumble of noise from Finn, as much as Patrick tried to pay attention, his mind kept going back to the four.

He'd most likely be making a call to Glenna's brother and or sister.

"Dad, look the van is gone."

Finally something that Finn said startled him out of his musings.

"I hope we don't find a mess at home." Glenna kept looking down each street or into each field as if they'd be parked in the middle of one.

"No, Beckworth would have called us."

"If they actually did their job." Glenna turned in her seat to look at him. "They're not the brightest stars, you know."

"Yeah." Finn agreed from the back.

Patrick told the two to wait in the car a moment. He walked around the house to make sure nothing was out of place. He checked the ground under all the windows. Nothing disturbed. He held up a hand to intake they needed to wait a bit longer while he checked the interior, though he didn't expect to find anything.

When they entered, Glenna went straight to the table to pull her laptop out without damaging the frame and art that she didn't want to remove.

"Where's Finn going?" He asked as the boy rushed by him.

"He's letting the kids out of their kennels."

A bark and a loud hiss followed Glenna's words. Louder was the crash and then Horace shot into the kitchen faster than she'd ever seen him move, Agnes hot on his tail.

Finn wandered in a second later. "I think they had words. They were staring daggers at each other when I went in to let them out. Man, they're just like siblings."

He shook his head in wonder. Then pinned his dad with a stare, the likes of many Glenna had seen from his father.

"You didn't hear a word I said about the game."

Glenna glanced between the two men. "I think your dad has something to tell us."

She stood and went to the coffee pot, seemed like they were going to need something with caffeine.

"Glenna is correct, have a seat and I'll tell you what I have learned."

"When?" Glenna and Finn chorused.

"From the game."

"What?" Again the question was chorused.

"I saw the four in the parking lot after the game. They were gone by the time we got to the cars."

"What?" another chorus.

He frowned at her as she placed the cup of coffee in front of him. "If you two would stop interrupting me, I'll explain."

Glenna patted Finn's shoulder as she passed behind him to her chair. She sipped, not saying a word. Finn sipped his hot chocolate, which he'd made himself in the microwave.

"Anyway, since they were there, they weren't here, which is why the place hasn't been ransacked." He turned to Finn and the love that shown warmed her heart. "And I have a dad thing going on, meaning I've learned over the years to hear the important things my son has to say, even if I'm also mulling over a case."

Finn gave him a skeptical look, then grinned. "If you say so, Dad."

"Really? You regaled us on how your catch was the pivotal moment of the game." He held up his hand to interrupt whatever his son was about to say. "To which, I full heartedly agree. I'm very proud of you son."

Patrick paused a moment to beam at his son, Glenna's heart melted a little more.

"As I was saying, there was something about the four. It was obvious they were watching us. In plain sight. Safe in the thought that they were wearing masks I wouldn't recognize them. But I memorized everything I could about them as the four of them were beating me to a pulp."

Glenna shuddered at the image his words brought to her mind. She reached for her phone. "I'm calling Reagan."

Patrick hissed out his breath. "Good, I thought you were going to call Beckworth and Jones."

"I'm pretty sure we've established the pair of them are rather worthless, Dad."

Patrick laughed.

"It's on speaker."

"Do you fucking know what time it is?"

Glenna, winced. She'd forgotten. "Sorry, Reagan, I didn't think. We have a break in the case. Oh, and Finn's here."

"Glenna, I've heard the F word before." Amusement laced Finn's words.

"Sorry Finn. So what is up?" The next words were muffled as her sister apparently told her husband who'd been rude enough to call in the middle of the night. *"It's Glenna."*

"I believe, and it's not just a hunch, I'm all but ninety-nine percent sure we saw the ring of art thieves or gang whatever they call themselves."

"You believe, not just a hunch? Did you see them or not. I thought they all had ski masks on."

"They did, but they couldn't mask their body builds, height weight all that, if you know what I mean. When someone is coming at you with the intent to kill or maim..." Glenna heard his indrawn breath. "...you remember the every detail about your attackers."

"Agreed. Where did you see them?"

"Finn's regional final football game."

"What? Why would they be there? They just showed up out of the blue?"

Patrick waved her to let him speak, he ran through the events since the hospital, or rather the van's close proximity to everywhere they went.

"At first I didn't notice them. As we walked toward our cars I noticed these four guys were just standing there staring at us. So I stared back and took in their stances, builds, etc. The fact activity played out all around them, yet they were focused on our small little group as we neared. I felt fear in my gut that my family was going to be hurt. I glanced to Finn to answer a question when I looked back to where they'd been seconds before, they were gone. For a moment I thought I'd imagined seeing them. Until I saw the ever present van peeling out of the parking lot."

"Oh, I saw that. I meant to mention it," Finn said. "By the time we got to the car though, I had already forgotten—lost in the moment of winning I guess."

"Don't worry about it, Finn, it sounds like the vehicle has turned into a fixture, which is what they want. They want all of you to know they're watching and become so blasé about them, so it's no longer a distraction. They want to throw you off then they can sneak in and snatch the painting."

"My thoughts exactly."

"Now if we could put names to their builds."

And then sounding like he was moving around as he spoke, Paco said, *"there were four of them when you were jumped the other day?"*

Glenna felt bad, it was so late, or early in the morning in D.C. where Reagan and Paco lived most of the time. He was probably making coffee.

"Yet there were only three during the break in."

A pause. Reagan must be thinking. That always boded ill for the bad guys. Glenna grinned. Patrick gave her a curious look but didn't comment. Instead he answered Reagan, though it was more a statement.

"Yes, one of the four that day was short, a little chubbier and definitely not an exercise buff of any kind. I think he was probably the driver the night of the break in. He was also the coward who held my arms."

"He held your arms, Dad? What a bas..." Finn chanced a look at Glenna. "What scum. You could have been killed."

"I have two strong legs, and I used them to my advantage, with him as leverage." He had been staring at the phone as if he could see Reagan and Paco. Now he looked his son in the eyes. "I'm fine."

For a full minute the two stared at each other. What was conveyed between the two, could only be the connection between father and son.

"Did Beckworth ever come up with area surveillance around Glenna's shop?"

Paco's question broke the silence. Glenna started, she hadn't even thought about street cameras. She'd been too upset about Alex.

"When he took my statement at the hospital he said the parking lot between Effie's and Glenna's camera angle focused more on the lot than the rear entrance of either establishment. There were three men in black that approached from the west but then went out of range."

"Doesn't give us anything new, what about on the street?"

"No, they entered the lot as if they'd crossed from the side street on the opposite side of Lincoln Avenue."

"Where there are no cameras."

"The city council voted to have them on the main road where all the shops were. It would be a waste of tax payers' money to put them on the side streets." Glenna shrugged at her phone. "Calistoga is small, sis."

There was a sigh on the other end. *"They probably stayed in their black garb anyway."*

"True. I've been thinking. They have to know art. The website for *Blackmans House* has pictures from past events. I plan to go over them with Patrick and see if he recognizes anything about the men maybe come up with some names for you. Then you can add them to your list of things to look for on the dark web and see what you can find."

"They're not going to be using their real names, Glenna. What I don't understand is, it takes a lot of money to just hang around here. Food, lodging, rental van. They have to be rich so why are they stealing art? Or is taking the pieces that lucrative?"

"The *Madonna and child* is priceless, Finn."

"Even so, you'd be surprised what the rich do. Some may have a lot of money, but they've extended themselves so much that when the economy takes a dip they find themselves scrambling. On the other hand they have all that money can buy, but they crave excitement. The more dangerous the better. Most turn to

*extreme survivalist stuff like Bear Grylls. Maybe art
theft is their excitement," said Paco.*

"We're looking for four rich spoiled playboys, out
stealing art for fun?" Glenna couldn't fathom the idea
Paco suggested.

*"Pretty much. Once you two get us some names we
can run with them, even if you don't I've set traps out to
flag any mention of the piece on the Dark Web."*

"I'll have them, if possible, for you in the morning.
And by the time we arrive Wednesday morning we'll
have a plan," Patrick said.

"I thought you were coming in on Tuesday?"

"We're taking the redeye Tuesday night. We'll be
in Brooklyn around five in the a.m." Glenna felt tired
even thinking about it. She could never sleep on a
plane.

Glenna caught Finn yawning, the poor kid had
had a few long emotional and physical days. She stood
and placed a hand on his shoulder.

"Come on Finn, off to bed with you. We'll fill you
in first thing. We've got a full weekend ahead."

"I'm fine, really."

"Son, Glenna is right. You need your sleep, and
we're almost through here. I'm going to need your help
in the morning."

Glenna called Horace and followed Finn into his
room. The cat followed, she eyed the dog, raised her
head and turned and disappeared into Glenna's room.
Snobby cat.

"Finn, I promise we will keep you up to date with
everything. I think your dad is going to need your
help." She held up her hand. "I know that's what he
said just to placate you to go to bed, but I *really* think
he is hurting more than he lets on. The plan is this,
you and I will be one step of head of him the rest of the
weekend."

Finn grinned. "Deal."

Glenna returned to the kitchen in time to hear the
last of the conversation between Patrick and her sister.

"In light of the fact the culprits are watching our every move, I would rather Finn not go anywhere on his own, like school. I don't have a list of who can or cannot take Finn out of school."

"I thought that was mandatory? I know it is at Gabby's school."

"This is a laid back area. It probably is mandatory and no one bothers to enforce it."

"I agree, missing Monday and Tuesday is a good idea. I'm sure you've already talked to his teachers for his school work while he's in Brooklyn."

"I was planning to do that on Monday, I'll just tell them he's out until we return. It's late. I apologize for the late night or should I say early morning call? We'll talk again tomorrow. Glenna and I will check on her cottage and the shop, then bring you up to date on any developments."

Good nights and good mornings were offered all around and the connection went dead. Glenna raised a brow at Patrick, he had the same *what now* expression. She figured more coffee was in order. She knew he wouldn't sleep until they had scoured the events page on *Blackman's* Site.

"The search will be much faster if we do it together. You do your connections, I'll do the traditional and Google anything or one we find on the Site."

She grinned as she busied herself finding a snack to go with the coffee. Something that wasn't chock full of empty calories, she was feeling the effects of not exercising.

"God, I'm feeling out of shape," Patrick said. "Make it something healthy."

He was reading her mind again and she felt a sense of family. They had a lot to do over the weekend. She took a deep breath as she pulled some things out of the fridge. Sometime during the last twenty-four hours she'd stopped thinking of their coupleness as of a trial. She would wait until all this business was over before filling him in.

She wanted to make sure this time.

She placed a plate of mostly fruits with a few crackers and cheese on the table, then refilled their coffee. After she logged on, she looked over the top of her laptop at Patrick.

"Now that we have somewhere to search or at least a lead, no matter how far-fetched it seems, I feel we're at least in a little control." She tapped a couple of keys until she reached the search engine.

His brows drew together. "There is something about one of them, I wasn't close enough to really *look* at their faces but one of them was familiar. And whatever it is, is so close I swear I could taste it."

"I hate when that happens. Bitter taste."

She sipped her coffee and got to work.

"Bingo!"

Chapter Nineteen

Patrick had been trying to figure out why one of the men looked so familiar. While she worked, he'd searched his computer for clues. When he'd been about to throw his hands up in defeat the answer almost jumped out and hit him over the head.

He loved to startle her. She almost jumped out of her seat and the little squeal sent tingles of the dangerous kind up his spine. He grinned at her. She was so cute. It had been so quiet the only sound the tick of the wall clock. How long had they sat both lost in concentration?

She had her hand over her heart. "What?"

"Airline."

She didn't answer, just gave him a tilt of the head and one raised brow as if to say *continue.*

"You know the major airline in the UK?"

"Branson Airways?"

"Yes, that's where he comes from. Raymond Branson. I have to admit I have always had a fascination for airplanes of every kind. I've seen his picture enough times to recognize him." He looked back to his screen and read. "'Branson founded the airlines in 2005 and began operations in 2008. The young man was only 30 when he started his endeavor. And at 42 he's now one of the richest men in the world'."

"And he's part of an art ring?"

He lifted a shoulder. "I'm pretty sure he wouldn't deem to be anything but the leader. As your sister said, he must be in it for the thrill. He certainly doesn't need the money."

"Wow." She tapped on her computer a moment, then her eyes widened. "Listen to this. 'Branson CEO of Branson Airways made a large contribution to the Louvre's renovation of the galleries devoted to the northern European paintings from the 17th to the 19th century."

"All of a sudden it doesn't seem so unbelievable."

She continued to read but shook her head in the negative. He felt that thrill when a case was coming together, getting close to the end when he could tie it up in a neat package and hand it over to his superiors.

He glanced above her head at the clock, three in the a.m. "Glenna, if we're going to clean up your shop and do everything else on our to-do list, we better catch some shut eye."

She held up one finger. "There was a gala for the kick off of the renovations. Branson was there. There's several pictures."

"I would imagine there would be if he was a *large contributor.*"

She stared at the screen. He didn't think she was going to say anything more, but as he was about to move from the table her words halted him. Her eyes went wide. "I know these guys. Even Raymond, I hadn't paid much attention to him tonight. But yeah I recognize him, and there are three couples with him. I've seen all of them at several art functions in New York."

He scooted his chair around so he could see her screen. "Which ones?"

She pointed to a blond beach boy type. "That's John or Jim, something that starts with a J, I think, Lewis. He's big in investments on Wall Street. His wife is some supermodel from *Victoria Secrets*. Man, her dress must have cost more than I make in a year."

He could believe that, the woman sitting next to him was a knock out. Then Glenna pointed to a guy with totally opposite coloring, more Italian, dark eyes, skin, and hair. The woman next to him had flame hair, another beauty.

"That's Monroe Dyson, I'm sure you know what family he's from. And his wife is an Eisenhower from money in New York. And Edwardo Bertarelli. He's in pharmaceuticals. I don't know much about his wife. I know her name is Karen and I've spoken with her on a few occasions. Very nice."

"Study the people at all the tables in this picture. The occupants all look slightly bored. Except at the table with Raymond and these three couples, they clearly have a history."

Glenna was quiet as she did as he suggested. Then she nodded. "There were three in black that night. And the fourth guy was probably the driver they had waiting. I would bet my last dollar the four men at that table are our thieves. Something else, they're a perfect foil for each other. One's dark, one's light, one's ginger, and Raymond is a perfect blend of each. It's sort of *Stepford Wivesish*. Creepy."

He chuckled. "Yeah, creepy. We better get to bed."

He wiggled his eye brows at her, she just grinned back. They both logged off, then he stood and pulled her up with him, and the momentum, as he'd intended, brought her into his arms. The impact caught him by surprise. His throat closed off with emotion. He'd *never* felt this way since Finn was born. The immediate love of his son had almost brought him to his knees. And now this small dark, with the delectable streaks, haired woman did the same. He wasn't sure what to do, he had made her a promise that he wouldn't seduce her during their trial period. He wasn't sure he was strong enough.

He lifted one hand to her cheek and bent his head slowly until he could look into her deep green eyes. He swore there was love there, just as he let his lips gently rub over hers. He kept it light and easy. Or would have if she hadn't run her hands up his back and pulled him in, efficiently taking control.

God. He opened his mouth to her and lost himself in her. He bent, placing one hand under her knees and as he started to pick her up his body screamed at him to stop. Talk about a shocking dose of reality.

About the same time, she pushed with one hand, and brought one of her legs to the floor and awkwardly crawled out of his attempted romantic *carry the woman off to bed* move.

They both straightened, chests heaving trying to catch some air. He didn't want to admit it, but she probably saved him from a trip to the ER. Best to keep it light.

"If I weren't so beat up, I'd pursue this and continue on to bed. But missy, you're safe tonight."

She gave a mock pout. "Damn!"

*****

She yawned, such a long big one her jaw popped. She rubbed a hand over her cheek as she entered the kitchen. Had she even slept? She'd tossed and turned all night thinking about what might have happened if Patrick's injuries hadn't reminded them in a brutal way that he was *far* from healed. Love. She knew she saw it in his eyes. She wanted to tell him that this farce of a trial was just that, because as far as she was concerned... They were a couple.

A few more things had to be cleared out of the way before she could let him know. The biggest obstacle had been dealt with, she had come to terms with his baggage as he had hers. Patrick saw Glenna for who *she* was. No more comparison between her and Joyce.

That left two obstacles. One, his law enforcement, but she was *slowly* coming to terms with the fact she and Finn together could get through any worry. Two, the last obstacle, Raymond and his small ring of bandits.

She sighed. Since she'd returned from New York and her sting at the altar, it seemed as if life had gone into hyper drive. As if it had been years and not just a few weeks.

The sausage sizzled, she stirred the eggs to make them fluffy, and with her other hand she pushed the toaster lever and the bread dropped into the slots. Finn reached over her to try for a mushroom sautéing in the small pan. As usual he'd caught her by surprise and she dropped the spatula into the eggs.

"I am so going to have a heart attack one of these days if you guys keep creeping up on me." She smacked his hand, rescued the spatula, and used it as a pointer. "Sit. Breakfast will be done soon."

"What's in line for today?"

She thought about it for a moment, but as she was about to answer Patrick walked in and did it for her.

"Several things, one is going to Nanna and Móraí's to bring them up to speed about our trip to New York. They may also have a few questions concerning that statement about Glenna being your mom, after all we're only supposed to be a trial couple."

The boy's eyes widened. "I'm sorry, it just sort of slipped out. Besides, I don't think either one of you are still thinking of it as a trial couple anymore."

Patrick grinned, and Glenna swore his hand started to reach out as if it longed to ruffle the boys' hair. He'd probably done that when Finn was younger. Now though, it probably wouldn't go over so well.

"No, but we promised we would visit. Though we will probably need to go to *Glenna's Surprisingly Vintage* first." He glanced at his phone in his hand, then shoved it in his pocket. "We need to hustle after we eat. The cleaners will be there at nine."

"Don't we have to find a place for the picture?" Finn asked.

"That is on the agenda also."

"I have an idea about that." Glenna served the plates all around. "I'll fill you two in on the way."

Patrick frowned at her. "You know, you're not here to serve us. We are capable of helping."

"I know, but I'm enjoying having someone to cook for. It's boring and I really don't cook that much when I'm on my own. So humor me and enjoy it while it *lasts.*"

Her last word seemed to placate him because he grinned and got down to the business of eating. He seemed to move a little better. She wondered if he'd gotten any more sleep than she had, his eyes did look a little shadowed and heavy, as hers felt.

It seemed like only minutes after they'd climbed into the 4Runner that they were pulling into the parking lot at the shop. Before they could even turn off the engine, Effie blew out of the Bistro's front door in a blur of, Glenna wasn't sure, but it seemed a combination of orange, pink and bright green.

"What the hell is that?"

"Language, son. That's Glenna's person."

"Her what?"

"I'm sitting right here guys. Ask Rebekah, she'll know what that is."

Finn shrugged and pushed his door open. Glenna did the same, as the ball of colorful energy launched herself into her arms.

"Glenna. It's been ages. I swear it has anyway." She stepped away and looked at Patrick. "And how are you, handsome?"

But before Patrick had even started to replay, Effie had turned her attention to Finn, he returned her stare warily.

"And you must be Finnegan."

"No one calls me that."

Effie raised her brow. "Finny it is then."

"Ack, no one would dare call me that."

Effie put her hands on her hips in Glenna's strong woman stance, except it looked more like a demanding child on her friend.

"I *dare*. Now come on Finny and parents, let's go meet the cleaners and get this show on the road. And I want nothing left out as you explain to me what is going on."

Glenna reached for Patrick's hand and then followed in her colorful wake. What would she do without Effie? She'd be bored, that was for sure.

*****

Patrick blew some air through his teeth, he hadn't done a damn thing, yet he was exhausted. He was glad they had a few days before they flew off to New York. He needed to be in top form when they set the bait.

He looked out the window of the Bistro as the traffic slithered down the main street of Calistoga. So far, the day had been productive, and now they were in the process of hiding the art. They'd told no one their plan. Glenna had told them on the way that morning that Effie had been with her when she'd bought her laptop case and purchased the same. They were going to do the switch.

Patrick hadn't seen any of the four suspects, but he was sure if he looked hard enough he'd spot the van. Glenna had made it known in her art circle she'd be attending the Gala. She'd also hinted she may have something of value with her.

The original plan would stay the same, let them think they're in disagreement about the art, black market, or to give it back to the country of origin.

"Do you see anything?"

Glenna's voice startled him, luckily he'd just sat his cup down. Finn was fixated on Effie as she moved around the Bistro talking to the patrons. She looked like she belonged in a parade on Main Street *Disney* with the rest of Tinkerbell's friends.

"No, just keeping an eye out. They may have gone back to New York now you've set the ball in motion by posting on your art forum you may have something to share at the gala. But they could be here watching for all we know."

Glenna glanced around. Her gaze pausing on each of the single men in turn. None of them looked like the men they'd seen on line. Most were either fiddling with their smart phone, tablet or on their laptops. Seemed that was the new look of the millenniums.

What ever happened to conversation?

"I've been trying to think of all the times I've ran into them over the years. They've never given me a second glance. Even though I don't come from *money*,

I do run in the same collector groups and belong too many of the same associations. Yet, until I came on their radar with the Madonna and Child I doubt they'd ever heard of *Glenna's Surprisingly Vintage.*

"The one thing I do remember of my impressions is of spoiled, rich, and self-absorbed men, who have nothing better to do than hang at the gym in the mornings and spend their evenings with booze and women, most likely not their wives, and I'm sure gambling. And what bigger gamble than to pit yourselves against the law to steal famous artifacts?"

"You know when we first came to the conclusion Raymond and his friends may be our art theft ring, I've had my doubts but the more we talk it through the more it's not sounding like such an implausible idea. They're bored and this is a hobby for them."

"Exactly."

Finn finally focused on the conversation, or maybe he'd been listening the entire time. "Sounds like some of the spoiled kids at school, the ones who live in the big houses on the hill. The things they do because as they say *there's nothing to do in this valley.* Mostly they tend to do recreational drugs and race their cars out in the sticks where the law won't be around."

Patrick had been about to question how Finn knew these things, then realized it had been the same when he went to school. There were the same social levels as there was in everyday society. You had your street thugs, your middle class band geeks or football jocks, then you had your holier than thou rich who thought they were above it all.

"Can I get you another round?" Effie startled the three of them out of their thoughts. Then she raised her voice to carry over the shop. "Then I'll grab my laptop and we'll go over the mock up ads for the shops."

"Great, because we need to get going. We have a lot to do before I take Patrick and Finn home to meet *The Elders.*"

Effie's eyes widen and she took on an even more elfish aura, if that were possible. "I knew you were taking a trip." She wiggled her brow in a *you know* kind of clandestine way. "You're taking them to the family? Is there something you're not telling me?"

"Actually," Patrick began, but Glenna placed a hand on his arm.

"Let's get our drinks and we'll talk while were looking at the graphics Karen sent you."

They figured if they mixed business with the switch if anyone was watching, they'd think it was just that, business. Glenna had explained earlier that because of their shop proximity they came up with slogans to share cost of ads. Coffee and Art, sort of stuff. They encouraged their customers to stop for a cuppa and then browse the antiques.

Effie paused in indecision, clearly she was curious. She bit her lip and started to walk away, then turned her face squished, the only term he could think of, up in consternation. Then with resolve she twirled in a kaleidoscope of shimmering colors and went to get drinks and the laptop. A few minutes later a chair had been pulled over and drinks and laptops covered the table.

"Before we do anything, I want to hear."

Patrick raised a brow at Glenna. This was her friend, her news. Finn grinned like a fool. He was worried his son would be hurt if Glenna didn't return their love and she walked away when all of this was over.

He'd seen love in her eyes, and he would take the risk.

"Sometime today would be good," Effie said.

Glenna reached around her screen to grab Finn's hand, and then did the same to Patrick with her other hand. She smiled, and his stomach did a little jig when he saw her eyes glisten. Her throat worked with emotion, and he knew where her heart was concerned, he needn't have worried.

"We're going to be a family."

"Shut the front door!" Effie's voice could probably be heard at the nation's capital. "You mean the two of you are getting married?"

"And she's adopting me!" Finn added.

Which was the first either Glenna or Patrick had heard that. Not that the thought hadn't woven its way through his thoughts. After all, Joyce had never been his mother and never would be. He needed a mother.

"That's exactly what it means." Even though they were still doing the couple trial might as well starting thinking in larger terms.

"Oh, I'm so happy for you."

Effie slid out of her chair to give Glenna a hug and then she put her arm around Finn and gave him a kiss on the cheek, and his face flushed. Effie gave him a hug also, her small arm barely able to cross his back. The other patrons were starting to take notice, and he wasn't sure if that were a good thing. Though they were prepared for the *switch* to be seamless, the less attention the better.

"When you get back from *The Elders* let's do lunch."

"We may have to have a picnic at the shop, it's opening the day after we return."

"Have you had any calls from the ad for an assistant?"

"Not yet, but it's only been a few days. I hope to have someone by the time I get home. The marvel of cell phones, you can be anywhere to conduct business. I'll have to do phone interviews."

"If you'd like, I could conduct the follow up interview with anyone you like." Effie sipped her, whatever the foamy concoction was. "Let's decide on an ad, then I better get back to work, the place is filling up for our busy hour."

Finn and Patrick talked a bit about the upcoming trip while Glenna and Effie busied themselves looking through the graphics. He knew when they found something, they both gasped at the same time and said, "This one."

"That was easy, no discussion or anything," said Finn. "Man. No two girls at my school can *ever* agree on anything, it is so annoying."

Patrick wasn't sure if he needed to be concerned about Finn's interest in girls or not. The last little while his son had been talking a lot about the opposite gender, in particular his friend Rebekah. Was he ready for Finn to have a girlfriend? He glanced over at Glenna who was currently busy tapping in an email. His gut jumped and his whole body tightened in wanting.

No, Finn was *not* ready for these feelings. And what? He was sixteen. The age of raging hormones. Good God, Patrick was so *not* ready.

"Okay, we'll let you get back to work, we need to head out." Glenna's voice brought him out of his musings, and he was ready to be pulled from them. He would think about his son growing up later. When they'd wrapped up the case.

Glenna and Effie slid their laptops back into each other's cases, as they were identical and left them on the table. Glenna gave her friend a hug, then Effie, being Effie, gave Patrick and Finn big hugs also.

"Have a safe trip."

Then she picked up Glenna's case and walked to the back.

And Glenna grabbed the other bag went to the car. Switch done and hopefully none the wiser. Effie would put the art in her safe in the back of the store. Safe for now.

Chapter Twenty

"Hurry Finn we've got an hour drive to the airport."

Patrick held the back door open for Glenna she maneuvered past him juggling her carry on, laptop bag, while pulling her big suitcase. She glanced up and saw his raised brow.

"What?"

"We're only going to be gone a week."

She looked at her case, it wasn't that big. "I was frugal with my outfits, and I talked to Jessica and she has a gown for me to wear to the Gala so I didn't have to pack one."

"Well thank heavens for that."

She narrowed her eyes. "Are we being sarcastic?"

He threw his free hand over his heart. "Promise, I am truly grateful. I'm not sure we have room for one more bag."

She paused considering him for a moment. Then just continued to the back of the 4Runner only to find that Patrick had been serious. And he had felt the need to *remind* her they'd only be gone a week. Good grief, what was with all these bags?

"Here let me put those in. You can keep your carry-on in the front seat with you."

Though she knew he meant it as a question, it came more like a statement. While he figured out how to stow her bag, she opened the passenger door and put her carry-on and laptop on the seat, then went to do one last sweep of the house. She passed Finn on the way, his back pack slung over one shoulder. No bag, she glanced back at Patrick staring at the back of the SUV with concentration trying to arrange everything. Finn must have brought out his bag earlier.

Agnes was staying with her second favorite person, if Glenna was still the first, Effie. Agnes seemed to think they were the same species, which Glenna admitted sometimes Effie did resemble a feline. When she wasn't going for the *Tinkerbell* or elf look.

Horace was in the local Doggy Day Care so that Patrick's parents didn't have to worry about him. And he would have other friends to play with. They'd checked on her house after they'd dropped him off. Mr. Grumpy Pants had no new snoopers, as he'd called them, to report.

Glenna wore a smile as she climbed into her side of the SUV. She tossed a look over her shoulder to see Finn already fastened in, his nose stuck in his smart phone tapping away.

She felt Patrick's gaze on her. She turned to him and he grinned. "Ready for our first family vacation?"

"I'd hardly call it a vacation, we're going to be working."

"Yeah, but it is going to be a blast," Finn said. "I get to go to the range with Dad and I am going to meet the famous *Elders*." Apparently, Finn was paying more attention than she'd thought.

"What he said." Patrick pulled out on to the street. "It will be good to see Tyler and Keira, and then there's the range..."

"It must be a guy thing. I see nothing fun about firing guns and hiding around buildings shooting at silhouettes and trying figure out which are good silhouettes and which are the bad ones." She gave a chuckle. "Like, are you a good witch or a bad witch."

She felt both of them staring at her, she turned to Patrick. "What?"

"I'm damn glad you chuckle and don't giggle."

"Yeah, giggling girls are annoying."

"I did giggle."

"No that was a definite chuckle."

"Yeah, chuckle."

She really didn't pay attention whether she laughed, chuckled, or giggled. But apparently she didn't giggle. Which brought her to the thought they were going to New York to catch a ring of rich spoiled men who had a hobby of stealing art and had no apparent qualms of killing if someone got in the way. And they were talking about chuckling.

"Okay, where did you just go?"

"I was thinking that we are embarking on what could be a very dangerous trip and we're making light of things."

"Glenna, that's how you make it through the day. If you didn't find humor and good in the everyday stuff, then you'd never survive. When it's time I'll be focused. But we're on our way to the airport and we're a family." He paused as if waiting to see if she were going to contradict him. "Anyone watching, like the van following us, don't turn, wouldn't know that we're going to New York for anything other than pleasure."

"They're following us?"

Finn answered before Patrick could. "Yeah, they were parked in the same place they were Friday when we saw them."

She inhaled, she could do this also. She'd known they would probably be followed. Having it confirmed caused a ripple of unease to run over her. She was not used to this cat and mouse stuff. How did her family handle it?

Like Patrick.

They found the humor and good in the everyday...

*****

Bags boarded. They settled in the waiting area for their flight, Glenna eased out a sigh of a relief. Part one of their journey down. She reminded herself to think of normal things, and her mind wandered to the other day on the way home from switching the art with Effie. When they'd stopped at Patrick's family home.

His parents hadn't thought anything amiss about their whirlwind courtship, took it in stride as if there was nothing out of the ordinary going on. Their warm

welcome still made her smile. They were excited to
have another daughter they'd said. After Margaret
Kathleen, they'd wanted another child but had never
been *blessed* with one. But then his dad had remarked
how they had barely been able to keep up with the two
they had.

"Now this is what I like to see, a smile on that
beautiful face. What are you thinking now?"

"About your parents. They didn't ask any
questions, just took it in their stride we're a couple."

"Dad did take me aside and give me the talk..."

"Ah, doesn't he realize you already know about
the birds and the bees? You already have Finn."

It was Patrick's turn to chuckle. "A talk about how
women like a little bling."

"Bling?"

"Yeah, Da is always trying to keep with the times
you know. He wanted to know *when* I would be giving
you a ring. I explained that with everything going on, I
hadn't had the chance to pick up one up and when I
was in the hospital I had to ask you then, instead of
doing it as I'd planned."

"As you'd planned?"

"I told him I had planned out a big production.
But the beating made me realize life is too short and I
couldn't wait."

His green eyes returned her stare. She read in
them sincerity and love. Emotion clogged her throat
and she couldn't say anything.

"Hey, let's not cry. I'm not good with crying
women."

She swallowed. "I'm scared."

"I know. We don't know what we'll find in New
York, I'm sure they know you'll be at the Gala. After
all, they've seen you at these functions in the past.
Only they don't realize you know who they are."

"No." She smiled at him and put her hand on his
cheek. "I'm scared because I'm falling so hard for you,
Finn, and the rest of your family. I'm scared I'll mess it
up. And I'll hurt you or I'll be hurt."

"Love's worth the risk."

"Yes."

"Hey guys, could you knock that lovey-dovey stuff off? You're embarrassing the kid here."

Her hand dropped, but warmth spread through her body and she was sure her fair skin had turned an unbecoming shade of puce. The overhead announced their flight, a good time to gather her things. Patrick did things to her that made her forget where she was. The gate area of a very public airport was not the place to have an intimate moment.

Finn and Patrick were two large to curl themselves into middle or window seats, hence the isle seats and Glenna didn't mind the middle. Once everything was stowed it was only a matter of moments before the plane was in order for take-off. They had planned to go through pictures of the four men, who hit the European news often, so all three of them would recognize them.

Although it hadn't been completely confirmed, Glenna had a deep-to-her-core belief the four were who they were looking to set up with their bait.

None of them looked like a criminals but *The Black Cats* were. Reagan had found the name on the Dark Web, though they're real names weren't used, the descriptions and background fit to perfection.

Reagan had found a tidbit about how, at times, they would contact someone who knew the area well to be their driver. Places the men weren't familiar with, Calistoga a good example as all were from the UK.

*****

The flight had gone by in a flash, much to Patrick's delight. He hated flying. He did not have the build that folded comfortably into a business class seat. He leaned his head in and breathed in the scent that was all Glenna, fresh, young, with a hint of berries. He turned his attention to his son who currently had his head back on the head rest, head set on, mouth open slightly snoring.

At least they had been able to sleep. His mind had been too busy going over the plan to get close to the men so they could over hear their discussion about selling the art or giving it back to the country of origin. At least now they knew who to get close to, the problem would be *not* reacting.

When the pilot announced the descent, he nudged the two sleepy heads awake to start gathering their bags, laptops, phones, and anything else. Glenna came awake slowly, her eyes blinked, then slid down again she sighed and snuggled into him again.

Finn came awake instantly stretched the best he could in the confined area, grinned at his dad, ready for their grand adventured.

"Hey, should we just sit here and go to the next destination?"

Glenna didn't move, just hummed deep in her throat, more growl. His gut twisted as desire shot through him. He shifted in his seat, now was not the time to have an erection. Until he'd met Glenna, it really hadn't been a problem. Now however it *popped* up at the most inappropriate times.

Again she stirred and this time she sat up and rubbed her eyes, breathed in deep and finally opened her eyes and gave him a sexy sleepy grin.

"Good morning." Then her brow furrowed. "I slept? I never sleep on planes. I didn't snore or drool or anything did I?"

"Terribly, the entire plane rumbled. And look at my shoulder, it's drenched in drool."

Her eyes widened and shot to his shoulder, before she realized he was joking. She gave him a punch in the arm.

Finn leaned over. "Do I have to separate you two?"

Patrick chuckled, Glenna just leaned over and smiled at him.

At the pick-up curb, bags in tow they found Tyler waiting for them. He grabbed Glenna swung her around as if he hadn't seen her for years instead of weeks.

Patrick waited until he sat her down, then he stepped in and gave his friend a one armed man hug with a thump on the back.

"Tyler meet my son, Finn." Finn shook Tyler's proffered hand.

"Now that we have all your stuff crammed in the back, let's get this show on the road. The *Elders* have a spread ready."

"It's six in the morning." Glenna raised a brow in Patrick's direction. "I can't believe... never mind, I can. It's exactly what Ma would do. Anyone else joining us?"

"Everyone was invited, but when I left the house only Keira, Lucy and I had arrived."

"Lucy?" Finn questioned from the back seat.

"Our daughter she's three going on twenty."

"At least she no longer bites ankles." Glenna chuckled.

Patrick sat back and let the chatter filter around him. He hadn't known he'd been waiting for Glenna his entire life. As soon as they took care of the threat against her, he could make her his and they'd be a real family.

Glenna's childhood home was deep in a residential area of Brooklyn, Patrick hadn't known existed. It was one of the larger homes on the block, and it looked well-kept and lived in. He was looking forward to meeting her family, and hearing all the stories. At Quantico, Tyler had been full of them about his childhood. He wanted to hear all about the young cheerleader, Glenna.

They were led into the kitchen the moment they arrived. According to Glenna, this was the hive of the house. Finn looked a little overwhelmed, seemed like the family had arrived.

"Glenna." A woman that could only be her mother enfolded her in a bear hug. Keeping one arm around her daughter she turned. "And you two must be Patrick and Finn."

He held out his hand, but she ignored it and left Glenna and wrapped her arms around him in a hug. "Welcome."

Then to Finn's surprise gave him a bear hug also. "Aren't you the handsome fellow? Gabby, Sophie come meet Finn."

Two giggling teens rushed in from the other room and slid to a stop and cranked their heads back to look up to Finn. He had to be at least a foot taller than both.

"Wow, you're huge."

A tall man stepped forward and placed a hand on the young girl's shoulder. "Sophie, that was rude."

Patrick figured this was David Solomon, Glenna's sister Christine's husband, the man wasn't a small man himself. And the woman standing next to him holding a chubby little tawny head guy must be Christine.

"Facts are facts, my son's from Scottish and Irish stock, he's either going to take after a highlander or a rugby player, both are *huge*." Patrick held his hand out to the man.

Patrick felt as overwhelmed by all the introductions as Finn looked. It was going to take a few days to place the right names with the right faces. Martha, Glenna's ma as she called her, rushed everyone to seats so her breakfast wouldn't cool off too much. The meal was all chatter and chaos and he could see that his son was enjoying himself. The boy was so used to solitary meals with his dad, this must be a novelty.

It was a colorful bouquet of chaos.

Chapter Twenty-One

It wasn't long before Glenna and her sisters were helping their mother clean up, the men left to talk in the living room. Glenna glanced over her shoulder as they left. At the same moment Patrick paused and half turned to regard her. She grinned to reassure him. Her family could be overwhelming, but he'd be fine.

"I like Patrick." Jessica rinsed a dish then placed it in the washer. "Finn is a nice boy."

Christine had been busy clearing the rest of the table, and brought an armload to the sink. Once they were all on the counter she pulled Glenna into a hug.

"I'm so glad to see you happy after that bun boy turned out to be such a..." She stepped away leaving her hands on Glenna's shoulders. "I can't think of a word to call him."

"Gay." Keira piped up leaning a hip on the edge of the table. "He had no intention of marrying her.

"No, he was after my..." Glenna wiggled her brows. "Etchings."

It was so good to be home with her family. They healed her almost as much as Patrick had.

"It's good to see you so happy, I was worried." Jessica looked around the room. "Reagan hasn't changed. If there's dishes to do, she disappears."

Glenna chuckled, that was an understatement. "She's probably in talking strategy with the guys."

Jessica tilted her head in confusion. Glenna hadn't realized that Tyler and Reagan hadn't filled the family in.

Keira shrugged. "We thought it was your place to explain."

By the time Glenna finished filling her mother and sisters, not to mention the little generals who were trying keep the toddlers in check, what was going on in her adventurous life, the kitchen sparkled.

It was time to gather with the male and Reagan portion of the family. And she was ready for the big announcement. She knew she'd pull off the engagement, because to her it had become real when Finn had announced to his grandparents, Glenna was going to be his mom.

"It's about time you guys finished in the kitchen. What did you do, remodel?" Reagan wanted to know.

It was interesting to see how her sisters and sister-in-law bee-lined to their spouses. Glenna settled on Patrick's knee as there wasn't a spare chair in the room.

Lucy played with *Frozen* figurines, chattering, oblivious to those around her. Ben was trying to help his cousin, Freddie, stand using the ottoman for the younger toddler to hold on to, which looked a little awkward as Ben was barely standing himself. Gabby and Sophie were in deep conversation with Finn.

Her family was growing. She hoped to have a little one to play with the cousins before they all grew up.

Where the hell had that thought come from? She'd never even thought about children before. Until Patrick and Finn had barreled into her life.

"Out with it sis." Tyler leaned against the piano. Keira snuggled to his side. "You're regarding everyone as if you have some type of dire announcement to make."

She placed an arm around Patrick's shoulder.

As if feeling Glenna's attention Finn stood, came to stand on the other side of his dad. She glanced around the group. "I was trying to decide if I should share our news or wait for a time when Matt and Bryn are here."

"They're so busy right now. The organizations they work for are going through a large overall. Making sure the security is beefed up and all that. I doubt they're going to have time," Reagan said.

"They send their love, though," Martha added. "Why don't we get them on Skype? Gabby can you grab the laptop from my office?"

"Sure Nana." And the girl was off and returned in only moments.

Love so overwhelming punched Glenna in the stomach. This was what family was.

Matt appeared on the laptop screen, with Bryn slightly behind him. She must be leaning down so their faces were cheek to cheek.

"Hey, what's up?" Glenna's brother's voice filtered over the room.

"Your sister has something to tell us." Her father announced.

No reason to wait, so with no preamble, "Patrick and I are engaged or well we will be after all of this is over."

Squeals from Gabby and Sophie almost deafened the group. Finn squeezed where his hand rested on his dad's shoulder.

Silence. Not what she had expected. She'd thought everyone would be happy. But stunned was the word. Though she couldn't blame them. After all, it wasn't that long ago they'd all been gathered for her wedding to another man.

"You mean, for this case you're working on?" Her dad asked.

"Glenna's going to be my mom." As Finn put his other hand on her shoulder. "I can't wait, it's going to be awesome."

Again, silence. For two minutes and then the little generals looked at each other. Seemed to take Finn's measure, Gabby nodded. She stepped up to him and cranked her head back to look up at him.

"Welcome to the family." Then she lowered her gaze to Glenna. "You *are* going to have your wedding here?"

Bemused Glenna tilted her head at Patrick in question.

"We can have a small party in California after, but Mum and Da would love to visit here for the wedding."

"And Aunt Margaret Kathleen and her family," Finn added.

She returned her attention to Gabby and Sophie who'd joined her cousin. "I guess that will be a yes."

Again the squeal had the adults cringing, and the toddlers giggling. Gabby reached for Finn's hand, Sophie for the other one.

"Come on, we have plans to make."

As the led the boy out of the room, Patrick said to no one in particular. "Should I be scared?"

Jessica laughed. "No, they're our resident party planners. They're already planning what courses to take when they go to college. Business and marketing. I have a feeling they'll take Manhattan by storm when they're older."

Right before Finn rounded the corner out of the room they heard him comment. "There has to be bagpipes and Dad has to wear our family tartan."

Glenna smiled. Her heart was bursting with happiness. She just wished there wasn't *The Black Cats* to deal with. Such a harmless name for dangerous spoiled rich playboys.

Tyler had already noticed a van lurking, must be their surveillance vehicle of choice.

The rest of the afternoon was jam packed with planning what they needed to do before the big event on Sunday. The next day she'd have a girl's shopping day with her sister's, except Reagan who'd be with the guys at the range preparing for battle. Though Glenna couldn't think how that would be needed at a five star hotel function with a bunch of rich art patrons. But what did she know? Friday would be a tourist day, she would be showing Patrick and Finn around her old haunts and all the must sees of Manhattan. Including John Jay College of Criminal justice.

Saturday, the weekend festivities would begin with a brunch at the *Tavern on the Green* in Central Park with local artist's work displayed for sale, which would kick off a swirl of artsy activities going late into the evening with the yearly gala wrapping things up on Sunday late afternoon.

Patrick and Glenna would be staying at the hotel where the event would be held Saturday night, they wanted to be as visible as possible, letting everyone know about the stolen Bellini art. Or to be more precise, let as many people *overhear* them debating the merits of whether to let it go to the highest bidder, or return it for the reward.

There was always the slim chance *The Black Cats* were not the culprits.

It had been a long night and morning. About lunch time, Glenna wanted nothing more than a nap. And as usual, her mother sensed exactly what she needed and drew a halt to the gathering with orders to let the travelers rest.

Patrick returned after going in search of Finn. "He's deep in conversation about our wedding. I hope you didn't have any ideas, because I don't think we get any say in the event."

Glenna giggled and threw a hand over her mouth. "Sorry, I don't think I've giggled since high school, and that was a *giggle* and not a chuckle. I must be more tired than I thought. Come on, I'm going to lay down and rest. And before you say you don't need to, remember even though you look better, you're still recovering."

"Actually, I was going to ask if I could join you." He waggled his eyebrows at her.

"Come on."

She led him to Tyler's old room, she was next door in her old room she'd shared with Reagan. Finn was in the basement in Matt's old room. She opened the door for Patrick and gave him a gentle shove, keeping a hand on the knob intending to shut the door, but he had other ideas.

He grasped her shoulders and pulled her up against his chest, with his hand he reached over her shoulder and closed the door with a small snap.

"Now I have you to myself, finally."

His head lowered, his lips gently rubbed over her lips lasting only seconds before deepening into a tangle of tongues. Moments before, she'd been so tired she'd hardly been able to walk to the rooms. Now all she wanted to do was get her hands under his shirt and feel his strong back under her fingers. She followed thought with action.

His muscles tensed at the first contact of skin on skin. His shirt slid up his back along with her hands and it seemed easy enough to continue and take it over his head and off. Her hands and his head caught in a tangle of fabric.

After a moment of struggle Patrick was free and the erotic moment dissolved into a fit of chuckles. His hands went to her shoulders and he leaned down to kiss her forehead.

"Glenna, girl. I believe we're too tired to follow through with our intentions."

"I have a feeling when I realized I was in Tyler's old room, in my parents' home doing the nasty, it would have been a cold water bucket of wake up call. And besides it's just creepy to even think about, now I'm not in your arms and I can think."

Patrick grinned. "You're right, but just wait."

"What do you have in mind?"

"You'll find out when this is all over." He waved his hand toward the door. "Now go take your nap."

Chapter Twenty-Two

The last few days had been a whirl of laughter and family. With the ever present hint of danger following. Literally. Everywhere they went they got used to having the van in view. Blatant intrusion into their lives, with the tinted windows the occupants couldn't be seen to confirm their identities.

It was all about letting Glenna and Patrick *know* they couldn't do anything without them knowing. If they got on the subway, the vehicle was waiting at the exit. Creepy how they *knew* where they were going.

Glenna wondered if they thought she'd brought the *Madonna and Child* with her. They must have figured out as she had done, it was small enough to fit into her laptop bag.

A knock on her door interrupted her thoughts. It opened before she could answer. Her mother slipped in.

"Glenna, that black van is out front again. They're going to know you're going to that fancy brunch."

"Ma that is the reason we're here. I'm sure they'll be following us around all day as they have been."

"Well I don't like it. It's bad enough I have to worry about Tyler, Keira, Dav... Well you know what I mean. I never thought I'd have to worry about you. I thought I finally had a child who had picked a safe profession, and now look."

Glenna caught her mother in a hug and kissed her on the cheek.

"Ma, I'm pretty sure I'll be back to my safe and boring career soon. It was just a matter of luck or bad luck that I ended up with that picture. I don't think the people who owned it even realized it was an original Bellini or it wouldn't have been in that 'grab box' as it was listed. Besides, have you seen my bodyguard? Patrick? We'll be fine."

Her mom brushed a stray tear away from her cheek. "I better let you get ready, Patrick is already in the kitchen having a cup with Fred."

Glenna smiled. Her family had welcomed Finn and Patrick. She wanted to get this all behind her so she could start her new life. Being with her law enforcement part of the family the last few days, and seeing how well Patrick blended right in, had gone a long way to erase her fears.

Glenna put on the borrowed slim black dress Jessica saved for just these occasions. Classic and she could dress it up or down. As it was brunch in the park she decided to keep it not too dressy, but elegant enough to shout class. She pulled on her strappy sandals, decided to go with silver bangle bracelets, looped earrings and a simple chain with a small emerald in a silver shamrock.

She grabbed her purse and went in search of her date.

For late fall, the weather was perfect for a walk in the park. They'd opted to take a Lyft instead of the subway in their finery. They entered the side gate to Tavern on the Green, the spread of food was impressive as always, as were the art displays scattered around the outdoor patio.

Glenna let herself slip into her art persona. She was in her element, and recognized several people from other events. She hadn't been to the annual weekend event for a few years, but the same people attended. She steered Patrick toward a couple of older women whom she knew to be the gossips of the art community.

They were conveniently browsing the tray of pastries. Glenna angled her body to give her attention to Patrick, but close enough the ladies could hear.

"Really? It's a Bellini, we should put it out on the Dark web. My sister has contacts, can you..."

"Shush, let's discuss this later. Now's not the place." He glanced around as if to see if someone was listening, took her arm and led her to a private area.

Bent his head close. "Keep talking, we've got their attention, they're trying to be sneaky but they're moving this way."

Glenna could almost feel the women approaching, but when the person came into view, it was one of their *suspects*. If they were correct it was Raymond the one Reagan thought was the leader. A shimmer of unease ran through her, though she'd seen the man at these events before. *Breathe Glenna.*

She nudged Patrick. He was good he didn't even blink. The man didn't actually approach them, just stood by the table as if trying to decide what appetizer was the tastiest.

Another ripple of uneasiness raced over her, and suddenly she had the feeling Raymond and his cats saw through their ruse. So what? The important part of the day was to set the trap. With that in mind, she tugged Patrick's arm until he leaned so she could whisper in his ear.

Soft, as if not wanting to be heard, but loud enough their companion could hear, she said. "I believe that is a Bellini over there. It has the same style as..." she let her eyes widen. She took a moment to glance in Raymond's direction. "Let's go see."

"Excuse us." Patrick took her hand and led the way toward the displays.

"I can feel his eyes on us."

"Which one's the Bellini?"

"I was just playing things by ear, just take me to that one over there and I'll pretend to be disappointed."

Though the piece was a gorgeous Venetian, Glenna wasn't familiar with the artist. She picked up the brochure next to it and read the artist was actually a student at NYU studying the style of Giovanni Bellini and similar Venetian artists of the 1400 and 1500's. She'd have to follow him on his social media—his work was magnificent.

"Like it?"

She turned to see a young man standing beside her. "Very much so, is this yours?"

"Yes. I was going to display my attempt at the Madonna and Child I've seen at the Met. Bellini was a little obsessed, there are so many around."

"I've heard one was lost during the war." Glenna saw that Raymond had followed and lingered nearby she let her eyes wander over the crowd looking for the other three.

"There was one in Afghanistan?" The young artist's question brought her attention back to him.

Patrick didn't chuckle, but his words were laced in humor. "Wrong war. The painting was lost during the Nazi occupation."

"Oh, I never was good with history, unless of course it was art. I love the Renaissance period. It's next on my course of studies."

"I must say..." Glenna brought the brochure up to read the name. "Jeremy, you have a raw talent."

"Thank you." He smiled and then spotted someone looking at another one of his painting. "If you'll excuse me."

He half bowed at the waist toward them, then headed in the direction of his other admirers.

"Fake or sincere?"

"What?" Glenna asked.

"The kid, he couldn't have been much older than Finn. He has talent but I got the idea he's trying too hard to be like one of the men he admires so much. He's just a couple hundred years out of his league."

"I thought it was endearing." She stood up on tiptoe and kissed his cheek, then whispered. "Raymond listened to every word. He didn't miss the mention I dropped."

He pulled her up, so her feet actually left the ground and gave her a sound lip smack. "If we're going to make a public display we might as well do it with gusto." Then he lowered his voice. "I haven't noticed his partners in crime."

"Neither..." Across the patio, she saw the others walk in from the little coffee shop in the rear. "There they are now, better late than never I guess."

Raymond noticed his friends at the same time, and made his way toward them.

"You know I've been thinking..." Glenna started.

"Oh, oh. I've come to realize when you start *thinking* things get crazy."

She pressed her lips together to keep from laughing and gave him a bump on the arm. She glanced around to make sure no one paid attention, though just to be cautious she sidestepped them into a corner of the patio with their backs to the perimeter and a good view of the patrons of art.

"We're being serious here. As I was *saying*, I've been thinking. We came up with the plan to lure them with the painting, but that was before... I'm ninety-nine percent sure they know or they are almost certain we have the painting. Do we need to change our plan a little?"

"Good point." He took his attention from surveying the crowd and grinned down at her. "The plan is to move the art to the salon when we get home. Let's drop the hint that you're going to do a one night show of it before we return it to the country of origin, instead of pretending there's a possibility we may seek a high bidder on the Dark Web."

"You're right, I don't think they would buy that. Even if those gossip ladies repeat it." She followed his example and studying everyone. "Oh, since there is *nothing* illegal about contacting the country to return the art, and having a one night reception we no longer have to *whisper* it. Why don't I make an announcement tomorrow night?"

Glenna didn't know if Patrick contemplated the crowd or his answer. After a moment he snaked an arm around her and then said. "Not a bad idea, though I'm not sure we want to force their hand by giving them a reason to get their hands on it before we go home. We're here for few more days."

"What do you think we should do then?"

"I agree we should let people know, just not in a formal announcement. Let's just continue what we planned, just with a different dialogue." He tugged her into his side, kissed the top of her head without taking his attention from the four men he'd been keeping an eye on. "You're excited about your discovery and you want to surprise the public with a showing."

"Oh, I like it." The possibilities flew across her mind. "Let's go, I have some planning and it does no good over here in a corner where no one can hear."

Once again they found themselves in the midst of phenomenal displays of local artists. The talented flocked to New York, making it hard to get noticed. So many choices for the patrons of art.

Glenna loved the energy, the different eccentricities, and the talent. How she'd wished she were as gifted. Whenever this thought crossed her mind, she reminded herself how *talented* she was for finding a home for others' art.

Patrick had a slight frown on his face, most likely trying to figure out the abstract piece he was studying. Before she could tell him her thoughts on the framed chaos of colors, two prominent Californian patrons sidled up to the display next to them. Glenna didn't want to miss an opportunity.

She leaned in, "Patrick, this is what I want to do."

He frowned, she tilted her head back a little and rolled her eyes in the direction of the couple next to them. Enlightenment etched over his features.

"And what is that?" His tone indulgent.

"We could have a reception. One night. Maybe by invitation only. Make a huge deal out of my discovery."

When she saw him try to suppress a grin, he gazed over her shoulder on the couple. She knew she had their attention and pressed on.

"It could be in the center of the display cases. We could serve appetizers and wine." She threw her hand to her chest, trying not to be overly dramatic. "Since the piece was taken from the flak tower in Berlin-

Friedrichshain we could contact Berlin to let them know we have the piece and what we're doing. Maybe we could ask for one of their historians to visit and recount how the painting was lost, and what they've done to locate it."

"Sort of display and lecture on stolen artifacts?"

"You catch on quick for an art novice."

"I have my moments." His tone dry as the desert in the middle of August.

Glenna didn't need to turn, she could feel the heat of their bodies, as they'd edged up almost touching her back. She was in the process of coming up with more to keep their attention when they inserted themselves into the conversation.

"Darling, we couldn't help but overhear a bit of your conversation."

The man placed his arm around his wife. Glenna remembered them from a gallery event in LA a few months ago. "Yes, what did you find?"

Glenna let out a sigh as if she'd been caught with her hand in the proverbial cookie jar. "Oh, I didn't realize you were there. I'm trying to keep it a secret until I have everything organized."

Together as if a single unit, they leaned closer. The woman glanced to her husband then back to Glenna. "We will not say a word. This is just so exciting. Especially since the showing would be close to home."

Glenna hadn't realized they'd recognized her. She didn't need to act flattered. She was. They were moneyed from the Hollywood. He was a producer of some kind. She was far from a movie buff. For all she knew one of the top producers in the industry could be standing in front of her. But she did know that they were huge contributors to the arts.

"You know my shop?"

"*Glenna's Surprisingly Vintage*, of course, I visit whenever I'm in wine country." She paused, a sad look crossed her face. "I was very fond of Alexis. I'm very sorry to hear what happened to her and your precious boutique. Do you know what they were after?"

The conversation had taken a different direction, Glenna didn't know how to respond. Were they involved with *The Black Cats* in some way? Or were they just curious. Usually Glenna wasn't paranoid, but since the break-in, she looked for ulterior motives where there weren't any. Luckily Patrick took the lead.

"We have an idea. It's what we were discussing."

Again the couple inched forward, Glenna swore they were literally joined at the hip. The way they moved in tandem. She'd watched them earlier and had the same impression.

"And what were you discussing?" The man shifted his gaze to encompass the patio area, his eyes narrowed. "Whatever you do, don't let them in on it."

Though Glenna took a quick peek to see who he'd been starring at, their suspects, she still asked. "Who?"

"Branson, Lewis, Bertarelli, and Dyson."

The woman giggled. "He calls them the four musketeers."

Something ran over her. Maybe a combination of dread and excitement, she wasn't sure. She just knew they were closing in.

Patrick pretended he wasn't interested in the four, he didn't even glance in their direction. "We really aren't ready to tell anyone."

"You can trust us," the woman.

Patrick chuckled. "I've learned to do the opposite when someone promises that."

The woman's lip jutted out. "Honestly."

Spoken in a tone that led Glenna to believe the woman wasn't used to not getting her way. Maybe now would be a good time for a lesson. That is, if they weren't trying to spread the tale.

"Come on, Babe. I don't want the news out, but they've been around the galleries, I think they'd be happy to keep our little secret." Glenna tilted her head. "You know, maybe they could help us."

"Yes, yes, yes."

The woman chanted. As she bounced her husband went along for the ride. Glenna blinked. Weird. Twiddle Dee and Twiddle Dumb floated across her mind. So distracted, she started when Patrick cleared his throat to bring her back to the conversation.

"Can I speak with you in private?"

Glenna smiled at the couple. "Give us one moment."

Once they were almost out of ear shot, again the tandem movement as their bodies swayed in Glenna and Patrick's direction. The couple's full attention on them.

"Glenna, we aren't ready to let everyone know about..." he lowered his voice a notch. "...art you've found. We don't want another break in."

Glenna leaned to the side to consider the couple then whispered. "I think they can be trusted to keep it quiet. They've been around the art circuit for years."

This time Patrick twisted to view the couple, currently pretending to have their attention on the young artists' work. He turned back and leaned in to Glenna, lips grazing her cheek to whisper in her ear. "They'll spread the word, exactly what we need."

Glenna turned her head "yes" breathed a second before her lips met his. Before long an intent tango of tongues swept her away until her entire body thrummed with desire.

A moment later, they couple moved closer. "Excuse us." The man's voice broke over them, a tidal wave of cold water.

Glenna swallowed, good lord. How had she'd completely forgotten they were in a very public place. Patrick could make her forget her own name. Yet he slipped an arm around her shoulders and steered them toward the waiting couple as if this sort of thing happened every day.

"Let's take a walk around the park for a moment."

Without waiting for an answer, Patrick led Glenna through the side gate by the coffee shop in the back of the patio area. She felt the attention of the men standing only feet away from the exit. She'd bet they would follow.

Yet when they found their way across the street with the other couple, Glenna realized the men weren't following and the Van was parked not far away and empty for a change.

Unless the other couple was bugged, which Glenna now doubted they had anything to do with the men, they couldn't hear the conversation.

"Okay, what is all this secrecy about?" The man still wedged to his wife's side, asked.

Sticking as close to the truth about her find as she could. She filled them in about the *Bellini Madonna and Child*.

"We are trying to find the agency in charge of the stolen artifacts from Berlin. I'm not sure, but I believe all the countries were victims of the Nazi occupation have organizations tracking down their lost treasures." She grinned up at Patrick. "Meanwhile, I figure I might as well use the art to my advantage. What a great way to introduce more patrons to my boutique?"

The woman was clearly excited, the couple quivered in excitement.

"What are you thinking? I'm the party planner for the art association in our area, I could help."

"Oh, wonderful." Glenna reached for the woman's free hand. "We're thinking of doing a special showing and hopefully have a historian from Berlin visit with stories about all the art that went missing during the occupation."

The woman gave her hand a little squeeze before she let go. Then, miracle of miracles, stepped away from her husband to dig through her purse. She produced a card and handed it to Glenna.

"Here, call me when you have the date set. I'm thrilled to be involved in such a momentous occasion."

They watched the couple sway as one as they sashayed to the brunch still in full swing.

"I sort of feel bad. She was genuinely excited for us to invite her help."

"Why can't you have the showing? It's the perfect trap. We'll have plain clothes everywhere watching their every move, because they will be there. Then Raymond Brandon his ring of thief's will be behind bars. And we'll return the piece to Berlin. It's a great idea Glenna, go for it."

Glenna regarded the card, then slipped it in her clutch. "I think I will."

Chapter Twenty-Three

Glenna flopped onto the bed, not even taking in her luxurious surroundings. Exhausted to her bones she just wanted to sleep until the Gala the next evening. The whirlwind activities of rubbing shoulders with artists and patrons from gallery to gallery ending at the Met ordinarily wouldn't have been so draining. However, the constant awareness of being watched, and keeping alert to watch for anything suspicious had taken a toll.

Her arms stretched above her head she let out a groan, muscles protesting at the pull. She'd just close her eyes for a moment before she got ready for dinner. At least it would be just the two of them and they could relax. She hadn't decided where to take Patrick, it wasn't like he was new to New York, he *had* attended The City University of New York.

Still she'd wanted to treat him to something special. She'd think about it in a minute...

*****

Towel firmly wrapped around his waist, Patrick contemplated Glenna. He rubbed his hair dry. He really didn't want to wake her, actually he did, but not for dinner. Swallowing down his desire he reached for his jeans. He wouldn't listen to objections, they'd order in. Besides it would be nice to be alone with her.

He'd just zipped up his jeans when the beautiful lump on the bed stirred. A soft groan slipped from her lips two seconds before her lids lifted and the green of Ireland pinned him. He sucked in his breath and let it slip out again through his teeth.

"Look at you. I have my own highlander."

She pushed herself into a sitting position. Her gaze traveled from the top of his head to his bare toes, heat sizzling in its wake. He dropped the towel he'd used on his hair. The mattress dipped with his knee. The motion made it easy for him as the object of his desires rolled into him.

In one movement, he reached over so he leaned straddling her in the process, until she lay back again on the bed. Several moments could have been an eternity as he drank in the sight of her. She didn't say anything, apparently content to have his attention. Careful to keep his weight on his knees, and bracing with one hand, he lifted his other to slip a slim black strap off her shoulder. Something he'd wanted to do all day. The little black number she'd been wearing clung to every curve to perfection.

Now all he could do was think about peeling it inch by inch until she was naked under his searching hands. And what was he doing just thinking it. The way she watched him, he was damn sure it was what she wanted.

With that thought in mind, he shifted to his side, then began his journey. The other strap went down, his lips trailing in its wake. His finger hooked in the V of the neck of the dress and pulled it down. God. Braless.

As any red-blooded man would do, he dipped his head and caught a nipple in his mouth. His hand captured her other breast.

*****

Glenna couldn't breathe. All the air had left when his lips and tongue gently caressed then sucked her nipple. When was the last time she'd had any type of intimacy? Years. And this was no one night stand, this was overwhelming.

When she woke and saw him standing over her, towel in hand, bare chested—now she knew the true meaning of a six-pack—his jeans unbuttoned at the top, holes in the knees. She thought she'd gone to highlander heaven.

He was taking her thoughts away with his questing hands and tongue. She remembered saying something about a highlander, but it was lost at the moment.

"You okay?"

His face so close the words had brushed over her lips. Was she okay?

"I'm not sure."

He leaned his forehead on hers a moment then his hand moved from her breast, leaving her skin to quiver in the cool air. Now he cupped her cheek.

"If you're not ready, we can wait."

"I don't want to wait. I'm just scared. I haven't felt like this for anyone before. I've had flirtations, but Patrick, I don't think, I know I love you and I don't want to ruin everything. What happens if I can't make love?"

"Glenna we'll stop whenever you don't feel comfortable. Just tell me." He waited until she nodded. "How does that feel?"

He raised a brow at her. Again he moved his hand, softly running his fingers down her arm.

"Good."

"And this?" He walked his fingers along the fabric of the dress that still lay across her rib cage.

She couldn't say anything. The hum worked its way up her throat and tumbled out in a groan.

"And this?"

He repositioned himself onto his knees and worked the silky black fabric over her hips, his fingers skimming her skin in the process. She heard him suck in air when he realized she hadn't worn any panties. She'd thought about these moments that morning as she'd pulled on her dress over her bare skin. She hadn't wanted anything so much in her life, or been so scared to follow through.

"And this?" His voice low and gruff.

"Indescribable."

He growled and bent his head, his tongue circled and dipped into her navel.

Shivering she pushed him, his look of surprise brought her up on her elbows. She wasn't sure if it actually happened but she tried to raise a brow at him, nodding toward his jeans.

"You're overdressed."

Then he grinned, stood and shucked his pants. She pushed herself into a sitting position in order to have a better view. He'd been sans underwear also. He gazed down at her, standing strong, tall, and full of desire for her. She gulped down the emotion that threatened to overwhelm her. She blinked her eyes to keep the moisture at bay. God, he was the most beautiful sight she'd ever seen.

"Come here." She placed her hands on his hips and pulled him into her.

As he had done a few moments before, she nibbled along his taut stomach relishing in the texture of his skin. Her fingers worked the way around to his fine ass and kneaded.

He placed his hands on her shoulders and gave her a small shove until she lay back on the bed. He waited a moment while she shimmied up to the top of the bed, then he crawled over her. His hands placed on either side of her face, he dipped his head enough to give her a feathered kiss on the lips before moving on to her cheeks, nose, forehead, nothing was safe from his exploring lips.

Sometime during his assessment of her body he'd shifted to the side of her to lay along the length of her. His hands were following along in the wake of his lips. Need settled in the pit of her soul, gripping her with an emotion she wasn't coherent enough to name. She only knew that if he didn't take her soon, she'd wither and die. She'd think about how dumb that sounded later when she could actually think.

When had she fallen in love with him? She knew she'd been on her way and almost there. The emotions running over her in the aftermath of his questing hands stole away her thoughts, and she gladly turned herself over to the sensations.

It took a moment for her to realize he wasn't touching her, she opened to eyes to find him looking down at her with a tenderness that made her heart ache with want.

"I didn't..." he sucked in air. "...come prepared."

"What?" Her mind refused to work. A moment later it dawned. "Oh, it's been so long. I'm safe."

He placed his hand on her stomach, her skin quivered and her muscles tightened. She had to press her legs together to still the need.

"I'm... not... sure I can stop."

"It's up to you." His arms vibrated holding himself to look down at her. "I'm clean also. Of course, I have been waiting for you."

He trailed his finger up the center of her until he cupped her face and dipped in for a kiss that started tender, but quickly turned to an urgency that stole her breath away.

All thoughts of consequences and responsibilities flew out through the gently swaying curtains.

When he entered her, the dam broke and tears swelled and slid down her cheeks. He took his time, kissing away the wetness and keeping a steady rhythm. The need caught deep in her chest until she was bursting, she bucked her hips trying urging him on, but he keep to his pace.

They peaked together, had his mouth not found hers at that same moment, she was sure her cry of release would have brought the hotel security.

For a moment neither of them moved, his head rested on her forehead, their breathing ragged. Hearts pounding as one. He shifted a fraction so his body lay to the side of her, his arms still held her.

They must have fallen asleep because the next rational moment, Glenna felt the cold seeping from the breeze coming through the open window. Her shiver woke him, he reached for the blanket that was sprawled on the side of the bed to fling it over the both of them.

"Let's just stay here the rest of the weekend." He nuzzled the side of her neck and she had to swallow to keep herself from hurling herself at him again. "I do need fuel to continue."

She chuckled. "Order Pizza?"

"Sounds good." He didn't move other than snaking an arm for the phone.

*****

Finn watched the two girls pouring over their notes. He hadn't known what to expect when he met his soon-to-be step-family. His dad may say that this was a trial period for them all, but he knew deep in his heart that Glenna was his dad's soulmate and meant to be his mother. There'd been a connection since the moment she'd entered their home with Agnes.

Now here he was with two new cousins who had all but high jacked him into helping to plan the wedding, though no one had discussed it with the bride. He had a feeling where Gabby and Sophie were concerned the Beckett family was inclined to indulge them.

He had always wanted a big boisterous family like Rebekah had, now it looks as if he'd get his wish. Yet there had been a few times over the last couple of hours listening to the girls chatter over fabrics, styles, and colors he'd thought of the cliché *be careful what you wish for, it just might come true!*

"Let's go."

Gabby grabbed the notebook she'd been busily scribbling in, Sophie close on her heals. They stopped at the door, in unison looked over their shoulders and raised a brow at him. Did they practice that?

"Are you coming?"

"Ah, I didn't hear where we are going."

And again, in unison, they studied the ceiling for what he didn't know, then returned their attention to him.

Then as if he were the dumbest boy on earth Sophie instructed him of their plans. "We're going to the backyard to stage the wedding."

He waited for the *duh* but at least she hadn't done that. Of course, he had no idea what she meant by *stage*. *W*asn't that what they did in the movies?

"Stage?"

Again they tossed their attention to the ceiling. He looked up to see what was so damn interesting. Just a white ceiling.

"Come on, we'll explain while were doing it."

Gabby reached for his hand, Sophie for the other. They led him through the house and out the back door. Luckily he'd still had his jacket on, he hadn't adapted yet to the cooler climate.

Sophie walked to the far corner of the yard, spread her arms and twirled to look at them. She crossed an arm across her midriff and resting her other arm's elbow on it, she cupped her chin with her hand.

"Picture it, the music stage situated here at an angle in the corner. It'll allow for more seating."

Gabby walked over and stood next to her and surveyed the yard. Finn wondered what they were seeing. Both girls walked around him to the other side by the gate. Turned and surveyed from that vantage point. If he hadn't known better he would have asked if this was their first time in the *Elders'* back yard.

"Yes, that will work."

Gabby then turned a little to the side to regard the side of the yard where they were standing, just in front of the Arbor. The area they were regarding was to the left.

"Food tables here. As we had for Mom's wedding."

"Yes." Sophie wandering around the yard a bit.

Finn was content to just watch, it was very intriguing. They *were* little generals as the family called them. They had a goal and they were strategically planning every detail. He couldn't wait to entertain Rebekah with his adventure.

"Finn, what do you think? This is staging." Again Finn waited for Sophie to say *duh*. Instead she continued. "The process of selecting, designing, adapting to, or modifying the space for the event."

He had a feeling she'd read that somewhere, or learned it in a class. They were taking some kind of class for event planning. They had their entire careers planned out. He had no idea what he wanted to be, he had an idea to follow in his dad's footsteps, but yet that idea kept changing.

"What do I think? I have walked into one crazy ambitious family, especially my new cousins."

"And?" Gabby gave him a grin.

"I like it."

*****

Great advantage point. From the windshield of the van he had an excellent view of the backyard where the young punk just walked out with two girls. He lowered his brow, what the hell were they doing?

Fascinated he watched them walk from one corner to survey the yard here then to the other side. All the while they kept up some kind of dialogue, he could tell they were explaining something to the kid. What with all the arms flaying and pointing this way and that.

He got out of the van and quietly closed the door, not latching it. Just enough so the light above the windshield didn't stay on. Then he made his way to the back and unlocked the doors, inching one opened for easy access.

If he timed it just right he could surprise the kid as he threw the black bag over his head. He'd wait until the girls were occupied and the kid came close to the gate. A huge tree would block him from their view. He couldn't have done better if he'd planned out the scene himself.

Then someone would have to sit up and take notice of him.

His thoughts were a jumbled mess as they flew from one scenario to another. No. He had to stop this. He sucked in his breath. Concentrate. He was getting himself worked up and nothing good ever came when he let that happen. He needed a cool head, because for his plan to work, he needed the kid. He closed his eyes and counted to ten.

When he opened them he almost squealed in delight. The kid stood by the gate. Almost like the boy was delivering himself to him. He searched the back yard for the girls. Perfect they were occupied arguing about something in the far corner.

Quietly he walked to the boy, he was taller up close. No matter. Again, it was if everything was ready for him. The gate was unlatched, he eased it open sucking in his breath in hopes it wouldn't alert anyone.

He waited two beats, when his target didn't move he launched the bag over his head. Taking advantage of the boy's surprise, he grabbed him around the waist firmly keeping his arm over the fabric of the bag. He hauled him away from the gate, not an easy task with the boy struggling. If the kid's arms hadn't been anchored under his hold he doubted he would have managed to get him to the van.

The bat waited on the bed of the van. He held tight with the one arm, his other snaked out, grabbed the handle of the bat, then bam—the boy went peacefully into the back of the van as planned.

He surveyed the area as he walked to the front of the van, that's when he realized he'd been so intent reaching his goal he hadn't noticed the screeching emanating from the yard where he'd just snatched the damn kid. Those two girls would alert the entire neighborhood if he didn't hurry.

He jumped in and slammed the vehicle into gear and slammed the pedal to floor. He'd barely gotten out of there before the girls got to the space the van had vacated. Not that they'd been able to stop him, but being able to identify him was not in the plan.

Especially since *no one* knew he had been following the Cat Boys, whatever the hell they called themselves, every step of their adventure.

Right before he careened around the corner, he took a moment to check the rear view mirror. They weren't standing in the road watching him leave as he'd expected. They'd gone in the house for help he supposed. He shrugged. Let them try and find him. He'd covered his tracks.

*****

Gabby grabbed Sophie by the arm as they watched the van take off right before they'd reached the back of it.

"Come on, I'll call my mom, you run and find Papa and Nana."

Gabby reached for her phone in her back pocket pulling the door open, she let her cousin enter first. While she waited for her mother to answer, she could hear Sophie pounding through the house hollering like a banshee. One of Paco's favorite sayings, not that she even knew what a banshee was. Their new soon to be cousin had been kidnapped and what was Gabby doing? Thinking about Banshee's. She shook her head and clicked off, her mother wasn't answering she'd have to call someone else. Before she had time to call Paco or Uncle Tyler her ring tone for her mother sounded. *Bad to the Bone.*

Reagan's voice filtered through. "Sorry, couldn't find my phone. What's up Gab?"

She straightened her back sucked in a breath and let it out.

"Gabby?"

"Someone took Finn."

"What?"

Gabby quickly explained what they'd been doing in the backyard. "Finn was checking the gate, you know how sometimes it sticks and Soph and I were arguing about where the band platform should be...."

"Gabby..."

"Sorry anyway we heard this weird sort of grunt thud sound and turned and we saw some guy wrestling Finn across the road. The guy had put some kind of black bag over Finn's head. We ran after him." She swallowed. "Mom he hit him over the head with a bat and threw him in the back of the van and took off."

"Tell me all you can about the man and the vehicle. Take a deep breath and close your eyes and describe the scene."

Gabby did as told and relived the scene. "I swear it was the black van that's been in front of our house ever since Aunt Glenna came home. The guy had his back to us when he used the bat, then he slammed the door and went on the far side of the van to get in the driver's side. He was parked across the street facing the wrong way. Anyway, I got the plate number."

She rattled off the plate id. Concentrated on anything else she could remember. "If it hadn't had a license plate I would have thought it was a new vehicle, there were no dents, and it was clean as if just washed."

"Good girl," her mother said. "You and Sophie stay inside the house. Where's Nana and Papa?"

Gabby looked up when they walked in. "Sophie went and found them, they're here now."

"Let me talk to Nana."

Gabby handed the phone to her nana. She put her arm around her cousin's shoulder the younger girl shivered, and Gabby knew she needed to distract her, she could see the tears swimming in her eyes. There was no time for hysterics. She'd called her mom, whom Gabby considered her own personal wonder woman, she'd take care of Finn.

"Come on Soph, let's go in the living room and finish up our plans it will give us something to do and keep our mind off Finn."

*****

Finn had a mother of a headache. When he tried to move, he discovered two things. His hands were tied behind a chair and he faced a stranger that was currently sitting across from him, smirking. Smirking? What the hell? Where was he? He glanced around the room and it looked like something out of a horror movie. It was the type of basement that he always screamed in his mind at the girl *don't go in the basement.*

"I was beginning to think I'd hit you a little too hard."

Well, that explained the drums currently playing a vigorous concert in his head. He refused to ask the obvious *where am I?* It wasn't like the guy would tell him. He could only imagine this had something to do with the art thieves. The only thing was, this guy wasn't one of the men in the pictures his dad had shown him. Could they have been wrong about who the culprits were?

"Cat got your tongue?" The guy chuckled, sounding a little too much like *Chucky.* "Pretty funny under the circumstances."

Finn had to pull himself out of his horror movie comparison of the situation or he'd scare himself to death. His father would be so proud if that happened. He pulled himself out of the slouching position, with his hands tied it wasn't easy. Two days earlier he'd been put through a quick tutorial of how to handle exactly what he was going through. *Think Finn.* Which was a bit hard with hammer time going on in his head.

Keep him talking.

"Cat? So you are part of The Black Cat's then?"

"No. I just happened to be at the right place at the right time. They needed someone to give them details of some of the properties around Calistoga, and since I happened to know the area real estate, they made me an offer."

Okay so maybe the guy had hit him a little too hard, but he couldn't make any sense out of what he had just told him. Lame he knew but the "Huh?" came out before he could pull it back.

"The four of them were at one of my favorite Irish bars in Midtown talking about taking their ladies to Napa to do a wine tour." He chuckled, again a chill rained down Finn's spine. "They were bellyaching about how bored they were going to be. Then one of them leans in speaking real low, and just at the right moment the band stops for break and I was able to hear. The guy had heard about a priceless piece of art. The minute they started talking about where it was at, I knew it was *Glenna's Surprisingly Vintage*. It had to be. I heard enough to know they needed my knowledge of the building that Glenna owned.

"I took the opportunity to introduce myself, of course they never bothered telling me their names, just smiled and shook my hand. All would have been fine, except the bastards were too dumb to find the secret way to the basement."

"Wait we thought there were only four of them."

"I'm not part of their little group. After I gave them the information, not that they used it, I didn't have anything to do with them. I just made sure I watched."

Finn stopped struggling, he knew about the basement? He stared at the man. "You know Glenna?"

"Yeah. She thinks she'll never see me again. She's got another think coming because I'm far from through with her. If she thinks what I did to her before was bad, she just needs to wait."

"Who are you? Are you the guy she was going to marry?"

"Oh, no, I'm not Lance Gordon." He chuckled again causing a ripple of dread to run over Finn. "For one thing I'm definitely not gay, and another, Glenna hasn't seen me in what? About ten years."

Finn had no clue who this guy could be. The only thing he knew, was he had to get away and warn

Glenna. This guy had an agenda, one that didn't bode well for his future step mom.

He wiggled his hands, yeah the rope was lose. The guy had no clue how to tie a knot. Even so, Finn knew he had to be careful, you just never knew what a nut job was going to do. He'd seen enough of them on TV, he wasn't talking movies either. The nightly news was full of them.

"If she hasn't seen you in ten years, why are you so interested in her now?"

The guy paused his pacing and stared at him as if he'd said something completely dumb. He shook his head and continued. The steps were measured as if the guy counted each.

Think Finn, stall or things aren't going to go well.

"Okay, so that was a dumb question."

Reagan had said, the best thing would be to ask leading questions that required more than a yes or a no. If you could actually get your captor to talk. Until he started pacing, the guy had been a regular Mr. Chatty. Finn just needed to figure how to start him talking again.

"How did you get them to take you to California? There's lots of people there that wouldn't *know* their plan they could get information from." Finn waited a beat. "Why drag you, an unknown from New York to drive the car in Calistoga?"

Finn had been known to watch a crime show now and again.

"Since I knew the floor plan of the exact shop they were discussing, I made myself valuable. It's the way of the world, son." The guy frowned as if something just struck him. "They didn't drag me to California. They didn't even know I was there. And neither did you. It was fun to make you think their van was everywhere. Most the time it was me watching. They left the area not long after the beating. They watched the house for a day or so, but then they left and I filled their spot, son."

Finn fought the words back, he didn't want to antagonize him by telling him not to call him *son*. It was just a word.

"You had something they needed. Knowledge. Okay I get it. But couldn't you have just *shown* them a map?" Finn was grasping, it sounded like he only had one meeting with the four art thieves. He had to keep him talking.

Finn continued to work the ropes, he could almost slip one hand out.

The pacing stopped again and the guy turned to glare down on him. He'd said something to piss him off, he could tell.

"What does it matter to you? If they had listened to me in the bar, they wouldn't have bungled the job and now they're trying to figure out how to get the art." He walked over to a small basement window. "I don't give a fuck about their plan. I just used them to watch Glenna."

The rope slipped over Finn's hand and he was able to get both hands free. Holding the rope so it didn't drop, he tried to figure a plan. He would only have one chance, and it had to be a surprise. He tried to shove the rope in his back pocket and discovered his phone. He'd been so preoccupied he hadn't felt it in his back pocket.

The guy was pretty lame as a kidnapper to leave a phone on the victim. When they'd gone to the gun range Tyler, Keira, Reagan, and Paco had given him their numbers, just in case. None of them thought he'd need the numbers. Damn he wished he didn't.

"What now?"

"I call your daddy." He grinned. "Of course, I'm pretty sure he knows you're gone by now. I'm just letting him stew."

"My dad doesn't stew easily."

Finn sized the man up. He was at least three inches shorter than Finn. He wasn't as muscled either. Finn could take him down. Especially if he caught him at the right moment. He glanced around the room while the guy continued to pace and mumble. He didn't see any guns laying around, that was a good thing.

"If you know Glenna then you must have something in common like art."

"Now I do. I've traveled all over the world. I've seen some of the finest exhibits. She'll be impressed. And my knowledge helped me into the inner circles where Glenna felt most comfortable. Oh, yeah, I would see her from time to time." He frowned. "Until now, I haven't dared visit California."

He swirled from the window startling Finn, he almost dropped the rope. Thank God he hadn't. The guy pointed a finger at him. "Only then did I find I hadn't needed to leave. Glenna knew it had been all her fault. She hadn't turned me into the authorities."

Finn didn't have a clue what the guy babbled about, he didn't care. Let him ramble. The guy was barely tall enough to see out of the high window, he stood caught up in his own thoughts. Finn took advantage, pulled out his phone. Careful not to move too much or make any noise, he kept the phone low to his side. Dividing his attention between the man and his phone he first turned the sound off so it wouldn't ring. Thank goodness no one had called so far, but maybe they were tracking the signal.

He glanced at the muttering man, he had enough time. He called Tyler, muted it and set it on the chair just enough under his butt cheek so it wouldn't fall on the floor, but hopefully enough Tyler could hear the conversation.

"Are we still in Brooklyn?"

The man jumped, if Finn wasn't so scared he would have laughed.

"You don't need to know where we are."

"What are you going to tell my dad when you call him?"

"Nothing until I have Glenna with me."

The guy was a total loon. "You think Glenna is a toy to give to you in exchange for me? We're people, and you do know that most of Glenna's family are cops or special agents, right?"

That made him pause, had he not thought of that? Again, the thought the man was a complete loon crossed Finn's mind.

Chapter Twenty-Four

The door banged on the wall as Glenna pushed through it, knowing Patrick was close on her heals. This was her fault. Guilt burned in the pit of her stomach. Finn, the most precious person in the world. Not just to his father but to her. She loved that boy as if he were her own. And she'd planned to be a wonderful mom to him, and what did she do? Put him right in the crosshairs.

"Glenna, come sit, I have tea." Her mother's answer to just about everything.

"Here son, I have a shot of Jameson's for you." Her dad's answer to everything.

The two were settled in with their beverages, not necessarily of choice, across from what looked like a command center. Three agents set across form the Elders with there laptops, and smart phones, typing away with a grunt here and there.

These were *not* her family. Anyway, they weren't when they were in work mode. Tyler, Keira, and Reagan were deep in their thoughts and she would not disturb them. They were the one chance Finn had.

Where.... And as if she'd brought him in on her thoughts Paco came through the back door.

"Gabby?"

The girl had been in the corner with Sophie bent over something. "Do you know if the gate was open? Did you hear anything?"

Gabby had probably already answered the same questions over and over again, so Glenna was surprised when the teen didn't roll her eyes. Instead she walked over to her stepdad, pursed her lips in concentration trying to remember if she'd left anything out.

"Soph, come here."

The girls were about two years different in age, yet no one would know it. They were together as if the best of friends not to mention sisters, far more than cousins. Though they weren't even really blood relatives, just by marriage. Glenna felt the moisture gather a moment before a tear slipped down her cheek. She'd wanted Finn to be the big brother the girls didn't have. He was only a few months older than Gabby.

Why hadn't she insisted on staying at a hotel instead of with Patrick? Instead she'd let him take her to his home for protection, where she'd fallen so hard for him and his irresistible family.

"Sophie, Finn was checking the lock, right?"

"Yeah, I noticed the other day it either stuck and you couldn't get it open or the darn thing wouldn't click shut. I had asked him to check it out." She sniffed. "If he hadn't been by the gate he'd be here...."

"Don't you dare blame yourself young lady. If it hadn't been at the gate it would have been another time." This from Gabby, who was a young lady herself.

Glenna turned in her seat and reached for Sophie's hand. "Soph, it was a blessing you both were there. The two of you were able to see the van. If it had been another time when he was by himself, we wouldn't have a clue. You two are heroes. Don't you forget that?"

Patrick who'd shot down his whiskey the minute he sat, had a dazed look on his face. Her father poured him another, and he tossed it back without hesitation. Would he ever forgive her?

The girls continued to go over things with Paco. Glenna watched the other three, intent on what was happening on their screens. Tyler had on a headset listening to what, she had no idea.

"Good boy." Tyler grinned. "Somehow the kid was able to call me. I'm listening to the conversation."

Patrick pinned him with a stare, the first indication he'd been listening. "Which one of the bastards have him?"

"From what I can tell, none of them." He switched his attention to Glenna. "He wants you."

Uneasiness raced through her. Who would want her? Lance? He hadn't seemed violent. And he had never wanted *her*. Thoughts of the men who'd she come in contact with over the years flew through her mind. Other than customers, she really had only dated off and on after Danny. He'd ruined her for relationships. Until Patrick, and now she'd ruined things by bringing danger to his son.

Danny.

"Can I listen for a moment? See if I recognize the voice."

She slipped out of her chair, walked around the table to where Tyler handed her the headset, she fit it over her head and listened. Finn sounded good, he kept up a running dialogue.

She was going to throw up. She grabbed the back of Tyler's chair, her knees wobbled. She'd never forget that voice as he stood over her and called her vile names with each pound of his fist.

Danny.

She pulled the headphones off and threw them down on the table, she needed to get out. She ran out the back door even though her legs felt like gelatin. She heard Patrick calling her name. But she didn't care. That lunatic had Finn. She'd never forgive herself.

Please God don't let him hurt Finn.

*****

Patrick couldn't believe he'd let his son come into the danger zone *again*. He reached for the third shot of whiskey Glenna's dad had poured and realized if he kept going he wouldn't be good for anyone especially his son. He left it untouched.

Startled out of his reverie, the thud of the headset hitting the table brought his attention to his surroundings and the fact that all color had drained from Glenna's face. She took off out the door, the rest of her family stared after her in confusion.

"Look up Danny Collins, he's the bastard who'd raped Glenna, he's the one who must have Finn."

Then he took off after Glenna. Shit poor agent, that's what he was. He let his emotions and his love for Glenna distract him.

He caught her as she was about to leave through the gate where Finn had been taken. He wrapped his arms around the front of her and pulled her back against his chest. Her hands were pulling at his trying to move them, luckily she faced away from him, or he was sure she'd kick him in the shins. What did she think she could do?

"Glenna, you're going to hurt yourself."

He kissed the top of her head, held tight to ride out her emotions. He would not let her go until she had it all out. She continued to flay and kick, his arms were soaking up the rain fall of tears.

Several minutes passed before she ran out of steam and she went limp. If he hadn't been holding her tight the dead weight would have let her slip through his arms. Instead he gently turned her around, keeping his hands firmly, but gently on her shoulders. He bent enough to look into her face.

"We'll get him. He will not hurt you again."

Her eyes widened. She tried to wrench free. He held firm.

"I'm not worried about me." Anger vibrated her shoulders with each word. "I'm worried about Finn."

"I know honey. Your family is the best, and you and I are going to walk right back in there and help. We'll find Finn before Danny does anything."

She sniffed. "I don't understand why this is happening, how would Danny even know about Finn. Does he have something to do with *The Black Cats?*" She placed a hand over his heart and dropped her head to rest on it. "Your heart is racing. Here I am going on like it's all about me and Finn's your son. I'm sorry."

"Glenna look at me."

He felt her sigh more than heard it, she finally raised her head, her eyes glazed with worry. He knew she loved his son almost as much as he did. He glanced up at the window of the kitchen, they were both needed. But first he had to make sure Glenna didn't blame herself. This was all on him. She'd done nothing but follow her heart even though she'd been scared.

"That's better. We will figure out what, if anything, Danny was doing with the other men, but first we're going to rescue *our* son."

He saw her throat work in a swallow and if he hadn't been watching her closely he'd have missed the affirmative nod of her head. She stepped away, he let his hands drop a moment before she turned to return to the house.

"You're not to blame for this, Glenna." He called after her retreating back, but she never broke stride.

He closed his eyes a moment to send up a prayer, to whatever God wanted to listen, that Finn would be okay. A hopeful feeling passed over him. He'd made sure his son was trained in defense and he'd had a crash course just the other day about situations, like kidnapping, Finn was a smart kid. He'd use what he learned.

Hell he already had. He'd called Tyler, they were tracing the signal right now.

The back door blew open, only a heartbeat after it had swallowed Glenna. Tyler leaped the two stairs landing in a run.

"Come on, we have a location."

Patrick didn't need to be asked twice. He fell in step behind Keira who had been right on her husband's heals. Out of the corner of his eye, he saw Glenna coming out also. He stopped, turned to block her way.

"Don't' do this Patrick. You're wasting time." She sidestepped him and followed the other two.

He opened his mouth, but the words telling her she'd be in harm's way stuck in his throat as he turned to catch up. Emotions warred in his gut. She *knew* Danny, she could help with insight into his motives. On the other hand, he'd need to divide his worry. Again he tried to force the words out to tell her to stop before she climbed into her brother's SUV.

Then he realized, two things at once. He wasn't alone and he needed her by his side.

Patrick lost track of how many turns Tyler had taken, it was as if he followed a maze. He gave up trying to figure out where they were going. It had been too long since he lived in New York, and back then he'd only visited Brooklyn a handful of times. He didn't know the area. He'd trust the man who did. He looked over to Glenna, she was staring straight ahead. He knew she wasn't watching the road. He laid a hand over hers where it rested on her thigh. She closed her eyes and then tipped her head to regard him.

"You're right, we'll get the bastard and Finn will be fine."

"He's a smart kid." Tyler's voice floated from the front. "He knew we would be able to track his phone, but mostly hear the conversation."

Keira changed the subject. "Glenna when we have Finn, I believe you and your sisters need to have a talk."

Patrick felt the muscles in Glenna's thigh tighten in understanding. He'd thought she'd talked to her mother about the rape the other day while he was at the gun range. Maybe she hadn't.

"Yes we do. I should have talked to all of you after I talked to Ma the other day." Her body seemed to relax against him. "It felt good to finally have a mother's shoulder to cry on. I have no idea why I held it in."

"You're very lucky you have a mother. Don't *ever* take her for granted. She loves all of her kids and she's *always* there for you." Keira twisted in her seat to look over her shoulder to look at Glenna. "Thank you for sharing her with your motherless sister-in-law."

Glenna reach out to pat Keira's arm. "Ma loves you."

"We're getting close." Tyler chuckled. "I don't think Finn's kidnapper realized that the questions Finn was asking helped describe where he was being kept. We know he's in a basement and Danny is or was at the time, looking out the window toward the street."

"Meaning we're going to park around the block and rely on Reagan and Paco who are still monitoring the situation." Keira had again taken up the reigns of the conversation.

Patrick took out his phone and called Reagan tapping the speaker button, he laid it on the console so everyone could hear.

"We're around the corner from the location," Tyler said as soon as she answered.

"Good, Finn's been keeping a running conversation. The guy is still at the window so you'll need to go around to the back." Reagan's voice filtered over the inside of the vehicle.

Paco's voice sounded muffled like he stood across the kitchen. *"There is a lot of rustling going on next to the phone. We're not sure, but I think the young man is probably restrained and he's working whatever has his wrists."*

Glenna let out a soft gasp. "Oh, I hope he's not going to do something rash, like try to take Danny down. The man may not be as tall as Finn, but he has muscles. Or he did when I knew him. He was almost obsessed with working out."

"We can hope his middle has gone to a bit of a pot."

"You're saying he might have gone soft?"

"Glenna, I'm saying I have faith in my boy."

He gave her leg a squeeze to emphasize his words. All the while tapping down his panic.

"Whatever he's doing, he's keeping it cool Glen... He's a smart one. From the description we've been able to put together the basement door is close to the rear of

the house. Don't wait too long. We don't want the
bastard to catch on to Finn, or notice the phone."

Reagan gave them a few more instruction about
the floor plan then disconnected.

Patrick tried not to think about what could
happen if Danny Collins noticed what Finn was up to,
yes time to go. His hand went to the door, Keira
noticed.

"Wait can't just waltz in there. We need a plan."

"I thought we did have a plan, go in and get Finn."
Patrick knew better, and also knew he was thinking
like a parent not an agent. He pulled air into his lungs.
"You're right. We assume, probably correctly but we
have to be sure, that he's working on his own agenda.
There isn't any possible reason *The Black Cats* would
take Finn, why would they? No this is about Glenna."

He felt Glenna's body tense at his words. It wasn't
her fault, but he didn't have time to reassure her, that
would need to come later. Now it was all about Finn,
getting him out of that basement safe.

"Right. I need to help. I know I'm not an agent so
what can I do?" Glenna wanted to know.

"You stay put." Tyler turned in his seat to look at
her. "We have phones, we'll put them on vibrate. I
agree with Patrick, the art thieves are probably not
involved. But things will go south pretty damn fast if
they show up and surprise us. You watch. Text if
anything is going on."

"I hate to point this out, but you've parked around
the corner, if I stay put I can't *watch* anything."

Tyler frowned, and Patrick knew he'd forgotten
that fact also. Patrick maneuvered to look out the back
of the SUV. There was a small park across the street
which would afford a view of the street the front of the
house faced. She'd be in plain sight, but not be able to
be seen from the window where Danny stood.

"There." Patrick pointed to a bench facing the
swing set. "You can sit in the park, no one would even
notice. With it being on a corner you'd be able to see
vehicles coming from all directions."

The other three took in where he pointed. Both Keira and Tyler nodded, Glenna still contemplated. Finally she nodded. She opened her door.

"I'll go now. Stay here until I'm on the bench."

Patrick grabbed her forearm to pull her back in the car. "One more thing."

He reached a hand around the back of her neck to bring her in and kissed her fast and hard. Then he let her go. She hesitated for a moment.

"Be careful." Then the door snapped shut.

They watched as she followed their instructions. She glanced around then gave them a thumbs up.

"Now let's go get your boy."

There was an alley behind the houses, conveniently giving them an avenue to approach the house unobserved. Once they reached the backyard, they found the gate broken. Tyler hopped it, Patrick followed, much to Patrick's surprise, Keira had no trouble clearing the crumbling wood.

A screen hanging askew from its frame was the first challenge. The goal of surprise would be spoiled with the screech of a rusty hinge. Patrick held up a hand. He walked around the back of the house looking for a window that may be a better entry.

Nothing.

Keira placed a hand on the screen and inched it away. Too slow for Patrick, he tapped down his impatience. Better be slow and safe than alert the man holding his son. After what seemed like hours, Keira had the screen wide enough for them to enter. Once the door was open. She grasped the knob, Patrick sucked in his breath and prayed the damn thing was unlocked.

The Gods must be watching because it was.

Once the three of them were in, it was only a matter of seconds before they heard the voices from the basement. By hand signals they agreed to wait at the top of the stairs and listen.

*****

Finn figured he'd been there about a year.
Glenna's family had to have a signal and be on their
way. If they weren't already outside somewhere. The
guy was back to his pacing, and Finn just wanted to
stick his foot out and trip him. Unfortunately, as if the
bugger read his mind, he gave Finn a wide berth never
close enough.

Then he heard it. A creak. The guy was blathering
on about Glenna and what he was going to do to her.
As if his dad would actually hand her over in exchange
for Finn.

Finn had tuned him out, he needed to keep a cool
head if he was going to come out of this alive. With the
running commentary going on, Finn knew the man
hadn't heard the sound.

Now was the time.

As soon as the guy was in front of him. Finn
jumped from his seat, rope in hand, wrapped it around
the guys neck. As intended, the guy was completely
caught off guard, his hands went to his neck to grasp
the rope.

"Hold it right there."

Finn held tight but maneuvered around so he
could see Tyler. Keira and his dad right behind, three
guns—he had no clue what kind—pointed at the man
who'd stopped struggling the minute he'd heard Tyler's
voice.

"You didn't take into consideration Glenna's
family. Trained agents. Stupid of you." Finn gave a
little tug on the rope.

Finn felt the moment the man sagged in defeat. In
fact, he almost lost his balance. One minute the man
was standing on his own, the next he was dead weight.
Luckily, his dad stepped in and took over.

While he put the cuffs on, Tyler read the man the
Miranda.

His dad clapped a hand on his shoulder and gave
a squeeze. "Good job."

Finn was caught off guard by the emotion his dad's words held. Almost eye to eye, he could see the tears in his dad's eyes about two seconds before he was pulled into a bear hug. The likes of which he hadn't seen since he was a kid.

Before he deemed it not cool to be hugged by one of your parents.

Today, he welcomed the warmth of his dad's arms around him, giving him the strength he hadn't realized had zapped out of him. He rested his head on his dad's shoulder and hugged him in return. How long they stood in an embrace Finn wasn't sure, but in hours or maybe it was only minutes he felt another pair of arms encircle him and his father

"Finn." Glenna's voice tugged on his name. "Are you okay?"

*****

Glenna's heart still beat in triple time. She wasn't sure it would ever return to its normal place. She couldn't have lived with herself if anything had happened to Patrick's son.

Before long, officers filled every nook and cranny of the place. Doing this that and the other. Reagan had called in their location soon after the three had left the house. So the officers had been on standby, out of sight of the house.

"Come on, let's get out of their way." Glenna still held Finn's hand. She gave it a tug and led the way around the working CSI people.

"I'll be out in a few." Patrick's voice trailed them up the stairs.

She paused the minute they reached the backyard, it had less people milling around. She couldn't wait, and pulled Finn in for another hug. She admitted it was more to assure herself he was alright than anything else.

While she'd been in the park waiting for hours, okay only a ten or fifteen minutes, she'd thought about letting Patrick and Finn go, let them go on with their lives. Then she realized they were hers, and they loved her as much as she loved them.

Love was complicated, messy, and hard. She'd kept her heart safe from hurt for long enough it was time to suck it up and take the risk.

It was time to get *The Black Cats*, grab life back, and enjoy the ups and downs of living with Patrick and Finn.

Chapter Twenty-Five

Glenna sipped her tea and watched the show. *The Elders* were fussing, one of their favorite things to do, over Finn. Was he okay? Did he need anything? A warm cup of milk? Oh, he was old enough her dad was sure he could handle a shot of Jameson.

At the last, she felt Patrick stiffen. Not saying anything she'd reached for his hand and clasped it firmly. He looked down at her with a frown. She just smiled and shook her head.

Sure enough Finn held a cup of tea, not Jameson, as Glenna knew would happen. Her dad may think whiskey was the cure all for everything, but her ma would never let it happen to anyone in the household under twenty-one.

All of a sudden, Glenna felt drained. The events of the day began to hit her, she glanced at the clock to see it was well after midnight. She stifled a yawn, but not before Patrick saw. He snaked an arm around her shoulders and straightened away from the counter they'd been leaning against.

"I think it's time to get Glenna back to the hotel. We don't want anyone to know we've been gone."

"Those cat fellows probably know about that bastard that took Finn by now..." her dad began.

"No, they don't. That guy just wanted Glenna." Finn startled everyone.

"Really? It's just a coincidence that he found you at the same time?" She asked.

Finn shrugged. "I'm not very clear about the exact connection, the guy was sort of raving like a lunatic. But he met them somehow, since he was in real estate they asked for information about Calistoga. When he realized they were talking about *Glenna's Surprisingly Vintage* he gave them information about your shop and how it had a secret basement. Since then, he's been keeping tabs on you through them." His chuckle filled the air. "He was pretty disgruntled that they didn't find the hidden door. Oh, and get this, you know how we thought they were changing vans using different colors to throw us off? Well sometimes he was the one watching, in fact they left for New York a day or two before us. He was the one who followed us to the airport."

Patrick looked at her, his expression must match hers, *surprise*.

"No wonder it seemed like they were everywhere even ahead of us sometimes." Glenna shook her head.

"Especially here in Brooklyn and Manhattan with all the traffic. It's seemed impossible for them to be everywhere. I had assumed they had two vans and they'd split up." Patrick again was on the same wavelength as if reading her mind.

"I'm just glad he's behind bars, now at least we know who and what we're dealing with, *The Black Cats.*" Glenna smiled, she knew they'd be ready for them.

"I think it's time we get back to the hotel so no one notices we didn't stay there." Patrick repeated.

Patrick regarded Glenna. She tried not to blush, memories of what had happened in their hotel room, before they received the call, scampered over her. All of a sudden she had a burst of energy, and she wanted nothing more than to be in his arms.

"I don't understand why you can't just stay here?" her dad asked.

Her mother stopped fussing for a moment to stare at her, and Glenna felt the heat begin in her chest and travel to the top of her head when she saw the dawning filter over her mother's face.

"Fred, I guess they're right. They need to finish what they started."

Her dad looked first to her mother and then to her in bewilderment. "Couldn't they just go first thing in the morning before anyone noticed?"

"No, dear. I think it is best they go tonight. You two run along and give us the low-down tomorrow after the big event."

Finn grinned into his tea cup. It seemed like the only one in the crowded room who didn't understand what her and Patrick were anxious to get to their room and *do* was her father. Mortifying was what it was to have Tyler smirking, Reagan and Keira grinning. And Paco was trying hard not to look as embarrassed as she felt.

"Well okay then." Her dad said as he walked them to the door. "We'll see you tom... I guess it's tonight that we'll see you. Take care."

He gave her a hug and shook Patrick's hand, or would have if Patrick hadn't pulled him in for a proper hug.

They traveled the distance in silence. She wasn't sure what he was thinking, though she had an idea it was the same thing she was. Once they reached their room, the door had barely closed and been locked before he pulled her into his arms. This time no words were spoken.

He said plenty with his hands and mouth. She followed his example and let her hands and lips wander over his shoulders, chest, and flat belly, then dropped lower. It was a tangle of hands, but somehow they managed to explore each other until they knew every sensitive spot on the other's body. Though Glenna was sure they'd find even more as the years passed.

*****

Glenna fell back onto the bed and let out a sigh. "I love you, Patrick. Can you forgive..."

He stopped her word with a gentle kiss. "Don't ever think there is anything to forgive. You *cannot* control the actions of others. You and Finn were right when you both said it would be safer for him to be prepared. If I hadn't listened to you, I don't know what would have happened."

She rolled to her side a placed a hand on his cheek. "Oh Patrick."

"Ssh. Because of you, I allowed my son to take a quick defense lesson with Reagan and Tyler. Something I would never have done. It's over. Finn is fine. I could beat myself up because I didn't leave him home with Mum and Da." He kissed her nose. "Again, because of you, I realize I *can't* control the world. It's dangerous..."

"Wait, because of me?" She struggled to sit up against the backboard. "I'm the one who's been carrying on about how dangerous your job is."

"Yes, and I've been saying what?"

"That you're doing your best to take the bad guys down. You're trained and even if you weren't an agent you could be struck by a car and any manner of things. So you've always believed."

He shook his head, what she saw on his face surprised her. He'd always sounded so confident. Vulnerable, was written over him at the moment. She swallowed.

"I may believe that as far as I'm concerned. But not where my loved ones are. I thought the threat was to you. I stayed close, thinking Finn was safe with your family. Because of you, I've come to believe my words. Being kept in the dark and bubble wrapping those I love is more dangerous than educating them on the dangers of life. Thank you. Because of you, Finn is home at your parents snuggled in a warm safe bed, hopefully, asleep."

He lay on his side, elbow on the bed his head propped on his hand, looking up at her. She couldn't resist and leaned down and kissed the tip of his nose, as he'd done to her earlier.

"And because of you, I believe I can handle the everyday worry of your job. You *know* what you're doing and I have faith." Before they turned even mushier she changed the subject. "Let's get some rest.

We've had a long day, and we have some under cover duties."

She slipped down next to him, snuggled in and prepared to sleep when his phone rang. She glanced at the digital clock on the bed side. Two in the a.m. was never good for a call.

He swung his legs over the side of the bed as he reached for the phone, he tapped to connect. His eyebrow raised and looked down at her. "Thank you for calling Mr. Gr... Barlow, I'll have someone there in a moment."

He tapped off. "That was Mr. Grumpy Pants. You have a visitor currently checking out your house again."

She struggled to sit up again. "Call Beckworth, then tell me what my neighbor said. Oh, and I thought he didn't have a phone?"

After he set his phone on the table he situated himself next to her, draped an arm behind her and pulled her in.

"I gave him a burner phone I had laying around so he could let me know if anything happened at your house. Anyway, Mr. Grumpy Pants got up for a glass of water and noticed a light bobbing around—his words—in your house. Said it made him seasick to watch and we damn well better get someone to get the varmint—his words—away from his quiet neighborhood."

"I'm sure he said something about me bringing it to the neighborhood."

"I wasn't going to mention that part." He chuckled. "Beckworth wasn't happy about the early morning call, but he said he was on it."

"I guess when you have money, you can fly anywhere day or night. They must have left right after the last gallery showing this afternoon."

"Yesterday afternoon. Mr. Grumpy Pants didn't say lights, he said light. It could be someone else after the painting now that we've let it be known, more or less, that you have it."

"We better get some sleep."

Chapter Twenty-Six

"About ready?" Patrick's voice filtered through the door.

Ready? She wasn't sure. She took a deep breath, tonight was the big Gala, where they'd make sure the rumor about here *piece of art* made the rounds. Was she ready? She looked ready, her reflection indicated she was. On the inside not so much. In the last couple of months her life had taken turns she'd never imagined.

Not long ago she'd been ready to walk down the aisle with a man she'd planned to spend the rest of her life with. A man who might have gone through her most personal things and prized possessions a few hours earlier.

It was humiliating to admit how wrong she'd been about Lance Gordon. Sourness burned in the pit of her belly. And *humiliating* didn't even come close to how she'd felt about Danny Collins and his stunt to make her pay for some unknown injustice.

"Hey, you okay?"

Now there was a thread of worry in Patrick's voice. How could he want her after the proof that she brought out the worst in men. Yet he did want her. He was tender and kind. A good man. She sucked in her doubts. She'd make sure he didn't regret his decision of falling for her.

Yes, he brought out the best in her and together they'd make a wonderful warm home for Finn. And *maybe* more children? Her heart pounded at the thought. With a smile on her face she pulled open the door. Patrick stumbled in a bit, as he'd been leaning against it.

"Hey." Then he stepped away and she felt his eyes travel from her hair where's she'd pulled into a knot on the top of her head, down to her peacock blue toenails.

"Wow. I'm going to be the envy of every red blooded male at the gala."

He held out his elbow to escort her as if she were at the entrance of a ballroom instead of leaving the bathroom.

"I think I better keep you to myself. Let's turn some music on, we can dance here. I don't want to share you."

Happiness bubbled, replacing the last drop of sour in her stomach. "Sounds delightful. But let's get the bad guys taken care of first. Then I'll save all my dances for you."

He looked so disappointed, a laugh burst out before she could control it. She gathered up her clutch.

"Oh, did Beckworth call while I was getting ready?"

"Yes, I was going to wait to tell you after the event."

She stilled, a feeling of unease traveled over her. "What happened?"

"They missed whoever it was, though Mr. Grumpy Pants is sure it was the *young fop*. I'm sorry Glenna, they said he pretty much trashed your place and then moved on to your shop."

"My shop? Did he break things there?"

"Whoever it was must have had a key. There was no damage to the door. Beckworth said that a few of the boxes in your office were strewn all over the place, but nothing broken. They were apparently in the process of going through the closet with the secret door when Beckworth arrived. The guy must have heard them and slipped into to the showroom. As the officers came in the back door, they saw the closet was opened and went to investigate giving the culprit plenty of time to escape out the front."

"I've never given anyone other than Effie a key, there hasn't been a need." She sighed and rubbed a thumb between her brows. "I did have a spare key at the cottage. The guy must have found my keys and used them."

"Now your smile has turned to a frown and I'm sorry for that. I wish I could shield you from all the unhappiness."

She drew in a deep breath, something she'd been doing a lot of since her failed wedding day. Enough was enough already.

"Well life isn't always going to be rosy. But let's grab every bit of happiness we can. Let's go have a good time. Drop a few more hints. *The Black Cats* know we have the art, so let's let them know where and when they can find it. It will be like a puzzle and if they put it all together they'll win the prize."

"Except we'll be the real winners because we'll be the ones to nab them before they get away with the treasure."

"Come on, I feel like dancing."

A few minutes later, they stood at the entrance into the Manhattan Ballroom at the New York Grand Hyatt. Spectacular was all she could say. These artsy types knew how to throw a party. She glanced up in time to see Patrick's amazed expression a second before he masked it to one of politeness. After all they were there on an agenda. But hey, it wasn't like they couldn't have a little fun.

"Let's mingle before dinner. Have some fun. Isn't that what we're supposed to be doing?"

"Yes it is." Again he stuck out elbow, she took it as they sauntered around the room greeting people.

She led the way to all the known gossips and accidently let tidbits of her discovery here and there and the showing she was planning. Though *The Black Cats* were there and mingling, they stayed close almost following in their wake. If they had an idea that Patrick and the authorities knew their identity and were following them as close, they might not have been so blatant or cocky!

Everything was extraordinary, the room, the dinner and absolutely *no* dry chicken for the

Blackmans Antiquities House Gala, nor was there any ordinary dish served. There were choices of mouthwatering Moroccan, Curry, and Thai. She'd had the Spicy Thai soup for her appetizer, she needed the recipe. Not that she'd be able to do it justice. She just wanted to sit and veg until she was ready to pop.

Patrick, a true meat and potatoes kind of guy, picked through his food a little on the leery side. However, in the end he was a fan of the cuisine. He slid his chair back an inch and turned to regard her.

"What?"

"The food, what do you call it?" He snapped his fingers. "Presentation was interesting. I must say they had everything beautiful, the drizzles and all, but I think I'm going to need a burger later to fill up."

Glenna noticed the music had started and turned to look at the few couples making their way around the hard wood floor. She smiled as she watched them sway. She stood grabbing his hand in the process.

"It's a slow dance. Besides, exercise helps the digestion."

He raised a brow, but let himself be led to the floor. They swayed along with the others. The orchestra obviously had known there should be no rigorous melodies after such a meal.

It felt wonderful to be wrapped in his arms, the fairy lights twinkled giving a romantic essence to the evening. She could stay like that forever. Until reality danced by them. Raymond with a beautiful redhead had come to claim a space on the dance floor. Right next to them. Glenna had a feeling it wasn't by accident.

Apparently neither did Patrick, as the thought crossed her mind he leaned in and whispered just loud enough for the other couple to hear. They were that close.

"We should fly home tomorrow so we can get started on plans for the showing."

As their reservations were for the next afternoon, she knew his words were for their benefit. She took his lead.

"I'm not sure Patrick, Finn's having a good time with his new cousins. And I wanted you to get to know the rest of my family, not just Tyler."

"We'll come back for Christmas." He rested his chin on the top of her head for a moment. She savored the feeling. "I just want the art taken care of and in the proper hands."

Glenna wasn't sure how to respond. They hadn't really alluded to the fact someone had broken into her shop for the painting. The art community was huge, but when it came to news about one of their own, and though she wasn't an artist herself, Glenna was included in their elite group. The break-in had been a topic throughout the weekend.

On the one hand, they let it drop about the painting, but on the other one she maintained her conviction she hadn't known what they were after since nothing was stolen. Patrick was careful to make it sound like the painting was there for the taking if they'd wanted it, he just didn't mention it was in a hidden basement.

She realized that he had waltzed them away from the eavesdropping couple, saving her from responding. Thank goodness. She wasn't good at this undercover stuff. She'd be glad to be back in her little shop running next door for lattes, chatting her customers up, and enjoying her life with her new family.

Soon.

"Let's..." Patrick started as the orchestra struck up the next song. That just so happened to be the tango. He gave her a wicked grin. "You're in for it now."

"What?"

"Finn and Rebekah gave me a quick lesson before we left."

With that he swung their clasped hands up and let them lead the way to the side of the floor, then slipped his arm around her. Using their other hands to traverse the way they'd come. And in true tango form, he dipped her. A feeling of falling swept over her, but he kept a comforting hold on her the entire time. She'd never danced the tango before, but he led the way with ease.

When the song ended, there was a light round of applause, she felt her face burn with the knowledge they'd been center stage and she'd been so involved trying not to trip over her own two feet she hadn't even noticed.

Patrick gave a wave in thanks and led her off the dance floor, not stopping until they were at the elevator and had to wait. When they were on their floor, he still didn't utter a word, but continued to their door slid the card in and once the door was shut he wrapped her in his arms.

"I couldn't take it another moment, I needed you here in my arms."

She tilted her head back and raised a brow at him. "I was in your arms."

"Yeah, but I couldn't do this."

His hands found her zipper and slid it down, then made quick work of skimming the rest her dress off her shoulders letting it pool around her feet. Her skin tingled in the trail of his fingers, her stomach muscled tightened in want. She'd *never* had these sensations with anyone before.

"Do you think when I'm old and gray I'll still have this incredible sensitivity to your touch?"

"I'm counting on it."

He silenced any more conversation by capturing her mouth with his.

*****

"Do we have everything?"

Patrick couldn't believe everything they were taking home. He swore they had twice as much as when they arrived. Glenna's family... well there wasn't really any word he could think of to describe them. He felt it a privilege to know Tyler and now he was going to be his brother-in-law. That is, as soon as he formally asked his sister to marry him. He was almost a hundred percent sure she knew that the pretense of their, as she called it, coupleness had *never* been a pretense for him. Or for her. To be on the safe side, he'd incorporated Finn to help him come up with something suitably romantic to ask her.

After all the art painting bait was set and completed, then he'd sweep her off her feet. As Glenna had said they'd always known she had the painting, but now they knew it was going to be on display for their pleasure and ease of taking it. Or so they thought.

He'd be waiting.

"Yes dad, we have everything."

His son's words startled him out of his thoughts and it took him a moment to remember what he'd said. He'd never been so antsy to get a case over with, he usually enjoyed the chase and the capture a bit of a letdown. This time the capture was going to be the enjoyment.

"Then let's get this show on the road and get home. You have school."

He chuckled at Finn's groan, especially since he knew the boy loved school. Sometimes he thought it was because of Rebekah, which worried him as they were too young, but they seemed to be only friends. Good, he hoped it stayed that way.

"Say your goodbyes."

Patrick and Glenna held hands and watched Finn grin, he wrapped an arm around each of his soon-to-be new cousins.

"See you two at Christmas. We'll finish our plans. I'll check into what we discussed."

Patrick glanced down at Glenna, who took that moment to do the same to him. Her expression was as curious as he felt. What had those kids been *discussing*?

They had a long flight, he'd see if he could get it out of him. Though his son was one of the few people he knew that could keep a secret.

*****

A tired threesome de-boarded the plane in the wee hours of the morning at the Oakland airport. Patrick was not looking forward to the hour drive home. They needed a *Beam me up Scotty* moment. Glenna and Finn had both slipped into dreamland the moment the SUV turned toward home. He wished he could do the same, but at least this would give him some time to think.

They needed to set the stage, which was planned for that weekend. When the general public were involved in that *stage* it was always tricky. They would need to advertise the event therefore innocent people would be around and may be in harm's way.

Beckworth and Jones were dropping by later in the afternoon and they were going to brainstorm.

Patrick blinked, finally. He'd never been so glad to pull into his driveway. A few hours' sleep and he'd feel like a new man. He woke up his slumbering passengers and after several minutes of grumbling they helped take in the luggage and all their other treasures from their trip.

He'd pick up Horace from Doggy Day care after he slept, and he was sure Effie was good with Agnes a little longer. They hadn't told anyone the exact time they'd be home, hopefully they'd have a few undisturbed hours of sleep.

"Let's get some rest we can put everything away later."

"Thanks Dad." Finn tossed over his shoulder on his way to his room. He didn't need any persuading.

"Let's go."

Glenna looked at him in surprise, she'd been heading toward the room she'd been using. He grabbed her hand, it seemed silly to take separate rooms. After a moment she slipped her hand in his and together they dropped onto the bed. Patrick pulled her close and it seemed like a minute later Finn was standing over the bed.

"Hey you guys going to sleep all day? Beckworth and Jones are here."

He pried his eyes open, after a moment they focused enough to see he'd slept about two hours longer than planned. Glenna mumbled and rolled over. For a moment he thought of letting her sleep. Then he imagined how upset she'd be if they left her out of the planning.

"Glenna," he whispered in her ear.

She ignored him. Finn looked amused, but he was no help. He just stood with his arms folded.

Louder this time. "Glenna, Beckworth and Jones are here."

This time her eyes opened as if she'd been prodded by a cow prod and sat up in one motion, almost dislodging him from the bed, as he'd been leaning over her.

"Oh my." She noticed Finn, and put a hand to her hair. "Oh Finn. I must look a wreck. Give me a minute."

She crawled out of bed, stopped, turned, and pointed at them. "And don't you dare discuss anything important until I'm there."

Then she continued onto the bathroom. Good thing he hadn't let her sleep.

*****

"Thanks for coming over. I think we'll have our ducks in a row in time." Patrick waved the officers off. It was a productive and informative afternoon. Much to his surprise, his experience with the two men in the past hadn't been that industrious.

Glenna paced the living room, then come to a stop in her strong woman stance. "What I want to know is

where does Danny fit into all of this? Danny is in real
estate."

"He hasn't said much to the authorities in New
York. Let's concentrate on reeling in *The Black Cats*,
then we can piece everything together."

"I hate to say this, but from the bits and pieces
we've been told of the conversation between Finn and
that man, he's been obsessed with you all these years.
It was a huge coincidence he happened to be in the
right place at the right time to jump on the band
wagon."

"Where though? He hasn't been in the area for
years. There's no way he could have continued in real
estate and me not know about it."

Patrick stopped her pacing by grabbing her
shoulders and looking down at her. "I remember Finn
said something about Danny meeting them in an Irish
bar in New York. But I do know you're driving yourself
nuts. I think he's a little insane. Let the investigators
do their jobs. We'll know the answers soon enough."

He waited until she nodded. "We have some
planning to do. You go call the woman, I forget her
name, who volunteered to help plan."

"You know, I would enjoy this showing much
more if we weren't setting the stage for a robbery for
the night before."

He pulled her in and hugged her, resting his head
on the top of hers. "I know, Glenna. Soon this will be
over and then you'll find out just how boring I am and
leave me for Mr. Grumpy Pants."

She laughed as he'd intended. Then she gave him
a quick kiss on the cheek. "I need a shower, then let's
go get Agnes and Horace."

She stopped at the hallway and looked over her
shoulder a slightly horrified expression. "Finn's game
is Friday night."

He hadn't forgotten. But with everything going on,
he hadn't brought it up. "If you're too nervous you
don't have to go."

"What?" She swung fully to face him. "Of course I have to go."

Chapter Twenty-Seven

Indian summer had struck the Napa Valley for Finn's game. Only a slight breeze marred the perfect football evening. Glenna had purchased an American Canyon hoodie for the occasion in anticipation of a cool November evening. As soon as the sun dipped behind the east hills, she was sure she'd be glad of the warmth.

"I get so nervous at these things." Patrick's mother shook her head. "I know it's just a football game, but it's Finn, you know?"

Glenna grinned at the older woman, she remembered well when her ma and dad had attended Tyler's games. You'd think he was in the Olympics' or something the way she carried on.

She patted Patrick's mother's leg. "Finn will do awesome. I know he's practiced enough since we got back."

Caroline's grin faded to a frown. "I never asked how that trip went."

Glenna again patted her knee again. "It accomplished what we set out for and tomorrow evening, hopefully, it will be over."

They hadn't told Patrick's parents about Finn, he was safe, and there would be no point in upsetting them after the fact. Finn had wholeheartedly agreed. He loved his grandparents and didn't want to cause them a moment of alarm. Glenna was proud of the boy, he would be a fine man like his father someday. She swiped at the aggravating tear that slid down her cheek and turned away so Caroline wouldn't see it. Too late.

"Why are you crying, did something happen?"

Glenna chuckled. "I just get a little emotional when I think what a wonderful young man that boy is."

As intended, Finn's nana puffed up her chest like a proud peacock. "Yes he will be a fine man too."

Patrick arrived with an arm load of snacks and a drinks to share at that moment. His sister and family trailed him and for the next several moments it was chaos trying to seat everyone while trying to protect the goodies from spilling over the bleachers. Waste of money to scatter them as Patrick's father proclaimed several times. Glenna hadn't realized how much she'd missed her crazy family until she'd met Patrick's family.

The game ended with a blast of the school cannon. Time to cheer.

"Wow, close game." Margaret Kathleen proclaimed as they climbed from the bleachers after the American Canyon win of 21 to 20 over their opponent.

Glenna's heart had stopped several times. She hadn't realized how much she wanted Finn's team to win. It was just a high school football game.

It had come to symbolize normalcy. That's the only reason she could think of. She was about to say something along those lines to Patrick when she spotted the men. She stopped and Patrick bumped into her and if he hadn't grabbed her shoulders she'd most likely would have toppled headfirst down the stairs.

"Darlin', you can't just stop without warning." His words came out on a chuckle.

Oh how she didn't want the normal to end. "What are they doing here?"

"Who?" But he'd followed her line a vision. His body bunched, she felt his chest tense.

"They are not going to ruin this night for Finn."

Patrick moved around her and was down the stairs before she could stop him. The rest of their group followed. Glenna raced to catch him and grabbed Patrick's hand to make him stop. She glanced across the field. Finn was celebrating with his teammates unaware of the four men watching.

"They're not going to confront us, they still don't know we have any clue of their identities. They're only here to keep an eye on us. If they wanted us to know they were around, they would have parked the van in plain view."

Patrick slowed his pace a bit. "You're right. If we didn't know what they looked like, they would blend in with the crowd." He snapped his fingers. "Blend and watch. They're making sure we don't do anything with the painting."

"They don't want us to recognize them from the gala, then we'd be suspicious." She raised a brow at him. "Yet they're suspicious of us."

Patrick's dad's long legs carried him passed them. She could hear Patrick's sister and her family rushing behind her. Patrick's family reached the boy before they did. Finn's móraí one step ahead. He pulled the boy into a bear hug. By then Glenna was close enough to hear what Patrick's dad said.

"Great job my boy. Let's go celebrate."

Hugs were flying left and right.

Glenna watched Patrick's expression slip into proud as they followed in the family's wake at a more leisurely pace. When they reached the group his dad was in the process of steering Finn toward the cars. "Come on Finn my boy. Let's go."

Without further conversation they turned in unison, out of the corner of her eye she saw Patrick's parents and sister and her family do the same.

It was the hardest thing Glenna had done in a long time. Not turn around to see what the men were doing. She didn't want them to even suspect they were on to them.

Once in the car, the three of them followed Patrick's parents to the local Italian restaurant.

Finn leaned forward in his seat, as much as his seatbelt would let him, to tap his dad on the shoulder. Patrick glanced at him in the rear view mirror.

"Did you see those guys at the game?"

Glenna twisted in her seat. "You saw them? We were hoping you didn't."

"Why? They were just watching." He shrugged back into the vinyl. "I didn't see them until after the game. They had their full attention on you two. You may want to call those police dudes and tell them to watch the shop, they're behind us in the van. Once we're at the restaurant they may believe it's a good time to strike, instead of tomorrow night."

"Good idea. I'll give them a call. We have a life to live and I don't plan to let those four ruin it." Again Patrick glanced in the mirror at Finn. "Thanks for being observant. It is a good quality to have. "

Finn shrugged. "I want my new life to start as a family with Glenna. If you'd get off your ass and ask her properly."

Surprise rippled over her, not that she hadn't known that their 'fake' coupleness wasn't the real deal. It had been the real deal since almost the beginning in her mind. It was good to know Finn felt the same way. They were going to be a family.

Patrick's only response was a chuckle as they turned into the parking lot behind the others.

*****

Nerves tingled in every portion of her body. She just wished she were anticipating something joyous not dreading the next few hours. So many things could go wrong.

"Glenna, nothing is going to happen. Finn is at Rebekah's studying. Beckworth, Jones and several other officers from other precincts in the area are surrounding the shop at the moment. Not to mention several of my fellow agents are outside waiting to make sure no one is following us."

That made her laugh. They'd seen the van dogging their movements since they'd returned from Brooklyn a few days ago, not to mention their appearance at the game. Even though the men didn't know they'd been spotted. It was like they were taunting them. Knowing the Calistoga PD had absolutely no evidence on them.

They *hopefully* didn't realize that some of the traffic on their street was now federal and local officers policing the area. Or they just plain didn't care.

What did it matter?

*****

"A lot of traffic all of a sudden."

Jason's voice filtered from the back seat of the van where he paid only marginal attention to the house they were watching. He was more interested in the magazine he was flipping through.

Raymond darted a look in the rearview mirror at him. His friend wasn't saying anything that hadn't crossed his mind. Monroe shifted in the passenger seat so he could talk to Jason in the back.

"Don't you think that's because of that bastard who used us? A few innocent questions about the area, and he used it to follow and gain knowledge on us. And he could use that against us. I'm glad we had the good sense not to give him names. "

Raymond felt the familiar rage boil. This was his baby, he'd formed his ring of art thieves and for years they'd had an outlet from their boring, predictable and high pressured careers. It had also served as a release for his anger. Anger he'd never understood, however, for as long as he remembered it simmered under the surface of every action or thought. When he was young he would take it out on unsuspecting innocents, from the kids that lived in the ghetto, or if desperate, to the neighborhood animals. When he'd come close to venting it on one of his peers, he'd realized he needed something. And had formed *The Black Cats*.

Until now, no one suspected. Until *now,* no one had been hurt either. Something he'd been trying to stay away from, more because when people were murdered it caused the men and women in blue to sit up and take notice.

He must admit though, his adrenalin pumped knowing that nabbing the painting from under everyone's noses would be more dangerous than any of their other heists because they were being watched. Glenna and her bodyguard, fiancé, whatever the hell he was, had set the bait and they were going to grab it… just not when they planned. The *Cats* would do it when they planned.

*****

Patrick's eyes had finally adjusted to the dark. He'd insisted that Glenna wait at the Bistro with Effie. It would be natural for her to be busy with the appetizers and everything else they had planned for the next day. He looked at his phone for the hundredth time. How long would the bastards wait before they made their move? It was almost midnight.

His phone vibrated, startling him. It hit the floor with a thud, thank heavens for protectors. The text spread on the screen.

Have you heard anything? Anyone seen anyone? Effie and I are finished and I'm not sure what you want me to do.

He'd been so certain they'd strike by now. But then they were smart, not your bumbling idiots you sometimes saw on television. These men were used to negotiating high priced deals in the board room with corporate sharks, getting what they wanted and walking away with committing all kinds of who knew what. Patrick was positive they were as lethal in their business dealings.

Or maybe they kept their crime to art theft.

I will have one of the officers follow you home to make sure you're safe. Do not come over here, I want them to think the shop is, and has been, empty all evening.

He stood to the side of the window and watched Effie and one of her employees, walk Glenna out to her car. He smiled, leave it to Glenna's eclectic friend to make sure they had a bodyguard. Even if he didn't look that tough with his man bun and the skateboard dangling from his fingertips.

As soon as Glenna pulled out, the guy watched Effie get in her car and do the same. Only then did he throw his board on the side walk and down the street he flew.

Patrick breathed a sigh of relief as he watched a dark sedan discreetly pull onto the street behind Glenna and another one for Effie. He went back to his seat. At least Glenna would be safe. And Finn was staying at a friend's so he could study. That was his story and Finn was sticking by it, Patrick allowed a chuckle before returning to his current situation. The waiting was driving him crazy. This was worse than a stake out when he was in the safety of his car and watching.

He felt like a sitting duck, he had no idea when they'd show up, would they come in the front? Mostly likely the back. Should he be waiting with gun at the ready? Hide so they were all in and looking before he caught them by surprise? The other officers were watching and would enter almost immediately.

Nothing could happen to him, unless the trigger happy one shot him as he'd done to poor Alex. Patrick wouldn't think about that. He wasn't dumb, he had Kevlar on.

*****

Glenna swore she could see a trail in the carpet where she'd been pacing. She stopped at the doorway of the kitchen to see what time it was. After three in the a. m. She hadn't heard from Patrick or any of the other officers. She'd been instructed when she came home to go to bed. If the van guys were watching to see when she arrived home, they'd feel safe to go to the shop once the lights went out.

Patrick's SUV was parked next to her car in the drive. He'd caught a lift to the shop with Beckworth, in hopes no one would realize he was there and not home.

She was beginning to think they were the ones being duped not the other way around. She sidled up to the picture window in the living room, making sure she couldn't be seen she peered out looking for the van. And there it was.

If it was across the street were all four in it? Or was it empty so they'd think they weren't going to the shop that night?

This waiting was driving her bananas.

She didn't want to distract Patrick with a text. Especially if they were making their move. She settled into the overstuffed chair to curl up and wait.

"Glenna?"

Startled awake, it took her a moment to realize it was light. Morning. She sat up and stretched and looked at Finn.

"What time is it?"

"It's early only about seven. Where's dad?"

"I don't know. I must have fallen asleep waiting." Every muscle in her body felt stiff, and it took a moment to struggle out of the cozy chair. Even after Finn took pity on her and helped haul her up.

"I thought you'd both be hustling around getting ready for the showing, bad guys in jail, and all that."

"I have no idea about the bad guys. I haven't heard from your dad. Is the van still outside?"

Finn went to the side of the window and peered out careful not to be seen. "Yes. They weren't there when I got home a few minutes ago."

Patrick.

Dread ran over Glenna. He'd held up the last time, still four against one. Yet, he was only human and she knew that they weren't afraid to use a gun. This time other officers were there for back up.

"If something had happened, you'd know. My guess is Dad did the same you did, fell asleep waiting for them and they did a no show." He raised his brow at her as if that were significant and she should know what he meant.

She knew what *no show* meant, but her mind was still too muddled with worry and an added dollop of sleepiness.

"Which means, we guessed wrong they never planned to take the painting last night..."

"If they weren't outside watching I would say the idea of nabbing the art had cooled and they'd decided to cut their losses."

Patrick had come in the back so quietly neither of them had heard him. Glenna jumped and almost fell into the chair she'd just vacated. Finn had the good sense to grab her to keep her upright.

"I swear I'm never going to make old age around here. Because I'll have a heart attack long before that."

"Did they even bother to drive by the shop?" Finn asked.

"Not that anyone saw. But early this morning I think most of the officers were asleep at their posts. I struggled to stay awake by walking the shop every fifteen to thirty minutes."

"I'm sorry. I fell asleep waiting. Finn just woke me up."

"The van there when you got home?" Patrick spoke to Finn over his shoulder. He stood in front of the picture window in full view. "They aren't being secretive about watching us, we might as well let them know we're aware. But then we'd have to be blind not to be aware."

"What now?" Glenna just wanted it to be over.

She'd been so excited to have nothing hanging over them for the showing. They had the consulate representatives meeting them in the morning to make the exchange. Tonight though, they would be the experts on stolen artifacts and how the black market worked. A mini workshop on the subject would kick off the event.

"Do you think they'll be blatant enough to attend?"

Patrick turned from his post at the window and walked back and slid onto the couch. His weariness almost palpable. He ran a hand through his hair.

"I think they might."

"Really?" The surprise in Finn's voice matched hers.

"Why would they risk it?" She finally gave in and plopped back into the cozy chair.

Finn sat next to Patrick on the couch and folded his arms. "Do they think we're still clueless to their identities?"

Patrick looked over to Glenna in question, but she had no answers. She shrugged. "I'm not sure what to think."

"They are either incredibly arrogant thinking that no matter what they do we'll never have enough evidence to bring them in, you know flaunting it in our faces or..." He scratched his chin, something she'd noticed Finn doing when he was thinking. "What?"

"Sorry, you and Finn are so much alike. You both scratch your chin, or tug on your ear when you think."

Patrick turned to look at Finn who just raised his brow and shoulders in a full body shrug.

"Well as I was saying, if they're not flaunting, then they think we're the stupidest bungling officers since the *Keystone Cops*, and we're clueless."

"Who?" Finn asked.

"Who what?" Patrick looked thoroughly confused.

"The *Keystone Cops* is an old black and white film series from the early 1900's," Glenna explained.

He looked at his dad in awe. "You know about this how?"

He elbowed his son in the ribs, and by the *hoof* Finn gave it wasn't as playful as it looked. "I watch old reruns on that classic station on cable."

Glenna decided they needed to focus on the problem at hand, they were all tired and easily distracted. They couldn't afford to be. Her assistant needed justice and the arrogant bad guys needed to be put away for good.

"Okay guys, I think we better all get some rest. Effie and I have things under control. I told her we'd be at the shop around two since the event starts at five. I had planned on a long exhausting night. I thought they'd make their move. I didn't realize we'd be stood up."

Patrick chuckled, indicating how punchy he was from his lack of sleep. "Let's try for four hours of sleep. Let them sit out there and stew."

"Won't Beckworth or your parents call to find out what happened?" Okay so Glenna wasn't thinking either. "Okay that was dumb. You've talked to Beckworth, he's probably doing the same. But I'm sure you're parents are antsy."

"I called them on my way home. I even touched base with your law enforcement family. We're good for some uninterrupted shut eye."

"I've had a good night's sleep. I need to finish up one more paper and then I'll call Rebekah and let her know what's going on." Finn stood and shook his head. "I swear she's acting like this is her favorite crime series come to life."

He left the room before either could comment. Patrick pulled himself up as slowly as Glenna, then they walked to the bedroom for some needed sleep. Sleep that Glenna had an idea they were going to need to face the rest of the day and night.

Because once she met with the consulate in the morning, she wouldn't have possession of what they wanted.

Chapter Twenty-Eight

Pleasure tingled over her, Glenna had always dreamt of a grand showing, ever since she'd opened her *Glenna's Surprisingly Vintage.* Anger simmered almost spoiling the moment for her. This moment was supposed to be one of the best of her life, yet the fact the four men who were responsible for her assistant's murder, were across the room drinking *her* champagne, mingling, and acting like any of her other patron's, threatened to ruin it.

Except they weren't the innocent, nice people they portrayed themselves to be.

Frustration tossed itself into the mix boiling in her belly. And what a combination it was. She felt her vision blur, and the terrible thing was the fact she wasn't sure if they were tears of joy or sadness.

Alex had talked about an event just like this to help bring more tourists and patrons of art to their little town, a community that had been struggling since the devastating fires had swept over the valley recently.

Glenna liked to think that Alex had help guide her and Effie as they had planned the showing. In fact, the two of them had reminisced about the times they'd had with the young woman before the bastards had robbed her of her future.

She straightened. She would *not* let them ruin this moment for her. True, if it weren't for the discovery of the treasure she hadn't known she had until the murder and break in, there wouldn't be this event. Eventually she would have, and she'd like to think she would have had the event then. In fact, she would have discovered the picture far sooner if she hadn't been distracted by the devastatingly romantic Lance Gordon. He could have a wonderful career on Broadway with his acting abilities.

She'd been so susceptible to his charm. More so, because she'd finally realized she was ready to move on after the violation of Danny Collins. Only to be betrayed by Lance. She glanced over to where Patrick stood talking to the woman who'd come to give the presentation on the piece that would be returned to her country. She smiled and decided it was time to make her way over, start directing everyone to their seats they'd sat a few seats around the main attraction. An easel held the painting in the middle of the showroom. Although, there would be many who would have to stand.

Finn must have read her mind, he began the process for her. He'd touch a person on their shoulder, then gesture with his other hand to urge them toward a chair. He was going to be a wonderful man, just like his father.

"Hey, there you are." Patrick slung an arm around her shoulders, comfort and warmth immediately helped wipe away the anger and frustration leaving pleasure to wrap around her. "I thought you were going to linger by the door all afternoon."

"I wanted to make sure everyone felt welcomed, but I think everyone is here." She turned to the other woman and smiled. "It's your time for the spot light. I'm so glad you could join us today, Ms. Schröder."

"Please, call me Adele. And are you kidding me? I wouldn't have missed this. It is always such an exciting moment to recover some of our country's missing treasures."

Adele smiled at them, Glenna had imagined someone much older would be the expert. She glanced around at her guests and decided this young vibrant woman could probably make growing weeds interesting. She was as excited as her patrons to hear the lecture.

"Good, then I assume you're ready to begin?"

"I hope you don't regret you've invited me when all your lovely guests are falling asleep in their chairs."

Glenna laughed. "I'm sure that will *not* happen."

Glenna and Patrick gathered the stragglers that Finn and Rebekah hadn't settled yet, into the area designed for the presentation. Glenna wasn't sure what to expect. She was about to find out. She walked to stand by the center of attention, the *Madonna and Child*.

"Welcome everyone. I'm so happy you could join us today, but more than that I'm excited to introduce you to Ms. Adele Schröder. She is Berlin's top art expert, but her specialty is the recovery of the lost art stolen during the Nazi occupation." Glenna held her hand toward Adele. "I turn the time over to you."

"Thank you, Glenna, for inviting me. I'm very pleased to visit your beautiful town. Well, as Glenna said, I am a boring researcher. However, it's anything but boring. I love to find treasures and this…" She turned to gaze at the painting. "Is a lovely piece that Berlin is very excited to reclaim. We already have a spot of honor at the Gemäldegalerie which translates *Old Master Paintings*…"

Glenna had read the presentation prior, as it was a custom to send it along to the host first to make sure it fit the demographics of the audience. This was the first showing of this magnitude for Glenna, she'd been thrilled when she read the speech.

Since she had reviewed it, she felt free to gaze about at the patrons making note where Raymond Branson, Jason Lewis, Edwardo Bertarelli, and Monroe Dyson were. They weren't together, but stationed around the perimeter almost as if they were the guards. Did they know, or have an idea they were being watched by the several undercover agents also attending.

Glenna hadn't met the agents, they could be anyone in the crowd. Patrick had done that on purpose. He hadn't wanted her or any of his family to react differently if they happened to run into one of them. For all Glenna knew she'd had several conversations with many of them.

The room grew quiet and Glenna realized Adele had finished and waited for her. Glenna felt the warmth seep up her collar. Such a big day and she was lost in her thoughts. Good Grief.

She took the two steps to the art expert's side. "Thank you so much. What a wonderful museum you have. I don't know about all of you but I could lose myself in a museum full of art treasures."

As intended everyone smiled and some even nodded in agreement. After that Adele was left to mingle and chat more about her passion, art. Glenna made her way to Patrick's side. He was with his parents, she'd been surprised when they'd arrived. She hadn't taken them for the artsy type, and by the way their expressions, she'd been right.

"Glenna." The relief was evident in Caroline's voice. "What a lovely reception, or should I say showing?"

Glenna smiled. "Either is correct. I'm glad you both could attend."

"When Patrick told us about it, we had to see this piece of art, see what all the fuss was about." Patrick's father glanced toward the easel holding the main attraction. "It's... I'm not sure how to describe it. I thought it would be an old stuffy painting. What was all the fuss about? If you know what I mean. Seeing it in this setting in a place of honor, the lighting just right it takes my breath away."

This time the warmth that spread through her was one of pride from hearing Kendal's words of praise. She slipped her hand into Patrick's and tried to reign in her emotion.

Her voice still wobbled a little when she said, "Thank you." She wanted to express how his words affected her, but they clogged in her throat as she blinked the tears away. Kendal only smiled warmly at her and patted her shoulder.

Patrick cleared his throat and nodded toward Raymond still at his post by the back door. "The four of them haven't moved since the presentation started.

Almost as if they are the guards. I'm not sure what to make of it, unless that's what they want someone to think, but who?"

At that moment Adele walked over to Raymond at his post and he nodded, put his hand to his ear. Did he have an earpiece? Glenna glanced up at Patrick his gaze fixed on the pair, a frown on his face.

When Adele nodded and turned to return to the painting with Raymond on her heals, Glenna felt a moment of dread.

"Stay here." Patrick didn't wait for an answer.

"What's that all about?" Patrick's mother wanted to know.

"I'm not sure, but it can't be good."

Patrick followed the two and once they were at the painting, not wanting them to know he followed he stopped by the first person he saw.

"Enjoying the showing?" He asked the older woman, who had jewels dripping from ears, throat, to wrists. Patrick was pretty sure the dollar amount would be more than the value of his home.

She had been intent on her brochure and started as she looked at him. After a brief pause she smiled. "Why yes, young man. It's just what our community needed now that the valley is rebuilding after the fires."

Young man? How old was she? Patrick wasn't that *young*. Still it was nice to hear. Smiling down at the woman. He tried to engage her in light chatter while trying to listen to Raymond and Adele.

From what he could hear Adele did indeed think Raymond was security. She was currently giving him instructions on the transport scheduled to take place the following morning with a member from the Berlin consulate. She informed the man she would be meeting the gentleman at the shop at nine.

Patrick noticed that Raymond did not correct her assumption that he would be in attendance for the meeting. Patrick wondered what the man planned.

Was he going to pretend to be the security transport? With all the *real* security that would be in attendance, that wasn't going to happen. He searched the crowd and saw the other three men, still standing on the perimeter.

The only action Patrick could do at the moment was to wait and watch. His least favorite part of his job.

*****

Patrick smiled. Glenna just plopped down on one of the vacated chairs across the room. She took off her impossibly high heels, and he heard her sigh from where he stood. How she'd managed to walk on the damn things was a secret of womanhood he'd probably never understand. They looked damn good on her though, so he wouldn't complain if she insisted she wear them.

Effie sat next to Glenna chattering away, giving him time to make sure the place was void of any lingering patrons. He wouldn't put it past the men to find a hiding place and wait the night through.

If that was their plan or whatever plan they had for the exchange they would have a surprise. He would check the basement, though they hadn't found it the night they'd broken in, that didn't mean Danny hadn't informed them in more detail where to locate the door. No one was clear how involved he was with them. From what the New York authorities had found, he'd just chatted with them one time.

"Agent McGinnis, we've swept the entire place. No one hiding any nooks or crannies." Agent Southerland smiled. At least she'd worn sensible shoes. "We're going to head home, if they're watching, they'll expect everyone to be gone soon. Are you sure you don't want one of us taking Ms. Schröder back to her hotel?"

"No that's fine. And thank you for taking one of your Sunday's to help me out."

"No problem, I'd actually planned to attend when I heard about it in the paper. These kinds of jobs are hardly something to complain about. After all, it would have looked strange if I hadn't tried all the delicious foods. The only bummer, I had to pretend I don't drink."

Patrick chuckled. "If you're riding with one of the others, you could always enjoy a glass of wine before you leave."

"Tempting though that may be, Agent Caines is waiting for me. But thank you."

"See you next week in the office."

She tossed him a grin as she left. He walked over and secured the door, then went to where Glenna and Effie chatted with Adele.

"Are you ladies ready to go? I believe we'll leave this mess for in the morning, when we're doing the 'exchange'."

Glenna grimaced. "I don't know, I'll dream about the mess all night."

"You can do this Glenna. You won't see it once you walk out the door. It's not going anywhere. You look like you didn't sleep last night." Effie raised a brow waiting for her to argue.

"Effie, don't let her move. I'm going to check our secret."

"Secret?" Adele stood. "I need to see this."

Adele followed Patrick through the showroom to the back store room. He heard her give a small gasp of surprise when he went to the closet to reveal the hidden door.

"A cellar built during the prohibition period."

"Oh, I've read about things like the prohibition, in the 1920's and early 30's, right?"

"That is correct, I'll just be a minute."

"I'm not waiting. I want to see this."

She was right on his heels, he just hoped the men weren't waiting. He reached behind him and pulled his Glock from his waist band.

"Are you expecting trouble? No one knows this is down here."

"The guys after the painting know it's down here but haven't found the passage." He paused and lowered his voice before he started down the stairs. "That we know of, they may have been snooping today."

"And intend to wait the night in the basement, safe and undetected." He heard a hint of excitement in her voice.

She wouldn't be so intrigued if they were lying in wait.

"Hang on until I give you the go ahead."

She nodded, but he barely saw her. The only light filtered from the storeroom above. Gun in both hands, arms stretched ahead leading his way into the room. Standing in one place he swept his arms in a semi-circle making sure the room was empty. Still not satisfied he reached to pull the string. Bright light flooded the room to reveal boxes of all shapes and sizes filled with Glenna's treasures. He wondered how many more rare art pieces she had she might not be aware of, he hoped none.

He turned to give Adele the go ahead and she was already at the bottom of the stairs. At least she'd been quiet. He didn't say anything just gave her a look.

"When you turned the light on, I could see no one was here."

"They could have been hiding."

Of course, the room empty of hiding places didn't lend any credence to his warning. He shrugged and went to investigate beneath the stairs, though he could see through the frame work no one was there. He wanted to reassure himself he didn't leave a square inch unsearched.

"What are in all these?"

Adele was bending over a box full of who knew what. Getting dust all over her slacks, he didn't think she cared. If he didn't steer her away from the box and back to Glenna and Effie, they may be down here for hours.

"We better get you back to the hotel. We don't want those watching to think anything is up."

Disappointment shown in her eyes as she straightened. "You're right. I left my bag in the showroom."

He waited until she was almost up the stairs before he pulled the string to turn the lone bulb off then he followed. He locked the door and pulled the items in front giving it an ordinary closet appearance.

Adela returned to the store room with Glenna and Effie in her wake. She looked around at the room.

"At least there are no windows in here."

"We're hoping they believe the story about the exchange in the morning. They won't think anything of your *briefcase* after all you brought it to the showing."

Glenna had placed the easel and painting in the storeroom as soon as the last patrons had left. He knew she hadn't wanted to wait until this moment in case they were watching.

"I am still curious as to why they would believe that we would have to exchange this painting with the consulate when I'm the country's art expert? It is not unheard of for me to reach out to patrons who have art that one or our museums would like to display."

"Glenna made a big deal when we were at the Gala..."

"I'm sorry I missed that, I do try to attend. Sorry for interrupting."

"It was an event." Though he was thinking of Finn's near escape. "We tried to lay the ground work for everyone to think Berlin would send an ambassador to retrieve it, and that having you as a guest for the showing was just that, you're our guest and have nothing to do with the exchange."

"That sounds plausible, and as I *am* the expert of course I'd want to be in attendance to make sure the person picking it up for the consulate knew how to handle it." She set her case on the table to open it revealing packing for the painting. "I did tell anyone who brought the subject up tomorrow's the plan. I'm not sure I talked to any of your thieves though."

Together Glenna and Patrick answered. "You did."

Glenna gave him a grin and though it was hardly the time or the place, desire ripped over him. He swallowed and glanced away he clamped his jaw tight, then he caught Effie's knowing grin. Damn. How embarrassing.

"Let's get going, or they're going to think something is up," Effie said breaking through the tension. Although, Patrick was fairly sure he was the only one who felt it.

The painting was safe in Adele's case. Glenna and Effie on one side of her, and Patrick on the other, they walked to the car. Keeping up the chatter about Berlin, and anything else they could think of, as they didn't know where the men were watching. And they were *watching.* Patrick could feel the back of his neck prickle. A sure sign.

He opened the door for Adele, then the other two women. Once he settled into the driver's seat he called the station on his handless phone to let them know they were on the move. Other agents were also in place. He hoped.

He didn't think the men would confront them in front of the shop. He wasn't too sure about the route to the hotel. Adele was correct to worry about whether they'd bought the story. There was no reason Adele couldn't transport the treasure. Though with the value of the painting, they had sent a man with her. He had been at the showing, but left shortly after so as not to draw attention. He was waiting at the hotel and would take over security as soon as they dropped her off. The scene in the showroom the day he'd met Glenna passed through his mind and he shivered. He didn't want another death over a painting. Senseless. Murder usually was.

*****

"And there they go."

Raymond drummed his fingers on the steering wheel as they watched from their post across from the shop down the side street. A perfect view of the activities.

"They're going to drop her off to her bodyguard at the hotel. What's our next move?" Jason twisted in his seat to include Monroe in the back.

"They think we are going to try to either take the Madonna tonight or in the morning during transport." Monroe leaned forward.

Raymond met his eyes in the mirror. "You don't think they've left it in the shop."

"No. I don't think there's a consulate meeting either."

"Why would they need one?" Jason asked. "I know the painting is priceless but this Adele Shruder, or whatever her name is, came to lecture, so why not just have her bring it back with her to Berlin."

"Why would she have a guard with her if she came to the states to lecture?" Raymond asked.

Monroe moved his hand from the back of the Raymond's seat and settled back into his former position. He slouched against the door, legs along the bench seat. "I believe they think they're pulling the wool over our eyes."

Raymond grinned in the review mirror at his friend. He turned and finally removed a hand from the wheel to fist bump Jason in the shoulder.

"Ow."

"Oh baby, I barely touched you."

"Yeah right."

"Guys. Focus." Monroe didn't so much as move with the command. "The way that agent boyfriend of Glenna's keeps watching us, I have a feeling they suspect."

"No, I don't think so. Glenna and her law enforcement bodyguard were definitely preoccupied with each other at the Gala." He chuckled.

"Does anyone know about our hobby?" Worry threaded through Jason's words. "I thought we agreed no one know but the four of us? Yet somehow we let our guard down to ask that guy questions about the area."

"Yeah, except, I'm not sure how much he heard us talking about our hobby before he realized we were talking about Calistoga, that's what seemed to draw his attention." Raymond tightened his grip on the wheel. "To answer your question, no. My assistant thinks the only reason we're here is the winery."

"Speaking of which, the vineyard itself mostly survived the fire, it was just the house and the outbuildings. I think it's a great investment." Monroe asked.

"I do too," Edwardo said.

The others paused to stare, it was the first words they'd heard from Edwardo all evening. When he'd first joined their little ring of *Cats*. They found out quickly it would never be Eddie. He always had their back and had become a valuable partner in their nefarious activities and legitimate dealings alike. But talking? He listened and observed.

Finally, Raymond looked at Jason. "What are your thoughts?"

"It will take a lot of work, but yeah I think it will be a great investment. Damn good wine also."

Raymond grinned. "True."

He started the engine and eased onto the road. The other car was well out of sight. They knew where the hotel was, no need to give themselves away.

"What's the plan?" Monroe asked.

"After they drop her off, we'll find a way in and take it before anyone knows." Raymond wasn't sure how yet, but they'd brainstorm and come up with a plan they always did.

"You don't have a plan do you?" Jason sighed and then laughed. "But hell, that's the fun isn't it. I mean we don't need the fucking money."

"We also don't want to be stuck in some American prison either." Monroe, the voice of reason from the backseat spoke up. "Is this painting really worth it? I mean, even if we buy into the fact the agent is *only* the boyfriend he's trained for things like this. I have a bad feeling."

Raymond pulled into the lot and found a parking spot far from the building and any street lamps. Once he'd backed in so they had a view of the hotel he turned the car off. Only then did he twist in his seat to see not only Edwardo in the passenger seat, but those in the back, all were his best friends. Jason and Monroe he'd known his entire privileged life. Edwardo they'd gathered into their circle years earlier.

"I've thought about that. This is the first time we've ever consulted an outsider. It was only a chance conversation on the other coast and yet it didn't go well. This was the first time we've ever been interrupted during a heist, and that didn't go well...."

He fell silent. He scratched his ear while he thought, was it worth it? If they were caught it wouldn't just be for theft, it would be for murder.

"It's a matter of pride," he finally stated.

"Yeah yours. I say we cut our losses." Monroe ground the words out. "As Jason said we don't need the money. Is it fucking worth it? If we do get away with it, this has caused so much uproar already they'll be watching the Dark web for any sales, we'll have to sit on it for a few years before we can reap any rewards for our efforts."

Raymond felt the twist of his guts. The adrenalin that pumped through his veins at the thought of outwitting the authorities raced through him. He refused to think he wasn't using the excellent judgement he usually did in high risk situations. He would not let it be personal.

He was a shark when it came to the board room. He had more money than God, he had all the beautiful women he wanted. Did he need another notch in his heist belt?

"True, we'll have to sit on it. But are any of you ready to let the authorities win?"

"Yeah. If we're caught we won't see the light of day for years. Raymond, think, Are we ready to face that?" Jason asked.

Monroe shifted again to lean in between the front seats. "I know that you've got a stubborn streak wider than the English Channel, but dude, prison? Really? You're a pretty boy, think about what happens to rich guys like us in prison."

"We won't go to that kind of prison. We'll be sent back to England. And shall I point out, between the four of us we have a team of lawyers that will throw any evidence *they* think they have on us out the window." He grinned at his friends. "I mean, why the fuck do we pay them so much if they're not the best?"

Raymond heard Jason draw in a sigh. "You know, I hate to leave a job unfinished."

Then he heard the leather rustle from the back where Monroe settled into his slouch. "Yeah, then we lay low for a while."

Edwardo regarded Raymond who twisted to throw a look in the back at the other two and shrugged and gave an affirmative grunt.

Chapter Twenty-Nine

One of the agents had spotted the car parked across the street from the showing. They had watched the men climb in and wait. The four may think they were the only ones watching, but they weren't.

Standing by the front door of the hotel, Patrick's nerves prickled as they had earlier. Something was going to happen he knew it. There were no other cars on the street it wasn't hard to spot the car the moment it turned into the lot.

"They just pulled in and parked as far from the light as possible, if I hadn't watched where they went, I'd have had a hard time noticing them." Patrick informed the other agent at the back of the hotel.

He was glad they'd had enough time to move Adele and her man to the room across the hall. In the room registered in her name, there were two agents in place.

So far, things were going as planned. Patrick knew that didn't mean things could slide down a rabbit hole fast. It was going to be a long night, he was sure they wouldn't make their move now, it wasn't that late in the evening. Many guests would be returning from dinner and others may have plans for the next few hours. But at least the Madonna and Child was safe and would be on its way home to Berlin early in the a.m.

Effie and Glenna were with Adele, as Glenna refused to go home. Patrick had agreed because he couldn't push down a little niggle that he'd missed something, or the feeling that the other shoe was about to drop. Glenna should have been safe at home.

He was sure all of the men were in the car waiting. They weren't the type to resort to kidnapping to exchange for the painting, it was the thrill of taking it from underneath everyone's noses. Yet, he didn't want to take any chances with her being at the house alone if he were wrong. Finn was at one of his football buddies home for the night, he would be safe. Besides the four had seen how kidnapping had gone down, or had they? No one really knew where Danny fit in, if he did. The man wasn't forthcoming with the authorities. The last Patrick had heard, since his plan to capture Glenna, he'd had some kind of mental melt down. No answers from that corner.

Patrick didn't like mysteries or lose ends. When the four were in custody he'd find out.

*****

Patrick paced carefully to stay out of view of the lobby windows. He was antsy, he knew they had a solid plan, but something was off. His gut twisted. Things were going too smooth.

Too anticlimactic. That's what it was.

And still there was that pesky little worry of something he was missing.

He stopped just to the side of the window, the car was still in its same place, his vision had adjusted with the darkening night and he could barely make out the figures, mostly because they moved from time to time, unlike headrests. He started to turn just as one of the car doors opened.

"They're on the move," he said.

"We're ready." A woman's voice filtered into his ear.

The one thing that had bothered him from the get go had been, how did Raymond and his band of cat burglars know the room number? He wouldn't be surprised if they were hackers and had somehow got passed the firewalls of the hotel. Didn't matter.

"Everything in place?" he asked.

There was a pause and some rustling. "Yes, I'm going to have a robe on over my clothes, give him the impression we're relaxing, etc. Adele will be in the shower. She couldn't sleep, you know. And if they insist she get out, they have a surprise when they find Agent Coleman instead."

Patrick smiled but didn't reply. No one wanted to tackle the former Raiders' wide receiver.

He watched from his place as they drew closer, he needed to get to his post. The elevator doors slid closed as the automatic front door opened. He hadn't seen who walked through the door. Which meant they hadn't seen him either.

As he walked by room 342, he gave a brief knock, the signal he was on his way to the end of the hall where it turned. There were agents stationed throughout the nooks and crannies of the boutique hotel but mostly on the third floor.

*****

So far it had been a piece of cake, the woman at the registration desk hadn't paid any attention to the men entering. Obviously they couldn't have put on their masks before entering even if though they'd waited until around midnight. They'd found hotels were suspicious of men entering in the middle of the night.

Unless of course, you're in a major city, here in the laid back town of Calistoga, better to hide in plain sight. They just needed to keep their faces down, that way surveillance would get the tops of the heads. Look at no one, especially any personnel. No reason to make it easy for anyone to give a good description of them.

Once in the elevator without a word they pulled their masks from their back pockets and slipped them over their heads. They'd formed a routine over the years. From the moment they left the car until the moment they were inside there wasn't a word spoken, and then only instructions or questions. Voices could be traced as easily as a face.

Technology while wonderful for their various legitimate businesses was not their friend for their first love. The thrill of stealing priceless art or artifacts under the very noses of the protectors.

Raymond stood to the side of room 342 Jason on the other, Edwardo behind Monroe, he knocked, schooled his voice to a different register.

"Room service."

The woman's voice filtered through the wood panel. "We didn't order anything."

Monroe knocked again. "It was ordered for you by a…" Rustle of paper that his friend had had in his back pocket for their little charade. "Glenna Beckett, there's a note."

They heard the bump and a click as the woman undid the lock, the door crept open. Monroe ready, kicked the door the rest of the way open. The woman jumped out of the way with a screech.

"What are you doing?" her voice wavered.

What the fuck?

"Where's the art woman from Berlin?" Raymond felt his gut clench.

The woman swallowed. "She's taking a shower."

He nodded to Jason, he walked to the bathroom door where now that he listened could hear the shower going. His gut eased a fraction. He still didn't like the fact they hadn't known about this other person. An assistant? She wasn't at the showing earlier. He'd made a point to study everyone who'd attended.

Monroe was moving around the room checking to make sure no one else hid in a closet or other hiding place. Another rock hit the bottom of his stomach at the same time he realized there had been no guard at the door. They'd been prepared to deal with him. Before he could form another thought the bathroom door blew open knocking Jason on his ass. And the largest man he'd had the misfortune to see other than on the big screen, stood gun ready.

Monroe stopped midstride, Raymond turned to leave. Their most important rule: at the first sign of trouble all men for themselves and get the hell out of dodge.

The problem with getting the hell out of dodge was that the pass was blocked with an impressive wall of men with guns pointed at his chest.

"Stop! Federal Agents." As if they'd needed to announce themselves.

The Madonna and Child had been a jinx for them since Monroe had visited the bar and heard about the piece from Lance Gordon.

*****

Something wasn't right. Patrick always trusted his gut. It clenched. He knew the other shoe was about to drop. He kept to his post. He could see the agents enter, anticlimactic. The thieves weren't usually violent. The murder of Alex hadn't been planned, and from the tapes it seemed like knee jerk reaction at the interruption. He wasn't even sure they were armed as they had been the night at Glenna's shop.

Yet the hair on the back of his neck stood at attention. "I'm going to stay at my post to make sure there are no surprises."

"Gut telling you something?" Came the woman's voice.

He could hear the commotion with the agents cuffing and reciting the Miranda. Yes very innocuous.

He peered around the corner and that's when he noticed another man lurking at the other end of the hall. Somehow he didn't think the man was a gawker, especially as the hotel had informed the occupants of the floor with as much of the details as they could. It had been left to them if they wanted to go out for the evening or check into a vacant room on another floor if available. As they hadn't known what time something would happen, if anything.

Yet the man stood intent on the happenings. And damn, but he looked familiar. Patrick settled against the wall, he couldn't see anything from this vantage point but he needed to think. Where had he seen him?

A moment later he glanced around to peer down the hall, most the officers had either gone back down or were in the room. The hall was empty. The man had gone. Maybe he was just a gawker. He holstered his gun and made his way to the room.

As expected most the excitement had died down and agents were in the process of finishing up.

"Enroute." The women's voice piped up in his ear and startled him after the stretch of silence.

"I'm on my way in a few. Going to check on our guest with the painting." He glanced around a last time and made his way across the hall.

He gave a quick two knocks a pause and another knock. The door opened cautiously, and Adele's guard's face appeared. Patrick wondered again how much security training the man had had before they dubbed him trained enough to protect Adele and her treasures when she traveled around the world. He looked white as a sheet.

"Come in." His voice even shook.

Nerves of steel the man did not have.

"How are things here?"

"They'd be fine if the flu hadn't decided to bite me in the ass. I'm glad I had your help tonight." The man slipped into the overstuffed chair in the little sitting room. "I'm weak as a fucking puppy. You must think I'm a wimp."

Patrick tried not to look as guilty as he felt about his earlier thoughts, as the man echoed them. That made him feel a bit safer leaving Glenna at the hotel while he drove to his office.

"Sucks. Sorry, are you going to be okay to fly in the morning?"

Patrick knew it wasn't charitable of him, but he wanted the damn painting out of his jurisdiction, it had caused enough harm. Even if they guy felt as sick as he looked, Patrick wanted him on that early flight.

"Hopefully, this is just a twenty-four hour thing." The man regarded Patrick for a moment. "Even if it's not, I'll make sure Adele and her painting are safe and on their way home."

"Do you need me to get you anything before I leave?" He asked as an afterthought he didn't have the time, but it seemed like the decent thing to do.

"No. Before the showing, we stopped at the market and picked me up a few things." He started to push up from the chair, then apparently thought better of the idea and slumped into the cushions. "Things should be quiet around here now. Especially since your agent Coleman has offered to stay until we leave for the airport. You better get going if you want to finish up tonight."

He wanted to stay, make sure. That niggle was very persistent. But he couldn't think what lose end there could be. Danny was in custody in New York, and the spoiled rich boys were on their way to the Federal offices in San Francisco now.

"Oh, hi." Glenna had walked through from the other room of the suite. "I thought you were gone by now."

Effie resplendent in iridescent pinks and blues tonight followed a step behind.

"I wanted to check in, make sure you're okay." To Effie, he said, "Adele has an early flight, do you want me to drop you off on my way to San Fran?"

"Effie is going to take me home. With all the excitement I haven't really had time to talk to Adele. We're going to stay a little while and then we'll head out."

"I think it's so cute the way he worries over you." Effie commented, then went over and held her hand to the guards head. "You feel warm, do you want a Tylenol?"

Effie and the guard? Patrick almost grinned, the two couldn't have been more opposite. But then the old cliché...

Patrick looked down at Glenna kissed the top of her head. "Be careful and I'll call you from the office."

Patrick shut the door of the suite and started toward the elevator. His gut twisted with indecision. He needed to follow the others, but he really didn't want to leave Glenna even if Coleman was staying. There would be no way he'd leave if he didn't know they were safe.

He paused before stepping in the elevator, just to be safe he'd take another sweep around the floor and make sure he wasn't over thinking everything. He needed to prove to himself the little niggle was prodding him to be overly cautious and there wasn't really anything else going on.

*****

Waiting.

He hated waiting. It had been hours since the showing, it had been all he could do not to rip the painting from the easel and take off. Patience. He was good at that, hadn't he been patient for what, two years now? He should have had it by now, but no, Glenna had forgotten about the box of treasures she'd gotten from the garage sale. Apparently he'd been too convincing in his pursuit of her when he'd swept her off in the romance of planning a wedding.

Who knew that would have been so easy?

The inner circles of the art community were a tight knit group, and Lance Gordon was one of their community. It was what he did, acquired treasures, usually legally but The Madonna and Child had tempted him to move to the other side of the law. He'd heard about the art expert Glenna had flown in from Berlin had been keeping track since.

If you had the computer skills he did, it wasn't hard to find things like travel itineraries. He had watched from afar from the moment their plane had touched down.

And now was his time. The agents were gone with the four men, and soon Glenna's boyfriend would be gone. It had been pure luck that he'd seen him knock on the door across the hall, now he *knew* where the painting was.

He couldn't believe how things were turning out. After months of searching, almost getting caught by Glenna's nosey neighbor, not to mention those *Black Cats* had scared him off the night he'd planned to search the basement he'd just found out about. The night they'd shot Glenna's assistant Alex.

He'd liked the girl.

It had thrown a monkey wrench into his plans because then the place was crawling with cops and agents.

Yeah he'd been patient in spite of the fact he hated waiting. And tonight he'd be rewarded by his perseverance. He still hadn't figured out how the men knew about the painting, nor did he know who they were. Every time he caught a glimpse of them, they either had their black ski masks on, or they were parked in a shadow.

Didn't matter. He had a plan. That would be to get rid of the Neanderthal he'd seen entering the Berlin woman's room. All the agents, except the boyfriend were gone, but he hadn't seen the huge man since the commotion. He had to be somewhere.

Fuck.

The boyfriend just rounded the corner. Had he slipped in to the alcove in time? Luckily these boutique hotels were frillier with billowing, or at least this one did, curtains at the window. He stepped behind the fabric and held his breath. The man paused and looked his way, but after a moment moved on.

He waited another few seconds before he let out his breath.

*****

Patrick reached the end of the hall and let out a frustrated breath. Nothing. No sign of anyone let alone the man he'd seen at the opposite of his hiding place. He'd only caught a glimpse of him, but something raised a flag. There was just a touch of recognition. He'd seen him somewhere, or he could have seen a picture.

He made his way around the floor again, trying to settle the pitching in his gut that he was missing a piece of the puzzle. He gave a brief knock on the door. Glenna called out to inquire who it was. Then unlocked the door to let him in, but he didn't enter. He needed to get to the office.

"Are you sure you don't want me to drop you off?" He leaned in and gave her a quick kiss.

Her smile almost dislodged the unease, but then it settled in with a vengeance. He didn't want to leave, but then he looked at the former football player dwarfing the overstuffed chair where he lounged. The other guy must have gone to his room, with the threat over.

"We're not going to stay much longer. You go get what you need done I'll see you at home."

Home he liked the sound of that. "Okay, you take care."

He started to turn, then thought better of it. He needed to let Agent Coleman in on his concerns. Even if they were unfounded.

"I just need to let Coleman know something, then I'll be on my way."

He walked over to the man, who didn't so much as move a muscle just looked up from his sports magazine with a bored expression and a lift of a brow. As if Patrick was interrupting the reading of a masterpiece.

After he described what he had seen of the man. The guy straightened and listened intently. Not that Patrick had had an up close and personal, so it was more a general description.

"I'll keep a look out, McGinnis. The British dude has gone to bed. I told him I'd stay until they left for the airport." Verifying what the guard had told him.

The man let his attention return to the magazine again. Patrick got the distinct impression Coleman was more alert than he let on. Hopefully, Patrick was seeing dragons where there weren't any.

As he pulled out of the lot and headed south, toward San Francisco. His mind wouldn't stop going over the day, and it all came back to the unknown man.

They had Danny boy, they had the play boys, who else was there?

Lance Gordon. It was the man bun, he'd remembered making fun of it when he'd seen the man's picture.

He'd still been interested, hadn't Lance gone through Glenna's house again? Patrick slammed on his breaks. The blast of a horn indicated the people behind him weren't appreciative of his driving skills. He pulled to the side of the road to let them pass, and ignored the finger, knowing he deserved the gesture.

He made sure no other traffic was coming and flipped a U-turn.

How hadn't he known? Because he was focused on *The Black Cats* and nothing else. Using his hands free, he put a call through to the station to let them know he would be delayed and why. They'd contact Coleman, he'd removed his earpiece, not that it would have worked this far from the hotel.

Thank God he'd only gone a few miles.

*****

Lance called the front desk. "Hey, I just saw some guy sneaking around the third floor. I thought all the excitement was over, anyway that's what the busboy who knocked on my door a few minutes ago said."

"Sir, it is. It is. I'm sorry for the inconvenience. I'm sure it's just one of the other hotel guests."

Lance sucked in his breath and then inspiration struck.

"With a gun?"

"Oh. I'll call the officer who's still here."

He didn't correct her, he'd been almost positive the agent was still lingering. Now he knew. And the minute the guy left the room, he'd slip in. Earlier, he'd taken advantage after he'd seen the boyfriend right before everything went down. He slipped down to the registration desk and created a key card with the information from the room where Glenna and the art expert were laying low.

He stood at the end of the hall praying the guy would check the opposite direction first. No luck, but Lance was ready. The agent had him by six inches and a good fifty pounds, but anyone could be felled if they were caught unaware. All this ran through his mind in a split second as the man rounded the corner, hand on the gun in his holster, though probably because he didn't want to alarm anyone, by pulling it out.

Lance pulled his own gun out, waited until the man was by him, then he slipped out of his hiding place, reached up and brought the butt down on the back of the man's head. The way someone who'd been in prison had bragged was the *correct* way to knock someone senseless without killing the bastard. Of course, the prison bird was drunk and spouting all this at a bar. Lance took a moment to watch for any movement. When there was none, he took off as quietly as possible toward the door that separated him from his treasure.

He drew in his breath and slipped the card in. When it blinked green, he pushed down the handle and used his shoulder to slowly open the door. The room was dim, so he stood in the entry to get his bearings. The women were chatting in the sitting area. He took a step and stopped.

Three? He hadn't noticed Effie slip in earlier, and she was *hard* to miss. He'd really liked her also, too bad he hadn't liked Glenna. That wasn't fair, she was nice enough, she just had what he wanted, and he'd been detached from her in order to keep his bearings. Not wanting to let any emotion come into play when he found the painting. He didn't want his conscience to get in the way.

It was now or never.

"Good evening ladies."

It was gratifying to see all three start and gape at him.

"Lance?"

"Your true love." Keeping the gun level on them he tilted his head to the side and winked at Glenna. "Though I hear I have competition."

"Lance?" This time it was Effie.

The woman from Berlin calmly sipped her wine. Did this happen a lot in her line of work? It was a bit disconcerting to have no one take you seriously when you had a gun pointed at them.

"It's the man bun." The woman said.

He felt his arms drop a fraction. "What?"

He straitened his arms, he took the stance he'd seen on *NCIS*, one of the only police shows he watched. He probably couldn't hit the side of the barn, but they didn't need to know that.

The woman chuckled at his question. "Your man bun and come on, you look like you just walked out of men's fashion magazine. How can we take you serious?"

He straightened his shoulders. "I needed to blend in, so no one found me suspicious."

"It probably worked in the lobby. But I'm sorry, Glenna, Effie, are you shaking in your heels?"

And then the bitch had the audacity to outright laugh.

"Shut up." He pointed the gun at her forehead. "Carefully stand and get the painting and I'll slip out before your bear of an agent gets back. I don't want to hurt anyone."

Instead Glenna stood. "Lance put that thing down. We'll forget all about this, just leave."

Effie stood, and then the other damn woman did also. This was getting out of hand. If he took a shot, he may hit one of them. Worse it would draw attention.

"Effie, Glenna both of you sit or I'll shoot your art expert." He kept his focus on the woman. "You go get the painting now."

All three women sat down. He was running out of time and he needed to get the upper hand. Damnit he was out of his element. This painting must be cursed or something, first the professional men were caught and now it wasn't looking good for him. He may be a computer wizard, business man, and antiquities dealer but he was not a criminal.

He wasn't until that moment.

"Is the damn Madonna and Child cursed or jinxed or something?" He blurted and then felt his eyes go wide, he hadn't meant to say that out loud.

"Actually there have been rumors about several of the pieces stolen during the Nazi occupation. It's been said that the artists' ghost watches over their work to make sure it finds its way home."

Normally he wasn't a superstitious man, but he couldn't discount the chill that just scampered down his spine. Nor could he discount all the bad luck that all of them had encountered since they'd discovered Glenna had it in her possession.

"Lance." The sharp command in Glenna's voice brought his attention back to the present. "Put that thing down before you hurt someone. I know you're not going to shoot us. And Adelle is not going to get the painting for you. It's going back to Berlin in the morning as planned."

So that was the woman's name.

"Adelle, I'm afraid Glenna is wrong. I can and will shoot one of you if you do not get the painting." When she didn't move he took a sidestep bringing himself to Effie's chair, he redirected his gun to point at her head. "Now."

Adelle looked at his gun visibly shaking, but still pointed were it wouldn't miss Effie if it went off. He saw her throat work in a swallow, then she sat her glass down and stood.

"Fine, but you'll have to deal with the consequences."

As he watched her walk into the other room he pondered her words, what had she meant? Stealing the painting or was there really a curse? The fine hairs on his arms prickled against his shirt and it was all he could do to repress the shiver that wanted to overcome him.

His turn to swallow, he looked down at Effie, big mistake. Large blue eyes stared directly at him, her ponytail as usual a mop on her head, tilted to the side.

"Lance, you're not going to shoot me." When he didn't move, she sighed. "You know you're shaking like a leaf. Are you going to be able to live with yourself if that thing goes off?"

"Lance, she's right." Glenna inched forward in her seat, he made himself keep focus on Effie. "You're not a bad person. What I want to know, why?"

Without breaking eye connection with her friend, he replied to Glenna. "Why? What do you mean? That Madonna and Child is worth a fucking million or more dollars on the Dark web."

"Why didn't you just ask me about the painting? Why go all of the trouble for two years to get me to marry you, just so you could find the painting?"

"Do I need to repeat myself about the worth?"

"No, but that doesn't answer my question. You could have just asked. I had no clue what I had, or what the worth was. All you had to do was ask if you could see some of my things. I knew you were part of the art community and into art and treasures, one of the many things we had in common."

Frustration ran over him. He'd gone to all the trouble and headache to con her into falling in love with him, though now he knew she'd more fallen in love with the idea of love than him. Still he could have just *asked* her? Really?

"Well what are you going to do now?"

Adelle brought his attention to her. She stood at the door leading to the bedroom her own gun pointed at his chest.

"Drop the gun and nothing bad will happen." She shrugged her shoulders somehow without the gun wavering. "Berlin takes their treasures very serious. Do you think they'd send someone untrained to bring home one of their priceless pieces of art? Not to mention I have security with me."

Startled he glanced around, what did she mean security? What to do?

Well this had gone to hell in a hand basket in a hurry. If he didn't think fast he'd be in the cell next to the boys.

He felt sweat pool at the small of his back. Awareness ran through his veins, and not the exciting kind. The kind where you know you should be having a little movie in your head about your life. Isn't that what they said that your life flashes right before you die? He seemed to have a blank reel of film.

*****

Patrick blew into the lot, slammed on the brakes in front of the hotel. Threw the car in Park, but didn't bother turning it off. He waived the valet off as he ran, the glass door barely having enough time to open for his entrance. He paused at the desk. "Grab your master key." He didn't wait for the girl he punched the elevator button by the time the door slid open she was at his side.

"The agent called you?"

He had been intent on watching the numbers change, took an hour or so it seemed just to reach two. He should have taken the stairs. Then it registered what she'd said. He looked down at her and frowned.

"What?"

"We had a call about some guy on the third floor snooping around with a gun, I called Agent Coleman and he said he'd check it out." She raised a brow. "He never called me to let me know what was going on, I assumed that was why you were here."

Dread ran through him. Lance had to have called to distract the agent.

He held an arm out to stop her from leaving the elevator. "Let me have the key, you need to go back to your desk. Call the number I gave you earlier and let Officer Beckworth know I need backup."

He stepped out, gun at the ready. He glanced both ways. He didn't have the time but he needed to at least have a looksee. He turned left walking softly but swiftly. At the L of the hall he made sure the other hall was clear, then retraced his steps and continued to the other end where another turn was. That was where he found Agent Coleman, struggling to stand. Blood dripped through hair from a head wound.

"Whoa." Patrick holstered his gun, leaned down and gripped the man's elbow and hauled him up. Steadied him. "Back-up should be coming."

He glanced around, spotted a chair in one of the many alcoves. He helped the agent over to sit. He didn't have time to question him, he could figure out what had happened.

"Stay here."

When Agent Coleman didn't put up a resistance, Patrick paused. Maybe he should call an ambulance. He looked a little more closely, but Coleman had his head down in his hands elbows resting on his knees for support.

He hesitated.

"Go, I'll be fine."

Patrick could barely make out the other man's words, but he didn't need any more encouragement, he took off at a trot toward room 341, across from where everything went down earlier.

He leaned in to listen. No sound of a commotion. Could be good or bad. He went to slip the card in, but the door hadn't shut all the way, the upper latch was holding it open a fraction. He carefully nudged the door open, slowly hoping the thing was well oiled.

The room came into view, and his heart dropped to his toes at the scene. No one was hurt thank God, but he'd pretty much walked into a Mexican standoff. Gordon had his gun on Effie, though it wavered a little as he looked toward Adele, who had her gun trained at his chest.

Then he glanced to Glenna who had her eyes on him. He nodded in a way he hoped conveyed not to give him away.

He held the door and gently helped it close as soundlessly as possible. The good thing about hotels, their floors rarely creaked or groaned, he took a few steps in, Effie cast him a discrete glance out of the corner of her eye. If Adele noticed him, she didn't so much as blink. Gordon had his back to him.

"We could stand here all night. You're not getting the painting." Adele kept Gordon's attention. "And you're not going to shoot Effie or anyone for that matter, you're just not a killer."

Patrick took another step, then another.

"Lance, come on. You don't want to go to prison. You have a world class collection. Is this piece worth it? Don't make things any worse than they are." The gun in Gordon's hand shook as he listened to Glenna's entreaty. The arm holding the weapon started to drop, but then he brought it back up and straightened his shoulders.

Damn, Patrick had hoped he'd give in. Things could get tricky when your perp had a gun pointed at someone. Even though he was behind Gordon if he grabbed him from behind he could pull the trigger in reflex. He'd planned to grab him from behind pinning the arm with the gun to his side. But it was still up and pointed.

He drew in his breath took a step to bring him directly behind the other man and placed the barrel of his Glock at the back of Gordon's head.

"Federal Agent, keep both hands where I can see them, slowly lay your weapon on the ground." He gave a little tap where his gun aimed. "No quick movements."

Gordon's arm didn't move, but the gun hit the ground with a thud. Thank God it didn't discharge.

"Keep your arms up."

Patrick holstered his gun, Adele kept hers trained on Gordon's chest. He pulled both arms behind Glenna's ex and cuffed him. At that moment the door blew open. Beckworth and Jones had arrived.

Chapter Thirty

Finn ruffled Horace's shaggy body as Agnes sauntered over titled her head and he swore the cat purred "*Well?*"

He chuckled and scratched behind her ears. "You two are just like siblings, if one has something the other has, they want to be included too."

A knock on the door interrupted his thoughts. He knew it would be Rebekah, they were cooking dinner. It would be interesting to see how things turned out.

Hopefully not burnt.

He opened the door and she stood there with her arms full. "Hey, here let me take that, or is there more in the car."

She handed him the bag, bent to give attention to the two pets demanding it.

"I didn't think they did this, dogs and cats are not supposed to live in harmony."

"Yeah, they're pretty modern minded."

"Oh, and no that's all there is, let's get started." She leaned a hip on the counter glanced at her phone. Then turned to the sink and started to wash her hands. "Glenna leaves the shop soon, right?"

"Yeah normally, but I asked Effie to give us a call when she was on her way."

"Good, what about your dad?"

"He's getting things ready at the bar."

"Good." She pointed at the sink. "You're turn. You'll be handling food because this will be a joint effort."

He grinned. He actually liked to cook. Sometimes when his dad worked late he'd have dinner ready for him. He paused letting the water rush over his hands. He'd now have Glenna to cook for him and his dad. His grinned widened.

"You know, since all the *Law and Order* stuff went down all you do is grin like the court jester."

"I'm going to have a mom!"

She folded her arms and raised a brow at him. "Believe me, moms aren't always all their cracked up to be."

He considered her for a moment. He picked up the lettuce and placed it in the colander to rinse. "From what I observed about my new cousins, girls and their moms have a complicated relationship."

She nudged his arm with her elbow. "Look at you all grown up and wise. You're right. I love my mom to pieces but sometimes..."

"Alexa play *Imagine Dragons*."

He smiled as he worked beside his best friend. They were making pasta one of Rebekah's specialties. It had to be perfect for his dad's big night.

"What happens if she says, no?" He'd not let himself think of the possibility but now he couldn't help it, Glenna had been so adamant that she couldn't handle the worry of his dad's job.

"Are you kidding me? Glenna adores you and your dad. The first time I met her, she had that love struck look in her eyes whenever she looked at either one of you. Now back to work. Dinner isn't going to cook itself."

*****

"Come on, one latte." Effie stood at the back door. "Do you have plans?"

"No, but now I have someone to go *home* to, seems like that's all I think about all day. Home. I had planned to move back to the cottage, but Patrick said there was no hurry. Not exactly an invitation to stay." Glenna grabbed her bag, checked the time on her phone.

"And you want him to get so used to you being there, he'll make it permanent. And that's why you've been neglecting me, your best friend." Effie stuck her lip out like a pouting Gnome. She had a pointy hat on, in red for the holiday's, with a tinkling little bell. She'd look at home in the middle of someone's garden.

"Okay, one latte, and then I need to go home and fix dinner for the guys." She grinned. "The guys. I'm so happy. Pinch me and see if I wake up."

Effie being Effie did just that.

"Ouch, that hurt."

"Well, see you're awake." She threw an arm around Glenna's waist and gave a squeeze. "I'm so happy for you, girlfriend. Now who am I going to hang out with?"

"You're part of my family, so me. I'm not going anywhere. Maybe Patrick has a friend..."

"Don't even think about it."

Glenna chuckled, she wasn't sure who or what would be Effie's soulmate, but hopefully she'd find someone soon.

"I just remembered I need to call a supplier. I'll call while I grab our drinks. Settle in at our table."

Glenna settled in at their favorite corner by the window. Her mind turned to what she'd make for dinner. She'd forgotten to take any meat out. She thought maybe she had some shrimp in the freezer that usually worked because they thawed quickly.

*****

Glenna pulled in the drive, disappointment ruffled through her as she noticed the 4Runner wasn't parked in its usual spot. The lights shown from the kitchen, shadows danced letting her know at least Finn was home, and probably Rebekah. She hadn't decided if she should be worried about their relationship or not. They seemed to be just friends. But once in a while she'd catch the girl looking at Finn like he was as good as chocolate.

They were far to young... she'd think about it later, right now she just wanted to go relax.

She opened the door and almost stumbled over Horace. He was planted in her path. She grinned when she noticed he looked up at her with a rose stem clamped in his mouth, the blossom drooping out the side. She glanced around the room noticing the romantic setting. The lights low, the table set for a formal dinner. And roses graced the center. Had she interrupted a romantic moment for the two kids? No, because Horace had been waiting for *her*.

"Glenna, here let me take your bag." Finn didn't wait and took the purse off her arm.

Rebekah walked in from the other room. "Hi. We thought it would be nice to fix dinner for you and Mr. McGinnis. The two of you have had a hard couple of months."

Glenna raised her brow at the girl. What was going on? Did Patrick know about this?

"Dad will be here soon, would you like some wine while you wait?" Finn asked in a formal voice.

"I'm fine thanks. I'll wait for Patrick." He pulled the chair out for her to sit at the table. "What have you two cooked up? Smells divine whatever it is."

"Pasta with a creamy tomato basil sauce." Rebekah went to the stove, lifted a lid. "Almost done."

At that moment Finn's phone did its little jingle signaling a call from his dad. He answered, then frowned. Once he tapped off he turned to Glenna.

"I'm sorry, looks like Dad's been held up. Welcome to my life." He chuckled. "More food for us, right?"

"Here, let me help you guys." Glenna started to stand.

"Sit, we're waiting on you, even if it is the just the three of us." Rebekah's statement brooked no argument.

Glenna settled into her seat again and watched the two bring the food, which did smell wonderful. Once they were all seated, Finn's eyes widened.

"Oh, I almost forgot. Dad wanted you to meet him at the *Hydro Grill* for dessert and a drink. He feels bad he's missing dinner."

"Did he know about this?" she swept her hand over the food.

"No, I think he assumed you made dinner like you always do." He frowned at Rebekah. "I guess we should have let him know ahead of time. He'd have made sure he was home."

"Sometimes the best made plans go awry." Glenna picked up her fork and dipped into the pasta. "I am not going to let it stop me from enjoying my dinner."

"Good. Then we'll clean up and you can go meet Dad."

"Oh, no you cooked. I'm not feeling like going out. I'll give him a call and tell him we'll go tomorrow."

She almost didn't see it, her attention had been on the most excellent sauce she'd tasted, but she looked up in time to see the look that passed between the too. Panic. Why? Were they hoping for the adults to leave them alone?

"What's up you two?" She carefully placed her fork down. Was she reading too much into this? They were teenagers, and hormones raged oh, how she remembered.

"Aw, nothing. Just that dad will be disappointed. He's said a couple of times this week how he'd been so busy being back in the good graces of his bosses that he hadn't had any time to do anything with you."

Glenna regarded Finn for a moment, his expression... she couldn't read it, she turned to Rebekah who at the moment was contemplating her dinner as if it carried the answer to world peace. Something was up, she just couldn't place her finger on it.

"Okay, if you two are sure." She picked up her fork and indicated the table in general. "You have worked hard already. I feel guilty leaving you the dishes also."

"That's what dishwashers are good for." Finn grinned and then dug into his dinner.

The meal turned out to be relaxed and fun. The two kids regaled her with stories about school, the eccentricities of their teachers and classmates. By the time it was over her face hurt from smiling.

She looked down at her business attire, she really didn't want to go to the bar dressed as she was.

"What time did your dad say he'd be at the Hydro?"

Finn paused, his hands full of dishes he'd been taking to the sink to rinse. "He didn't really say, just after we were done."

"Okay, I'll give him a call."

She'd already tapped in his number before she'd left the room. Maybe she could talk him into coming home and they'd snuggle up in front of the television.

"Hey." He voice caused tingles to run the course of her veins. "I've got a table, are you on your way?"

The eagerness in his voice changed her mind. She'd enjoy a drink.

*****

She frowned as she pulled into the lot. Only a few other cars, besides the 4Runner, were there. The place was usually jammed full, the bar was always hopping. Maybe everyone was last minute Christmas shopping.

She got another surprise when she walked through the door. Except for a string quartet, the place was empty. Patrick walked to meet her, he held out his hand.

"Dance before dessert?"

Right on que the music filled the air with a popular tune from *Disney's Beauty and the Beast.* Romance. Patrick knew her. He held her close as their bodies swayed, she had to swallow down the emotion.

This was how it felt when you were in *love* and the romance was the bonus. In that moment she could feel Patrick's emotions, his arms held her firm, but they trembled a little also. As if he held his desire in check.

After the dance he led her to a table that was decorated similar to the one at home had been. He held the chair for her and then went to the other side.

"Very romantic."

"I try to please." Patrick grinned.

The lights were low, even though she saw a twinkle from one of the roses in the vase, she leaned in to get a better look. Was that a ring?

Patrick plucked the rose from the vase and got down on one knee. Before she could respond, the front door opened and Finn walked in, trailed by Horace and Agnes. Finn joined his dad on one knee. Horace plopped his butt on the ground next to Finn, and Agnes just sauntered around looking bored. Out of the corner of her eye she saw movement and turned, there stood Rebekah ready with a camera. She turned her attention to the two men in front of her. She could feel the tears trailing down her cheeks by then. How long they'd been flowing she didn't know, nor did she care.

"Will you be my wife?" Patrick asked.

Without giving her a chance to answer, Finn asked. "Will you be my mom?"

And Horace gave a short bark.

Agnes paused to sniff at her feet then rubbed across her calf.

She swallowed and pushed her chair out and got down on her own knees. She held her arms out.

"Group hug."

The men leaned in, Horace did his best to horn in on the action.

She whispered, "You had me at dance before dessert."

Epilogue

Valentine's Day, a year later

Glenna gazed out the window, the same window she'd been looking out almost two years ago. Such a different scene, the feeling today was joy. And today she knew exactly where her groom was. At the moment he was probably drinking Jameson with her dad and brothers.

February in Brooklyn, what had Patrick been thinking? It was too cold for a winter wedding. Thank goodness the weather Gods had determined this would be an unseasonably warm February in Brooklyn. Still there were outdoor patio heaters strategically placed around the yard.

She grinned at the sight through the glass, the generals were growing up, and most definitely still in charge. And by damn the kids had outdone themselves blending the heaters seamlessly into the décor. They'd enlisted Finn and Rebekah for the occasion. Glenna was glad the girls' parents had let her attend.

Glenna turned as the door opened to let her sisters' spill in. Effie brought up the rear looking like cotton candy on a stick. Glenna blinked, Jessica had spent an hour on her makeup she, didn't want the wrath of her sister if she ruined the painstaking work.

"I love a man in a kilt." Effie wiggled her brows as all the women hummed a growl of agreement.

"Wait until you see the groom, sister dear, you're going to faint." Christine put an arm around her pulling her in for a careful hug. "I'm so happy for you. Patrick is such a doll."

Glenna raised her brow, she wasn't sure if he'd appreciate being compared to a doll. But he was a hottie. She glanced out the window at her new son hurrying around, his kilt flapping in the wind. He was going to break several hearts on his way to manhood.

"Darling, Finn and the little generals have out done themselves." Her mother joined her and Christine at the window. "Rebekah too. Are her parents in the floral business? She's a pro, just look at those arrangements."

"I have no idea, she doesn't talk about them much." Glenna for not the first time, wondered about the girls' home life.

Now was the time of joy, she had a life time to find out about the girl, and she planned to.

She faced the others again. "I'm so glad our entire family was able to attend. I promise that Patrick, Finn and I plan to visit more often. As long as all of you know you have an open invitation to visit us on the west coast."

"And free latte's when you visit the Bistro."

"Okay, I'm there. I know David would love to visit. All that lovely wine," Christine said.

"I've never been on the west coast."

Glenna turned her attention to her newest sister in law. Bryn, at last, was coming out of her Irish shell. Of course, she had always been able to down the Jameson with the guys. Glenna couldn't wait to get to know her better.

"I expect you and Matt to visit soon then."

"I promise. Maybe we could all do a vacation together, sort of a family one. It would be fun."

Glenna looked to her twin. "She says it would be fun. Spoken like a true only child."

Reagan grinned and threw an arm around Bryn. "Oh my dear. You have no idea. However..." she raised her brow at the room in general. "We have grown up a lot since our last family vacation."

Glenna grinned at her mother when she threw a hand over her heart in mock pain. "Bryn, you have *no idea*, oh, the drama."

"I think it sounds like a great idea," Jessica said.

From there, with Effie directing, the plans flew back and forth until a date in the fall was set. By the time a knock signaled that things were ready, Glenna's jaw hurt from grinning.

Happy. Could a heart really burst with happiness because Glenna had the feeling she was about to find out.

*****

Patrick stood at the garden arbor where Rebekah had thrown every color and kind of flower over it until you couldn't see the wood and somehow made it look as if they'd naturally grown there.

His thoughts were scurrying everywhere. He was nervous. He was a tough, federal agent able to face down the bad guys and yet he was nervous of a little imp of an antiquities shop owner.

He was afraid he'd let her down in some way. She'd had reservations about giving him her love. He'd been everything she'd been determined to stay away from. He'd bulldozed those barriers down and he'd never forgive himself if he hurt her.

Finn laid a hand on his shoulder and leaned in to whisper. "She loves you Dad, that's what matters. You love her. We're going to be a family, now smile before you scare the children."

Finn chuckled at his own joke, and straightened. Patrick grinned at his son. "Thanks for the pep talk, if that's what it was. But you're right. Love, that's what matters, I'll make sure she's happy."

At that moment, Glenna appeared at the back door on her dad's arm. A vision in white. She took his breath away, and his doubts. As clichéd as it was, this was the first day of the rest of their lives. There'd be ups and downs but it would be a good life.

*****

Dazed, she was a married woman. Her heart hadn't burst yet, but her happiness was spilling over even her fingertips tingled with it.

Glenna hung on to her new husband as she gazed around the festivities. Her entire family, along with Patrick's, were there. Life. This is what family was all about. Tyler held Lucy high letting her giggle. Kiera stood with her arm around his waist, her other arm over her protruding belly. Their family was growing even though they were both agents, somehow they made it work.

Reagan and Paco stood listening to what looked like a lecture from Gabby. They held hands, Paco kept grinning at his wife, then back to Gabby. The girl didn't seem to notice, she was too earnest about her subject, her hands flew as she emphasized points.

Glenna let her focus wander to Jessica, her beautiful school teacher slash soccer mom, sister. Even though Ben wasn't very old, he'd been playing soccer since he could walk. Now he held his mom's hand as he pulled her toward Gabe, grinning with every step.

And there was Sophie who seemed to be giving the same lecture to her parents, David and Christine. Even though she bounced her little brother, Freddie on her hip, she didn't let that stop her from gesturing to make some point or another. The look on the boys' face was one of pure joy, as he laughed at his big sister.

Matt, where was... awe she should have known. He had his wife over in a relatively quiet corner nibbling on her neck while Bryn tried to push him away. Judging by Bryn's wide grin, she wasn't protesting too much.

She felt someone brush up to her side and turned to see Finn. He wrapped an arm around her. Flanked by her two favorite men she couldn't have been happier.

Before she could voice her emotions to Patrick, her dad took a position on the small corner stage the little generals had set for the Celtic band to use. The dance music would be starting soon, and so would the traditional dance with her dad. She swiped the tear from her eye, as she tried to focus on her dad. He tapped his glass with a fork or spoon, she couldn't tell. He would have been loud enough without the microphone he'd held the glass to. It was a wonder the neighborhood dogs didn't howl in protest at the sound.

He set the glass on a little table knowing he had everyone's attention. He adjusted the mic on the stand.

"You know when I held Glenna in my arms for the first time, while her mother held her sister, I didn't picture her in white as I walked her to her future. No, all I could think of was 'What were we thinking? Six children how am I ever going to afford food, clothes, and college?'"

As anticipated his words drew a chuckle. He gazed out at the packed back yard for a moment until he spotted his wife.

"Martha we did good! Here we are blessed with the best family ever. I couldn't have picked better life-long partners for our children than they found on their own. And now we are doubly blessed to have grandchildren."

"I have a toast, fair warning it's a long one." Again everyone chuckled on cue.

He raised his glass and this time found Glenna's gaze. She felt the warmth of her father's love to her toes. He was right, the Beckett's were blessed. Sure they had their problems like everyone else, but they *always* had each other's backs.

"Congratulations to my beautiful daughter and her new family."

He took a sip along with everyone else. Glenna knew what was coming he'd made a tradition of giving a toast one sentence and sip at a time. She was just grateful everyone was sipping fine bubbly that Finn had procured for the wedding from his summer employer, and not Jameson.

"Welcome to my new son-in-law and new grandson."

Sip.

"May you have a long and happy life together."
Sip.
"And bring us many more grandbabies."
Sip. Glenna raised her brow and glanced up at Patrick. His grin told her, he was all for the making of grandbabies.

"To the next generation."

As everyone took a sip, her dad relinquished the stage so the band could begin. Everyone cleared off the small dance floor that had been set up. And the first strains of music trailed over the yard.

A moment later her dad was at her elbow.

"I believe this is our dance, Glenna girl."

She almost broke down at that, he hadn't called her that since she was in high school. So many memories came floating back as they waltzed around the dance floor. Why had she moved so far away? She again made herself a promise to visit more often.

"He's a good man." His words broke into her thoughts.

"Yes he is. And he is raising a good young man."

"Finn's a good boy. I am so happy for you. Please know you can still come to your dad if you ever need to."

This time she had to choke the words around the emotion. "A girl always needs her daddy."

She hadn't noticed the song had ended and she was still swaying with her dad. Her new husband was there, she hadn't even noticed him dancing with her mother. But Martha was standing beside him. Glenna held out her arms and gave her mom a tight hug, then turned and stepped into Patrick's arms.

"Well wife, you're stuck with me now."

"And I couldn't be happier." He looked a little wavery as she gazed up at him, must be the tears blocking her view. "We're going to have a good life you, me and Finn."

"And the many more grandbabies for your father."

His chuckle warmed her from the tip of her toes to the tingling top of her head. He leaned in and his lips warm and solid caught hers. The music, the chatter, and laughter faded into the background, until only the two of them existed.

Glenna held on and enjoyed. Life with Patrick would always be an adventure.

The End!

The Beckett Series
By Mary Martinez

The Beckett's have a strong sense of family and honor. When one of their own is threatened, their bond is as strong as a badge of steel.

Disappear *Book I*

After two years undercover as an FBI agent to infiltrate a crime organization and discover the identity of a hit man, Tyler Beckett's cover is blown. Tyler's new assignment is to protect the only witness who can identify the mysterious killer. If only he didn't find her so attractive. Each day it becomes harder to keep his objective, especially since he knows the interest is mutual.

Keira Cavanaugh is the only witness to a hit ordered by a crime boss. The safe house is compromised and the same hit man shoots Tyler. Fearing Tyler is dead, Keira plans revenge on the crime organization. She must fake her own suicide in order to survive.

When Tyler discovers what Keira plans, he realizes he must stop her before he loses her for good.

Innocent *Book II*

All Jessica wants is a home and a family. So how did she suddenly find herself falsely accused of a felony and then kidnapped by a hit man?

Jessica Beckett loves her job teaching high school algebra. That is until Coach Brinley makes her life miserable because she actually has the audacity to fail his three staring football jocks. Maybe if they'd done their homework they would have passed. She refuses to be intimidated. He on the other hand refuses to admit defeat and manipulates the boys into accusing her of sex in exchange for passing grades.

Gabriel Despain loves his job as FBI agent. But falling for his partner's sister has complicated a great partnership. It would be a lot easier to ignore his feelings if Jessica hadn't found herself in trouble. Now he must keep her safe. And if he can't remain objective, they both might get killed.

Quiet *Book III*

Christine Beckett's dream of partnership in a prestigious New York City law firm has finally come to fruition. She has financial security, a loving family, and owns her home, why does she need a man?

Detective Solomon has worked with Tyler Beckett on several cases, he almost feels he is part of the Beckett clan. He considers them his good friends, except for Christine who seems to look down her professional nose at him.

Christine receives a threatening note and her townhouse echoes with mysterious cries in the night. That is when the handsome and irritating detective insists he temporarily move in to protect her. To add insult, it is with her family's blessing.

Illusion *Book IV* Utopian the Beginning

Special Agent Reagan Beckett left Brooklyn for San Francisco ten years ago—and on bad terms with her family. When the World Banking Association (WBA), one of the biggest worldwide financial institutions, is targeted by domestic terrorists, Reagan is called to join the team with two others in New York City. Now she would be home for an extended visit.

Special Agent Paco Luis Perez has heard of the legendary Tyler Beckett and looks forward to working with the man on the assignment in New York. However, when he reads Beckett's dossier on his flight from D.C., he discovers the Beckett he expected to meet isn't Tyler.

NYPD Detective Spencer Alexander Williams III, a member of the gang terrorist task force, reluctantly agrees to consult on the domestic terrorist case as the local liaison. He has never liked working with a team; he learns more on his own. But they need his uncanny knack to anticipate the gang's movements.

As soon as Reagan receives information on the assignment, she researches her new partners. But does she know enough to literally trust these men with her life?

Profit *Book V* *Utopian the Conclusion*

Matt Beckett is the Chief Financial officer for World Banking Association (WBA). Over a year ago an agency known as the HEAD group tried to take over the WBA. Matt's sister, Reagan Beckett, a member of a Federal Special Task Force took out one of the key players, a serial killer known as *The Headman.* Now the founder of HEAD, Andrew Phillips, is back and ready to finish what he'd started with a new and dastardly key player from the Dark web.

Matt doesn't have any desire to be involved in any cloak and dagger stuff. He'd rather leave that to the other law enforcement Beckett's. Unfortunately, it doesn't look like he'll have a choice.

Bryn Connelly is the Chief Audit Executive also for the WBA. She had been one of *The Headman's* targets and thought her days of danger were over. However, she finds herself working with laid back Matt Beckett, much to her dismay.

Matt couldn't be more delighted when Reagan informs him he'll be working the lovely Bryn. He's been trying to catch her eye for five years, now. However, their sleuthing quickly lands them in a precarious position.

It's up to Matt and Bryn to finish what Reagan and her team started, but can he win the *lovely* Bryn and save the day? Or will he lose her forever if the WBA falls into the wrong hands?

Abandoned *Book VI*

Glenna Beckett loves her family dearly, but being the youngest of six can be overwhelming. Moving across country helped her learn who she was outside the family. She's built a successful business in the form of a quaint shop on Main Street of Calistoga, that sells a bit of everything vintage, the new age term for antique. What more does she need?

Then he walked into her shop. International playboy, Lance Gordon. After a whirlwind courtship he asks her to marry him. Burying a niggle of doubt in the pit of her tummy, she says yes. He's even agreed to have the wedding in Brooklyn so her family can attend. But he never arrives.

Glenna refused to believe she'd been abandoned at the altar and asks her brother, Tyler, to contact an agent friend on the West Coast to search for Lance.

Patrick McGinnis can't believe he's walking into a prissy shop in the high end of the Napa Valley searching for a missing groom. The bride, Glenna Beckett, is everything he feared, drop dead gorgeous, and a spoiled brat. Not that he'd ever tell her brother that. He hates wild goose chases, and this mission is exactly that. Patrick's certain the playboy fiancé is off wooing some other delectable creature.

Unfortunately, once Patrick started to dig, he finds there's more to the tale and it will take all his skills as an agent to keep Glenna safe. Especially when the case takes a turn and threatens the safety of his son, Finn.

Stay tuned for the Next Generation

Thank you for reading!

Dear Reader,
I hope you enjoyed the sixth book of my Beckett
Series, *Abandoned.* The Beckett's are like family to me.
I know where they live, I've walked their
neighborhoods, hung out at some of their favorite
spots!

I really hope you enjoyed getting to know Glenna,
Patrick and Finn. I love feedback and would love to
hear from you. Tell me what you liked, didn't like, or
would to like to have read. You can write me at
marylmartinez3@gmail.com or you can visit me on my
web site MaryMartinez.com.

I have a favor to ask you, as I said I love feedback. If
you're reading this letter, I can only assume you're at
the end of my book. Here's the favor, if you're so
inclined, I'd love a review of *Abandoned*, letting me
know if you liked it or hated it, either way I'd love your
honest opinion.

Reviews are very hard to come by these days. Most
readers are off to the next book almost before they've
finished reading 'the end'. You, the reader, have the
power now to make or break a book. If you have the
time, here is a link to my author page on Amazon:
http://www.amazon.com/-/e/B006MWJ1T6, where
you can find all of my books.

Thank you so much for spending time with the
characters from *Abandoned*. Hope to see you again
soon.

In appreciation,
Mary Martinez

About the Author

Mary lives in Magna, a little town west of Salt Lake City, Utah. Together with her husband, she has six grown children, and six wonderful grandsons and five beautiful granddaughters. She loves to spend time with family and friends--she includes good books as friends!

Mary and her husband love to travel, especially to the Caribbean for relaxing, and Italy for the wine. And most recently she discovered she was Irish and Scottish, of course they had to visit Ireland and Scotland. Mary fell in love with both, but the green hills of Ireland felt like home. With the experience from the exotic places she has visited, she is able to fill her books with colorful descriptions of cities, painting a colorful backdrop for her characters. One of her favorite US destinations is New York/Brooklyn, where her beloved Beckett's live. When she visits, she can wander their neighborhoods, favorite parks, and visit their favorite pub, Putnum's.

They are avid concert 'Ho's'! Yes, they pretty much want to do them all. They love outdoor amphitheaters the best and attend as many during the warmer months as possible.

Mary writes mostly romantic suspense, romance, women's fiction, and she has just begun to dabble in young adult mystery. She is a member of Romance Writers of America (RWA). During her writing career she has been a conference coordinator, workshop presenter, and chapter president for the Utah Chapter of RWA. In 2007 she was presented with the Utah RWA service award in acknowledgment and appreciation for outstanding service. Mary has also participated in numerous library panels on writing and co-presented a workshop on writing a series at the League of Utah Writers conference.

Mary and her husband are also enthusiastic college football fans. They have season tickets to the UTES, University of Utah Football and they tailgate every game. They love tailgating so much, that they were married at a tailgating in 1999.
GO UTES!

Video Bio: www.youtube.com/watch?v=ISsOcM0kyzY

Visit her website for more information:
www.marymartinez.com

Made in the USA
San Bernardino, CA
13 March 2018